WITHOUT CONSCIENCE

Also By Michael Kerr

DI Matt Barnes Series
A REASON TO KILL
LETHAL INTENT
A NEED TO KILL
CHOSEN TO KILL
A PASSION TO KILL
RAISED TO KILL
DRIVEN TO KILL

The Joe Logan Series
AFTERMATH
ATONEMENT
ABSOLUTION
ALLEGIANCE
ABDUCTION
ACCUSED

The Laura Scott Series
A DEADLY COMPULSION
THE SIGN OF FEAR
THE TROPHY ROOM

Other Crime Thrillers
DEADLY REPRISAL
DEADLY REQUITAL
BLACK ROCK BAY
A HUNGER WITHIN
THE SNAKE PIT
A DEADLY STATE OF MIND
TAKEN BY FORCE
DARK NEEDS AND EVIL DEEDS
DEADLY OBSESSION
COFFEE CRIME CAFE
A DARKNESS WITHIN
PLAIN EVIL
DEADLY PURPOSE

WITHOUT CONSCIENCE

BY

MICHAEL KERR

ISBN 979-8642899410

'**Twill** vex thy soul to hear what I shall speak;

for I must talk of murders, rapes, and massacres,

acts of black night, abominable deeds,

complots of mischief, treason, villainies,

ruthful to hear, yet piteously perform'd.

~ SHAKESPEARE

(Titus Andronicus)

CHAPTER ONE

Blink.

The motionless figure had been totally unaware of time passing, but was now fully alert again. The wristwatch LCD glowed green at the touch of a button. Over forty minutes had ticked by since the predator had hunkered down and slipped into a trancelike state, unmoving behind bushes that crowded one side of the narrow, asphalt-topped path.

The night and attendant mist united, seemingly conspiring to cloak the still form in cloying darkness, for it to appear as a nebulous shape that could have been a gargoyle carved from granite, eroded and soft-edged from the passage of time and effects of weather, ostensibly engaged in stony introspection.

As the time drew near, the tension mounted, becoming almost unbearable in an exquisite way, as a rush of adrenaline welled up; a bubbling pressure cooker of heightened emotions that caused muscles to twitch randomly on hearing the muffled slap of trainer-clad feet approaching, growing louder by the second.

The only thoughts were of Caroline, which brought a vision of her beautiful features to mind; a face framed by flame-coloured hair; a face that was so radiant, even with the treacherous, insincere smile on the perfectly-sculpted lips that spoke honey-coated lies.

This would be the culmination of a great deal of patient planning and preparation, which was the necessary foreplay to yet another successful kill.

Pushing up, back scraping against the rough bark of the tree, to flex both legs to relieve aching knees and cramped thigh and calf muscles that complained from having been at rest for too long. The sharpened branch shook in a white-knuckled grip as the moment – and the unwary runner – drew ever nearer.

Moving forward now, slowly, and with the stealth of a cat, to stop again behind a screen of evergreen foliage.

This was no dummy run. The waiting was over. She would soon be dead. One small sigh of contentment, and the words, "Thank you Lord for that which I am about to receive," whispered almost soundlessly. It was Showtime.

She stopped. Why would she do that? There was no way she could have heard anything, or seen any movement. No matter, she was near enough, standing less than ten feet away and looking about her in the gloom like a skittish thoroughbred filly that was on the verge of bolting. But it was now far too late to escape her fate. Unknowingly, she was just scant seconds from being taken.

It was still dark when the strident clamour of the alarm clock dissolved a dream in which Karen had been swimming in a warm ocean, chaperoned by several sinuous, glossy-skinned bottle-nose dolphins. She awoke to the reality of another early autumnal day, swathed in bedclothes, not the azure waters of the Caribbean. And unbeknown to her this would not be like any other day, but a truly exceptional and extraordinary one: the one on which she would die. She had been selected. It was not personal. Karen was just unfortunate, in that she loosely resembled someone else, was available, and her status, looks and predictability combined to make her a soft target.

Sitting up, she threw the duvet back and swung her legs out of bed. Reached out to silence the nerve-jangling sound of the alarm. It was five a.m. On automatic, she went for a pee, then donned her sweats and scuffed Nikes and finger-combed her long, auburn hair back to fix in a ponytail with a bobble as she hurried downstairs and went to the fridge and drank a mouthful of OJ straight from the carton.

Karen Perry believed in the old saying; 'No pain, no gain'. Running was her passion. She especially loved the peace and quiet of early morning, which was a time of day she moved through with consummate ease.

"Guard the house, Russ," Karen said, bending to stroke the large ginger Tom that had adopted her six months ago and moved in. He was of indeterminate age, had an ugly scar on his nose, and was missing the tip of his right ear, presumably due to some dispute over territory, or maybe in combat for the favours of a local female of the species. Karen thought of him as a fur-clad warrior, so had named him after Russell Crowe, the hunky Aussie actor who had once starred in the epic Oscar-winning movie, Gladiator.

Closing the door for what would be the last time, Karen skipped down the steps of the Victorian terrace house. It was cold. Patches of thin fog hung listlessly like grey rags in windless air that the waning moonlight penetrated only sporadically. Blurry yellow circles of sodium-vapour-powered street lamps appeared suspended and without support, in semblance of hazy miniature suns in a far-off quadrant of the heavens.

After stretching, taking deep breaths and running on the spot for a minute, Karen set off down the street towards the northern entrance of the park, which was just a few hundred yards away. Once inside the immense tract of land – that she thought of as a haven from the oppression of urban London sprawl – she ran fast, finding a rhythm as her heart rate increased and her body became filmed in perspiration.

Karen aimed at completing three miles each morning; a goal only ever curtailed if she slept in, which was a rare event. Her usually pre-dawn activity was more than just exercise, she found it a cleansing and therapeutic occupation, preparing her for the hustle and bustle of the city, which with full daylight would awaken like a wild and noisy beast.

The lake was covered by a luminescent blanket; a raft of what could have been undulating cigarette smoke. She breathed evenly and followed her well-trodden route. There was no sound, and yet a rash of goose pimples rose on her bare arms. She had the sudden sensation of being watched, and so looked about her without slowing, but saw no one. It was just an instinctive feeling, and yet she could not shake the presentiment that she was no longer alone. Should she turn back and head for home? She had never been accosted or felt in danger before. But for some reason she now felt at risk. Was that a figure up ahead? Probably just a vagrant. No need to be irrational. If he approached, she would just run away. No average man could catch her, so unless he was an Usain Bolt type there was nothing to worry about. She squinted through the murk. The figure was no more than a slender, solitary bush. Her thudding heart lessened its drum roll in her ears, and she felt foolish for allowing her imagination to conjure up a false sense of danger.

Moving on, drawing level with a deep thicket of rhododendron, a sudden, quick movement caught from the corner of the eye attracted her attention. She stopped, more curious than afraid, to stand stock-still, alarm heightening her senses as she looked and listened. After maybe twenty seconds had passed, she shrugged and made to set off again. She was spooked, but commonsense told her that any movement would most likely have been made by a nocturnal animal foraging for food; maybe a fox or badger.

The figure exploded out from the foliage, rushed forward and grabbed at her, hissing a staccato of expletives as she twisted out of reach.

Taking off like a greyhound out of a trap, not looking back, kicking her heels, and arms close to her sides and her legs working like the pistons of a well-oiled machine, Karen determined to put as much distance as possible between her and whoever had attempted to assault her.

Fate in the form of a loose shoe lace intervened. She stood on it, tripped, lost her footing and fell heavily, crashing on to her knees before rolling sideways off the path and down a bank of wet grass, gasping with shock as she broke through the low layer of ground fog and splashed into the icy water beneath it. She gulped a mouthful of air as she surfaced, before a crushing, pinching pain bit into her neck, and her face was pushed back under the water. She thrashed and fought to break free, but to no avail. Holding her breath, she arched her neck back, only for her head to be driven down even deeper. With her heart pounding like a racing engine in her chest, and her lungs aching for air, she realised that someone was attempting to drown her. She was going to be murdered, and there was absolutely nothing that she could do to prevent it happening. Red motes danced behind her eyelids, and she involuntarily, finally had to gasp for breath, knowing that all she would inhale would be the chill lake water. She choked and gagged as the liquid was drawn down her throat. And as blackness deeper than a starless night encroached, numbing her brain, she was dragged up and backwards, to be dumped coughing and spluttering onto the sloping bank.

An overwhelming sense of relief filled her, even as hands clawed at her sopping sweat pants and pulled them down to below her knees. This was an opportunist rapist, not a killer. She had no strength, was in shock, unable to scream or to do anything. If some lowlife was going to use her to get his rocks off, then so be it. She would have to just suffer it and be glad to escape with her life.

A hand clamped over her nose and mouth a split second before a paralysing agony made every muscle in her body contract and stiffen in rebuke. Her mind bellowed at the outrage that was being visited upon her. Gloved fingers dug into her throat. She could not breathe; needed to open her mouth to protest and give vent to the terrible pain and fear, but was too stupefied. No sound could escape her compressed windpipe. White noise fizzed in her ears, and an oily film dimmed her vision to wash over her consciousness and enshroud her in what was to become eternal darkness.

The shadowy figure worked feverishly at the body, pausing every few seconds to snatch glances in every direction, in the manner of a cautious animal at a watering hole, or a beast with its fresh kill, gorging warily, knowing that other predators would in all likelihood be fast approaching, wanting a share of the spoils.

After no more than sixty seconds, the hunter hurried away, to be enveloped, as if ingested by the mantle of fog.

CHAPTER TWO

Detective Chief Inspector Barney Bowen switched the kettle on, before going across the office to sit behind his desk and wait for it to boil. It was eight a.m., and his view from the second-floor office window was of a gunmetal grey sky, fronted by even darker, greyer buildings. The days were short now; high summer no more than a distant memory. Barney's wife, Anna, wanted to relocate to Portugal or Spain when he retired, to be done once and for all with the harsh British winters. The premise was tempting, but Barney knew that he would most likely die of boredom. He needed purpose to stimulate him and keep him from mentally seizing up. He determined to meet her part way and spend a month or two each year in a rental villa or condo. The last thing he wanted to do was live permanently in an ex-pat community, having to drink bottled water, avoid spicy spik food – that would play havoc with his ulcer – and wonder when the next Basque Separatist bomb would go off. Plus, he could live without moving to a country where the masses floated their boats by watching bulls being speared, tormented and put to the sword. Although that disgusting practise was now being outlawed in some areas.

"Good morning, boss," Detective Sergeant Mike Cook said, breezing into the office, to shuck off his old, scuffed, black leather jacket and drape it over the back of a swivel chair.

"What's good about it?" Barney said, wishing he was still at home in bed, snuggled up to Anna. The kettle began to whistle. He got up and went over to the small Formica-topped table in the corner of the room to make tea.

"Everything," Mike said, watching Barney brew, and then taking the proffered mug over to his desk. "I choose to think of all the people who are worse off than me, and it makes me feel a lucky bastard to be reasonably fit, have a job, and be able to enjoy the luxury of a roof over my head."

"Such philosophical wisdom for a copper. I think I'm going to puke," Barney said before sipping noisily at the strong tea.

Mike's phone trilled and they both glared at it with distaste, as if a dog turd had materialised from thin air on the desktop to offend their questionable sensibilities.

Mike picked up. "Detective Sergeant Cook," he said, then, "Yes," and after a pause. "Where?"

Barney watched as his DS frowned, reached for a ball-point and began to scribble on a notepad. He knew by the look on the younger man's face that it was bad news. Mike's cheek muscles were bunching as he gritted his teeth, which was always a sign of trouble.

"We've got another murder in Regent's Park, boss," Mike said as he racked the phone. "Same MO as that jogger last month. And in almost the same spot."

"Jesus wept," Barney said before gulping his tea, scalding his mouth and coughing, his chest cramping on the hot liquid. He slammed the mug down on the desktop, got up and retrieved his coat from a hook on the back of the door. "Tell me about it."

Mike grabbed his jacket and followed Barney out of the office, "A guy was walking his dog and saw a body lying next to the boating lake at about seven a.m.," he said, chasing after Barney, who was power-walking toward the lifts. "He didn't have his mobile, so left the park and waved down a passing patrol car. They accompanied him back to the scene. The uniforms confirmed that it was the body of a young woman, and arranged for all the park's exits to be covered. A few ginger beers, local vagrants and a few joggers were stopped and questioned."

"And?"

"And no credible suspect as yet. The doer could have been long gone. There's a CSI team and a pathologist already there."

Mike pulled up behind several vehicles, including a crime scene investigators' Ford transit van. Crime scene tape was strung like bunting from trees to secure the area, and the static and chatter from radios, flashing blue roof lights, the large white incident tent that was already erected, and the overall-clad figures doing a fingertip search along the lake's bank combined to disrupt the normal tranquillity, broadcasting that this was now the location of a serious crime.

Barney and Mike got out of the unmarked Sierra and walked over to where a uniform raised a hand to stop them.

"Who's in charge here?" Barney said, brusquely showing the young constable his warrant card.

"DS Starkey is the Crime Scene Coordinator, sir. Over there," the PC said, pointing to a burly officer in baggy white Tyvek overalls, who was standing talking to two other technicians; a cigarette dancing between his lips. The trio looked like animated snowmen.

"The duty pathologist's in the tent," Jack Starkey said, recognising Barney and Mike as he began walking towards them, pausing to flick his cigarette end into the glassy water behind him. "It's Battle-axe Beatty."

Barney grinned. He knew Jane Beatty of old, and had long since come to know that her air of aloof detachment was just a professional persona that she pulled on with her jumpsuit and gloves. When not working – and in the company of people that she knew and liked – Jane had a wicked sense of humour and was good fun to be around.

The whir and flashing of a camera ceased. The forensic photographer exited the tent. Barney and Mike entered to find Jane knelt next to the body, a probe thermometer in hand. She jotted the reading on a form and then stood up, grunted and proceeded to massage the small of her back. The preliminary examination had been completed.

"We're going to have to stop meeting like this," Barney said, smiling at the petite pathologist, whose slim figure and short, blonde hair were obscured by the oversize hooded garment she wore.

"Christ, if it isn't Barnaby of the Yard," she said with a smile. "Are you still taking money under false pretences? I thought they'd have put you out to grass by now."

"I go next March," Barney said. "You're invited to my retirement bash. We'll need a pro to carve the meat."

"I'll come in my greens, masked, wearing my wellies and gloves and wielding a scalpel."

"Better than a strippogram...unless—"

"Stop, Barnaby. Don't even go there."

"Too late, Jane. I just imagined you slicing and dicing a roast, swinging your hips to some raunchy Tina Turner number, and wearing a black lacy bra, matching panties and fishnet stockings."

"In a changing world, you're a constant," Jane said. "You make Dirty Harry look positively clean."

Barney laughed aloud. "I'll take that as a compliment. What happened to the decedent?" The preamble of small talk was over.

"It's the same M.O. as the last one."

Barney studied the pale, blood-spattered corpse. The young woman's emerald eyes were staring, as though she could see through the canvas roof, up to some distant point far above it. Her mouth was drawn back in a frozen grimace of terror and pain; an indelible moment sculpted on to her alabaster-white face. Looking down from her head in a slow sweep, Barney saw that the girl's sweat top had been pulled up to her neck, revealing small breasts – their nipples taped over, presumably to prevent the friction of movement against material causing soreness. Why not wear a bra? – and a gaping rent below her sternum that was awash with blood.

"He took her heart," Jane said in little more than a whisper.

Barney nodded and continued his visual inspection. The pants were down to the corpse's ankles, knees apart. A length of branch protruded from between her legs: Excalibur in the stone.

"The sick bastard," Barney said, his voice thick with anger and disgust. "Anything else?"

"No. What you see is what you get," Jane said, hiking her shoulders. "She's been in the lake. Probably attempted to get away. He then impaled her with the branch, strangled her, and hacked her heart out. She hasn't been dead for too long. Anything else will show up when I do the cut."

A little later the corpse was tagged and bagged and taken to the mortuary in Holborn, where Jane was based.

"Are you thinking what I am, boss?" Mike said after they had pushed through the gathering crowd of media vultures, who could smell blood and death with more acuity than any carrion eater on an African plain.

"Yes. But I wish I wasn't," Barney said as they drove out of the park and became a small segment of the steel serpent that was traffic moving in slow motion. "We have two murders that may or may not have been committed by the same maniac. And we need to explore all possible avenues before jumping to the conclusion that a serial killer has started up."

"The tabloids will have a field day," Mike observed, giving a cab driver the finger and hitting the horn as he was cut up. "As soon as they know how this one died, they'll write it up as *'The Ripper of Regent's Park strikes again'*, or something along those lines."

Barney lit a cigarette and took a deep drag. "That's Detective Superintendent Hotshot Pearce's problem, not ours," he said, exhaling the blue smoke onto the dash and inside of the windscreen. "He loves to head up press conferences, and he's pretty good at deflecting the shit that the media throws at us. He knows the MIM chapter and verse." The Murder Investigation Manual covered all aspects and procedures of strategy regarding murder cases, including a section on how to 'work' the Fourth Estate.

"He's a royal pain in the arse?" Mike said, screwing his face in lemon-sucking fashion.

"No sweat," Barney said. "He doesn't like to get his hands dirty. It's down to me, you and the squad to collar this nutter. Pearce'll take any kudos going, and we'll take all the flak, as per usual."

"We've still got zilch on the first one."

"I know," Barney said. "I know."

The following morning at ten-thirty a.m., an orderly ushered them into the white-tiled autopsy suite in which Jane Beatty had just finished up with the green-skinned cadaver of a middle-aged woman, who had been strangled to death by her husband and left to rot under the matrimonial bed of their Deptford maisonette. The guy had taken off with his teenage mistress for a two-week holiday in Tenerife. The late woman's sister had become suspicious after repeatedly phoning and calling at the house. After several days of not being able to contact her sister, she broke a window to gain entry. The smell had led her to the bedroom, as surely as the Bisto Kids were drawn along the curling vapours of a gravy trail. The corpse was on its back, stuck to the floorboards, and maggots had been free ranging, feasting undisturbed on the overripe flesh.

Mike looked away from the abomination, which had its face peeled back to disclose the plum-coloured bruises that her husband's fingers and thumbs had left on the throat tissue, as silent witness to his act.

"Over here," Jane said, beckoning them across to a gurney at the end of the room, on which the covered corpse of the young woman found in Regent's Park reposed. Jane pulled the sheet back to partly reveal the naked body. The 'Y' cut and unrelated chest wound had been roughly stitched, and the aluminium table on which the PM had been performed would shortly be hosed down by an assistant, for the runoff pans below it to be awash with a melange of blood and other noxious body fluids.

"You're late," Jane continued. "I got through with her five minutes ago."

Barney hiked his rounded shoulders. "Have you got anything new for us?"

"Not much more than you already know," Jane said, holding up the bloody sharpened stake that she had removed from the body. "This was rammed up into her stomach ante mortem, and would have caused death by massive internal haemorrhaging, had she been left to die. The removal of the heart was clumsy but effective. It had been cut partially free and manually ripped out in a hurry. I think that a knife with approximately a six-inch serrated blade was used. Liver temp' taken at the scene and back here, plus the lack of any significant lividity, indicate that she had only been dead for a short period of time when I got to her."

"Had she been raped?" Barney said.

"No evidence of vaginal, rectal or oral penetration, other than the branch. And no traces of semen. Toxicology might find something, but I doubt it. I don't think she was drugged. This seems to have been a frenzied attack, with the sole purpose of inserting the stake, strangling her, and removing the heart. I'll get the paperwork to you ASAP."

"Is that it, Jane?"

"I'm afraid so, Barnaby. She had a little water in her lungs. I would guess she fell, or maybe threw herself into the lake in a bid to escape. She was impaled on the bank next to the water and then asphyxiated before he did the wet work. Do you have an ID on her?"

"Yeah. Her mobile phone was found at the scene. We've confirmed that she was Karen Perry, a twenty-three-year-old. She was single and lived nearby. Running in the park before dawn was something that she'd been doing most mornings for several years."

"I hope that you find whoever did this before he does it again," Jane said, letting her eyes play on the young woman's face, that until so recently had been animated and vital, and was now just cold and set, bereft of life. "It's the same psycho that killed the last one."

"Is that definite?" Barney said.

"Yes. No doubt. He's also right-handed; the knife cuts tell me that. And I think that tests will show that he used the same knife on both of his victims."

"Thanks, Jane, it all helps," Barney said, smiling weakly and heading for the door, where Mike was already standing, waiting, fighting with the waves of nausea that the smell of disinfectant and underlying corruption always conspired to make him suffer.

Back on the street, Mike put his hands on his knees and took deep breaths, trying to push the mostly imagined stink of death from his nose and lungs.

The tabloids had not been slow in picking up on the similarity of the two murders.

Headlines included: VLAD THE IMPALER-STYLE GHOUL STRIKES AGAIN IN HEART OF CITY. And: BUFFY THE VAMPIRE KILLER MANIAC IS LOOSE IN CAPITAL.

"I want you to work with Dr Mark Ross," Clive Pearce said, marching into Barney's office without knocking.

"Who the fuck is he?" Barney said, not bothering to stand up.

Mike picked up the nearest file on his desk and decamped, knowing that his boss and the Detective Superintendent were like oil and water at the best of times.

"He," Clive said, "is amongst other things a psychologist, lecturer, and probably the foremost criminal profiler in the UK at this present time. His expert assistance might just help us close this case before any other young women get mutilated and murdered."

Barney stared at the balding little man, whom he had known and disliked since they had both pounded the beat as rookie coppers almost thirty years ago.

Clive tried a smile. "C'mon, Barney, lighten up. This guy is the real deal. He used to be with the FBI. He has a gift for tracking down serial killers."

"If he's that good, why did he leave the bureau?"

"He never said why he'd walked. He married an English girl and ended up living this side of the pond. I think she had a lot to do with him quitting, but I don't know for sure. He now works at a maximum-security hospital for the criminally insane, down in Kent somewhere."

"We have home-grown psychologists that consult on this kind of case. Why bring a Yank on board?"

"Because Ross has been instrumental in putting away more serial killers than you or I have had hot dinners. He didn't learn his trade from reading books on human behaviour, swatting for degrees, or by just talking to patients, like most of the British consultants have. The guy has a gift that can't be taught. This sort of crime is rife over there. It's all part of the great American Dream that turned into a fucking nightmare. And this isn't a request, Barney. If Dr Ross agrees to help us with this, then I expect you to accord him all due professional courtesy and work with him. Okay?"

"Okay, Clive," Barney sighed, reining in his irritability, which manifested itself in him vigorously twisting his wedding band with his right index finger and thumb. "It might be interesting to see what he can do with what little we've got."

CHAPTER THREE

"You got hazelnuts?" Mark asked the deli owner, whose turban sported an assortment of badges and pins, mainly of Warner Brothers and Disney cartoon characters.

"I have walnuts, almonds, Brazil, coconuts, peanuts...in or out of shell. I have—"

"Whoa, Asif, just hold it right there a second. I said hazelnuts. I don't give a shit about pistachios, betel nuts, beechnuts, or any other goddamn nuts. Have you got hazelnuts?"

"Alas no, Dr Ross, that is the only nut that I am sorry to admit I have no stock of at the present time."

"Can you order some in?"

"Yes, indeed," Asif beamed. "I will consider it a priority and contact my wholesaler directly."

"Fine. Just give me some of your honey-roasted ham. I'll call back for the nuts in a couple of days."

Mark drove back to the flat with the wrapped, sliced ham secure in the folded thick wedge of Sunday newspapers that were lying on the passenger seat next to him. He parked up, walked across to the rear entrance and pressed the bell. Amy buzzed him in, and he took the stairs up to the third floor. The lift worked, but he opted for the exercise, intent on keeping as many muscles in his six-one frame as supple as possible, to maintain a certain level of fitness.

"Did you get the hazel nuts?" Amy said as he entered the kitchen, before going to him, interlocking her hands around his neck and kissing him on the lips.

He put his arms around her slim waist, let his hands drop to her buttocks, and enjoyed both the taste of her mouth and the feel of her shapely butt.

"No," he said when she broke away. "Asif tells me that most of Europe is in the throes of a Balkan hazel weevil infestation. It started in Turkey last year and has decimated eighty percent of all commercial growers. The tree rats will just have to dig up a few of the thousands that they've buried and forgotten about."

"They are *not* tree rats, they're gorgeous," Amy said, sticking her bottom lip out in a feigned pout.

Mark nodded. "You're right, they are gorgeous. They're like me, natives of the good old US of A."

Amy smiled. "I like them *despite* that. And I've never heard of Balkan hazel weevils."

Mark shrugged. "I'd never heard of Dutch elm disease, AIDS, SARS or Coronavirus until they caused so much havoc. Had you?"

"No, I suppose not."

"How about coffee on the balcony, while we browse through these?" Mark said, removing the ham from the newspapers and putting it in the fridge. "It's mild outdoors with the sun out."

"Fine. The java's ready. You pour while I go get my robe. I'm not hardy enough to sit out there like this."

"Shame," Mark smirked, admiring her figure, which was only covered by a thigh-length Buzz Lightyear nightshirt that proclaimed 'To infinity and beyond' across where her breasts punched the material out above the Toy Story character's visor-clad head.

"It's not *that* warm," Amy said, stepping out onto the small balcony to sit on a chair that Mark had dried the morning dew from with a wad of paper kitchen towel.

"I thought you Brits were hardy types, used to bad weather?" he said, wanting to go and put a sweater on, but not prepared to lose face.

"Not all of us," she said, shivering slightly and idly flicking through the pages of the morning's lie sheets. She felt her stomach clench as the craving for a cigarette did battle with her willpower. She was cutting back, with a view to quitting the habit, and was at her weakest in the morning. Her body demanded a fix to accompany that first cup of caffeine-rich Colombian blend filtered coffee. Damn it. She went in for her cigarettes and came back out feeling like a wimp, but lit up anyway.

They both read about the current investigation into the Regent's Park murders, dismayed at the tacky headlines that labelled the killer a stake-wielding monster; a night prowler who ripped the beating hearts from his luckless female victims' chests, probably to eat the organs raw and further feed his foul bloodlust.

They refrained from discussing the crimes. They both knew now, after this second slaying, that a pattern murderer was at work, and that the body count would rise until he was stopped. Mark had numerous physical and mental scars, which were vivid reminders of his confrontations with such brain-damaged individuals. He fought the inclination to go down that road again. It was chilling enough to read about violent death, without being personally caught up in the sordid machinations of murder.

"So, what's today's plan?" Mark said, folding his paper and tossing it on to the top of the small cast-iron table, sick of the doom, gloom and mass of puerile content that was deemed news.

"I thought we might go for a walk," Amy said, getting up from the chair and then hesitating to look down and watch a squirrel run from the trees that bordered three sides of the eight-flat complex, to cross the large lawn, climb up onto the bird table and search in vain for hazelnuts, before hanging upside down on the bird feeder and making do with peanuts.

"Where to?" Mark said.

"Around the lake. Then we could go for a pub lunch."

"Sounds fine. Are you staying over tonight?"

Amy gave him a 'we'll see' kind of shrug of the shoulders, picked up the empty mugs and padded back into the kitchen, her rubber-soled slippers squeaking on the new parquet flooring that they had laid themselves as a shared project just the weekend before.

Mark brought in the papers. Set them down on the coffee table in the lounge, and his eye caught the name of the cop heading up the park murders' investigation. He knew the guy, and had once helped him in an advisory capacity, and had made it clear that it was a never to be repeated exercise, and that in future the cop should use another consultant. Now, sitting on the edge of the settee, he quickly read the small print. His old instincts and considerable experience in the area of these types of crimes was still simmering on a back burner in his mind, and it was almost impossible to completely ignore what had been his field of expertise for such a meaningful part of his life. It was obvious that the unknown subject had an agenda. They always did. As so many of his kind, the killer was on a mission. Mark was sure that the two young women had not been taken just because they were alone and isolated. They fitted the killer's requirements, conforming precisely to predetermined parameters. The method of dispatching them also had an as yet hidden significance, which no doubt made sense to the mind of a lunatic. That the press had so many details of the M.O. was disturbing.

"Why are you reading that stuff?" Amy said, appearing behind him and looking over his shoulder.

"It still interests me, honey. I can't pretend that it doesn't. I loathe that dark world, but a side of me is still drawn to it."

"I know what you mean," Amy said. "I've been keeping up with the case, even though it scares the hell out of me."

"At least we're not involved. We can be voyeurs and play at being armchair sleuths. Treat it the same as though we were watching a TV movie, or reading a whodunit."

"Yes. It's terrible, but not our problem," she said. "I'll go get ready, and we can take that walk."

Amy took a quick shower, almost unconsciously checked her breasts for lumps, and then let her finger trace the dimpled scar tissue that was a permanent reminder that she would never have children. She had been a detective constable, working undercover vice, talking to local prostitutes and trying to connect with a pimp who was getting too big, too violent, and was into everything from child pornography to bent saunas. The guy was a Rasta; all dreadlocks and gold-capped teeth. His sobriquet was Shadow, due to his being as elusive as one. All went well until an ex-con recognised her. Word got back to Roland De Silva, (The Shadow), and shortly after, on being invited to a meet with him on the pretext of joining his string of girls, she was shot down in an alley. De Silva had just spat in her face, drawn a pistol and fired. Being wired assured an immediate response from other team members, who had been less than fifty yards away in an unmarked van.

Amy had survived being gut shot, but the soft-nosed bullet had necessitated a hysterectomy. She had not returned to duty. The physical damage healed, but she had been left with a fear that she knew would stop her from functioning at an acceptable level. Taking a medical retirement pension and turning her back on the force had been the most difficult decision she had ever had to make. It wasn't something she could readily come to terms with, even now. The experience had taken her spiralling into a state of near mental breakdown, accompanied by clinical depression. A psychiatrist – who she had seen at least once a week for over a year following the incident – helped her contend with the inner turmoil, understand the phases a victim went through, and get past it. Now, two years since the shooting, she was in a relationship with Mark, had a company, Sentinel Security Services, up and running, and was even taking flying lessons. Life was better than it had ever been, with certain fundamental reservations.

Dressed in sweater, jeans, trainers and quilted parka, Amy headed for the bedroom door, pausing to study the framed photo of Mark's late wife that he did not hide when she came to stay at his flat, which was on most weekends. He didn't pretend that Gemma was not still important, and she could live with that.

"I've got bread for the swans," Mark said. "Let's go."

Amy grinned. "Are you sure we can handle the excitement?"

Mark threw her a grave look. "Swans can be mean sons of bitches. They can break a man's legs with just one swipe of a wing."

"That's bullshit. Have you ever met anyone who got his leg broken by a swan's wing?"

"Can't say that I have. But I've never met anyone who was bitten in the ass by a snake. That doesn't mean it doesn't happen. Why? Would you rather go skydiving or bungee jumping?"

"Hell, no. It's just that I'm a little scared of becoming a middle-aged fuddy-duddy, who starts to think that a trip to the Victoria and Albert or playing Scrabble is a big deal."

"Neither of us are youngsters," Mark said. "We're almost middle-aged, ready or not."

"It's a state of mind," Amy said, absently running her fingers through the hair at her temples, which sported flashes of silver amongst the mainly mahogany crop. "I choose to be eighteen till I die. How about you?"

Mark grinned. "I'll buy that dream. C'mon, let's go give those swans hell."

CHAPTER FOUR

Caroline Sellars enjoyed a successful career as a BBC Radio 4 drama producer. The position afforded her with a high measure of artistic fulfilment within her chosen area of expertise, plus a much-appreciated anonymity when outside 'Aunties' portals. For almost five years she had been steadily gaining a reputation as being one of the most able producers in the business.

Life was a measured and pleasurable juggling act to Caroline. The significant other in her life, Simon Payne, a financial advisor, was as independent as herself, and the arrangement they had suited both of them. On an average of three evenings a week they would go for a meal together, take in a play or concert, and stay at one or the other's apartments. The commitment was shallow, and neither of them found any necessity to contemplate the relationship being more than an episode of indeterminable shelf life. As long as they enjoyed each other's company, and the sex was mutually satisfying, then they were happy to keep the status quo.

Caroline lived in a seventh-floor riverside apartment on Victoria Embankment with a superb view across the river to the Royal Festival Hall and the National Theatre; both of which were venues she patronised regularly.

All seemed orderly and predictable, until the first Saturday of September arrived and turned out to be the day that began a sinister and threatening period of her life, affecting all aspects of it. Her problem-free mind was now a place where dark, menacing shadows licked at her psyche, undermined her concentration and invaded her dreams.

The A4 size brown manila envelope was in her mailbox, along with bills, junk mail and an invitation to attend the first night of a play at the newly opened Teatro Theatre in Hampstead, which was being directed by an old friend, Nigel Alexander.

After locking the box, Caroline had taken the lift up to her apartment and made herself a cup of camomile tea, which seemed to calm her after a long day in the studio, where her biggest challenge was always the fragile egos of actors, who in the main were just lucky not to be 'resting'. Although most – especially the men – believed that they were always on the brink of being offered the part that would elevate them into the orbit of national awareness.

The envelope was bulky. Her name had been written on the front in red ink. There were no postage stamps or an address, so it had obviously been hand delivered. Inside was a folded copy of that day's *Mail*, with a yellow Post-it stuck to the front page. The message on it read: 'Keep this, you bitch. It will make sense in due course'. The newspaper's headline read: YOUNG NURSE BRUTALLY SLAIN IN REGENT'S PARK. Caroline thumbed through the pages, her fingers trembling. She felt threatened, but was unable to think of what meaning lay behind the cryptic, anonymous note, or the newspaper.

Over the following weeks she received two further notes in her mailbox, both simply stating: 'I'm watching you'.

Head in a metaphorical bucket of sand, Caroline had tried to ignore the unfathomable and senseless communications. But they took their toll. Was she being stalked? If so, by whom? She had no enemies that she knew of. It had been over eighteen months since she had knowingly upset anyone. She had told an actor, after he had unsuccessfully auditioned for a role, and subsequently approached her in a mean mood, that he was, in her personal estimation, in the wrong line of work, and that at best his performance had been wooden and second rate. He had gone on to find minor fame in a popular TV Soap, which had surprised her, but also surely negated any lasting grudge that he may have harboured. Simon had urged her to go to the police, but she had dismissed his advice. What would she tell them? That she had been sent a newspaper, followed by two notes informing her that she was being watched? Although nervous and perplexed, she tried to put the matter to the back of her mind, but failed.

With a now daily feeling of trepidation, Caroline opened her mailbox on the evening of October the seventh. She felt a cold, steel ball materializing in the pit of her stomach as she picked up a large envelope bearing her name in the now familiar bold red script.

Sitting in the lounge, she took a sip of neat Scotch, gasping as it burned a path of fire down her gullet. She tore the envelope open, pulled out the folded newspaper, and was not surprised to see a Post-it adhered to the front page. The message on it read: 'When I did this, I imagined that it was you, Carrie', and below the writing a happy face had been drawn with lines radiating out from the grinning circle like the rays of the sun. She dropped the tabloid onto the top of the beech wood coffee table and fisted her hands against her mouth as she read the headline: SECOND HORRIFIC MURDER IN REGENT'S PARK.

Her mind immediately retrieved the front-page story from the first newspaper and made all the right connections. She now thought she knew why it had been sent to her. Someone had killed two young women, and was implying that they had died as scapegoats in her place. She gulped down the rest of the malt whisky, almost choking; coughing, and retching as the spirit seared her throat.

Why was she being terrorised? Who would kill innocent strangers and infer that she was at risk?

Numb with a creeping fear that she could hardly contain, Caroline read of the previous day's atrocity. A young woman had been attacked, mutilated and murdered, not far from the spot where the first body had been found. The details were sketchy, but made it quite clear that the police were considering this to be a carbon copy of the September killing.

Redheads, Caroline thought. Both of them had been redheads. They had also both been in their twenties, as she was. The first to die had been a young nurse. She had been stabbed with a wooden stake or sharpened branch, before being butchered. The press had made a big deal out of a modern-day Jack the Ripper prowling the night. Some of the details that were reported should have been withheld, but there were still coppers only too happy to take payment from journalists and part with sensitive information.

Panic bubbled up to overcome her. Standing up too quickly, she cracked her knees hard against the edge of the table, sending the now empty glass, newspaper and envelope onto the carpet. She hobbled to the apartment door, ignoring the pain in her rush to double-check that it was locked, and that the security chain was in place. Satisfied, she turned off the lights and went to the window, convinced that a dark figure would be standing below in the shadows, looking up. *I'm watching you*; the Post-its had warned. She gripped the translucent wand, gave it half a turn to tilt the blind's slats open a fraction, and peeked out and down. There was nothing to make her feel more nervous than she already was. People strolled along the embankment, but she could not see anyone who she considered to be lurking with unknown intent among the steady flow of traffic that fronted the reflection of lights on the otherwise dark stretch of river. She closed the blind, picked her mobile up off the coffee table and phoned Simon. Told him in a jumbled rush about the current newspaper and note, and asked if he would come around. She was terrified; too scared to be alone.

"Have you called the police?" Simon said when she finally ran out of words and gave him chance to speak.

"No, not yet. I don't know what to do," she said.

"I'm on my way. We'll talk it through when I get there. But you'll have to report this. You know that, don't you?"

Caroline just grunted, ended the call and went back over to the picture window to pull the heavy drapes together before turning the light back on. The maroon, velvet curtains were striped with dust, due to hardly ever being drawn. Closing them as a secondary barrier, she felt as though she was cutting herself off from the outside world, and acknowledged that that was precisely what she was doing.

Although expecting Simon, her heart skipped when the intercom buzzed and broke the silence. After hearing his voice, she punched the button that released the lock on the main entrance door, to wait unmoving with her hand on the chain slide until he knocked and said, "It's me, Caroline. Open up."

She collapsed in his arms, and Simon held her, shocked at the visible change that had demolished the usual confidant and in-control personality he was used to. She was now like a frightened bird, trembling against him, staining the front of his jacket with tears.

After a while, Caroline wiped at her red-rimmed eyes and felt more together, feeding off Simon's strength of character and closeness, that pushed away the worst of her fear.

Sitting in the kitchen, she nursed another Scotch, watching in stony silence as Simon studied both of the newspapers, the envelopes, and the notes that she had received.

"Jesus Christ, Cally. Ring the police, or I will. Some maniac is on your case, killing those other women to scare you," Simon said, shaking his head after reading the macabre details.

"He's succeeded," she mumbled. "I'm petrified."

"Who would do this? Who do you know that would fixate on you in such a sick way?"

"I don't, Simon. I can't think of anyone who would wish me harm, or is capable of doing things like that," she said, nodding towards the newspapers.

"I'll stay here tonight," Simon said, getting up and walking around to the back of her chair, to massage her shoulders and neck in an effort to loosen the tension that was knotting her muscles into a hard, unyielding mass. "Better still, let's go to my place. You should stay there until this is resolved."

"I'll pack," she said, not putting up any argument; reluctant to linger another minute in what she no longer thought of as a safe sanctuary, but more a fortress under siege.

A malevolent chuckle erupted from the mouth of the figure hunched over the steering wheel of the dark green Toyota that followed the BMW to the flat in Russell Square, just a spit from the British Museum.

The whore and her stud could run, but they couldn't hide. Caroline Sellars would know a fear beyond any that her wildest dreams could begin to conjure up, before finally, slowly, she was afforded her just desserts. There was no hurry. You don't rush a gourmet meal in a top restaurant. It needs to be savoured; consumed at leisure with a glass or two of fine wine. The plan was to dismantle the bitch's life around her, and drive her to the point of total psychological meltdown. Only then would she be taken.

Inside Simon's flat, the couple talked for hours, but Caroline could not think of any plausible explanation to shed any light on the sinister events.

"Make the call, love," Simon said for the umpteenth time. "The implications of this are too dangerous to ignore. This isn't something that will go away. You can't just stick your head in the fucking sand."

"Tomorrow," she said. "I can't do it now. I've had too much Scotch, and I need to sleep on it."

They showered together before going to bed and making out. Caroline had suddenly needed release, to drain her of the tension that had locked her body up drum-tight. Sex was a temporary distraction from all consternation.

The following morning, at Simon's insistence, and feeling a degree calmer in daylight, Caroline phoned the police. She explained what had happened, and was put through to the incident room of the team dealing with the Park Murders investigation.

Barney knew that this was the break they had needed. It would appear that the woman was in some way a key to the killings. He remained outwardly calm as his nerves jumped with expectancy; somehow keeping his voice composed as he talked to a person who might just have answers that could result in an early arrest.

"Give me your address," Barney said, initially wanting to interview the woman in surroundings that she would feel comfortable in, and which might prove more conducive to his obtaining maximum information.

Armed with the address, he hung up. "Come on, Mike," he said. "We've got a lead."

"What have we got?" Mike said, following his boss out into the corridor.

"A woman who's been sent newspapers with headlines of the killings. It appears she's being stalked and threatened. Our boy is playing mind games with her."

Caroline could not help the two police officers, beyond giving them everything that she had found in her mailbox, which Mike bagged and labelled after first donning a pair of cellophane gloves.

"Why didn't you contact us after you received the first newspaper?" Barney said.

"Because I had no way of knowing that it was related to the lead story on the front page," Caroline said with a defensive edge to her voice. "The note just stated that it would make sense in time. Now, with the other newspaper and the note, it does. Although I have no idea why it's happening."

Barney nodded. "Please try to think of anyone who might bear you a grudge, or have any reason to wish you harm."

"I have thought, Inspector. I've racked my brain until it aches, and gone through both my work and personal relationships. I cannot imagine that a single person I know could be capable of these...these atrocities. I just don't know why anyone would want to hurt me. I don't understand any of it."

"We'll keep you under twenty-four-hour protection," Barney said. "It goes without saying that you may be at risk. Although if these notes that state he's watching you are on the level, then we may just pick him up. I would appreciate a full list of all your friends, acquaintances, work colleagues and, er, past...anyone who has been significant in your life."

"What do you think, boss?" Mike said, driving away from Simon Payne's flat, heading back to the Yard.

"I think we've got a real chance, is what I think. The killer has some sick motive. Caroline Sellars is a redhead in her twenties, physically similar to the two victims. Could be he's some old flame she dumped. Maybe he has a problem handling rejection. Or it might be someone at the Beeb who thinks she got promotion at his expense, which he believes he deserved. Whoever it is, knows her. It's personal. When we home in on him...case closed."

"Sounds simple," Mike said, his brow corrugating in a frown.

Barney twiddled with his wedding band. "I know. So why do I have bad vibes, and the feeling that it won't be?"

CHAPTER FIVE

Mark parked the Jeep Cherokee on the country road next to the eastern shore of Bewl Water. It was just a few minutes drive from the flat, which was situated on the edge of Bedgebury Forest, well back from the A268, out of sight and sound of traffic.

Holding hands, Mark and Amy followed a footpath around the large lake, stopping when they reached a small jetty, to sit on bleached planks with their feet dangling above the placid water, as they relished the tranquil surroundings.

"I think a small cottage over there would be a terrific weekend retreat," Amy said, pointing to a finger peninsula that poked out towards them from the far bank.

"I vant to be alone, eh?" Mark said, sounding more like Bela Lugosi than Greta Garbo.

"She never said that," Amy stated, smiling broadly at his bad impression.

"Who didn't say what?"

"Garbo didn't say 'I vant to be alone'. And if she had, it wouldn't have sounded like Dracula with a Yank accent," she said, gripping his arm and making as if to push him in the lake.

"You wouldn't dare," he said, knowing that she would, but counting on her wanting a pub lunch, and having the sense to realise that if he was soaked to the skin, then the outing would be curtailed.

"Next time," she said, turning her attention to unwrapping the part loaf of stale bread. "I wouldn't want to scare the wildfowl."

For the next thirty minutes they both tore slices of bread into small pieces and fed a dozen milling ducks, and two majestic swans that had glided across the lake like windblown galleons in full sail to see what they were missing.

"That's the birds sorted, now let's go and feed ourselves," Amy said, getting up and brushing crumbs from her lap onto the jetty, before carefully walking back along the aged and probably unsafe structure.

Mark drove to a thatch-roofed pub only a couple of miles from the lake. They ate a traditional Sunday lunch, comprising thick slices of roast beef, Yorkshire pudding and all the trimmings, to wash it down with a glass each of the house red.

They had only been back at the flat for twenty minutes when the landline phone rang. Mark had been pouring freshly brewed coffee, with Amy standing behind him, up close with her arms around his waist. She planned on them spending what was left of the afternoon in bed.

Mark turned into her, kissed the tip of her nose, then broke free, went through to the lounge and picked up, feeling slightly apprehensive, hoping that nothing had happened at the clinic to necessitate him having to go in.

"Yeah," he said.

"Dr Mark Ross?"

"Speaking."

"Detective Superintendent Clive Pearce. You once—"

"I once advised you on a case," Mark said, his interjection caustic and abrupt. "I also told you that it was a one-off. You're going to ask me to get involved with what I'm reading on the front pages, and the answer is no."

"Tell me that you haven't been following the case, Dr Ross," Clive said. "Give me your word that your profiling instincts didn't cut in and start coming up with theories on this, and that you didn't consider motive and..."

Mark held the phone away from his ear, almost ended the call, but then just stared at it as his mind raced and considered what the copper had said.

Clive Pearce closed his eyes, listened to the snake hiss of the line, but said nothing, knowing that cogs were turning in the other man's mind. If he pushed too hard, he would get nowhere. He would wait and see if the psychologist talked or thought himself into joining the team before he tried to reel him in with a hard sell.

"You know Amy, don't you?" Mark said, breaking the silence.

"Er, yes, of course. She was a damn good detective. How is she?"

Mark ignored the polite, patronising comment. "I'll talk it over with her and call you back," he said. "Don't be optimistic."

"Then I'll just hope, Dr Ross. We need to stop—"

"No sales pitch," Mark said. "I know the position. I also know that you have one or two very good consultants who you could utilise."

"They're not in the same league as you," Clive said. He was not above using downright flattery, if that was what it took.

"Later," Mark said, and hung up.

Amy had faced more danger than ninety-five percent of crime fighters would be unfortunate enough to come up against during their entire careers. Both she and Mark had found themselves drawn, as if magnetised or in some way tuned in to the same wavelength as the worst examples of humanity.

In Mark's case, his personal impressive record of being instrumental in running down serial killers – while with the FBI – had undoubtedly been responsible for the prevention of an incalculable loss of life. Was it his fate? Could it in some way be preordained that his life be somehow interwoven in a symbiotic existence with that which he hated? He felt as though he were one side of a coin, forever separate, yet still the obverse face of evil, having to live in the same pocket of small change with no choice in the matter. He was no Don Quixote intent on jousting at windmills and putting devotion and honour before his personal needs or aspirations. He had joined the bureau to be part of something noble, to make a difference, and had found that he had a talent for being able to 'see' and feel the nature of the beast. At first it had felt like a blessing, as though he were some kind of modern-day dragon slayer. But looking into the abyss became a curse, not a gift. Evil did indeed look back at you from the depths of the pit, to overwhelm the spirit and consume the soul. The final conflict that almost robbed him of sanity, and then his life, began to escape from the mental vault that he kept it locked away in. He forced it back, returned to the kitchen, picked up his coffee and sipped it.

"Who was it?" Amy said, stubbing out her fourth cigarette of the day on the presidential seal that was embossed on the bottom of a small ceramic ashtray.

Mark chewed absently at the inside of his right cheek. Went over to where she was sitting in the nook and settled opposite her. "That cop, Pearce."

Amy forgot about the cigarette end between her finger and thumb. She was transfixed. It was obvious to her why Clive Pearce had phoned.

"Did you tell him to stick it where the sun doesn't shine?" she said, looking down at the ashtray and letting go of the crumpled Superking filter.

"I said I'd get back to him, after we'd talked it through."

"What is there to talk about, for God's sake? You know what it can do to you. Why would you want to go down that road again?"

"It's not that easy to run away from what you are, Amy. I love you, and I value your point of view above anyone else's, so give it to me. Pearce knew that I would have studied the case, and wants to know what I think. That's all."

"If you want to do it enough, then you will," she said, crossing her arms and glaring at him; her body language unmistakable. "It's your call. But if you give him a little, then he'll want a whole lot more. You'll be sucked in up to your neck."

"I know if I don't help, and others die, I'll feel that I may have been able to make a difference and didn't. It's Catch-22."

Amy got up and went over to a shoulder-high corner unit, opened the leaded-glass door and withdrew a bottle of Three Barrels. Neither of them said a word as she poured large measures of the brandy into crystal tumblers and set them down on the tabletop.

"Official meeting," she said, retaking her seat. "Let's discuss it."

Mark readied himself for a verbal onslaught as he mulled over what he already thought of as a foregone conclusion. Only if Amy actually said 'no, please do not do this', would he be able to withhold any assistance.

He watched as she downed half the neat spirit before replacing the glass on the tabletop with the force and report of a high court judge's or auctioneer's gavel.

"OK, let's discuss it," he said.

"If you do it, then you don't step into that world alone," she said. "You take me on board, and we help each other through it. I will not sit back and watch you withdraw into a shell. If you want to be the Lone Ranger, then I'm going to be your Tonto, along for the ride."

"You'd look good in buckskins. Maybe if I wore a black mask we could really get into the roles."

"I should have pushed you in the lake when I had the chance."

They smiled, and their hands met across the table. A decision had been made without the need to argue or actually mull over the subject at great length.

"How about using my place as a base," Amy suggested. "It's nearer the action."

"Sounds good. I'll arrange to take a couple of days off. Can you?"

She nodded. "I have one client that I might need to see on Tuesday morning. Everything else can be handled by my operatives."

"Is that what you call your two guys, operatives?"

"That, or security specialists. What would you call them?"

"I know them, so I'd call them Petra and Jon. That's their names."

"If you're going to be pedantic, then Petra isn't a guy, she's a girl."

"Calling everyone guy is a long-term habit of mine. Women understand."

"Yes, they put it down to you being an uncouth Yank who doesn't know any better."

"Whatever."

They looked at back copies of the newspapers that Mark kept stacked in the small utility room and only threw out about once every three months, when the pile began to mimic the leaning tower of Pisa, assuming a dangerous cant that somehow defied gravity. Three hours later, with copious notes in front of him, Mark phoned Clive Pearce back.

"Yes, Dr Ross," Clive said, physically crossing his fingers, wanting the American to agree to assist them, and knowing that he could well be their best hope of bringing the case to an early and satisfactory conclusion.

"Call me Mark. You get two for the price of one on this. Amy and I will look at the book and work out a profile."

"The book?"

"The file, Clive. What I call the murder book. I need the whole nine yards. I want to see the crime scene reports and photographs; autopsy protocols and evidence analysis reports. I want every scrap of documentation. And I also want you to remember that in reality many serial killers remain at large, or take a long time to bring down. Don't expect miracles."

"Thanks, Dr, er...Mark. I've been in this business too long to expect divine intervention by way of a miracle. I just need to do everything that I can to give us an edge. Can you drop by the Yard and have a word with the squad that are investigating the case? I want them to have a game plan."

"Get the paperwork to Amy's place tomorrow morning. We'll go through it before I face the troops. OK?"

Mark gave Pearce Amy's address and phone number, then rang off. The old buzz was back. He felt like a kid with a new toy. He could hardly wait to study the case in depth. His new-found enthusiasm frightened him. He had always tried to believe that what he did was not who he was, but the boundaries seemed to blur and merge together too easily.

CHAPTER SIX

Clive delivered the files personally, and reacquainted himself with the profiler and the attractive ex-cop. He stayed for coffee, leaving his driver outside the smart Georgian terrace house adjacent to Richmond Park. He was a little envious of the property. Security companies were obviously raking it in, and he wished that he'd had the balls to quit the force and move into the private sector decades ago.

After Clive left, Mark and Amy sat in the oak-walled study – which Amy had subconsciously modelled as a near replica of her father's, only becoming aware of what she had recreated when it was almost completed – and set the document wallets on the large walnut desk.

"Plenty to look at," Amy said. "I'll go pick up a few groceries while you start in on it."

Mark nodded. The challenge before him was one that would necessitate facing personal demons he had thought to be vanquished. He was about to enter territory that he knew would both repulse and excite him in a strange unexplainable meld that only a very few people could appreciate, or even begin to understand.

Amy bent and kissed his bristly cheek. "I'll see you later," she said. "And if you go for a leak, have a shave. Or is that designer stubble?"

After she had left, and with only the solemn ticking of a large Victorian clock on the mantel of the Adam fireplace to break the silence, Mark found the resolve to confront the horror; to examine properly the fine details of the unsolved murders.

It was over two hours later when Amy re-entered the study. Mark had not moved from the chair since she had left, and his concentration on the paperwork, which was now strewn across the desktop, and even next to his feet on the carpet, was total. Thieves could have ransacked the house around him; such had been his intense focus on the mass of information.

"You ready for a cup of coffee?" Amy said.

No reply.

She went to him and put a hand on his shoulder.

Mark grunted, startled, the spell broken, and said, "You could give a guy a heart attack, creeping up like that."

"Just trying to get your attention. Next time I'll whistle Dixie, or ring a bell. Do you want coffee?"

"Uh, yeah. I could use a break," he said, stretching his arms and yawning.

Amy stepped forward and tipped out the contents of a large brown paper bag, which she had held concealed behind her back. What seemed like a thousand hazelnuts cascaded over his lap; the noise akin to gravel being dumped off the back of a truck.

"What the hell?" Mark said, shunting back in the chair.

"I called in at my local deli, and the owner looked at me as though I was a hod short of a brick when I asked about the current situation over hazelnuts. He seemed to think that the Balkan hazel weevil infestation was the product of a bad trip on acid. I said a friend had told me about it, and he gave me that 'You must have strange friends' look."

"He just hasn't heard about it, is all. These must be old stock," Mark said, grinning as he thought that if he were a squirrel, he would most likely believe that he had died and gone to that big tree in the sky, at the sight of so much expensive sustenance.

"While I make the coffee, you do penance for your fib and pick up all these disease-free nuts."

"Deal," he said.

"And don't think I don't know how many there are."

"You mean you've actually counted them?"

"No. But I know exactly how much they weigh."

"You're one sneaky broad."

"Once a cop, always a cop."

By midnight, Mark had a sketchy profile written out. Amy had spent half the evening reading through the files, while Mark tried to find and then think his way into the personality of an individual who would commit such blatantly shocking acts on women who were almost certainly strangers to him.

They talked it over, and Mark found Amy's views, as both a woman and a prior law enforcement officer, constructive and well thought through. He was ready to give the police a preliminary word picture of the type of psycho he thought they should be looking for. He had a tenuous, unexplainable sense of the man as an individual, which was taking shape at the edges of his mind.

Clive introduced Mark to the DCI handling the case. Amy had decided against accompanying him to the Yard. She preferred to stay in the background, and Mark had requested not to be named to the press. That had been his only stipulation, and Clive had assured him of anonymity.

The squad room was too quiet. All eyes were on him as he stood next to Clive and Barney and studied the impassive, sceptical faces of the team.

"Looks like a fuckin' ginger," DC Gary Shields whispered to DC Eddie McKay. "What does he know about real-life crime?"

Mark flicked a lock of long black hair back from his forehead and gave the coppers a broad Colgate smile. "Good morning," he said, well aware that the group regarded him with a mixture of suspicion and animosity, and no doubt thought that he was an unnecessary civilian presence in their midst. "I realise that you are the professionals who run down and apprehend the bad guys for a living. I'm not here to teach my grandma to suck eggs. But I may just be able to give you a little assistance; an insight into the type of person that you're looking for. Are there any questions before I begin? I'd rather clear the air before we get to it."

"Yeah," Eddie said, standing to address the now clean-shaven and immaculately, if casually dressed doctor. "What exactly is it that you do? Are you a profiler?"

"I was a criminal psychologist," Mark said. "I studied felons, and the patterns and motivational causes for their antisocial behaviour. A lot of these scumbags work to a pattern that can be anticipated. There's a ritual element to what they do, and many follow a predetermined blueprint. I attempted to get a handle on what made them tick, and to predict what their next move might be. If I can give you even one small lead or aspect to look at that you may not have considered, then it could conceivably help to identify the perpetrator."

The atmosphere lightened. He had put most of the cops at ease.

"And the answer to, am I a profiler, is," he continued after a pause. "I used to be. I was a federal agent working out of the Behavioural Science Unit at Quantico. Anything else?"

There were a few grunts and shaking of heads, but no further questions.

"OK, let's start with what we've got," Mark said, turning to the large wall-mounted whiteboard behind him, on which he added notes with a black marker pen as he talked. "Both vics were murdered in approximately the same location. And the bizarre methodology employed makes it reasonably safe to assume that we are dealing with the same deranged individual. The fact that the two women were young and had auburn hair is without doubt a factor. The light was poor, and I am convinced that rather than them just happening to be in the wrong place at the wrong time, they had been stalked. They were selected prey. This guy is redirecting anger from someone else, and venting uncontrollable urges on similar looking strangers."

"Have you any idea what type of person we're looking for?" DC Louise Callard said.

"It's early days," Mark said. "But at this point in time I would say a white male in his twenties or early thirties. He will almost certainly be single, with a pronounced personality disorder. He may well be a loner who avoids as much social contact as possible. His condition will determine what work he does, if any. He is apt to be employed in a field that affords him a certain level of isolation; apartness. Although I would imagine that he is of above average intelligence. This type usually blends well. He will probably keep himself in good physical shape. It is not a stretch to see him as a game player. The press and TV coverage of his actions will amuse and excite him; an added bonus. Rather than trying to conceal his kills, he chooses to leave them as a statement of what he is capable of. The grandstanding could ultimately be his downfall. His reason for killing is not apparent. I can only speculate at this stage that he is motivated by a real or imagined grievance. He has satisfied some inner need, and repeated the process for the emotional reward that it gave him. As I've already stated, this is anger, which is being channelled into revenge attacks. Vulnerable, similar victims are being targeted. The only problem at this stage is, that types can overlap. His disorder is not completely evident, yet."

"So, we're looking for a head case?" DC Gary Shields said.

There was a ripple of laughter.

"In simple terms, yes," Mark said. "He has an abnormal outlook on life. His psychopathic personality may take the form of a self-serving psychosis. He will be able to blame his actions on an event that has triggered this response from him. Although reasoning, and therefore the need to absolve himself of blame, will not figure."

"Do you believe that he will kill again?" Eddie said.

"Without a doubt. He has the taste for it now. He'll continue until he's stopped. Regent's Park would appear to be a place that he is familiar with, and that he has adopted as his killing ground. I suggest that when he feels safe to venture there again, you'll be served up with his next victim. This is a creep with a sadistic personality disorder; the type who thrives on violence, employing torture, mutilation and ultimately murder to turn his wheels. Inflicting physical and psychological pain is an obsession. Pattern murderers are, sadly, a part of life in the States. Over here they're still an exception to the rule. Just be aware that you are trying to find a killing machine; a freak who feeds on what he does and cannot be reasoned with or deterred."

"Why the sharpened branches in the vaginas, and the removal of the hearts, Doctor Ross?" Louise said.

"He hates women. Or to be more precise, hates one particular woman. To plunge a sharpened stake into the very centre of his victim's femininity is symbolic. He is attacking the object that he covets but is not allowed to possess. As for the hearts, that could also be emblematic. Maybe someone withheld their love, their heart. It broke his, and so he takes theirs, literally, to keep as trophies. You're looking for one sick puppy."

"Thanks, Doc," Barney said, shaking the tall man's hand as they left the building and went out into the car park. "If we get anything else, I'll give you a bell."

Mark nodded and walked off towards the Cherokee. He was meeting Amy at a pub in Chelsea, and was relieved to be away from the room full of cops, who he knew thought that profiling was in the main a crock of shit; the stuff that movies are made of. There was not much else he could offer them, yet. But he had been given the precise locations of where the bodies had been found, and planned to visit the crime scenes.

Barney returned to the incident room, impressed. He had not told the doctor about the latest development in the case. He'd wanted an assessment without the psychologist's prior knowledge of Caroline Sellars involvement. The Yank had been good. Now, he would bring his team up to speed and concentrate on staking out the park, and doing a full background check on everyone that Caroline had ever met since moving to the city several years previously. He would also visit Mark Ross later, to give him details of Caroline, who was a dead ringer for the two women that had been murdered.

"I have these Polaroids of the envelopes, and photocopies of the notes," Barney said, passing them to Mark after Amy had shown him into the study and he had told them about Caroline.

"You knew all this when I addressed your team, right?" Mark said.

"Yes. We'd only just got it, but I wanted to hear what your thoughts were on the two murders, without this lead."

Mark's voice was acerbic. "You don't have much time for profilers, do you?"

"Not a lot," Barney said. "The last time a psychologist assisted on a murder inquiry that I was heading up, he sent us in the wrong direction. We solved the case despite him and his half-baked theories. When we looked at everything that he had fed us, it was bullshit; more hindrance than help. He only succeeded in causing us to initially eliminate a suspect who ended up being the killer."

"Profiling is an aid. It doesn't offer a money back guarantee," Mark said. "All I can say is, that my department got it right more often than wrong. It's a technique that doesn't come with the name and address of the offender, but done properly it can narrow the field and save a lot of man hours and shoe leather."

"I know that you are better than that," Barney said. "You've narrowed it down to a list of one on many occasions."

"That was way back. I had some luck. What you have to remember is that a lot of serial killers never get caught. As you know, your average homicide is committed by someone who knows his victim, or can be linked to that person. Stranger-on-stranger killings don't offer the same luxury. Law enforcements' worst enemies are organised serial killers and professional hitmen. They can ply their trade over a long period, and the clever ones can outsmart us."

"How do you feel about this one, Doc—?"

"Make it, Mark. If we're going to be working together, forget the title. I only use it in the facility, or at seminars."

"Fine, I'm Barney."

Amy had excused herself to make coffee, and on returning with three mugs on a tray, she could sense the change of atmosphere in the room. The two men had begun to bond and could have been mistaken for old friends. She knew the DCI in passing, from her days on the force. He had the reputation of being a good cop, dependable, and not as starchy or anal retentive as many of his rank.

"As for this particular unknown subject," Mark said as Barney stirred two heaped spoonfuls of sugar into his coffee. "I think he's too cocksure for his own good. He likes to take calculated risks. He could have abducted the women, dealt with them at his leisure, and then dumped them. Instead, he chose to attack in the open. The high-risk factor is part of the thrill for him; an essential ingredient in his overall scheme. I also think that the dates are significant. He's struck on the first Friday of September and October. I expect the next to be on the first Friday in November."

"That could be coincidence," Barney said.

"I don't really believe in coincidence, Barney. I know it exists, but I choose to work on the premise that it doesn't. These are pattern murders, and the timing is part of the whole enchilada."

Mark looked down at the handwriting on the copies of photos and notes. "I take it your Document Section is examining these?"

"Yes. We have a forensic handwriting expert working on them."

"Good. It's amazing how much those guys can pick up from how someone writes. And if you want to keep Caroline Sellars alive, move her."

"She's already left her flat. She's staying with her boyfriend."

"The killer will know that," Mark said. "Believe me. He's a watcher who plans every detail. He will have expected her to run, and he'll know where she is. You need to put her in a safe house."

Barney nodded. He knew that Mark was right. That was why the flat in Russell Square was being staked out around-the-clock by armed officers.

"If you're using her as bait, then it's a dangerous game," Mark said. "He'll find a way to reach her."

"I hear what you say. I'll put it up to Pearce. He won't want to hang his arse out the window by leaving her at risk and maybe losing her."

"That's all I've got for now, Barney. I plan on taking a look at the crime scenes in the morning, at the approximate time that the victims were murdered, so warn your undercover boys that we'll be there. I don't want them to think that we're loitering with intent or just ghouls who get off on visiting the spots where the deeds were done."

It was pearly bright in the stark, cold glow of the moon as Mark parked up near the now indistinctive patch of ground where the first victim, Elaine Stanton, had been so cruelly mutilated and had leaked her lifeblood on and into the grass-carpeted soil: a location where children had played and would play again; where couples had strolled hand-in-hand, and where no visible sign now remained to denote the spot as being where a scene from hell had been enacted. The anonymous did not merit a memorial to stand as silent witness at the place they had fallen. Had the girl been a celebrity, or perhaps a police officer, then an engraved marker or plaque would in all likelihood have been on display in perpetuity.

An unseasonable forewarning of winter's approach was manifest in a sparkling layer of frost that covered every surface. Mark and Amy wore thick, quilted parkas and woollen gloves. They climbed out of the Cherokee and walked along the edge of the boating lake, passing where the second victim had been murdered.

"There isn't much in the way of cover," Amy said, her warm breath forming streams of vapour as it hit the chill air.

"He didn't care," Mark observed. "He was satisfied that no one else was in sight, and it was still dark when he struck."

"But both of the women were out running. They were young and fit. How do you suppose he got close enough to physically attack them?"

"He blended. Probably adopted the guise of a jogger himself. He could have passed within feet of them, and if he looked the part, they wouldn't have been alarmed."

"That simple, huh?"

"Yeah. If you know where someone will be, and at what time. If the coast hadn't been clear, he could have aborted, just carried on running and waited till the next morning, or the next. Also, the path leads through those bushes," Mark continued, pointing to the dark clumps of rhododendrons that were backed by trees that had already shed most of their leaves. "He could have been crouched in there like a spider in a web, waiting for them to come to him."

Amy clasped her arms to her body and looked about her, as if expecting a figure to materialise, jogging through the park towards them.

"You're sure he stalked them?"

"Positive. He selected them for their hair-colour, looks, age and build. He will have chosen them in daylight, then followed them to their homes and spent time familiarising himself with their habits. This is someone with a great deal of patience, who may have tailed dozens of likely candidates before finding suitable women who took early morning runs in the park."

"Do you think he'll be stupid enough to strike here again?"

"Maybe, but not necessarily. I think he's fixated on runners, though. They're soft targets, and he's found an M.O. that works for him. Any woman who fits the criteria is at risk if she puts herself in an isolated location between dusk and dawn. I have to believe that he's smart. He'll probably change the venue now. I would if I was him. He'll know that the first killing would have been viewed as an isolated incident, so the second wouldn't have been expected."

"Does visiting here help?" Amy said as they walked back to JC, as Mark referred to his Jeep Cherokee.

"Yes," he said. "It gives me a proper sense of the surroundings that he feels most comfortable in. He likes open spaces, and the dark."

Amy's brow knitted. "Isn't it just commonsense to use the cover of darkness and this sort of locale?"

"No. He could have taken them in their homes and during daylight hours if it had suited him. This is preference. He probably imagines himself a nocturnal predator; a creature of the night."

Amy took a vacuum flask from the holdall in the front foot well, filled the plastic cup and lid with piping hot black coffee and handed the cup to Mark before taking a sip of hers.

"Christ, I need a cigarette," she said.

Mark smiled. "It's all in the mind. Trust me on that, I'm a doctor. You don't need a cigarette; you just want one."

"Need, want, desire. The label doesn't alter the fact that I'm craving for a nicotine hit. And what do you know? You're a non-smoker."

"I got through two packs of Winston a day, back when I was with the bureau."

"You've never mentioned it. How did you stop?" Amy said, wondering just how many other facets of Mark's life were still unknown to her.

"I just decided to quit. Every time I took the pack out of my pocket, I counted to twenty, chose not to have one, and put it back. After about six months, I dumped the pack and flew without a safety net."

"No other help?"

"Yes, a colleague, Ritchie Weller. He died of lung cancer. That was an added incentive. When I was a rookie, straight out of the academy, I was assigned to Ritchie. He turned me into a half-decent agent. He chain-smoked, and at fifty he started coughing up blood. He was gone in less than a month. It was that quick. It was the day of his funeral that I decided to part company with tobacco. I realised that it was an expensive and ultimately painful way to commit suicide."

"You're a dark horse, Mark Ross," Amy said before finishing her coffee. "The longer I know you, the more I'm aware that I hardly know you at all."

"What you see is what you get, lady," he said, a mischievous grin forming on his craggy face. "Don't look for what isn't there to be found."

"Bullshit. At the right time and place, I want to hear all about you, to feel that there are no closed doors between us. Does that bother you?"

"Not at all. It should be fun. Have you any skeletons in *your* cupboard?"

"Maybe the odd one", she said, then changed the subject. "Now what?"

Mark shrugged as he drove out of the park and headed back towards Richmond, glad that he was leaving the city as the oncoming traffic became a metal and glass logjam. "I'll write up a more detailed profile based on what we have so far, and what I instinctively feel about the Unsub", he said. "And then we cross our fingers and hope that Barney and his team pick the guy up before he kills again."

"You think that they will?"

"Sadly, no."

CHAPTER SEVEN

This one was absolutely fucking perfect. Her hair was almost the same deep auburn shade. And from a distance – with eyes screwed almost shut to blur the image – her freckled, milk-white skin and even features gave the illusion that she actually was Caroline.

Six in a row had proved unsuitable. They had all made the grade physically, but only this one had gone jogging in the dark, and alone. Most kept to well-lit streets, and more often than not were accompanied. The killings were promoting a causal effect, and many women were beginning to take precautionary measures.

The woman now in sight was seated at a pavement table outside an eatery off Curzon Street. She was *the* one, now flagged for special attention. Her name was Judy Prescott. She lived alone in a second floor flat in Seville Street, and used the tube to commute between Knightsbridge and Green Park, Monday through Friday. Sitting opposite her in the same carriage that morning had been a thrill. Alighting at Green Park, she had crossed over Piccadilly and cut through Bolton Street to her place of work in an insurance office off Berkeley Square. Now, at almost twelve-forty p.m., she was on her lunch break, working her smartphone as she idly picked at a plate of chicken and pasta.

Judy was a creature of habit, and her early morning runs through Hyde Park had sealed her fate. She always left her flat at six a.m., entered the park, crossed Rotten Row and then picked up Serpentine Road. Her route was fixed. She would pass the pier and boat houses, to then cross the bridge and head back through the park to South Carriage Drive.

It would have been better if she had taken her exercise at night, but what the hell, beggars can't be choosers.

Reviewing the situation while sipping a double latte in Starbucks, keeping the prize in sight, it was amusing to think how inept the police were. They had moved Caroline to a safe house, but the boyfriend was still at the flat, and though unlikely, he might know where she was being stashed. When the time came, if he did have her address, he would talk. Of that there was no doubt. In the meantime, let the beautiful Caroline feel the claustrophobia of a caged bird; warm, safe, looked after, yet a prisoner, unable to spread her wings and fly freely. Her life had already been affected; the quality of it diminished to keep her in a continual state of fear.

Barney and Mike leafed through copies of the profile that Mark Ross had provided. It was early, and apart from the two of them, the incident room was empty. It would soon be hot, cluttered, noisy, and full of the smells of cheap aftershave lotion, more expensive perfume, and perspiration. Smoking was banned throughout the building, but some coppers bent rules they thought to be draconian, and the batteries in many of the ceiling-mounted smoke alarms were disconnected in the toilets.

After thirty minutes, Mike got up, stretched and said, "You want another coffee, boss?"

Barney nodded, pausing in his deliberation to empty a saucer – which he employed as an ashtray – into the waste bin next to his chair, before lighting up another cigarette, jabbing his glasses back up to the bridge of his nose, and going back to the report. He totally ignored the No Smoking policy. What would Big Brother do, shoot him?

The ex-FBI man had painted a chilling picture. It was a concise psychological evaluation, laid out in what was obviously a well practised format. Barney knew that the doctor would make out daily reports on patients at the facility where he worked. He also knew, from Clive, that the American had a double major in psychology and criminology, plus the practical experience of having specialised in hunting down ritual murderers for a living. It was difficult to imagine how any man could so fully immerse himself in a world that embraced homicidal insanity, or want to, without losing his own reason. Mark Ross was, or had been, a predator himself, who with an unexplainable understanding could almost see his quarry from just visiting murder scenes and examining the methodology used. It crossed Barney's mind that the line between hunter and hunted can be almost nonexistent.

"Do you buy Ross's line of thought?" Mike said, setting the two mugs of coffee down on the desktop.

Barney sat back and said, "Let's just say I wouldn't argue with it. He made a career out of doing this, and was rated as being among, if not the best."

"Gruesome."

"Yeah. The guy is like a sewer worker who explores the shit-filled tunnels of the human mind."

"Christ, boss, that's almost poetic in a distasteful sort of way," Mike said.

"Bollocks. That's just how I see it."

"Does what he's written help us, then?"

"You've read it."

"I know. But he writes in probabilities, nothing definite. The first murder could have been a one-off; a rape attempt that went wrong. Although that wouldn't explain the savagery involved. The second one confirmed that we had a real fruitcake. And we didn't need a trick-cyclist to tell us that."

"Ross is painting a picture of the *type* that did it. It's the only ball we've got to run with. He's positive that the Sellars woman is connected with whoever's doing this. He also confirms that it won't stop, and that the next killing will probably take place on the first Friday of the month and in a similar location to where we found the others."

"That's not a great leap of imagination, boss. It would follow the pattern. I just find it hard to swallow that he knows the mental state of the guy. He seems sure that this is someone in their twenties or thirties, white and a loner, who was abused physically and/or mentally in childhood. He then goes on to say that he suspects it to be an only child from a broken marriage, who may well have tortured animals as a kid, and had a predilection for starting fires. Isn't that the standard pitch of most profilers?"

"It's based on what they know from experience," Barney said. "This sick type of individual must fit a pattern that Ross has seen many times before."

"We need a lot more than he's given us."

"There would be more, if the murders had been committed inside the women's homes. All we have are corpses that have had their hearts cut out and sharpened branches rammed up their vaginas. So far, we've hardly any forensic evidence to work with. There was no matching hair, just a few fibres, and no prints or body fluids, other than those of the victims. Even scrapings from the fingernails came up blank. Neither of the women had managed to scratch their attacker. The scenes were clean."

Mike finished his coffee and said, "Knowing the type that we're looking for isn't going to stop it happening again, is it?"

"No. Unless we find the lunatic bearing a grudge against Caroline Sellars, and damn quick, then the tally will go up. Get the team together and make sure that they all familiarise themselves with this profile. I want them to know what type of sick bastard we're after."

By the third week of October, only one prime suspect had been found out of all the names of colleagues, friends and ex-lovers that Caroline had furnished.

Jason Tyler was a thirty-year-old city dealer; a single man who lived alone in an up-market loft conversion in Fulham, whom Caroline had suffered a brief affair with three years previously. She had ended it due to his brashness, flashes of bad temper, and above all, because of his almost narcissistic personality. She had come to think of him as immature; an overgrown ex-public schoolboy with only one real interest in life, himself.

The wealthy broker was good-looking, confident, and initially eminently desirable. Unfortunately, the candy coating covered a shallow and pretentious centre.

"What do you think, Caroline?" Barney said, facing her across the coffee table in the lounge of the safe house that she had been moved to, which was a fifties bungalow located on a quiet, tree lined avenue in west London.

"I think that Jason is basically a wimp. He would probably faint at the sight of blood. He's the last person I would suspect of being capable of murder."

"You did dump him, though. Right?"

"Yes. But he was too obsessed with himself to give a shit. He will have told all of his friends that he got bored and ditched me. It wasn't as though he was in love with me. I don't think he is capable of loving anyone but himself."

"He has no alibi for when either of the murders were committed. We have to assume that he may harbour you ill-will, and that whether you realise it or not, could have committed these crimes and sent you the threatening notes."

"How many single men would have an alibi for six o'clock in the bloody morning?" Caroline said sharply, her face reddening with impatience and anger. "I'm going mad, stuck in this rat hole. I feel like a prisoner, Inspector. My life is falling apart around me, and I haven't done anything to warrant it."

Standing up, Barney gave the young woman a hard look. "I can appreciate that you are being inconvenienced, Ms Sellars. Hopefully it won't be for too long. But having said that, you know that someone has picked you out and fixated on you. At some point if we don't apprehend him, he will try to kill you in a very unpleasant and probably protracted manner. We want to ensure that he doesn't find and harm you."

"I understand that. But how long—?"

"Is a piece of string?" Barney said. "Bear with us. The worst-case scenario is that you have to live under protection like that author Salman Rushdi did for so long. And like he did, you'll just have to adapt. The alternative is literally risking your life every second of every day. It's your choice. But to be realistic, I don't think you have one, do you?"

Caroline lowered her head and hugged her knees. Barney thought that she looked like a small, frightened child. She hadn't asked for any of this, but no one said life was fair.

"I'll keep in touch and let you know of any developments," Barney said in a gentler voice as he patted her awkwardly on the shoulder. "Just hang in there and try to think of this as time out."

Caroline looked up, met his eyes and saw compassion. "I needed to be reminded of the position I'm in," she said. "Thank you for laying it on the line. But I still don't think that Jason is the man that you're after."

"Maybe not," Barney said. "But we need to *know* that he isn't."

Barney left the bungalow, and Mike – who had stayed outside by the car and had been chatting to one of the armed Witness Protection officers – drove them back to the city.

"Stop when you find a decent looking pub and we'll have a sandwich and a pint," Barney said, glancing at his wristwatch and noting the date as well as the time. A part of him was already wishing his life away; he was almost looking forward to retirement. He had the gut feeling that this case would not only be his last big one, but that it was stacking up to be the worst and most grisly he had ever been involved with.

"Are you all right?" Mike said.

Barney had drifted; was staring down at the dashboard, his eyes unfocused. Mike had pulled into the car park of an old pub that had survived seemingly unchanged since the early eighteenth century. The crumbling brickwork and weathered marble colonnades of its exterior looked original, and had seen far better days.

"Uh, yeah, I was just wool-gathering," Barney said, regrouping. "Is this the best brown jug you could find?"

"It has character, and they serve a good pint," Mike said as he climbed out of the car.

CHAPTER EIGHT

From the little-used B road that ran along the southern lip of the valley, the grand house could have been mistaken for the stately home it had once been. Designed in part by Sir John Vanbrugh in 1716, it had, since 1958, served a far more lugubrious function, which was in all probability causing the many – but no more – Earls of Cranbrook to turn in their neglected family crypt.

Cranbrook House was now The Cranbrook Hospital for the Criminally Insane, whose inmates, in the main, were not impressed by their palatial and grandiose asylum. Mark had never ceased to be amazed by the establishment, and the lush setting that it seemed to grow from and be a part of. Being an American, he was in awe of British history, and in particular of many buildings that had been erected many centuries before his country had been colonised by whites. He showed his ID to the security guard, and at the touch of a button the chain-link gates rolled back to allow him entry to the grounds. On his right was the Great Lake, which abounded with mallards, swans, greylag and Canada geese, herons and crested grebes. The large expanse of water was also a haven for the bream, roach, perch, tench and giant pike that inhabited its depths.

Driving through the grey veils of morning mist, along the tree-lined avenue that stretched away from him arrow-straight, Mark thought the house a sombre, Gothic presence that squatted in threatening fashion in the distance. Its present-day function seemed fitting. As the fictional Hill House – so disturbingly used as a centrepiece by Shirley Jackson in her classic tale – Cranbrook held darkness within its walls. To those with imagination it could have been alive, and undoubtedly evil and insane. Even on brighter days, as the sun bathed it in ochre splendour, it exuded a singularly wicked presence. Could malevolence become somehow infused with the bricks, mortar and timber of such a residence? Had murder, mayhem, suicide and debauchery taken place within its environs down the centuries, for the pain, horror and violence to be soaked up like water or blood in a sponge?

Mark smiled to himself as he parked, exited the car and cast off the flight of fancy. At the entrance door to the hospital, he tapped in the four digit number to gain access to the west wing, where he collected his security keys from a dour-faced officer and took the stairs up to his office, which was situated on the third floor, above the residential dormitories, cells and the isolation ward.

After leafing through an inmate's file and making himself a coffee, Mark phoned E ward and asked Martin, one of the orderlies, to escort Billy Hicks to his office. In due course the inmate arrived, and thanking Martin, who then left, Mark motioned for Billy to take a seat.

Billy was due his six-monthly evaluation. It was an unnecessary but required part of his treatment plan, as it was termed. Mark knew that Billy had remained unchanged since the last formal interview back in May, but records had to be updated.

"Please don't do that, Billy," Mark said as the young man slid his hand down the front of his sweat pants and began to masturbate.

"S... Sorry, Dr Ross," Billy stammered, removing his hand and looking down petulantly to a spot on the floor between his feet.

"No need to be sorry, Billy. Just save it for your room. No one is shocked or impressed anymore by your jacking-off in front of them."

"Y... You hate me, don't you?" Billy came back. "You pretend that you c... care, but you despise me. He told me that you're p... planning to kill me."

"Who did, Billy?"

"The Visitor. He says th...that if I sleep, you'll murder me in my b... bed."

"We've been through this before, Billy. You know that the Visitor is just a symptom of your illness, don't you?"

"I've decided that I'm n... not ill, Dr Ross," Billy said, his eyes still cast down as he spoke. "It's you people who are a f... figment of my imagination. I don't know w... why I talk to you. You don't exist."

"Are you awake or asleep, Billy?"

"I'm asleep, tr... trapped in a dream by the drugs th...that are forced on me. Only the Visitor is real, and he t... tells me what's really happening."

Billy Hicks was twenty-six. He was tall, gaunt, and wore glasses issued by the hospital, which were fitted with thick plastic safety lenses that made his watery blue eyes appear too large and bulging under the strong magnification. His mousy hair receded from a high, domed brow, and his sharp hooked nose and protruding yellow teeth gave him the look of a rodent, which was accentuated by his quick, jerky movements and mannerisms.

It had been six years earlier that Billy came to believe that aliens were controlling his parents and younger sister, Vanessa's, minds. He had been twenty, and the Visitor, which appeared to him in the guise of a coal-black barn owl, had warned him that they would absorb him. He had no choice but to kill them. They were just entities that resembled, talked and acted like his family; impostors. The voice in his head could not be ignored.

He had phoned the police to report the fact that he had dispatched them. Killing the sleeping doppelgangers with an axe had been easy. He had crept into what had been his parents' bedroom, and standing at the side of his father's look-alike, brought the blade down with all his might. The body was still shuddering as he worked the sharp steel head free. And the other alien continued to sleep, lightly snoring and oblivious to what was taking place. A scything slash with the long-handled tool brought a truly deathly hush to the room.

The Vanessa thing had woken up and was sitting up in bed as he entered the room with the dripping axe. Pushing itself back against the headboard, crying out in terror and pleading in his sister's voice, had not swayed him from what had to do.

Confident that the aliens no longer posed a threat, Billy had admitted what he had done, not expecting a medal, but shocked to subsequently be incarcerated in a booby hatch and told that he would probably remain there for the rest of his life.

He had been diagnosed as suffering from acute paranoid schizophrenia, which in simple terms inferred that he was deranged, showing symptoms of delusional persecution and a disconnection between thoughts, feelings and actions. The vast majority of patients with the disease did not present a threat to society, and once diagnosed, their condition could be stabilised with suitable antipsychotic drugs. That was not the case with Billy. He was a highly dangerous individual, would always be considered as such, and would be monitored continuously and indefinitely. Only the large cocktail of medication administered daily kept him in a manageable and non-aggressive state of mind. Apart from Mark, Billy would only speak spontaneously to one of the male orderlies. Under normal circumstances he was at best surly and uncommunicative.

"Is there anything you want to talk about?" Mark said.

Billy gave him a sly glance before looking around furtively to check that the door was closed. "I know all ab... about the red-haired aliens who w... were terminated in Regent's park," he said, leaning forward and talking in a whisper.

Mark felt a sudden coldness in his innards, and fought to control his emotions and remain outwardly impassive, though his heartbeat quickened. "How do you know about them, Billy?"

"I r... read one of the orderlies' newspapers, and it w... was also on the radio."

"And what do you want to tell me about it?"

"Th... That whoever is doing it is a fu...fucking hero. But he has to be careful, or he'll end up being caught and p... put in a place like this."

"Okay, Billy. You can go back to the day room now and watch some TV," Mark said, pushing the call button under the top of his desk.

As the orderly opened the door, Billy rose and turned to leave. "Bye, Doc," he said. "I know it's still y... you in there. I can always tell by the eyes." He shambled out into the corridor, trying to think what day it was. One day a week they served liver and onions for lunch; his favourite.

Before the door closed, Mark saw that Billy's right hand was already down his stained pants, manipulating his ever-turgid member.

On the morning of the last Saturday in October, Mark drove to Amy's to spend the weekend. And being almost positive that a third murder would take place on the following Friday, he had cleared his desk, rescheduled a long-standing appointment, and arranged to be off duty on that day. The plan was to return to Richmond on Thursday evening, to put him within easy reach of the scene, when what to his mind was almost inevitable came to pass.

By-passing Sevenoaks, he joined the M25. Chris De Burgh's *Lady in Red* came on the car radio, immediately concentrating his mind on Gemma. She had been wearing a red dress when he had first seen her at a 'do' at the British Embassy in Washington, D.C. George W. Bush had still been President at the time, and was in attendance. Mark had been on short-term secondment to protection duties, during a period when the top dogs at headquarters thought that interdepartmental experience would give them more versatile, multi-layered agents. The idea had been lousy, lowering levels of effectiveness rather than enhancing them. FBI and Secret Service personnel were not interchangeable; rather two disparate species, whose similar external appearance in dark suits and neckties was all they had in common.

Mark had found himself focused-in on a young woman, attracted to her in a way that surprised him and played pinball with his hormones. She had felt his intense stare, looked around and made eye contact. Instead of politely averting his gaze, he smiled, and continued to appraise her.

They may never have seen each other again, but fate decreed that they should be together, at least for a short while. The next encounter was on the roof of The Kennedy Center during the intermission of the long running comedy: *Shear Madness*. It had been running in the Theater Lab since nineteen-eighty-seven, but Mark had never been to see it. Only at the insistence of Alma Merrill – a girl he had been dating sporadically for a year – had he weakened and gone along that evening.

Sipping Scotch on the rocks and watching the jets drift down over the Potomac to land at Reagan National, Mark had seen his Lady in Red again, wearing a black sheath dress on this occasion, and standing looking out towards the Watergate Complex.

The guy with her was Neil Kaplan, an investigative journalist with the *Post*, who Mark knew and determined at that moment to call the next day to find out the identity of the girl who had captivated his heart. It transpired that Neil had been her escort for the evening; no more than a good friend. He told Mark that her name was Gemma Sinclair, that she was English, an embassy official, and most importantly, single and not involved seriously with anyone. Through Neil, Gemma and Mark had met up a week later for a candlelit meal at the Bistro Françoise in Georgetown. If there was such a thing as love at first sight, then they were both smitten before the evening was over. Within six months they had married, and shortly after, Mark quit the bureau. His priorities had drastically altered. He was no longer alone and on a single-minded mission to seek out the beasts that existed in the underbelly of society.

The meeting with the Memorial Killer – who raped and strangled teenage girls and left them to be found at the Vietnam Veterans Memorial in Constitution Gardens – had been the final straw; the push that concentrated his mind and gave him the jolt needed to leave the darkness and step out into the light.

Pulling back from memories, that like a loop would play continuously if allowed, Mark took a route from the Tolworth underpass that would take him to Amy's via Hampton Court, through Teddington to Richmond Park.

His ghastly recollections would not be denied, though. They demanded to be relived. Having dug back into a past that was filled with more tragedy than happiness, which he normally suppressed, he gave in to the insistent clamouring. Driving on automatic, he found his thoughts drifting back to another time and place, and was returned to D.C.

It was a cold and rain-lashed night. He was standing, hands deep in his pants' pockets, oblivious to the elements as he stared down at the naked body of a teenage girl; the fifth victim of Ralph Hechinger, the Memorial Killer.

CHAPTER NINE

The Medical Examiner officially confirmed the obvious, that the victim was dead, before releasing the body. And after the crime scene technicians had finished up, Mark remained loitering in the driving rain for a while, alone and unmindful of being soaked to the skin as he closed his eyes and digested the facts of the case.

The ME had noted that traces of semen were apparent, and that bruising to the wrists indicated they had been bound at some stage. Together with the unusual posing of the corpse in a seated lotus position, it was an irrefutable fact that this was the fifth victim of the same killer.

The autopsy was carried out the following day, and was to result in a single significant find that had not been present in the four previous murders. It would prove to be the case-breaker. They had matching blonde hairs and semen samples from all five victims, which showed that the killer had not been concerned over leaving DNA. All Mark needed was a suspect to match to the trace evidence. The forensic proof was in itself enough to make a bullet-proof case to put before the District Attorney.

It was in combings from victim five's pubic hair that a single hair of non-human origin was found. It proved to be simian, from one of the anthropoid apes; an orangutan.

"The National Zoo," Mark said to his supervisor, Frank Sorvino, even before the ape's hair had been attributed to a specific species. "It has to be one of the employees."

"Walk me through it," Frank said, tapping a tightly held pencil on the desktop in an annoying staccato.

Mark scanned notes that he had made while rechecking the files on the dead girls. "All of the victims had visited the zoo during a six-week period before their deaths," he said. "The killer saw them there, selected them, and was able to either follow them home or somehow get their addresses. We need photographs and details of all keepers and vets that come into physical contact with the apes."

Frank stopped tapping with the pencil, tossed it aside and watched as it rolled off the desk and fell to the floor. "Could be anyone who frequents the place with the intention of selecting his victims," he said as he withdrew another pencil from a plastic desk organiser, rather than bending down to pick the first one up. "And it could've been on the victim, not a transfer from the killer. But it's worth running with."

Two hours later, Mark and Frank were sifting through faxes of employees work records and photographs. Of the ten that worked at one time or another with apes, four were women, and of the other six, only two had blond hair. Provisionally, it came down to two prime suspects. One was a forty-four-year-old married man with two daughters; the other a twenty-seven-year-old, whom a background check disclosed had a rap for aggravated assault on a girl, dating back to when he was at high school.

Mark had no doubt as to which of the men was the killer. Confirmation came by way of work attendance sheets, showing that one of the suspects, Vern Henton, had been off duty on the day that the fifth victim, sixteen-year-old Sheila Farnsworth, had been taken. Further investigation put Henton in Philadelphia at the time that Sheila had been abducted on her way to school. He had not returned to D.C. until after the girl's body had been discovered. It effectively ruled him out.

They approached the man they thought to be the killer as he parked his SUV in the driveway and walked up to the front door of his tract house in Marlow Heights.

"Ralph Hechinger. I am an armed federal agent," Mark shouted. "Stop where you are and put your hands—"

Mark stopped talking. Hechinger had immediately veered to his left without hesitation, to then dive headlong through a front window with his arms crossed in front of his face to protect it from the breaking glass.

The element of surprise was lost, and although they had placed the man's wife and daughters into protective custody as a precaution, and had an agent located inside the house, the bust had gone wrong, big time.

Shots split the air as Mark and four other agents crashed through the door. They careered down the hall and entered the living room, to stop in their tracks, met by the sight of Special Agent Will Carpenter. He was lying on his back, blood blossoming from a chest wound to stain his shirt in what looked like a crimson Rorschach blot resembling a six-pointed star. Standing over him, Hechinger leant forward and pressed the muzzle of a .45 up against the fallen man's forehead.

"There's nowhere to go from here, Ralph," Mark said, keeping his Smith & Wesson trained on the killer's face. "Just put the gun down and let's all walk away from this in one piece."

"No deal, fed," Ralph said in a calm and even voice. "I got urges, and did some terrible things, is all. There's no way back from the shit I'm in."

"Don't make me shoot you, Ralph," Mark said.

The balding zoo keeper actually smiled, and said, "How did you know it was me?"

"You left ape hairs on the last victim. After we found those, it was easy."

Ralph shook his head. "Forensics is taking away all the hard slog for you guys," he said. "But this is one of those times where no one wins. I'm going to count back from three, and then pull the trigger. I don't know if this guy is dying or not. But his only chance is if you shoot me before I blow his brains out."

"Don't do this, Ralph," Mark said, and could hear the quaver in his own voice, and feel the sweat oiling up the palms of his hands.

"What's your name, fed?" Ralph said.

"Ross...Mark Ross."

"Well, Mark, decision time," the middle-aged family man said. "Three...Two..."

The gunshot was deafening, like rolling thunder in a box canyon. Through Mark's eyes, time became a stop-motion film. A red hole appeared as the bullet punched out Hechinger's right eye, blowing him back, away from the wounded agent. The other agents fired, and the large, overweight zoo keeper pirouetted, spun around by the hot lead, to smash face-first into the wall behind him and drop, a dead weight, to hit the floor with a resonant thud of finality. The only movement was his left leg. It shuddered for a few seconds, then straightened out and became still.

Real time resumed. Mark lowered his gun as the other agents moved forward to secure the scene; one kicking the pistol away from the corpse's hand as another padded the sucking, wheezing hole in Will Carpenter's chest.

Will died during transit to ER, and Mark was devastated. He had been the team leader, and found it impossible to reconcile the fact that a friend and colleague had died, and that the killer had manipulated his actions, using him to affect what was in all but name a suicide to thwart due process.

The following week he had handed his badge and gun in to Frank Sorvino with a letter of resignation. It was as though he had crossed the thin line that separated love and hate. He turned his back on the world of pointless violence and death, to walk away from the talent he possessed to track down creatures that only existed to pursue their deviant need to abuse and kill their fellow man.

Soon after, Gemma had put in for a transfer back to the UK, and together they had started a new chapter of life in London. There followed a period of calmness and fulfilment that Mark had never previously known. Each day was somehow imbued with a warmth and texture that he had been unable to experience while continually trying to infiltrate the minds of homicidal maniacs, which in essence necessitated his thinking how they thought, to the point of almost assuming their identities in order to hunt them down.

Strident blasts of a car horn snapped him back into the present. He had stopped at traffic lights that were now glowing green. The street noises and music from his radio flooded back. He raised his hand in a spread-fingered gesture of apology to the irate driver behind him and then accelerated JC across the intersection, surprised to find that he was only a few minutes from Amy's. He mused over how time could lengthen or shorten in an unfathomable manner, depending on the level of boredom or engrossing occupation that engaged the mind. Time really could seem to fly by, or be drawn out interminably.

Amy met him at the door, to become a welcome, solid reality in his arms. He held her tightly, absorbing her presence and the individual subtle fragrances of her hair, skin and perfume. It struck him that a large part of his inner self had the ability to move forward and meet life on terms he had no control over. Optimism for what the future might hold triumphed over past setbacks. He truly believed that the facility to rise above and overcome adversity was a trait that had made mankind such successful survivors. Adapting to change was the key to the future.

"Are you all right? You look terrible," Amy said, pulling free to stand back slightly and study his face.

"Thanks. You look gorgeous," he said, dumping his soft, canvas Cardin holdall on the floor next to the mahogany telephone seat. "What does a guy have to do to get a coffee around here?"

After an early lunch, Amy broke her good news.

"I got my licence, Mark. I'm a certified pilot now. I can go up into the wide blue yonder whenever I get the urge, or can afford to."

"You never told me. When did some fool deem it safe to let you fly over an unsuspecting public?"

"Last Wednesday. I thought if I failed, then I could just book more lessons and not have to tell anyone I'd flunked."

"Congratulations. We'd better go out and celebrate this evening," Mark said, getting up and going around the table to kiss her.

"Sounds good. I'm going up this afternoon for half an hour. Do you want to come along for the ride?"

"The ride, yeah. The flight, no," he said, shaking his head. "I fly when there's no alternative."

"You mean to say you're scared of flying?"

"Scared doesn't do it justice. I'd rather wrestle alligators than be up there without a parachute."

"It's the safest—"

"Way to travel," Mark finished for her. "I know. All the stats say so. But I still feel a hell of a lot safer with both feet on the ground or driving JC. The chances of surviving a car crash are much better than nose-diving into a field, or dropping into the ocean from a great height. Add what happened to the World Trade Center and the Pentagon to the equation, and you've got a twenty-four-carat coward on your hands. I tend to think that if a terrorist or suicide bomber did manage to get past security, then he'd pick the flight that I was on."

"So, you won't come?"

"I didn't say that. I'll enjoy watching you show-off, from the safety of the bar."

"You might get an oil-smeared mug of tea or coffee. It's not a big operation."

The airfield near Mitcham had only been open for six months. It was small, but had all the facilities, including a bar; its panelled walls hung with paintings and prints of World War II fighter planes and bombers; a commemorative display of Spitfires, Hurricanes, Lancasters and the like.

"You said there was no bar," Mark said, on being led in and introduced to Sid, the steward.

"I didn't want you coming along just for the booze. I'll see you soon," Amy said, pecking him on the cheek and rushing off.

He ordered a large Scotch from Sid, and could tell from the old guy's clipped voice, military bearing and handlebar moustache that he was ex-RAF, and doubtless wholly responsible for the aviation-oriented gallery of magnificent flying machines.

Flying had given Amy a sense of freedom that was incomparable to anything else she had ever done. Apart from being with Mark, it was the biggest thrill she could imagine possible; an endeavour that rewarded her with pure delight.

After going through the pre-flight check and starting the engine, she spoke to the tower. "Cessna one five zero Foxtrot Charlie ready for taxi," she said, adrenaline coursing through her veins as the plangent roar of the engine reverberated throughout the cockpit.

"Roger, Cessna one five zero Foxtrot Charlie. You are cleared to taxi onto taxiway zero one right."

"Zero one right, Cessna one five zero Foxtrot Charlie," Amy said, nursing the throttle and turning the Cessna out on to the taxiway. Less than two hundred yards distant, she could see Mark. He was standing next to the white-painted cast-iron railings that fronted the decking of the covered porch of the bar. He raised a hand as if to toast her, and she knew that it would be gripping a glass of Black Label and ice.

Giving him a salute – that made her feel like a Biggles or Douglas Bader type – Amy then concentrated wholly on the task at hand.

With step-by-step instructions from the disembodied voice on the radio, Amy was soon straightening the nose wheel to line the plane up on the runway's centreline. Another quick check of instrumentation, followed by permission to take off, and she pushed the throttle forward. The light aircraft almost leapt, as if unleashed, to pounce like a big cat and rush along the concrete strip; its destination, the sky above.

Once high above the ground and settled into her short flight plan, Amy allowed a part of her mind to absorb and appreciate the exhilaration of being free from all earthly constraint. It was rare to feel truly alone and apart from the teeming world of uncertainty far below, in what now appeared as clusters of toy-town buildings, with the sprawl of London to the north and a patchwork quilt of green fields, pockets of wooded areas and arable land stretching to the southern horizon. Only scuba diving in the clear waters of the Indian Ocean, while on holiday three years before, had given her almost the same sense of emancipation. It would be nice to explore the depths with Mark by her side, to glide hand in hand through the blue; to be weightless and experience the equanimity and quietude together. She believed that such participation in surroundings at the outer frontiers of man's familiarity could promote a truly unique sense of bonding;

a sharing of danger and survival that would surely cement a relationship in a special, red-letter way.

All too soon she had landed, and although pleased to see Mark waiting outside the office, was saddened at once more being a captive of gravity.

Mark had been thrilled, watching the small plane cut through the vault of gunmetal grey sky. At times, weak sunlight had emblazoned it, glancing off the fuselage to give the aircraft the appearance of a silver dart. And more than once it had disappeared, puncturing sullen clouds, only to reappear as though cast out from the swollen mass; a thorn expelled from bruised flesh.

"Feel better for that?" he said, embracing her as she finally climbed down from the cockpit.

"Renewed. It's like a form of rebirth, if that makes sense."

"That's how I feel after a sauna and massage."

"When do you allow some bimbo to give you a body massage?"

"I haven't for years. But when I did, it was all done in good taste, and my towel covered my modesty at all times."

"You say," Amy said, finding it hard to believe, but wanting to.

"Yeah, I say, Doubting Thomas. And I'm taking the fifth on this line of questioning."

"Okay, let's go home, take a shower together and then have that celebratory meal."

"Where do you want to eat?"

"I thought we could try that new Italian restaurant, La Piazza. It's only a few minutes walk from the house. We can both enjoy a drink without drawing straws for who stays sober and drives."

"Sounds swell."

"Then...if you're a real good boy, I'll give you a full body massage, with no towels included."

"You got yourself a deal, lady," Mark said, already feeling aroused.

CHAPTER TEN

At seven a.m. on Friday morning, Mike phoned Barney's home number.

"Yes?" Anna Bowen said.

"It's Mike Cook, Mrs Bowen. Could I speak to the boss, please?"

"Sure, Mike, I'll get him," Anna said, then put the receiver down and went out through the kitchen door to where she could see Barney standing, smoking a cigarette and studying his beloved Koi carp in the large kidney-shaped pond that he used as a mental balm; a therapeutic escape from the harsh reality of his thankless job.

"Barney. Mike's on the phone," she shouted.

He waved and then made his way up the lawn to the house. Anna watched him. She thought how drawn and tired he looked. His steel-grey hair was beginning to thin; his shoulders seemed permanently drooped these days, and he had lost a little weight. She would be glad when he quit the force. He had given his life to police work and she wanted him to enjoy retirement. Her biggest fear was that he would die in harness. The years of stress and long hours had taken their toll. She could not help but think that his fight against crime had been as effective as rowing against the tide in a holed boat. The measures and deterrents in place did not work. Her view was that convicted criminals should be stripped of all rights and privileges, and that on leaving prison should not ever wish to do anything that would put them at risk of being incarcerated again. She was sick of hearing how badly done by they were while inside. No one forced them to steal and rape and commit murder. They should, in her opinion, be treated as they deserved to be…badly. If a person knew that if after serving a custodial sentence they so much as spat in the street, then they would be locked up for the rest of their life, she was sure that the crime rate would drop dramatically. Honest, law-abiding citizens deserved better protection from the lowlifes' that preyed upon them. A zero-tolerance policy against criminals should be adopted and adhered to. She got so mad with the ineffectual hot air that politicians fed to the masses. She would love to see a public referendum with a straightforward choice of yes or no to the reintroduction of the death penalty. The Government was supposedly there to serve the people but, in her view, only suppressed and dictated, and was therefore little more than a thinly veiled autocracy.

"Yeah, Mike, I was just about to leave. What's hit the fan to warrant the early call?" Barney said, still looking out towards the pond as he spoke.

"Vlad just struck again, boss. We've got another victim."

Barney's heart sank. "Where? We've got Regent's Park staked out; no pun intended."

"Change of venue. Hyde Park, near the boat houses next to the Serpentine. Same M.O., and by all accounts it's another jogger; a young redhead."

"I'll meet you there," Barney said, then hung up. Less than ten minutes later he was on his way.

The cold and overcast morning was a fitting scene for violent death. The forensic team were on site, and the distinctive white tent marked the spot of yet another atrocity. Barney pulled in behind the bunched mass of official vehicles on Serpentine Road and killed the engine.

"This is worse than the other two, boss, if that's possible," Mike said as he walked across to where Barney was ducking under a taut strand of crime scene tape.

"How do you mean, worse?"

"More mutilation. You better take a look for yourself."

Judy Prescott had foregone her early morning jog for a couple of weeks. But with life moving on, she had resumed her activity. There had been no further park murders, and the news was now full of equally disturbing events. Only the day before an old couple had been found murdered in sheltered accommodation in Chiswick. Jesus. They had been tied up and tortured by three teenage girls. Both corpses had been bound together back-to-back with duct tape. They were covered in cigarette burns, and had plastic shopping bags over their heads, taped to their necks to suffocate them. The girls had been seen leaving the flat and arrested shortly afterwards. The oldest was just sixteen. How sick was that?

Judy was approaching the boat houses when another jogger appeared through the blanket of early morning mist, breathing heavily, looking down at the ground and wearing a bright red bandanna tied around the forehead. As the runner passed by, Judy felt suddenly edgy and was about to turn around as a hand gripped her braided hair and jerked her backwards onto the ground.

Chest ballooning with pain as the impact with the solid asphalt forced the air from her lungs, Judy was stunned and could not gather

her wits immediately following the sudden attack. Strong fingers found her throat and dug into it, cutting off her breath. The moon face staring down at her bore a maniacal grin, and yet the shark-like eyes were flat, black, and devoid of emotion.

"Time to die, you whore," the thick, guttural voice said, breaking Judy's state of terror, freeing her muscles from the frozen state they had locked in.

Her assailant had straddled her hips and was leaning forward to add weight to the vicelike grip. Judy brought both of her knees up with all the force she could muster, simultaneously clawing at the grinning face with both hands. The pressure left her throat, leaving her suddenly free as her assailant fell back. She flipped over, gained her feet and made to run away. And as the elation of escape coursed through her, a sharp, paralysing pain between her shoulder blades drove her back down, to break her nose and front teeth as her face smashed on to the unyielding surface. Fighting to stay conscious, unable to even struggle, Judy felt her tracksuit bottoms being pulled down.

Somehow, sobbing, moaning, tasting her own blood and spitting out gritty pieces of shattered teeth, Judy pushed herself up onto her knees and tried to crawl away.

The explosive, piercing pain that pervaded her was so devastating that she could not even scream. She stopped, set in place; a living statue. It felt as though she had been impaled on a barbecue spit. After a few seconds her body relaxed, and she toppled sideways. Hands gripped and pulled her over onto her back, which caused her more agony as the object now inside her was forced sideways and driven even deeper under her own weight.

The realisation that she was going to die was a concept that made her mind scream with an unadulterated sense of dread that she had never before experienced. It was a sensation strong enough to distract her from the physical pain, as all else was washed away by the crushing awareness that imminent and inescapable nonexistence awaited. She hardly felt the pressure of the hands at her throat, and was dead when her top was lifted up to disclose her breasts, before the blade of a knife punctured the skin under her ribcage.

Barney pulled on a Tyvek suit and booties, that a CSI provided him with, before opening the tent flap and entering. For a full minute he let the abhorrent scene burn itself into his mind. The body of a young woman was on its side, facing him, knees drawn up. The expression on the face was a snarl. She seemed to be staring at him, though her glazed eyes were as sightless as those of a China doll. The corpse was covered in blood, and more pooled around it and ran off down a slight incline, to vanish at a point where the wall of the tent met the ground. A thick, dark length of tree branch protruded from between the cheeks of her bottom like a stiff tail, jutting out into the air at a right angle; her lips were swollen and split, disclosing broken teeth, and her nose was misshapen and bloody.

Barney left the tent and walked down to the lake's edge, to where Mike was standing, hands thrust deep in his trouser pockets as he hunched against the cold, damp air.

"Are you all right?" Barney said, lighting a cigarette as he looked out to where two geese slid through the curling tendrils of mist toward them in anticipation of a handout, only to show their disappointment by hissing and wagging stubby tail feathers when no treats were forthcoming.

"Yeah, boss. I just don't need to see her again. I had an Indian take-away and a few lagers last night, and I'm trying to keep it down and not contaminate the scene."

"She's beyond hurt now, Mike. We've just got to view her as evidence, and hope that we find something here that will help us prevent it from happening again."

Mike shivered involuntarily, only in part due to the low temperature. "I can't help thinking about how she is someone's wife, daughter, mother or whatever. I don't know how loved ones' come to terms with something like this. It's too gruesome to have to carry in your mind for the rest of your life."

"The nearest and dearest don't see this part of it," Barney said, dumping his half-smoked cigarette onto the dew-laden grass at his feet and sliding the sole of his shoe over it. "By the time they identify the body, it's cleaned up and laid out under a sheet. They don't get to see what we do, thank God."

They were silent for a while, each assimilating the new horror into their brains.

"Give Mark Ross a bell," Barney said, taking his notebook out to look up the Richmond number, where the psychologist had said he could be contacted.

"He was right about the date," Mike stated as he tapped the number Barney gave him out on his mobile phone.

Jane Beatty arrived, donned her one-piece jumpsuit, put booties and gloves on, and entered the tent. She carried what looked to be a small, green plastic suitcase or fish tackle box.

Barney had the fleeting thought of Jane as a ghoul, attracted by death, to indulge in her repugnant, chosen profession. He lit another cigarette and stayed at the lakeside for a while, to give Jane time to examine the body, before he would go and ask the usual, predictable questions.

After fifteen minutes, Barney took a deep breath and walked back up the incline to the tent, which was lit up and showed dark shadows flitting to and fro behind the illuminated canvas. It made him think back to his childhood, when at night he would make dark images of animals and birds appear on the walls of his bedroom by contorting his hands and fingers to bring to life magical moving forms. A light bulb and a play on shadows had probably given him more pleasure back then than all the expensive toys and state-of-the-art computer games available today could give kids. Youngsters nowadays could not even imagine a time before home computers and mobile phones; a time as remote to them as the Stone Age was to him.

"Morning, Barnaby," Jane said, glancing up as he hunkered down opposite her at the other side of the body, wearing a fresh pair of booties.

He nodded and manufactured a thin smile, but said nothing as the pathologist's attention immediately returned to what he imagined she regarded as little more than work material. It entered his mind that he may end up on a steel table himself, with Jane's gloved hand wielding a scalpel, to open up his naked body and remove, examine, weigh and section his internal organs. He shivered.

"Does doing this ever bother you?" Barney said, voicing his thoughts.

"Always," Jane said. "I try to handle them with dignity, and treat them with respect. I know that their essence has gone, and that all I'm dealing with is a shell, but I never let go of the thought that they had lived, hopefully loved and been loved, and passed through the same fleeting state of awareness and actuality that I'm still a part of. I can do what I do because I know that they are beyond discomfort. You have to disassociate, Barnaby. That's difficult to do at first, but it gets to be just a procedure. I try to do it with compassion. That's a personal choice. Some of my colleagues are so hardened that they seem to have forgotten what they're cutting on. To them it's just sacks of offal that never lived or breathed."

"I don't know how you can deal with corpses every day and still maintain a sense of balance, or be able to attach much importance to life, knowing how suddenly it can be snuffed out."

"It concentrates the mind," Jane said, gently holding the dead young woman's limp hand as she spoke. "I look on time as being the most precious commodity that any of us have, and don't take one second of it for granted. I try not to squander it by doing anything that I don't want to. That's why some people tend to judge me as being a little antisocial and preoccupied. I choose to do what I want, when I want, how I want, and with whom I want to do it with."

"That sounds like a good game plan."

"It is. But I sometimes wish that I could loosen up more. I seem to go through life without taking enough time out to smell the flowers."

"I don't think any of us get it right, Jane. In fact, I don't think that there is a right way. We've all got to do whatever pushes our buttons, and try not to do too many things that breed regret. It can sometimes be hard to fight your basic instincts."

"True. And this girl fought, Barnaby," Jane said, lifting the pallid hand up to show him the fingers. "The physical injuries suggest that she struggled violently. As you can see, some of her fingernails are bloodied. She must have scratched her attacker, which means we have every chance of retrieving DNA."

"That's a break," Barney said, his knees popping as he stood up too quickly. "Shit. I'll have to get back on the badminton court. I'm seizing up."

"When did you last play?" Jane said as she enclosed each of the corpse's hands in a polythene evidence bag, securing them with thick elastic bands around the wrists.

"Twenty years ago."

"I think you should find something less energetic to do."

"Such as?"

"Maybe walking or swimming."

"I feel as though I'm swimming against the tide every day, Jane."

Barney stayed inside the tent while Jane made notes and carried on examining the corpse. He backed off and watched her work, but said nothing else to distract her.

"Boss. I've got Dr Ross and Ms Egan outside," Mike said, poking his head into the tent, but not entering. He had the smell of blood and body waste up his nose and couldn't get rid of it. "Oh, and Jason Tyler, the guy that Caroline Sellars used to go out with, looks to be clean. He was at home when the uniforms called around. There was no evidence that he'd been out, and his car's engine was cold. But he was alone and had no alibi."

Barney nodded, turned back to Jane and said. "When you're finished, I'd like for two civilians to examine the scene, Jane."

"I'm through. You can bring them in now," she said, snapping shut the catches on her 'porta-morgue' and standing up.

Barney quickly introduced the pathologist to the psychologist and ex-copper, explaining Mark's background as a profiler.

Mark walked around the corpse. He was now back in full operational mode. It was as if the years since he had attended a major crime scene had melted away as quickly as butter on a hot skillet.

The amount of overt brutality and the manner in which the body had been abandoned with no regard to the victim's semi-nude state was a testament to the killer's rage. And yet it was a controlled rage. The tableau was ritualistic; a display that showed the workings of an organised if damaged mind.

"What caused the facial injuries?" Mark said to Jane.

"Impact with the asphalt," she said. "There are traces of grit in the lacerations to her right cheek, nose and lips. And her upper front incisors are broken. Whether she fell or had her head forcibly propelled, I won't know until I do the autopsy. There may be subjacent bruising under the skin at the back of the neck, if she was gripped and manipulated from behind."

"I'd like to be there when you do the cut. Is that a problem?" Mark said.

"Not many people call it that," Jane said, not yet decided whether she liked the tall American or not. He gave off no clue as to his emotions. She felt that the body at his feet was no more to him than an interesting specimen in a jar of formaldehyde, rather than the fresh corpse of what until so recently had been a vibrant, living individual, who should still be alive and enjoying life to the full. Even the man's hard, grey eyes failed to give a hint as to his feelings. It was as if what they saw and the light that conveyed it was absorbed into the black and non-reflecting reservoirs of the pupils. He was without question enigmatic and, she decided, potentially dangerous. "I don't think—"

"I'd appreciate you allowing Dr Ross to be present," Barney said. "I want him to have access to whatever he needs. It may just save us re-enacting this scene again."

"Make it official then, Barnaby. Put the request in on paper," Jane said, walking to the entrance to the tent and pulling the flap open. And to Mark: "Be at the mortuary for three o'clock, Dr Ross."

Mark had no time to answer. The flap dropped back into place. She was gone.

"Did he make any mistakes this time?" Mark said to Barney.

"No apparent latents in the coating of blood on the body. The technician is pretty sure that he wore gloves. There are just two footprints on the road, leading off into the grass, but with no discernible pattern left by the soles. There's a chance that he left us blood and tissue under the victim's fingernails, though. All we can do is pull Tyler in and have a doctor check him for fresh lacerations, and take samples for DNA comparison."

As they walked back towards the Cherokee, Barney lifted the tape for them to duck under, and stopped abruptly as a bright, blinding flash lit the matt-grey morning air in a sudden burst of harsh light. He knew it was a camera.

"Detective Chief Inspector Bowen, who are the two civilians with you?" Larry Holden said, appearing from a thick stand of laurel at the side of the road, raising his Canon to take another shot.

"Blind me again and I'll break that fucking camera on your thick skull and nick you for assault, Holden," Barney hissed through clenched teeth, approaching the paunchy, dishevelled little man with the purpose and speed of a pissed-off rhino.

"Hey, hey, easy, man," Larry said as he lowered the camera and backed up until the evergreen foliage brought him to a halt. "I'm just doing my job. You know I report it as it is, chief. Give me a break, huh?"

Larry Holden was a freelance stringer who liked to think he was a crime reporter, but spent the lion's share of his time as a paparazzo, determinedly dogging celebrities around the city's top restaurants and nightclubs, to take photographs of the subjects at play, while they were more relaxed and less guarded than usual. The media paid handsomely for candid shots of drunken actors or singers in a brawl, or in any way making fools of themselves. And to catch a glimpse of the thigh, crotch or tits of a female celeb was celluloid gold. Nothing deterred Larry from his quest to take the shot. The more his marks were surrounded by minders, the more he was drawn; a bee to the honey pot. He was less interested in the second leaguers who actually courted paparazzi attention. He needed the challenge and the big reward that the exceptional shot attracted. He had a smell for what he did, born of a past career in mainline journalism. Had his love for the bottle been less consuming, then he may have still been plying his trade from the relatively respectable offices of Canada Square at Canary Wharf.

Johnny Walker had a lot to answer for in Larry's book. Not the Radio DJ, but the amber nectar, that in both red and black label guises had proved to be the sly demon that had cost him both his job and marriage. Hannah had tried to put up with him, mainly for the sake of their daughter, Annette, but his countless empty promises to reform had eventually fallen on deaf ears, and now he was alone, left only with the need to take photos that would pay the bills, and a newshound's compulsion to dig out the nuggets of clandestine information that were deeply imbedded in supposedly solid rock walls of secrecy. His mission was to disclose the truth in all its less than attractive guises. He had paid a WPC handsomely for the tip-off that the Park Killer was expected to strike again on the first Friday of the month. From his small, tawdry flat he had monitored the police bands all through Thursday night, waiting for any transmissions that indicated an incident in any of the city's parks. His perseverance had been rewarded.

Leaving his battered Vauxhall outside the park, Larry had lowered his equipment bag over the railings and then, with difficulty, climbed the pointed palisade of defensive iron spikes and dropped down into the bushes that bordered it. He knew that the police would be guarding the murder scene, and that he would have to approach with stealth.

The dark side of dawn was his unwary ally, and he was soon crouched down close to the police vehicles with a view of the ghostly tent that seemed alive with the shadows of people flitting behind the lamp-lit canvas. And then Bowen and his sidekick had appeared, accompanied by a stranger to him.

"Stick to shadowing soap stars and pop singers, Holden." Barney said. "Why try to be an ace crime reporter when all those shallow egos are parading around, just waiting for you pack rats to snap them up for the Sunday supplements?"

"That's the bread and butter, chief," Larry said. "This is what I'm best at, uncovering the news as it happens."

"No comment, apart from bollocks. Do yourself a favour and vanish, before your camera ends up at the bottom of the Serpentine."

Larry knew instinctively that the tall guy with Bowen was the main event. And as he brushed past him, he reached out grasped the sleeve of his windbreaker and said to Mark, "Who are you?"

Mark's hand peeled the unshaven man's fingers back, holding them and exerting enough pressure to cause the junk-food-fat little snoop to drop to his knees and grunt in surprise and pain. The gravel that topped the tarmac bit through his trousers and dug into the skin of his kneecaps.

"Look if you must, but don't touch, buddy," Mark said, letting go of the man physically, but holding him in place with a stare that could have soured cream. "Who I am is no concern of yours."

Larry shuffled back, climbed to his feet and scurried off into the darkness of the shrubbery. Adrenaline burned in his muscles. The guy had a Yank accent, and his reluctance to be identified was fuel to Larry's fire.

"That was a little over the top, Mark," Amy said admonishingly. "He was only trying to do his job."

Mark hiked his shoulders. "He'll live. He should have kept his whisky breath out of my face."

Larry, still within earshot, smiled. An American, first name Mark, who was in some way involved with the Park Murders. He was on to something that would put him one up over the dickheads he used to work with. They had ostracised him, but he was still a better investigative reporter than most of them put together would ever be. Even on the outside, without the official contacts and machinery, he would get the scoop.

Back at his flat, Larry made a call. "Janice, I need something really quick," he said to WPC Janice Purvis.

"Use your hand and a Kleenex," she said.

"Funny girl. I mean info."

"Are you at home?"

"Yeah."

"I'll call you back. Give me ten minutes or so," she said, and disconnected.

Larry paced the room, sipping Scotch from a china mug that Annette had given him for a Christmas or birthday. He couldn't remember which, or how long ago. The vessel sported the yellow face of Bart Simpson on its side; the cartoon character's jaundiced appearance making his liver suspect in Larry's red-rimmed eyes. "It takes one to know one," he said aloud, having decided that Bart was a closet alcoholic.

The phone chirped and he snatched it up. "Janice?"

"Yeah. What is it you want?"

"The Park Murders. There's a Yank involved, working with DCI Bowen. I need to know what his connection is. His first name is Mark."

"That'll cost you, Larry."

"Double the usual if you come through today."

"Deal. I *know* who he is."

"You're an angel. Shoot."

"He's a criminal psychologist. An ex-FBI profiler now living over here and working at some nuthatch in Kent. He's a doctor of something or other, and his name is Mark Ross. He's consulting on the case."

"Anything else?"

"He's tight with an ex-cop; Amy Egan."

"Have they got any useful leads?"

"Not that I know of."

"Thanks, Janice. The cash will be in the post today. Unless you want to come over to my place one evening and collect it personally."

"Maybe when you're the last man left alive on the planet, Larry. But even that's doubtful."

"Stop playing hard to get. You know you want my body."

"In your wet dreams. Bye, Larry," Janice said, chuckling as she racked the phone.

CHAPTER ELEVEN

Amy poured coffee as Mark took a pew in the breakfast nook and mentally recalled every detail of the murder scene, his eyes unfocused as he stared into the middle distance.

"Did seeing that poor dead girl help in any way?" Amy said, placing the steaming mugs on coasters before slipping on to the bench opposite him.

"Yeah," he said, pulling his thoughts back to the kitchen, away from the carnage he had witnessed within the incident tent. "Being there gave me more insight and feeling for the killer than photos can convey. What did *you* feel and think?"

Amy closed her eyes and brought the scene back to mind with perfect, nauseating clarity. "The branch is phallic," she said in a clear monotone, in the same way that she had given evidence in witness boxes throughout her police career. "I believe that it was employed as a substitute for the penis. I can't understand why penetration isn't made physically. Why not rape them?"

"It could be love gone bad," Mark said. "That's why the heart is taken. But I agree with you over the branch. It must be someone who can't get it up."

"Or a woman," Amy said.

"What?"

"Just a thought."

"But Caroline Sellars isn't gay," Mark said, his eyebrows dipping in consternation.

Amy shrugged. "She might swing both ways."

"Jesus, Amy, you're right. I've been out of the game too long," he said, standing and pacing up and down the kitchen. "I got myself a fixed mindset on it being a male. In all probability it is, but I overlooked the alternative."

"All the evidence points to it being a man," Amy said.

"What evidence? We hardly have anything. Let's go over the murder book again," he said, taking his coffee through to the lounge where he had left the files on the first two victims, now punched and securely held in a ring binder, along with copies of all other statements and the autopsy reports.

Amy followed him, pulled the binder across the coffee table, turned it around and flicked through the contents until she came to

Caroline's statement and said, "She gave a list of all her ex-lovers, going back to when she first got laid, aged sixteen. The squad have checked them out, and only Jason Tyler fits the bill."

"I could be wrong, but I don't think they'll find he has any scratches, or that his DNA matches," Mark said. "These murders are planned over a lengthy period. If he was the perp, he would've had the foresight to construct bullet-proof alibis, and he didn't. We need to interview Caroline Sellars and eliminate any possibility of the killer being a heartbroken, homicidal dyke."

"Dyke isn't a very politically correct term these days," Amy said.

"How about a lovelorn, Sapphic sadist, then? Is that better PC?"

Amy grinned. "On second thoughts, let's stick with dyke."

"I'll go through it all again and allow for the possibility of it being a woman," Mark said. "Will you phone Barney and set up a meet with Caroline?"

"Could be awkward, with her being stashed away under armed guard."

"He'll arrange it. We're on a countdown again. If we're lucky we've got till the first Friday of December. Unless our sicko decides to step up the action."

"When do you want to see her?" Amy said.

"As soon as we're finished up at the morgue."

After reading through the files again, cover to cover, and allowing his mind to consider the hitherto overlooked concept of the killer being a scorned or jealous female, Mark went upstairs and changed into sweats and trainers. Back in the kitchen, he held Amy close for a long time, as she put her head on his chest and returned his embrace.

"I won't be long," he said, finally breaking away and walking to the door.

It was cold. The air was hardly warmed by a watery sun that was little more than a pale, diffused glow, impotent against the barrier of windblown clouds that almost screened its rays from London and the southeast of the country.

He jogged to nearby Richmond Park, invigorated by the raw gusts that cut through his running suit to raise his skin in tight, pimpled gooseflesh. The bare, dark fingers of defoliated trees that lined his route seemed to reach out, as if they were clutching, gnarled hands, attempting to snag his clothing and stop his flight through their midst. As he ran, he locked on to the immediate problem, to recall all his past experiences of sexually motivated homicides. In the case of the three park murders, a foreign body in the shape of a sharpened stake had been forced into the victims' vaginas, rather than a penis or fingers being employed. But everything pointed to the killer being male. White females made up the largest focus group for sexual predators' attention, and the attacks and subsequent torture and killing usually followed a period of stalking. As in common with many repeaters, the Park Killer would have targeted his victims carefully, after being satisfied that they conformed to a critical criterion; in this case the colour of hair, approximate age, height and general physical appearance being paramount.

Mark came to a halt and settled on a bench that overlooked part of the golf course. He took deep breaths and felt the sweat quickly cool on his body and in his hair as his burning calf and thigh muscles chastised him for subjecting them to a level of exercise that he had not indulged in for over a year. As his heart rate slowed and his ragged breath became even, he gathered his thoughts and considered the pertinent facts, listing them in his mind:

1. The murderer is a man or woman fixated on Caroline Sellars.

2. The victims were killed instead of Caroline. They were substitutes.

3. In all probability the killer knew, or had known Caroline well, and is feasibly an ex-lover or work colleague.

4. Although apparently disorganised, the crime scenes were in fact highly organised. The ritual taking of the women in selected locations conform to a set pattern. The crimes show careful planning.

5. The victims were dominated, controlled, and made to suffer before being killed.

6. The weapons had been brought to the scene specifically to carry out a pre-planned assault. The tree branches had been fashioned for one purpose, and left imbedded for maximum shock/horror effect. The knife used to remove the hearts had been retained...For further use?

7. The bodies were left abandoned as a graphic warning to Caroline Sellars; an explicit personal message for her to expect the same fate. It was an obvious ploy to instil terror; the primary reason for the killings.

8. How many? Were three his/her magic number? Would Caroline be next? Or would the slaughter continue?

9. Caroline is the key. Only she could lead them to the person who had targeted her. Her killer had made only one mistake, contacting her, not satisfied to remain totally anonymous. He/she had needed the quarry to know; to initially dominate and control her from a distance.

10. How long could the killer deny him/herself the ultimate prize? There would have been a plan in place from the outset. All actions would be part of a preconceived scheme to eventually abduct Caroline, take her to a place that afforded privacy, and subject her to a protracted period of humiliation, torture, and ultimately death.

Mark was shivering. Standing up, he stretched his tightening muscles, and then jogged back to Amy's house. He was sure that he could sense the crazed asshole's state of mind; love gone bad like rotten fruit mouldering in a bowl. This was not a serial killer with an uncontrollable urge to kill and kill again. This was an obsessional hatred for one specific person. Dark forces had been unleashed in a disturbed individual who was highly motivated by a need for retribution. And yet armed with all his profiling skills, Mark had no firm idea of the age, status, or even the gender of the person he was trying to mind hunt. Amy had thrown a spanner in the works, causing his mental cogwheels to be derailed from their tracks and grind to a halt. His theory of a single lone wolf male offender was now pie in the sky. The killer could just as easily be a disenchanted, middle-aged, married family man who had reached a crisis point in life and had anchored onto a past relationship with Caroline, however tenuous, and now blamed her for his present sensitivities. Or it could be – as Amy had observed – a woman who, not being able to possess Caroline within normal parameters, had determined to destroy her.

Back at the house, Mark showered and dressed and then made cheese, mushroom and chive omelettes for them both, which they washed down with what seemed mandatory mugs of coffee. After washing up, they went through to the lounge and looked out through the large picture window, entranced by the antics of two squirrels commandeering the bird table; one perched on the apex of the roof, as though a lookout, while the other used its sharp incisors as wire cutters and tried to bite through the mesh of the feeder that held a bounty of peanuts.

"I got hold of Barney. He'll meet us at the morgue and drive us to the safe house," Amy said, taking the empty mugs through to the kitchen and dumping them in the sink.

"Good," Mark said. "She's the only real lead in this case. You can talk to her first and see if she has any past girlfriends that were more than just friends."

"You think she would admit it?"

"She'll tell us anything and everything to get her life back and not be living in a world of fear. She's under sentence of death, and she knows it."

"So, you do think that it might be a woman?"

"I'm open to exploring all avenues. I see it as being a possibility we need to check out."

Mark pulled into the rear entrance of the mortuary in Holborn and parked in a slot near a ramp that led up to a grey metal door. He ignored the flaking remains of white painted letters, barely legible on the dark, cracked concrete that read: RE ERV D.

"Names, please," a metallic voice crackled over the intercom after Mark thumbed the bell push and looked up into the solitary black eye of the CCTV camera that was angled down from a wall bracket to capture all visitors and relay their images to monitors somewhere within the featureless and ugly building.

"Dr Mark Ross and Ms Amy Egan to see Dr Beatty," he said. And after a long pause there was a loud click and accompanying buzz to announce that the lock had been disengaged.

They entered the cold confines of the repository for the dead, which Amy thought of as being just a temporary stop on death's railway; a way station for the refrigerated travellers, before they were delivered to the terminus of dank grave or consumption by fire.

Jane met them in a small side room that was no less depressing for the bright prints that graced the walls, or the modern, inexpensive furniture. It reminded Amy of her dentist's waiting room.

Greeting them with a terse nod, Jane beckoned them to accompany her.

"I'll sit this part out," Amy said, picking up a year-old copy of Country Life from a neat, squared-off stack on an occasional table, noting that all the magazines were in mint condition, having probably never been read.

Mark followed the pathologist along a corridor and through swing doors into a large autopsy suite. He could smell death beneath the astringent layer of antiseptic that assaulted him, or imagined that he could.

"Well, Dr Ross, I think you're familiar with the procedure," Jane said. "I flipped through your book at lunch time, just to give me an insight as to where you were coming from."

"Please drop the title," he said. "I prefer just Mark."

"Okay, Just Mark. I'm Just Jane", she said, her mood lightening as she snapped on a fresh pair of latex gloves.

They both smiled, reaching an unspoken understanding, knowing that their individual, diverse talents might help to uncover the identity of the unknown killer. Mark sensed that his book had impressed her to a degree, judging by her current demeanour towards him. She had obviously decided that he had a more than decent track record in his field of expertise.

He had written *Missing Conscience* after leaving the bureau. A publishing house had approached him, having had commercial success with the work biographies of other ex-profilers. The mechanics of the hunt for serial killers had cornered a market that was in no small way thanks to such fiction novels as *Red Dragon* and *Silence of the Lambs* by Thomas Harris, that had also been made into movies and elevated the subject to a mass marketable level. The public obviously saw all FBI officers as being Will Graham and Clarice Starling types, and were hungry for the details of an occupation that pitted men and women against human monsters.

The advance on the book – though by no means large – had been a welcome supplementary windfall, coming at a time when his pension was only just enough to cover the basics of life. The decision to write the abridged memoirs was not wholly profit-based, though. In laying out his experiences on paper, one tortuous word after another, Mark had purged himself of certain events, diluting the terrible reality by giving it an outlet and flushing it from his system. The book was in its third reprint, and although there was no lack of encouragement for him to write a follow-up, he had declined. The project had been valid at the time, but was now behind him. He had, until now, put that part of his life into stasis, not realising that it was still an integral part of him; an ember glowing in the darkness, waiting for a cold draught to ignite it, and once ablaze, become a raging inferno within his soul.

The naked body of Judy Prescott, which had initially been recognised and identified at the scene by a local PC, was lying atop a stainless-steel table on her right side with approximately twelve inches of the branch still protruding rudely from between the cheeks of her buttocks.

"All external features have been noted and photographed," Jane said. "And due to the foreign body, I also had X-rays taken. Before proceeding with the internal examination in the orthodox way, I will now have to remove the object."

An assistant held the cadaver, his hands clamped onto its left hip as Jane grasped the home-made spear, to twist and pull it as though she were removing a drain rod from a blocked pipe. With an undignified sucking, flatulent sound and the release of stinking stomach gases, the branch relinquished its hold, and Jane tottered back two or three steps, holding the gore-covered stake two-handed.

Placing the makeshift weapon on a steel tray next to a ruler, Jane called across to a young, white-coated forensic photographer who had been at another work station taking photographs of a black teenager's body. The youth had been blasted in the face and chest by a shotgun, and as yet was still a John Doe. A group of school children had discovered the corpse, where it had washed up on the Thames foreshore in an advanced state of decomposition.

"Thanks, Brenda," Jane said a couple of minutes later, as the girl went back to the faceless youth, having taken several shots of the stake. Jane then measured the limb and placed it into a transparent plastic zip lock evidence bag.

"It is sixty-one centimetres long, and six centimetres in diameter at its thickest part," Jane said to Mark. "It had been inserted to a depth of thirty centimetres. This is almost identical to the stakes used on the other two victims."

Putting the bag down, Jane moved back to the body and eased the buttocks apart to examine the entry wound. Her assistant lifted the left leg to the side to give her better access. "This is interesting," she said, waiting for Mark to move into a position that afforded him an unrestricted view. "The first two victims were penetrated by way of the vagina. In this case, the point of the stake has ruptured the perineum between the anus and the vagina. And as the X-rays show, it broke through into the rectum and travelled up the alimentary canal into the stomach, causing massive haemorrhaging."

Mark had attempted to remain detached, but lack of recent exposure to the procedure allowed emotion to permeate in his mind. A rich imagination was part of his psychological armoury, and he could almost taste the fear and imagine the unendurable pain that the young woman had suffered as the thick tree limb had been savagely thrust inside her.

"Thanks, Alan," Jane said, and the assistant lowered the leg and turned the body on to its back, lifting the head off the cold steel to place a small, concave plastic block at the base of the neck, as if to give the corpse an angle of sight to watch its own imminent dissection. He then nodded and moved off to the far end of the suite, where yet another autopsy was in progress.

"I don't know what you're looking for, Mark. But I hope you find something that will help you catch this maniac," Jane said.

"We need a break," he said. "If you're to be spared performing a cut on number four in a few weeks."

Jane scowled. "Natural death, accidents and suicides are all part of a day's work," she said, lifting a scalpel from the top of a wheeled trolley next to the table. "But to have to deal with the results of what one sick human being has purposely inflicted on another person, like this, is depressing. Only having to work on babies and children is worse."

"It's like a jungle out there: predators hunting prey below the veneer of civilisation," Mark said. "These psychos hunt for the thrill of it, not for food. A wild animal's only motivation to kill is for sustenance, or as a defence mechanism. The resulting fear and pain that is caused are by-products, not a conscious part of the equation. It's only man that kills for the pure pleasure derived from the act."

"This girl was attempting to escape," Jane said. "She may have almost made it. I would imagine a scenario in which she fought and broke free after the initial assault, but stumbled and fell, resulting in her face striking the ground. The gravel and other debris in the lacerations to her nose, mouth and the palms of her hands point to that. Her assailant miscued with the branch, which indicates that she may have been moving, crawling away from him."

Mark watched as Jane made the Y-cut from shoulder to shoulder and opened the torso from the sternum to pubic mound. The morbid fascination that he had harboured as a rookie agent – when attending his first few autopsies – was now reduced to a level just short of disgust. He knew the procedure well enough to have performed it himself, albeit clumsily.

Jane exposed the lungs and examined the gaping, clotted cavity that should have housed the heart. "The heart was literally hacked out in a hurry," she said. "No finesse. Just cut and ripped savagely from the body, in the same manner employed on the other two victims."

Mark watched as Jane excised the lungs, oesophagus and trachea, not surprised to be told that the compression damage and bruising indicated manual strangulation. Next, the liver, spleen, the adrenals, stomach, pancreas and intestines were removed. Each organ was weighed, examined and sectioned. Samples from the stomach and urine from the bladder was retained for toxicological analysis.

"I think I've seen all that I need to," Mark said. "Barney can show me your write up and findings. I hope that we don't meet up again under these circumstances."

"Likewise," Jane said, nodding to Mark; the shaking of hands out of the question due to the blood coating her gloves.

The removal of the brain would be last. And as Mark left the autopsy suite, he recalled the sound that the small circular saw made as it bit through the skull, once the scalp had been peeled back. He had no particular wish to witness the routine ever again.

Barney was in the waiting room with Amy. He was pacing as though caged, glaring at the wall-mounted NO SMOKING sign with undisguised hostility. "Are you all done here?" he said to Mark.

"Yeah,"

"Good, let's go. These places give me the creeps, and I need a smoke."

Leaving JC in an NCP nearby, Mark and Amy climbed into the rear of the unmarked police car, and the circuitous route that Mike Cook drove to the west London safe house would have made many a cab driver proud of him. All he needed was a meter racing greedily to click up an extortionate fare.

"This is a one-off meet with the woman," Barney said. "Pearce okayed it. But we can't make a habit of compromising her location."

"No sweat," Mark said. "But you should move her every week. The killer will home-in on her if you don't."

"I doubt that," Barney said.

Mark smiled. "Doubt by definition is uncertainty; an inclination to disbelieve. I have *no* doubt whatsoever that when ready, the son of a bitch will run her down. It's rolling stones that gather no moss."

"You could be overreacting."

"Better safe..." Mark countered.

Mike parked the car next to the kerb on an avenue that ran parallel to the one in which the safe house was located. He stayed at the wheel as the others got out, and Amy and Mark followed Barney down a narrow walkway that led to a back alley that afforded access to the rear of properties, including the bungalow that Caroline was ensconced in. A workman was ostensibly repairing a fence, but the briefest of furtive glances in their direction was enough to cause Mark to suspect him of being an armed undercover cop, which he was.

Once inside the compact bungalow, they were led into the lounge by another officer in civvies who, wearing a T-shirt and cargo pants, looked young and good-looking enough to be a member of a boy-band.

Mark almost had to reach out and hold the door jamb for support as the woman got up from a settee to greet them. She wore a red blouse and black skirt, and although looking tired and tense, with dark, crescent smudges under her eyes, her facial features bore an uncanny resemblance to Gemma, his late wife.

CHAPTER TWELVE

Introductions over with, Mark and Barney retired to the kitchen, closing the door to give Amy privacy to talk to Caroline. The young cop – who Mark thought had eyes that had seen far more of life and death than his fresh face betrayed – brewed instant coffee for them, then made a test call on his two-way before sitting to the side of the locked back door, his hand on the holster of his shoulder rig, absently finding tactile comfort from the soft leather that encased a nine millimetre Glock 17.

"I take it you know why we're here, Caroline?" Amy said, sitting and facing the obviously distraught young woman, who had her hands in her lap, nervously clenching and unclenching them.

"Yes," she said. "DCI Bowen told me that Dr Ross is a specialist in this sort of thing."

"He is. And the more information he has, the sooner you'll be able to get your life back."

"What more can I tell you, that I've not already told the police?"

"The way in which the victims were murdered suggests that we could be looking for a woman."

"A woman!" Caroline said, astonished. "You think that some woman is terrorising me and killing people?"

"The crimes were sexual, in that vaginal penetration was made, though not by conventional means."

"I'm not gay, if that's what you're implying," Caroline said; a defensive sharpness to her voice.

"I'm not saying that you are," Amy said. "Only that it may be a woman that has fixated on you. It could be a total stranger, but that's unlikely, due to the correspondence you received. We can't discount the possibility of there being a female colleague or supposed friend who feels that you have rebuked her in some way."

"But I've never..." Caroline paused, and Amy saw a flash of doubt or recollection in her tired, emerald eyes.

"What? Tell me what you just thought or remembered, Caroline."

"It can't be relevant. It's too long ago."

"Please, let me be the judge of that. At this moment in time, everything and anything is relevant, believe me."

Caroline gathered her thoughts, frowning, and with her eyelids screwed tightly shut as she plucked a distant, unpleasant and embarrassing memory from where it had lain buried in her psyche.

Amy found that she was holding her breath as she waited what seemed an eternity, watching the mental struggle play out on Caroline Sellars' face.

"I was at university in Leeds," Caroline said eventually, her voice triggering Amy into releasing her breath and taking another. "I shared a flat with three other girls. It was great for nearly a year. We were like family...sisters, you know, sharing chores, makeup, clothes and secrets. We went everywhere together, and boyfriends were only a passing and usually brief diversion that seemed to put a damper on the fun."

Amy waited, but Caroline had gone glassy-eyed, presumably recalling an incident that had taken place up in Yorkshire, many miles and almost a decade away from the danger she now found herself in.

"What happened, Caroline?" Amy said in a low but firm voice.

"Uh, Judy and Fay were away one weekend. I remember it was late November or early December, and I was left with Ellen. We went out for an Indian meal, then on to a city pub. We both drank too much, and when we got back to the flat, Ellen got all maudlin over her mother, who had died that summer. I ended up cuddling her on the settee. Later, she didn't want to be alone, so I let her sleep with me."

Again, Amy waited as Caroline hesitated, biting her bottom lip as she tried to find precise words, obviously loathe to continue and divulge the details of an incident she had relegated to the part of her consciousness that stores memories of shame or guilt. She lowered her head, closed her eyes and continued without further prompting.

"I woke up, still a little drunk, and Ellen had her hand up my nightie, fondling my breasts. I don't know why, but I didn't stop her, and it got steamy. I kind of enjoyed it in a scary, weird way. I did things that I'd never done before or since with another woman. The next day I told her that I wasn't like that. I asked her to forget that it had happened, but she kept pestering me, telling me that she loved me, and talking graphically about the things we'd done to each other. In the end I moved out. I even had to be really nasty to her one day in the university bookshop. I suppose I caused a scene. That's it."

"Did she ever threaten you, or do anything?" Amy said.

"No. She found out where I was living and sent me letters for a while, but I just ripped them up unopened. A few months later she dropped out, left uni, and I never saw her again. I'm sure it wasn't related, though."

"What was her surname?"

"Garner."

"Describe her. Tell me what kind of person she is, or was?"

"She's...She *was* stocky, back then. Not fat, but heavily built. She always wore her hair very short. It was mousy. Her eyes seemed a little small for her face. They were distinctive, very dark like polished jet. I suppose you'd have to say she was unattractive. A lot of the guys called her Miss Piggy, behind her back. She was very...butch looking. I have some photographs from those days. She's in a couple of them. They're at my flat."

"That's good," Amy said. "Will you talk to Dr Ross now?"

"If you think it might help, yes."

Amy went through to the kitchen and asked Mark to join them. She had broken the ice, and when Mark sat in, Caroline recounted the details of her singular sexual episode with Ellen Garner. Talking to Amy had helped her overcome the repressed shame. She was now more fluent and open, though felt extremely embarrassed.

"To your knowledge, did Ellen bear grudges?" Mark said, finding it painful to look at Caroline. Even her expressions; the way she pursed her lips, frowned, and looked up toward the ceiling when searching for words, was reminiscent of Gemma. He was almost distracted from his line of thought, near to being overcome by a surge of impassioned memories that crowded in and threatened to engulf him. He felt awash with pain; drowning in an ocean of self-pity. The past could always turn around and bite you in the ass when you least expected it to.

"She once fell out with a guy in the downstairs flat," Caroline said. "He played grungy music, too loud and too late at night. When Ellen asked him to turn it down and show some consideration for other tenants, he told her to piss off and get a life. She seethed for over a week, and then lightened up. Her change of mood coincided with the guy having the paintwork of his car covered in brake fluid, and all four tyres slashed."

"And did she do it?" Mark said.

"She never admitted it. But her smug, self-satisfied attitude was proof enough to the rest of us that she had."

"Do you know where she came from? Or anything about her background?"

"She was a Yorkshire girl. I think from Hull, originally. But apart from knowing that her mother had died, she never talked to any of us about her past. I remember that her favourite saying was, 'OTM': Only Today Matters. Funny, she never even invited any of us to attend her mother's funeral. I don't even know if she went."

"I think we've covered all the bases, Gem...uh, Caroline."

"We'll need to arrange for DCI Bowen to recover those photos from your flat," Amy said.

"Do you really think that after all this time Ellen would do something like this?" Caroline said, directing the question to Mark.

"I believe that it's more a possibility than a probability," he said, wanting to leave, tortured by being in the same room with a woman who was unknowingly opening a scar on his heart, which now felt as if it was a fresh wound again, seeping grief-laced blood into his very soul. "But we obviously need to find her and determine it one way or the other."

"I feel so terribly guilty," Caroline said, her words heavy with self recrimination. "Those girls are being killed because of me."

"That's bullshit," Mark said, reaching out and taking her hand firmly between his much larger, stronger hands. "The only guilty party is the maniac who is committing these crimes. You are not responsible for the actions of a psychopath. None of us have any control over what these deranged freaks do. You are a victim, Caroline, so don't feel guilty, feel goddamn angry instead."

Amy stayed with Caroline for a while as Mark left the room and relayed what had been discussed to Barney.

"I'll have the photos lifted and get copies to you," Barney said. "Is there anything else?"

"Yeah," Mark said. "If you locate Ellen Garner, treat her as though she's a rabid dog. Don't underestimate her because of her gender. If she *is* the killer, then she will be extremely dangerous, and will kill again without hesitation."

Later, back at Amy's, Mark's thoughts flitted, as a bee or butterfly would from flower to flower in search of nectar. Gemma, Caroline Sellars, Amy, the park murders and the possibility of a female serial killer all jockeyed for position in his mind. With a force ten headache and building frustration over the case, he showered, letting the needle jets of hot water wash away some of the tension and relax his frayed nerves.

Amy stepped in beside him, put her arms around his waist and said, "Are you okay?"

"I will be," he said, turning to face her.

"I know what seeing Caroline Sellars did, Mark. I saw the resemblance, and I've only seen photographs of Gemma."

"Sorry, honey, but I—"

"You wouldn't be the man I love if you hadn't been affected. Let's try to back off the case for tonight. There's nothing more we can do until Barney checks out the Garner woman and gets the DNA results on Tyler. We should rustle up a meal together, put some Lionel Ritchie on, and try to chill out with a few large Scotches."

"Is that before or after?" Mark said, pulling her close.

"Before or after what?" Amy said, and then felt the pressure against her stomach, looked down and smiled. "No show without Punch, huh?"

"He's got a mind of his own. A naked babe in the shower always gets his attention."

"We'd better see to the little guy's needs, then."

"Less of the little," Mark said, finding her lips with his as she tilted her face up.

At that moment, kissing and embracing Amy, he experienced a sense of closure; was hit by an overpowering sense of acceptance. Life is nature, and nature has cycles. It repeats. You have to move on and get past things. Close out certain phases of it. He truly believed that most lives were like books. If they were doing the job intended, they furthered the plot, developed, and ultimately came to a conclusion. Wheels within wheels. A certain feeling of having reached the end of some weighty tome and pausing before beginning the next, invaded him. He now felt that he could look back on what had passed and leave it behind, not carry the burden on his shoulders as unnecessary baggage. The yoke of keen, harboured sorrow dissolved from his heavy heart, and he knew that at last he could continue life's journey unfettered. His phases seemed to be of ten-year periods, with subtle changes in priorities, and new perceptions. He could acknowledge the boy and young man he had once been, but in some way saw them as separate individuals, no longer a part of him, though he was obviously a product of all their experiences. For the very first time since Gemma's death he felt a distance expand and transform her from what had been a consuming and bitter daily onslaught of loss, to a sweet memory. The love he had had for her was still intact, but encapsulated and set aside, disentangled from what was now corporeal. He was at once liberated to give fully of himself to Amy, with no sense of betrayal to a lost and irrevocable past.

Gemma had been playing tennis on a warm spring day with a girlfriend from Middleburg, Virginia, who was on vacation in the UK. She had thrown herself sideways in an attempt to return a serve, and suffered massive heart attack. The friend had phoned the emergency services, and attempted to revive Gemma with CPR, but she was gone. All dreams can be snuffed out quicker than a candle. Gemma was taken from him in an instant. That she had not suffered was the only small comfort he could salvage from such a grievous event. Her passing gave him a new perspective; a cynical scrutiny of existence in general, in which he believed life and death to be a perverted lottery, in which at some point everyone became losers. But with time, and since meeting Amy, his outlook was again modified. He dared to envisage a positive future, though accepted that it would be of indeterminate duration.

"I love you, Amy," he said with a depth of sincerity that both of them knew had removed a shadow, and now allowed them to metaphorically bathe in the full light of the sun.

CHAPTER THIRTEEN

A near state of panic combined with the electric thrum of excitement had galvanised both mind and body into action as the bitch made a pathetic bid for freedom. She had crawled through the murk, across the dew-clad road, gasping and moaning.

"No. No. No" She repeated the word over and over in hardly more than a whisper. It would have been a very basic and dull mantra, had the element of sheer terror not lent the word erotic weight. If she had not tripped and fallen, then she would have escaped, but *if* was the difference between what might have been and what was.

A satisfying thrust of the sharpened branch was rewarded by a tremor that ran out of the speared body in unseen waves, to vibrate through hand, wrist and arm.

She had become still, posed on all fours, as if turned instantly to a solid sculpture of salt; the fate of Lot's wife for gazing upon the destruction of Sodom and Gomorrah. Slowly, as a felled tree will, she toppled on to her side.

A quick but sure look in every direction. No one. Fingers around the victim's soft throat; thumbs aching with the sustained pressure that sealed her windpipe and robbed her of all further hopes and fears and dreams and schemes. Knife now, sawing through the flesh and muscle under her ribcage. Hands inside, enveloped by slick, liquid warmth. Back on to the grass, away from the corpse, to place gloves, smooth-soled canvas trainers, knife and steaming trophy into a heavy-duty black plastic bin liner, before jogging back to the car.

Home, to strip off and look into the bathroom mirror at the damage where the whore-bitch-cow had left her mark, or in this case, marks. The iodine stung, staining the bloody scratches sulphurous yellow. The police would reclaim blood and skin samples from the corpse's fingernails. To have been so careful and now to have given up a genetic fingerprint was annoying, but their forensic evidence was worthless. There was no link to the victims, and no obvious connection to Caroline Sellars. No need to be a silly old worry bear. Wouldn't, shouldn't and couldn't be caught. Never, ever. The police were morons. One more kill, to instil even greater arse-puckering fear into the Jezebel Caroline, before taking her from under the coppers' noses and introducing her to Mr Stake and Mr Knife. It had to be a done deal before midnight on New Year's Eve. January first was to be a fresh start; a new year and a new beginning. The future held such possibilities, hope, and untold happiness; a renascence with all scores settled and consigned to the past.

Blink.

Now standing over the open chest freezer, with no memory of having left the bathroom, or of time passing. Icy vapour, numbing naked skin. Hand stuck to the hoar-frosted freezer bag containing the now solid heart, which felt like a small, frozen supermarket pullet.

Blink.

Daylight.

Sitting on the bed. Time lost again. several hours. The fugue periods were becoming more frequent and of longer duration. Probably a symptom of stress, which would relent when the business at hand was brought to a satisfactory conclusion. The capacity for, and execution of violent retribution was a release that sated a gnawing hunger. Vengeance was the only way to relieve the mental pain of being done wrong by. Natural justice had no equal.

While Mark got ready for the drive back to Kent, Amy went for milk and papers. Walking down the avenue to the mini-mart on the main road she was consumed with a sense of well-being. Mark had undergone a dramatic change. The part of him that cared for her had always been guarded. She had known that he loved her, but it was with a reservation, as though his past were a barricade that could not be stormed or dismantled. Standing under the shower in the circle of his arms, she had experienced an almost spiritual event as the invisible fortifications that protected his emotions crumbled and fell away, to symbolically be sluiced down the plug hole with the hot water and soapsuds. The change was indefinable, but momentous. She now felt as though she had been placed on a pedestal that had always been the gilded tower reserved for the memory of Gemma. For the first time during their relationship she could envisage a bright and happy future, with true commitment to hang their hats on.

On entering the shop, her high spirits were immediately dashed. Multiple images of Mark stared back at her from a rack of newspapers. His eyes radiated menace that had been directed towards the furtive photographer who had appeared from the darkness in front of them. Her own features were almost hidden behind Mark's shoulder, with just a startled eye and a spot of light highlighting a cheekbone. Mark's face had been the subject, and was lit in stark relief against the velvet blackness, which although unrecognisable, she knew to be a small and grisly corner of Hyde Park.

Walking back to the house with her full concentration on the article, she slammed into a lamppost, reeled away from it, and cursed under her breath as pain exploded in her shoulder. She plucked the dropped newspaper from the pavement, tucked it under her arm and jogged the last few yards to the open garden gate.

"That's all we need," Mark said after reading the report under the picture. "Thank Christ you can't be recognised."

"It's no big deal," Amy said without conviction.

"It could be. It gives the killer an edge. He or she now knows the identity of an individual who is on the case, big time. It takes away an advantage, and may make him...or her, more cautious."

He read part of the article for a third time, aloud: "Park murderer strikes again. Our exclusive photograph shows ex-FBI profiler Dr Mark Ross at the murder scene in Hyde Park. Official sources confirm that the now UK-based psychologist and supposedly retired manhunter – who also wrote the bestseller, *Missing Conscience* – is working as a police consultant, in an all-out bid to apprehend the..." Mark stopped and threw the newspaper on to the top of the kitchen table in disgust. "I'm out of this," he said. "My only stipulation was that I remain anonymous, and Barney blew it."

"It wasn't Barney's fault that a bloody photographer gate-crashed the crime scene," Amy said.

Mark smashed his right fist into the palm of his left hand. "Maybe not," he seethed. "But I don't work under these conditions."

"That's rubbish, Mark. You've got to take the cards that are dealt," Amy said, her voice as abrasive as sharkskin. "You're the best chance that Caroline Sellars has. If you walk away from it now and she ends up like the others, you'll have a hard time living with it."

"I'm not responsible for her life."

"You are in part. You took on a certain amount of accountability when you decided to stick your nose into this case. Caroline has got a lot more on the line than a bruised ego or hurt feelings."

"Why don't you just kick me in the balls?"

"I did, figuratively."

Mark sighed. "I thought that you didn't want me to get involved with this in the first place, uh?"

"I didn't. But that was then. We have to see it through, now. And you know it, so lighten up and get back on track."

Mark picked up his holdall and headed for the door. Amy followed him out to the car. He climbed in, opened the window and said, "Your place or mine on Saturday?"

Amy moved back from JC after kissing him good-bye for the fourth or fifth time. "Your place," she said as he keyed the engine to life. "We'll go feed those ducks again."

"No pushing people off jetties. Agreed?"

"No guarantees."

"I don't like unpredictable."

"Life is unpredictable. You'd better take a towel and a change of clothes in a carrier bag, just in case."

Mark grinned. "Take care," he said, pulling away from the kerb.

"And you. I'll give you a bell tonight."

"Missing you already."

Mark was in his office at the hospital playing catch-up with paperwork when his secretary buzzed him.

"Yeah, Ruth?"

"One of the orderlies, Martin, wants a word, Dr Ross. It's concerning one of your patients."

"Okay, put him through."

"Dr Ross?"

"Shoot, Martin."

"It's Billy Hicks, Doctor. He's in a state. Says he needs to talk to you urgently. He just saw your photo in a newspaper and went apesh...er, ballistic."

"Apeshit hits the spot, Martin. Tell him I'm on my way."

Billy was standing at the window in his room, wearing only underpants – that were pee-stained and grubby-grey, not the white that they had once been – and a pair of odd socks. He looked malnourished; bony, pale, covered in a welter of dark brown moles that rashed his back and neck. He was staring out through the bars and the thick, shatterproof plastic pane behind them, that did not open to allow fresh air invade, contaminate and play havoc with the thermostatically controlled temperature. It also negated the sound of birdsong, the wind buffeting tree trunks, whispering through their branches, and the distant buzz of traffic on an unseen road.

"What's the problem, Billy?" Mark said, entering the small room which had a stale-fart and sour sweat smell that caused him to

89

spontaneously begin to breathe through his mouth; nostrils closing down for the duration.

Billy whipped around, removing his hand from the front of his pants, as though he'd been caught with it in the cookie jar, and faced Mark. He did not make eye contact, but appeared to study Mark's outline from head to foot.

"Y... You've got an aura, Dr Ross, same as in the p... picture, look," he said, snatching up the crumpled newspaper from his unmade bed, to hold out at arms' length.

Mark studied the quivering front page, but could see nothing remarkable, save for the side of Amy's face peeping out from behind his shoulder in the photograph.

"Sit down Billy, and run this past me. I'm not following your line of thought."

Mark pulled up a plastic contour chair, which would have looked more at home in a garden or on a patio. Billy sat down on the edge of his bed and started to rock backwards and forwards like those big-beaked birds you stand next to a glass of water. He then began to scratch at his cheek with the nail of his middle finger, drawing blood.

"Stop that, please, Billy," Mark said.

Billy obeyed, tucking his hands into his armpits and clamping his arms tightly to his sides, to trap them and curtail their independent and wayward antics.

"Now, tell me what it is that's upsetting you."

"The auras. Everybody h... has auras, and I c... can see them."

Mark frowned. This was a new development. "You haven't mentioned this before," he said. "Tell me about it."

"The Visitor t... told me not to. He said that it's a secret," Billy said, eyes wide behind his grimy spectacle lenses, studying the grey vinyl floor covering as though it were alive with cockroaches, or something even worse.

"So why *are* you sharing it?" Mark said.

"Because you're in d... danger, Dr Ross. And if it's my secret, then I c... can tell it to who I want to. Now it's your s... secret as well."

"Can you explain what the secret is, Billy?"

"I've always s... seen colours around p... people and animals. It's like a th...thin, quarter inch outline. When I realised that no one else c... could see it, I knew that I had a g... gift. But I've never told anyone, till now," he said with a cunning, lopsided smile revealing his small, tartar-stained teeth.

"What do the colours mean, Billy?"

"Green is good, the darker the shade the healthier and safer someone is. But yellow isn't nice. You can't trust yellow. I know a lot about everyone I meet, just by the colour or mixture of colours that they're surrounded by."

"And what's my colour, Billy?"

"Dark red for danger, tinged with black for death."

"Meaning I'm in danger, and I'm going to die. Is that what you see?"

"You're in danger, and you *might* die," Billy said.

Mark noted that his patient was more relaxed, and that his stammer had completely gone. Billy was exuding a confidence that was uncharacteristic.

"When did you first notice this, uh, aura around me?"

"You always have one. It's usually turquoise, which is okay. It was only when I saw your picture in the paper that I saw the change."

"Do you know why it would change to a bad colour?"

"Yes. The Park Killer has seen the picture of you, and considers you a threat."

"What else do you know about the killer?"

"Nothing," Billy said, standing up and going back to the window to look out. "Murderers are surrounded by purple, though."

An interesting and unusual turn of events, Mark thought, never truly surprised, but still able to appreciate the hallucinatory workings of a malfunctioning intellect.

"Quick, Dr Ross, look at this," Billy said, pointing down towards the lawn outside.

"What do you see, Billy?" Mark said, getting up and moving to his side.

"That song thrush on the birdbath is about to die," Billy said in a small, sad voice. And as if on cue a sparrow hawk stooped out of the ash grey sky, knocked the thrush to the grass, then took off with its still living meal flapping weakly, mortally punctured by razor-sharp talons.

Mark's mouth was instantly powder dry, and the hairs on the back of his neck stiffened.

"You didn't believe me before," Billy observed, smiling at Mark and watching the swirling hues that emanated from him. "But I can see by your colour that you're beginning to."

"Will you look at some photographs for me, Billy?" Mark said.

"Sure, Dr Ross. But I want a favour in return."

"Such as?"

"An hour down by the lake. I want to sit and feel free for a while."

"That's out of bounds to you. You have an exercise area."

"Yeah, a fuckin' quadrangle with brick walls and barred windows to look at. I want a change from being with psychos and killers. It's called give and take; a compromise. A 'you scratch my back and I'll scratch yours' kind of situation. An hour by the lake won't hurt anyone. And I might even tell you the colour that's surrounding the young woman standing behind you in the newspaper picture."

Back at his desk, Mark tried to work out the odds of the thrush being taken by a hawk just a split-second following Billy's prophecy of its death. There were no odds. It was a zillion to one. Pure Twilight Zone stuff. He picked up the phone and waited almost three minutes before being patched through to Barney.

"Yeah, Mark?"

"I need a photo of Ellen Garner, and one of Jason Tyler, ASAP."

"I'll send you a fax," Barney said. "Have you got something?"

"I just need to see what they look like," Mark said.

"You might want to factor-in that fibres from two of the scenes came up identical," Barney said. "They're from carpeting that Toyota used in Corollas between oh-nine and oh-fifteen."

CHAPTER FOURTEEN

The car's windows were steamed up with his breath and smoke. The ashtray was full, and the temperature was freezing cold. He switched on the engine, and as he did, a column of ash dropped down onto his lap. "Shit!" He brushed at his trousers in the dark, then wound the window down two inches and threw the cigarette end out into the night. Breathing in the chill air, he coughed, brought up a mouthful of greasy, bitter phlegm, and cranked the window down further, to spit out a gobbet of what had the consistency of a prairie oyster, to aim at but miss the already extinguished butt of the cigarette.

This might well be a total waste of time, petrol and lost earnings, he thought. The Yank would probably tell him to piss off, or even try to do more than bend one of his fingers back this time. If or when the good doctor turned up, he decided to leave his camera in the car and try a friendly, low-key approach. He opened the glove box and scrabbled around until he found a fresh pack of cigarettes, to rip the cellophane off and impatiently pull out the foil and drop it, before plucking a cancer stick out with his finger and thumb nails, to fire it up with his Bic lighter as he wished that he was at home with a bottle of Scotch and the willpower to take a night off and watch TV, or read a pot-boiler. It would never happen. He liked to be out on the prowl, looking for the shot or scoop that would prove to be an international money-spinner. He seemed to have spent most of his adult years tear-arsing about and getting nowhere fast; maybe even going backwards. As he rubbed at the condensation on the inside of the windscreen with his coat sleeve to create a blurry circle to look out through, headlights blinded him for a second before arcing away. Brake lights flared ruby red for a couple of seconds, before blinking out as if they had been doused by the fine rain that had fallen for over two hours with no sign of respite. But his heart quickened. It was the black Cherokee he had been waiting for.

Mark pulled into the Residents Only car park and looked suspiciously at the old Vauxhall that his full beams swept over. As he climbed out of JC, he glanced across to where the unfamiliar car was parked under the sodium yellow glow of a globe-encased light that was atop a twenty-foot-high concrete post.

The driver's door opened, and Mark immediately recognised the lowlife photographer he'd last seen in Hyde Park, as the little man pulled his collar up against the rain and walked quickly towards him.

"No camera, see?" Larry said with an open-handed gesture. "I just want to talk to you for a minute. I—"

"You drove a long way for nothing, pally," Mark said. "I don't talk to the press, ever."

"Come on, get real," Larry came back. "You wrote a fucking book for Christ's sake. That doesn't promote anonymity. Blushing violet, you're not."

"That was on my terms, and a long time ago," Mark countered, surprised that he was being defensive. "It doesn't buy you jack shit."

"It made you high-profile for a while, and consulting on this investigation just opened the floodgates again."

"Only because you popped up out of the bushes with your Box Brownie."

"It's a top of the range Canon. And if I hadn't popped up, then someone else would have, sooner or later."

Mark turned, walked to the entrance door and slashed his card key through the slot above the handle.

"I don't misquote, and I do have ethics, Dr Ross," Larry shouted after him, as Mark pushed the door open, intent on ridding himself of what he considered to be a minor nuisance. "I'm freelance by choice," Larry continued. "I got sick of the politics and half truths served up with lashings of bias. I'll work with you on this, not against you. And anything you want off the record, will be."

"I've never met a newshound I could trust," Mark said, pausing and looking back to study the bedraggled, dishevelled, unshaven man, and seeing sincerity in his eyes that shone through, contradicting his seedy appearance. "I suppose you'll stick like glue whether I like it or not. Am I right?"

"You got it, Doc. When I smell a big story, I'm a regular bloodhound or leech. A lack of perseverance isn't among my many faults. And I know that you're hot."

"Larry, isn't it?" Mark said.

"Uh, yeah."

"Okay, Larry. Come on up and we'll see if we can work something out to our mutual benefit. I don't want to have to be looking for you behind every fence, pillar-box or tree from hereon in. I'd rather have you out in the open where I can keep an eye on you."

"You won't regret it," Larry said, beaming like a guy who'd fallen arse over tit in shit, to crawl out of it smelling of roses and with his pockets full of diamonds.

"If I do, *you* will. Comprende?"

Larry nodded. His fingers still ached a little from their first meeting, and he could sense the capacity for extreme violence in the tall American. Some people you didn't mess with. Ross was that sort of person.

Sitting in the kitchen, facing the psychologist across the table, Larry sipped at the two fingers of Scotch he had been offered and gratefully accepted. He was warm now. Mark – which was how the Yank said he preferred to be addressed – had taken his sodden coat away, then handed him a towel to dry his hair, face and hands with, before leaving the room, to return looking fresh in a blue chambray shirt, keenly pressed cream chinos, and tan-coloured moccasins on his otherwise bare feet.

"Tell me, why have you jumped back into the killing game, Mark? Why get involved? I thought you'd walked away from all of that crap when you quit the FBI. Your book made it clear that profiling was behind you; part of a past that you had no intention of revisiting."

"I did walk away. I wrote *Missing Conscience* to flush it all out of my system. It was akin to having stomach cramps, then taking a king-size dump, washing up and closing the bathroom door on the stink. I felt like a new person."

"What went wrong?"

"Same as after taking a dump. You eat again, and what goes around comes around."

"That's a simplification. Analogous answers are cute, but evasive," Larry said.

Mark grinned. "Okay, Larry. I weakened a couple of years back and profiled a case. Now I've been asked to help out again, and realise that it's a part of me, like the nose on my face. It's there, love it or hate it."

"What makes you different to a regular copper?"

"I'm not a cop. And what makes me different is that I am sometimes able to get into ritual murderers' heads. I somehow tune in to their wavelength. I have empathy for it."

"That sounds like a frightening talent."

Mark grimaced and said, "Tell me about it."

"And you enjoy going into the minds of raving homicidal lunatics?"

"No, it's a need. Like you have for booze. You might wake up hating yourself every morning, but you know that you'll go back for a hair of the dog. I suppose I'm like an alcoholic that has fallen off the wagon."

"How did—?"

"I knew that you were a lush from in the park the other day. Your breath was eighty proof, and your hands were trembling. Add to that eyes like piss-holes in snow, and the unshaven, unkempt look of first stage self neglect, and we've got a guy trying to blow his liver up."

"That bad, eh?"

"Worse. How old are you, Larry?"

"Forty-nine."

"You'd pass for sixty at least. All that's keeping you going is your work. And once the booze starts cutting into your brain and causing short-term memory loss, then you're all washed-up. I give you another five years at best before they find you lying stone-cold dead in your own vomit."

"You certainly know how to make friends and influence people."

"Another of my gifts."

"Can you find this killer?" Larry said, wanting to change the subject. He didn't need lecturing on his chosen shitty way of dealing with life.

"I don't know. This isn't a typical serial murderer. It's personal. The unsub has a known, intended victim lined up. The park killings are just fillers, to terrorise his mark."

"Who is the intended victim?"

"Forget who. It could cost the person his or her life."

"It has to be a look-alike," Larry mused, verbally. "The guy is killing young redheads. The motive must be rage. It's some fruitcake who's been blown out and can't handle rejection. If he can't have her, then no one else can. This is jealousy and hate that's got way out of control. You're looking for someone as crazy as a shithouse rat. How am I doing?"

"Very good. Behind those bleary eyes lurks a rapier-quick mind."

"So, I'm right?"

"This is off the record, OK?"

"OK."

"Well you're in the ballpark. Tell me, do you want to help save lives, or just make a few quid to blow on more hooch?"

"Both," Larry said without a second's hesitation. "But the priority is saving lives."

"What do you want from me, Larry? Spell it out."

"An exclusive interview and a photo shoot. I want you to tell me all that you can about the park murders without compromising anyone. And I'd like another exclusive after the case is resolved."

"And in return, you'll help me bait the son of a bitch, right?"

"How?"

"They say the pen is mightier than the sword. I'll think about how you can wield it while I freshen our drinks. Go and get your camera."

"We've got a deal, then?"

"Yeah, Larry," Mark said, sticking out his hand to cement it.

Larry nervously shook the offered hand. The two men held each other's gaze. Mark knew that he had an ally, if he was as good a judge of character as he believed himself to be.

Seated in the lounge, they talked till well past three in the morning. Larry took notes and photographs, only putting his camera aside when Mark said, "Enough, I ain't some movie star."

Rising, stretching as he yawned, Mark then took the now empty Scotch bottle and glasses through to the kitchen.

"Sleep on the couch, Larry. You're as drunk as a skunk," he said. They had agreed on the content of the exclusive interview that Larry would sell-on as soon as he had written it up.

"Thanks, Mark, I'm knackered. A couple of hours wouldn't hurt."

It was a little after seven a.m. and still dark when Mark rose, pulled on his robe and walked bare-foot through to the lounge from the bedroom. He rolled his head and groaned as bones cracked in his neck. His eyelids were malfunctioning, gummed with sleep. His mouth tasted like shit on toast. Too much Scotch. He was out of practise, and glad to be able to admit it.

Larry was gone. There was a scrawled message on a Post-it affixed to the coffee maker: 'Watch this space' was the succinct one-liner, with the newshound's mobile phone number written below it. Mark pulled the small yellow square off the pot and stuck it on the wall-mounted cork message board, then went for a shower while fresh coffee brewed. Once dressed, he turned on the TV and digi-box, watched the news and drank a steaming mug of coffee, black.

The fax machine came to beeping life. He carried his mug through to the lounge and hovered over the tray like a vulture impatiently waiting in line to pick at any titbits left at the scene of a kill.

The facsimiles of first Jason Tyler's face, then of a previously unseen female's face were disgorged, followed by a hand-written note from Barney:

Mark,

The shot of Tyler is recent. The one of Ellen

Garner (ringed) is the best of a bad bunch, taken

a decade ago.

Keep me up to date.

B.

"I can see egg y... yolk-yellow around this man's head, Dr Ross," Billy said, studying the faxes that faced him on the top of his bed, where Mark had placed them side by side. "He's arrogant, self-centred, and t... totally untrustworthy. But there's n...no sign of him being capable of hurting anyone."

"How about the other one?" Mark said, tapping the image of Ellen Garner, who was pictured standing between two other girls; one being Caroline.

Billy removed his glasses, wiped the lenses with the bottom of his T-shirt, replaced them, blinked rapidly and narrowed his eyes, concentrating on the broad-faced female with the manly haircut. "Bright red," he said, his voice spiked with excitement, stammer gone again. "Not just one red; a mixture of crimson, scarlet, ruby, vermilion, cherry, wine and blood. Every red I've ever seen."

"You said that red signified a person being in danger," Mark observed.

"It's subtle. In this case it's volatile. She *is* danger."

"Can you tell if she has murdered anyone, Billy?"

"I don't think she had when this picture was taken. But there's a rage within her. She is capable of violence. I'd need a current photograph to know if she has actually killed anyone."

"I'll try to get hold of one," Mark said. "What about the woman in the newspaper; the one who was standing behind me?"

"She's cool, Dr Ross. Mother of pearl; the sun behind clouds. That's like the Queen of diamonds in a pack of cards. She's mucho lucky in life and love at the moment."

Mark couldn't help but relax inwardly. Everyone likes to hear good news, whoever gives it. He didn't believe in gypsy fortune tellers, but would rather not hear bad news from them, or piss them off enough to hang a curse on him. Why take risks? If an old Romany wearing a shawl and all bent up with arthritis knocked at his door touting clothes pegs or even lucky dried dog turds, then he'd most likely buy some, just to keep on the right side of stuff he didn't understand. As a psychologist he would never admit it, but the truth was, he was as superstitious as the next person. He didn't walk under ladders, and was careful around mirrors.

"Now let's go for that walk down by the lake," Mark said, picking up the two sheets of copy paper and sliding them into a document wallet.

"Y... You mean it?" Billy whispered, his eyes bulging as his stammer resurfaced.

"A deal's a deal, Billy. I got it cleared. Get some warm clothes on and we'll take some time out."

Mark waited till Billy pulled on a grey pullover, blue jeans, and trainers (with Velcro fastenings, not laces), then took his donkey jacket from a plastic hook on the inside of the small closet. The deranged patient seemed like a small boy. Looks could be deceiving.

They walked side by side along the gravelled drive, then angled across the grass to a wooden bench that was sited near the lake's edge, facing out towards the large expanse of water. Sitting beneath the bare, drooping branches of a mature weeping willow, Billy appeared, erroneously, to be a happy, harmless young man taking the air on a country outing.

"I know I'm n... not, and never will be again in this life, but I feel s...so free here, Dr Ross," Billy said. "I'll keep this hour in a sp... special place, like a mosquito fixed in amber, and be able to hold it up in m...my mind whenever I want to examine it and relive what it was like."

William Blake had written: 'Cruelty has a human heart'. He was right, Mark thought. But sometimes the heart, or mind in this case, is not aware of the cruelty that it inflicts. He believed that to be the case with Billy Hicks. Billy was a deluded, dangerous individual, not au fait with his condition or shortcomings. It was almost impossible to watch the skinny, bespectacled patient gazing out at the lake, and accept that he truly believed that alien life forms had taken over his parents' and sister's brains. Or that he was in touch with a 'visitor', who appeared to him in the guise of a black owl. Knowing that Billy was mentally ill made Mark question his own grip on reality. How could he believe that this man was capable of seeing coloured auras around people; colours that denoted their personalities and emotional state, while at the same time dismissing out of hand the possibility of an avian visitor, or mind-controlling entities from outer space? The blind faith in God in various forms was shared by billions of people worldwide. Were aliens any less real or more ludicrous to embrace as an actuality? Mark decided that madness lay down that road, and concentrated on the still surface of the lake, and the reflections of the scudding clouds that swept over it.

"See those ducks over there, Billy?" Mark said, pointing to several mallards that kept up-ending to feed on the rich soup of small invertebrates below the surface.

"Yes, Dr Ross, I s... see them."

Mark pulled a bread wrapper containing several slices from the deep side pocket of his car coat. "Try them with this," he said, passing it to his ward. "I've yet to meet the daffy that can resist a free handout."

After a few minutes, Mark wandered off, leaving Billy to revel alone in his brief state of pseudo liberty. At a discreet distance, a hospital officer and two orderlies kept a watchful eye on the proceedings, ready to restrain Billy if he stepped out of line.

Later, back in the facility proper, Martin met them, to escort Billy back to the residential wing.

"Thanks for that, Dr Ross," Billy said. "I can't remember when I had a b... better time."

"You're welcome," Mark said, nearly adding that they might do it again; incorporate it into his treatment plan as a therapeutically viable avenue to pursue. But he bit the words back as they formed. If it happened, it happened. He would not promote false hope. It was amazing, though, that the time by the lake had – if only temporarily – given rise to a radical change in Billy Hicks. He was walking erect, shoulders back, not shuffling. And a previously unseen air of self esteem was evident in his demeanour. Mark watched as Billy strode side by side with Martin along the wide corridor. The young man's arms swung freely at his sides, his hands not down the front of his trousers, as was the norm.

Back in his office, Mark wrote up Billy's history sheet, detailing the results of the exercise, which had produced more positive reactions in the patient than all other previous treatments put together.

CHAPTER FIFTEEN

The girl at the till in Waterstones was a doe-eyed, anorexic looking little bitch with spiky orange hair, a stud in her bottom lip, and overlong fingernails that were varnished black. How long was she going to talk in hushed tones to the blue-rinsed old cow that had just traded in a book token for a flowery jacketed piece of romantic crap, which would no doubt be full of apolitical, asexual, afucking everything, that ignored all aspects of reality or anything that could be considered remotely controversial? Why were old farts attracted to a fantasy world without sex, violence, drugs, child abuse, and all the day-to-day variety of life in its ripe fullness and full ripeness? Did they reach an age where the fear of living and all that it implied bowed their spirits and turned their minds and guts to jelly? It was probably that the nearer to the grave they got, the darker aspects of dementia, cancer, and being a spit away from feeding the worms affected their outlook. Safe, uplifting, optimistic tales with, 'and then they lived happily ever after' endings must help them allay the dread of a near future that would manage all too well without them in it.

At last, the old bitch was heading off, no doubt to clog up a counter in another store, as though she were a fatty deposit, narrowing an artery and stopping the healthy flow of blood.

The assistant raised the corners of her mouth in a pseudo smile and said, "Can I help you?"

Oh, yes, you can help me. You can suffer a brain haemorrhage or go blind, just as soon as you've served me. "I hope so. Do you have a copy of Missing Conscience by Doctor Mark Ross?"

Turning to her terminal, 'Doe Eyes' punched in the relevant details.

Strange, how book stores were almost as quiet as public libraries. Both had the same ambience as a church. It was an effort not to weaken and look about for a sign that in large black letters on a white background would state, or more aptly demand: SILENCE.

"Yes, we have a copy of that. You'll find it on the first floor under true crime."

"Thank you," and a polite smile. It wouldn't do to just walk away without a word and give the dummy any reason whatsoever to remember the brief encounter. Though the cold weather had made disguise easy. A woollen hat, scarf, coat collar up, and glasses – not needed, just a prop – were not out of place.

The book was in good company, cheek to jowl with case histories of crimes, biographies of retired coppers, and hyped-up tales of has-been gangsters and killers its close neighbours. Same old drivel: Brady and Hindley, the Great Train Robbers, the Yorkshire Ripper, the Krays, Dr Harold Shipman, Ian Huntley, Fred West and his wife. The list was endless; mostly regurgitated accounts of crimes and of criminals who'd caught the media and publics' imagination. The morbid fascination for bloody murder and sexual deviance was alive and well. It would be fun to spend a few hours swapping dust jackets, to treat the geriatrics to some surprise; gory bedtime fare that would lurk, waiting like a fat spider to shock them with its dark, foreboding appearance.

Missing Conscience had a Gold FBI shield on the front cover. But it was inside the flap at the back where the main interest lay. The black and white author photograph showed Ross as he had looked several years ago. He was even-featured, dark-haired, and had the semblance of a smile playing on his lips, though no humour was discernible in his clear, penetrating eyes. Underneath the photo was a brief bio'.

ABOUT THE AUTHOR

A native of Colorado, Dr Mark Ross excelled as

a Special Agent with the FBI, attached to the

Behavioural Science Unit at Quantico.

He is now a criminal psychologist, living and

working in the UK.

Hands sweating. Must get home and read the book. This was the professional manhunter who had appeared on the front pages of newspapers. His sole and undivided attention and efforts would be channelled into solving the Park Murders.

He will not find me. I will read his words and understand how he operates. And if the time comes when I perceive him to be the slightest threat whatsoever, I will kill him.

It was hard to be patient and wait to be served. On this floor, the register was manned by a beanpole kid with raging acne, blue-black hair shorn at the sides with the longer top carefully styled to resemble an unmade bed, and an overbite that made him look and sound like Janet Street-Porter. *Count to ten...Count to ten.*

Twenty minutes later, sitting on the speeding, swaying tube with the metallic pounding sound of wheels on rails, the other commuters – who made an art form out of seeing everything whilst appearing to look straight ahead into the middle distance, or chattered inanely into brain-scrambling mobile phones – dissolved as the prologue and then first chapter were avariciously devoured.

Almost missed the station. The book was hard-hitting and gripping. All the more engrossing because these were the thoughts of a new enemy; a man who had been fool enough to set down for posterity how he worked, and explain his techniques.

Blink.

Back in the house, with no recollection of leaving the train or walking home. Now a sudden need to eat. Cold beans in a pan on the hob would do. Must get a grip and be more house-proud. Everything seemed to be coming apart of late. With the periods of blanks and the ongoing mission, the place was a fucking mess, especially the kitchen. The sink was piled high with pots and pans that had the remains of food set solid to them like dried puke. And the whole house stank like a landfill site.

Four hours of hard graft and the place was pristine. Cleanliness was next to godliness, so mum always used to say. Although that was hard to believe during her last year, as she had become incontinent and refused to wash, never mind take a bath or shower.

A glass of milk and a cheese sandwich smothered in brown sauce for tea. The milk tasted on the turn, and some of the bread had developed small, green florets like lichen on gravestones. Three slices were salvageable: 'waste not, want not' was another of mum's old sayings. How long had she been nonexistent? Not important. The past seemed as unreal as a half-forgotten dream. Memories were unreliable and became distorted by time. It was easy to rework events and make them more palatable. The whole of life could be recreated in the mind and made perfect, subtly manipulated, tweaked to suit, and altered like a poorly fitting garment.

Now, take the car to the supermarket and stock up. Then settle down with the book and see where Dr Mark was coming from. But first, a few minutes in the gallery with Caroline.

The effulgent glow from the orange light bulb gave the photographs in the alcove of the bedroom a gentle warmth. Over a hundred shots featuring Caroline were Blu-Tacked to the wallpaper. They depicted the cool and callous bitch: walking, alone and with others, eating, drinking, entering and leaving the BBC, at the door of her apartment block, at the theatre, in a pub, smiling, laughing and frowning. In all her guises she taunted and provoked. Her multiple images plagued, pleased, uplifted and depressed the spirit at once. She was a thorn to be removed, so that the wound could begin to knit and eventually heal over.

Blink.

Still standing at the foot of the bed. Caroline's many faces swam back into focus. An hour had gone by, leaving no memory of its passing. It must be a combination of fatigue and the new orange pills that the psychiatrist had prescribed for what the stupid bastard decreed was a mild form of schizophrenia. Would have to stop taking them. The side effects of antipsychotic drugs were unacceptable.

Shopping done, thank God. Snuggled up in bed, facing the gallery again and reading Dr Mark's journal. It was a How-to book, and should have been titled: *How to catch a Serial Killer*, or, *The Practical Guide to Profiling*. It contained sections on working a crime scene, gathering trace evidence, the methodology employed to isolate and apprehend the offender, and many more. Dr Mark called the unknown subjects he hunted, unsubs, and purported that they generally suffered from one or a combination of several personality disorders. It would be interesting to know how he had profiled the so-called Park Killer. He probably thought that he was hunting for a Looney Tune; a wacky, 'What's up, Doc?' cartoon rabbit, who was as mad as a March hare. These profiling pricks apparently relied heavily on the method employed to kill. They studied all the evidence, then stirred in a large helping of the magic ingredient, gut feeling. No wonder so many repeat killers were still on the loose. Their hunters misspent a lot of time looking for the proverbial needle in a haystack.

Finished. It had been a good read. Now to use its contents to build a self profile. Try to see how Dr Mark would evaluate and write up the killer.

Comfortable. In the living room at the old, scarred desk, with heavy curtains drawn against the night, and a green-shaded banker's lamp concentrating its light on the large notepad in front of it. A cracked and stained Star Wars mug full of sweet tea and *Missing Conscience* were at hand; the latter for instant reference.

A heading: THE PARK KILLER. Sub heading: Criminal Personality Programme.

With the book as a tool, it was a piece of cake, easy-peasy, lemon squeezy, no sweat. More aptly, a walk in the park. Ha! It was fun. First an index of sorts, prior to the actual formulation of the profile:

Behaviour: Principle is that behaviour reflects

unknown subject's personality.

The profiling process that follows is divided

into seven categories.

1. Evaluation of the criminal act.

2. Comprehensive evaluation of the specifics

   of the crime scene or scenes.

3. Comprehensive analysis of victim/victims.

4. Evaluation of preliminary police reports.

5. Evaluation of medical examiners autopsy

   protocol/protocols.

6. Development of a profile with critical offender characteristics.

7. Investigative suggestions predicted on construction of the profile.

Consult with local investigators and suggest proactive strategies they might employ to gain response from the unsub.

If there is a 'signature' aspect to the crime, the personality can be recognised

and predictions of past offence behaviour may be made from this insight.

Blink.

A feeling of having been away. Tea now cold. Eyes tingling with a sensation of pins and needles. Fucking medication. And there were pages of writing, compiled with no memory of having written them. Dizzy, and a little confused. Mouth dry. Must move. Need to take a piss and have a cigarette, and then read what had somehow been formulated and penned while on auto pilot, standby, or wherever the fuck it is that I go when someone switches the light off in my head.

Fifteen minutes later, composed, back at the desk.

"Are you sitting comfortably? Then I'll begin," said to the ether in the small, dismal room. "Eyes down and look in. Read and learn."

1. Evaluation of the criminal act itself.

Redirected rage, resulting in violent attack, mutilation and murder of victims. Hallmarks of Sadistic Personality Disorder. Unsub used physical and psychological pain to establish control and domination. Obsessed with person other than victims, who unsub has contacted to intimidate and make known his intentions. Victims were exemplars. The murders were not random.

2. Comprehensive evaluation of the specifics of the crime.

The scenes were open ground (city parks). The crimes were committed under cover of darkness. The choice of location was rational and made discovery of trace evidence impossible, in conditions that were contaminated by weather, and the fact that many other persons had frequented the sites.

Hairs and fibres collected from scenes to be cross matched.

The victims were physically attacked. A sharpened length of tree branch was forcibly inserted into their vaginas. They were manually strangled, and their hearts were removed with a serrated knife.

3. Comprehensive analysis of victim/victims.

Victims were unknown to each other and had no discernible connections.

All three (3) were young, slim, female redheads. They had been selected because:

a). Of their similarity to Caroline Sellars.

b). Due to their habit of jogging/running in isolated surroundings between dusk and dawn. Their professions and status were not a consideration.

4. Evaluation of preliminary police reports.

Not available, but presumed to be insubstantial - little more than time, date and place. No witnesses or survivors.

5. Evaluation of the medical examiner's autopsy protocols

Not available. Informed conjecture of findings is that:

a). Sharpened tree branches found in vaginas were inserted ante mortem.

b). External bruising to throat and subsequent internal inspection of trauma to windpipe and larynx would confirm that all three deaths were caused by manual strangulation.

c). Removal of hearts was post mortem with a sharp serrated blade.

d). Scrapings from under victim 3's fingernails would yield DNA from blood and tissue deposits.

6). Development of a profile with critical offender characteristics.

To follow.

7). Investigative suggestions predicted on construction of profile.

Follows profile.

Psychological profile of the Park Killer.

The unsub is not a serial/ritual killer in the accepted sense of the definition, and has contacted the intended PT: – Primary Target: Caroline Sellars.

The three victims (to date) were mutilated and murdered to instil fear in the PT. They all bore a physical resemblance to her. The unsub also shows traits conforming to a Schizoid Personality Disorder type, with sadistic tendencies, not fitting perfectly into a recognised type, and will tend to be introverted and would find it difficult to form lasting social relationships, should that be desired, which would be highly unlikely.

This individual may be a classic loner, with the possible exception being close family members. The perpetrator will be intelligent, but incapable of showing any genuine affection, and will be more likely attracted to solitary activities.

Given the nature of the crimes committed to date, there is every reason to believe that the unsub has no interest in physically indulging in sexual acts, may be impotent, and has fixated on the PT, and may believe that she has offended him/her, and is more than likely obsessed, and has formulated a plan to gain maximum mileage out of terrifying and dominating the intended prey before ultimately killing her.

The staged murders show a total lack of compassion, and an inability to feel guilt or remorse.

Physical aspects.

Historically, statistics show that the overwhelming majority of serial killers are Caucasian males aged between the ages of twenty and forty. The Park Killer is confident in his/her ability to physically overcome chosen victims, suggesting a comparatively fit, young person.

Investigative suggestions and predictions.

Eliminate all known friends and associates of the PT from inquiry. Suspects without cast-iron alibis are to be DNA profiled.

The unsub *does* know Caroline Sellars.

Previous victims were murdered on first Friday of consecutive months. It is highly likely that another murder will take place in a city park on the first Friday of December.

That was all, but should be enough. How much more could Dr Mark come up with than that? His profile would have reams of police reports and the details of three complete autopsy findings. But the bottom line was, they had no idea who they were looking for. It was tempting to work-up the profile on the computer and send the celebrated, hotshot Yank a copy. In fact, the urge to do it was irresistible. If the professional manhunter was sitting back feeling clever and thinking that he was on top of this case, then he was sadly mistaken. It would be fun to interact with him. The next understudy for Caroline would not be taken when or where the doctor and the plods expected. The first Friday of December would come and go without incident. The police and Dr Mark would breathe a sigh of relief, only to be suitably shocked, dismayed and even more confused when a day or two later, number four turned up. They were zeroed in on patterns, but their assumptions would not be rewarded. There was only one games master, and it was not the hired gun that the police thought might prove to be their salvation.

Blink.

In front of the alcove yet again. The multiple images of Caroline were evocative and disturbing. And yet they instigated an inner sense of expectation that lit up the darkness within, like the sun's rays breaking through parting clouds to bring warmth and light to the cool earth.

Time to go to bed and have sweet dreams. Snuggle up and imagine Roy Orbison's candy-coloured clown tiptoeing into the bedroom to sprinkle star dust and whisper, 'go to sleep, everything is all right'.

CHAPTER SIXTEEN

In the dream, Amy was walking along a wide, high-ceilinged hall, her short heels clipping on the mosaic, tiled floor, echoing rudely through the acres of walled-in space.

Broad shafts of light – akin to World War Two or Hollywood searchlights cutting through the night to signal yet another air raid, premiere or glitzy function – pierced the high windows at intervals, striping the way ahead with mote-filled celebration of the bright day outside that would not be denied. And as she decided that it must be a museum, antiquities and artefacts materialised to give sleep's fantasy venue appropriate props. Visitors plinked into existence as illusory dressing to a scene that could have been situated in London, Paris, Rome, New York, Cairo, or any of a thousand other museums.

Pausing, she looked down through the glass top of a large display case, and was intrigued by the remains of a mummified body. It was partly covered in tattered, tea stain-coloured bandages. A boy king, she thought, examining the exposed, shrunken face, with its sunken eyelids and too-large, dirty ivory teeth protruding from tightly moulded black lips. The leathery skin of the long dead Egyptian youth was a visible promise and curse to all who gazed upon it; that life and all its pettiness was but a fleeting torment. An epitaph that she had seen on an old gravestone crossed her mind: 'Where you walk now, so once did I. Where I am now, you soon will be'.

A sudden and awful sorrow pricked her heart and weakened her. She gripped the edge of what was a glass encased sarcophagus in the belly of a brick-built sepulchre. The museum was a place where the bygone, ancient and dead resided in a time warp in which the passage of millennia no longer played a part in their existence, but moved around them in hushed reverence.

The boy king's face began to rise, as bread dough in the sun will, to fill out and regain its prior form and vigour.

Fear and morbid fascination gripped Amy in equal parts, superseded by mind-numbing shock that threatened to unbalance her both physically and mentally.

The closed eyelids, now convex with substance behind them, sprung open to reveal sharp, hazel eyes that met Amy's in mutual recognition.

"It... can't...be," she whimpered in a distressed, choked voice, before sagging down to the cold, ice-slick tiled floor in a dead faint.

Rearing upright as the nightmare exploded into non-existence like an imploding light bulb in her befuddled mind, Amy kicked at the sheet and blankets that were bunched around her, clinging to her perspiration-soaked body. Hunched on the bed, head in hands, she sobbed long and hard until she was finally cried out and her stomach muscles ached with the contractions.

Darren still visited in both sweet dreams and fearsome nightmares. It was as a good or bad acid trip must be like, though she had never indulged in drugs. The memory of having nurtured him inside her body, given birth to him, and loved him with an intensity beyond any comparison that she could ever describe in mere words, spiked her brain with a pain that transcended mere physical discomfort. The strongest emotions defied all adequate description.

Darren had been four-years-old; a healthy, intelligent and happy young boy with everything to live for; the adventure of life still before him.

The sudden fever, vomiting, stiff neck and livid rash were quickly followed by unconsciousness. The pell-mell rush to the hospital, and then the interminable wait was all for nothing. The approach of the tall, solemn man in a white coat, with the message of death in his dark, work-weary eyes, was almost beyond her capacity to bear. It threatened her sanity. There was no memory of the doctor's actual words, only of the scream that percolated in her throat, trapped, bubbling, and to this day not released.

It had been meningococcal meningitis, as if a name for it mattered. At first, she had believed that it was a divine judgement, for falling pregnant at sixteen, out of wedlock. Maturity, and a loss of the faith she had once harboured, eventually dispelled that conviction. It was all just part of life's rich tapestry; the rollercoaster of human experience, complete with exhilarating, skyscraper-high peaks and dark, gut-wrenching, hell-deep troughs.

Her heart juddered then raced. She remained still for a long time, until the sweat had cooled and she began to shiver. Sometimes the dreams were more kind, like walking hand in hand with Darren along a sun-kissed beach, with the surf sparkling and the air full of his laughter as the foam tickled his feet, pulling the sand from between small and perfectly-formed pink toes. The scenarios were of endless variety.

Looking back, there had been a choice, get on or get out. Survive and let time dull the edge of the pain, or take an overdose, sit in a bath full of hot water and cut her wrists, to drift away painlessly into oblivion. She had chosen to live and get on. But it had been a close call.

The after-vision of the nightmare gradually faded. She showered, dressed, and was standing at the drainer with her hands on the cool stainless steel, looking out of the kitchen window as dawn broke. Light and day were liberation, away from the realm of the dark that fostered a lowliness of spirit within her, and allowed unwelcome thoughts to ferment unchecked.

Sipping tea, she watched as a three-legged squirrel made its way to the bird table. She had christened it Hoppy, and once more wondered how it had lost the limb and managed to fight off infection. Her heart went out to it. The rodent's ability to adapt after suffering such a terrible injury, was admirable. She smiled. Mark called it Stumpy, and had said that they should try to catch it and see if a vet could fix it up with a prosthesis. The smile died. She had not told Mark about Darren. There had seemed no need to, and yet it disturbed her on some level that she had consciously made the decision to keep it a secret from him. Perhaps this weekend she would rid herself of what felt a heavy burden; an invisible barrier between them, if only in her mind. He was more open, concealed less, and wore his heart on his sleeve, able to risk it being bruised or broken. Thoughts of their relationship being more, and the fleeting contemplation of not being able to have his child crossed her mind. The sudden music from her phone suspended further exploration in that direction.

"Hi, kiddo. How's life in foggy London?" Her mother – fifty-nine, going on sixteen – asked.

"Okay, Mum. Are you and dad all right?"

"We're fine and dandy. I need a hip replacement, but apart from that, everything is just rolling along nicely. Your father keeps griping on about how long it has been since you dropped in to see us, though."

"Dropped in! You live in the wilds of Cornwall, for Chr... Pete's sake."

"You could come for a weekend, soon, and bring that hunky American with you. He's sexier than Brad Pitt."

"Behave, Mum. And Mark is at least fifteen years younger than Pitt."

"Never use age as a yardstick, Amy. And remember, looks are only skin deep. I've met young at heart octogenarians, and old teenagers. Its frame of mind that counts, not numbers."

"And what else did you call for, Mum? I sense you're holding something back."

A pause and then, "I saw the picture of Mark in the newspaper the other day. And I recognised you half-hidden behind him. I've tried to mind my own business, but it goes against the grain. It worries me. Why are you involved with those terrible murders? Haven't you been through enough?"

"Mark's consulting on the case, Mum."

"You know how your being in the police force gave me ulcers. I—"

"Drink more milk and quit worrying, Mum. Mark is just working up a profile for them. We aren't out there attempting to catch the killer ourselves."

"Keep out of the newspapers, will you?" Helen said, more as a command than a request or recommendation. "Whoever is doing these awful things is not right in the head. Seeing your picture could be a red rag to a crazed bull."

"Okay, Mum," Amy said, not wanting to spend twenty minutes arguing a moot point. "I've got to go. I'll give you a call next week. Tell dad that I love him, and that we'll drop by soon."

"Will do, Kiddo. Give that sexy doctor a big hug from me. Love you."

"Love you too, Mum. Bye," Amy said and ended the call.

In the west London bungalow, with the sun still lying below the horizon, a nightmare had also jolted Caroline Sellars into wakefulness at almost the same time that Amy had been kicking at her bedclothes in somnolent agitation.

Caroline pushed herself up into a sitting position, back against the headboard, knees raised and arms hugging them. A night demon in the shape of Ellen Garner had chased her from sleep. She, (Caroline), had been running blindly through a moonlit forest, fleeing from the shambling, bulky figure of Ellen, who was stabbing at the night with a sharpened stake. However fast she ran; Caroline was losing ground. The gap between them was inexorably decreasing.

"There's nowhere to run," the voice shouted with evil mirth, floating to her on a breath of wind.

As the nearness of her attacker displaced the air, and the heavy odour of fetid breath overtook her and made her stomach heave, she had escaped by waking up with a cry dying on her lips.

Caroline looked at the grey square of window, then searched the room's shadows, fully expecting one of them to detach itself, take human form and shuffle towards her, knowing that if that happened, she would scream herself into madness. She had never had to look into the face of real fear; never been seriously ill; never suffered an accident of any note; and never been threatened or abused. Her closest encounter with alarm and panic had been when Jason lost his temper on occasion, to shout and sometimes break ornaments or furniture. She was not emotionally prepared to face serious adversity. And what if it wasn't Ellen? *Could* it be Jason? Who else had she ever given cause to torment her so much? Would she ever be safe again, or be able to return to her apartment? She thought not. Someone was intent on killing her.

CHAPTER SEVENTEEN

Parking alongside the Jeep Cherokee, Amy climbed out and hefted her large holdall from the rear seat.

Mark met her at the door, took the weighty bag, then kissed her gently on the lips as the door sighed back into its frame and self-locked. He smiled and said, "Miss me?"

"Like toothache."

"That much?"

"More," she giggled, taking the stairs up to the flat, with Mark close at her heels, admiring her shapely butt as it strained against the tight jeans she wore.

"Like two polecats in a corn sack," he said.

"What is?"

"Your ass."

"You know how to flatter a girl."

"I've told you before, it's a gift."

"I'd give it back, then. It's a crock."

"As in crock of shit?"

"Exactly."

"You think my social engineering skills are lacking?"

"Nonexistent."

"Maybe I'll do a home study course. Learn how to be a proper gent."

"Too late. I know you for who you really are, and I wouldn't want you any other way."

Mark gave her behind a firm pat. "Flattery will get you everywhere."

The flat was imbued with the comforting aroma of fresh coffee and the heavy fragrance of sandalwood and cedar spice emanating from a lit candle in a jar.

Mark dropped the holdall onto the settee, and as he turned, Amy's arms encircled his waist.

"I love you, Mark Ross," she said, feeling a weakness spread through her. She kissed him softly on the mouth, then increased the pressure, also pressing her breasts, stomach and thighs against him, wanting to be a part of the person she now loved above all else.

"You okay?" Mark said when she allowed him to come up for air.

"Yes. I'm just feeling very slushy, and maybe a little wanton."

"It's true then?"

"What is?"

"That absence makes the heart grow fonder."

"Yes, I've decided I want to cramp your style and see more of you."

"You want I should strip off?"

"Fool. I didn't mean see more of you in that sense," she said. "But it's one of your better ideas."

"Let's go to bed, now," Mark said. "I want to see more of you, too."

Standing next to the bed, undressing each other, their eager fingers were clumsy, rushing, as though they were inept teenagers, or tots frantically clawing at wrapping paper on Christmas presents.

"This must be about as good as it gets," Mark said a half hour later.

"Jack Nicholson," Amy said.

"Huh?"

"He starred in the movie: *As good as it gets.* It was a romantic comedy."

"Did it have a happy ending?"

"Yes."

"Mmmm."

"Mmmm, what?"

"I always wonder at the end of a movie with a happy ending, what happened next? Did one of them end up with Alzheimer's down the road? Or did the dame run off with a tennis pro or vacuum cleaner salesman after two years?"

"Cynic."

"I know. Another of my many questionable traits."

"The future will take care of itself. There's no point in trying to outguess it."

"True. Will you marry me?"

Amy was dumbfounded. She had not expected to ever hear Mark say those words. She opened her mouth, but no sound came out of it.

"Is that a yes, no, or a rain check?" Mark said, his voice relieving the tension and breaking the awkward sound of silence.

"I had a child," Amy whispered, now giving her mouth free rein to voice thoughts that slipped out uncensored. "His name was Darren."

"I want to know all about him," Mark said, seemingly unfazed as he reached out and traced her lips with his finger. "But it doesn't answer the question. Will you marry me, Amy? I love you, and weekends aren't enough anymore. I've started wishing the days away until I see you again."

"Yes," she said, the small word not seeming adequate enough to express such a monumental and life-altering decision.

They held each other again, tenderly, consumed by their own thoughts, both aflame with the concept of being together as a unit, their lives entwined and as near to achieving oneness as possible.

"What will your folks think?" Mark said.

"My dad's read your book about four times. I'm sure he'd like you to sign it for him, though he would never ask. You're larger than life in his eyes. He'll be chuffed."

"And your mum?"

"She fancies you like mad. You're up there with Brad Pitt, after dad, that is."

"I'm on a winner, then?"

"If you think that waking up next to me every morning is a prize, yes."

"Let's go and celebrate with coffee and a Danish."

"Where?"

"In the kitchen. I don't want to share you with anyone else for a while."

It was after another bout of lovemaking that, wearing robes, they padded through the flat to the kitchen.

"What's with the mug shots?" Amy said, seeing the faxes on the tabletop.

"Barney faxed them. The guy is Jason Tyler, and the broad is Ellen Garner," Mark said, staring at them as though a ring of colour might miraculously appear around their heads.

"Any help to you?"

"Do you want to hear a strange tale?"

"Yes. Is it a true one?"

Mark nodded. Poured the coffee, put the pastries on hold and went over to the table. Amy sat down opposite him.

"Once upon a time," he started, forcing a grin. "There was a young man committed to life in a secure hospital for the criminally insane."

"This sounds better than Snow White and the seven lecherous old dwarfs," Amy said.

"It will sound no less improbable. But like I said, this story is fact not fiction," Mark said as an unbidden picture formed in his mind of Snow White, asleep and lying semi-nude on an oak bed in a room that contained six other handmade beds, their headboards carved with rabbits, oak leaves and other cutesy fare. Gathered around the slumbering brunette with the Cupid's bow lips were a bunch of vertically challenged old diamond miners contemplating a gang-bang. He cleared his mind of the lurid scene before it became pornographic. "The patient's name is Billy," he continued, pushing back the image of Grumpy unbuckling his belt. "He has a special talent, I think. He purports to be able to see an aura around people, and the colour of it denotes their inclinations, emotions, and even their fate, to a degree."

"What is he serving life for?" Amy said.

"You don't want to know."

"Yes, I do. I'm unshockable. I want background."

"All right. An apparently mild-mannered and studious young man went bananas one night and split his parents' and then his sister's heads open with an axe, before...disposing of their brains."

"How?"

"He cooked them, and..." Mark pulled a face.

"Jesus, why?"

"He believed they were inhabited by aliens, and maintains that a black owl that he calls the Visitor told him to do it."

"Let me get this right, Mark," Amy said, unable to suppress a cheek-dimpling smile. "You have a lunatic murderer who has an imaginary non-human pal, who we'll call Olly Owl. Olly tells Bozo Billy to wipe out his family because little green men from another galaxy or dimension have relocated in their brains. He also sees colours around people, that he attributes meaning to. How am I doing so far?"

"Right on the money, honey."

"And you showed wonder boy the pics?"

"Correct."

"Mark, I really think that you're—"

"No, Amy. I'm not losing it. I'll explore any avenue open to me, if it might help find the killer."

"But this is off the wall, Mark. You sound like Mulder used to in the X-Files: 'The truth is out there'."

"He was right, it is. Do you read your horoscope in the papers or on the Internet?"

"I glance at it, occasionally. But that doesn't mean I believe what it says."

"What if instead of vague generalisations, one of these astrologists wrote something on the lines of: Scorpio: The sun, moon and the planet Zog are aligned in what can only be interpreted as a portent of doom. If you are a Scorpio, then be warned. Do not get out of bed tomorrow, or at very least, stay home. The chances of you being hit by a car, dying in a rail disaster, or even being driven into the pavement by a frozen slab of effluent from a high-flying 747 are all real possibilities. Be very afraid tomorrow, and extremely wary and careful."

"They don't write stuff like that."

"No, they're more responsible. There are so many people who *do* believe what they write, that they have to use constraint. Think how many thousands of work days would be lost if what I just said was printed, and all superstitious Scorpios' stayed home."

"I see the analogy to Billy. I'm a non-believer in the occult influence of stars and planets on human affairs, but if a well-known astrologer came up with that, then I would consider taking the day off. Better to be safe than hit by frozen shit being the best policy."

Mark told her of the bird being taken by the hawk, and of the colours that Billy saw around himself, Amy, and the pictures of the only two suspects that they had.

"You believe it, then?"

Mark shrugged. "I'm happy to add it to the mix. I think he has an ability. It's not something that I would admit to any of my colleagues, though. I don't fancy ending up in a rubber room."

"Have you got any further with the profile?"

"I've just developed a gut feeling that we're off base with Tyler and Garner. I don't think Tyler is killer material. And although the woman has the propensity to commit these offences, I'm almost positive that if she had held a grudge against Caroline, then she would have reacted at the time or soon after, not waited for so many years. It doesn't fit."

"Where does that leave us?"

"Who else could a woman bug to that extreme, other than an ex-lover or slighted work mate?"

"Hell, she could have picked up a psycho stalker, in the way a sheep collects ticks, without even knowing it. It seems to be an ever more popular pastime for nonentities with seriously fucked-up wiring. Look at what happened to Lennon and Jill Dando."

"Caroline isn't a high-profile celebrity, so I'll stick with the idea that the perp is more than likely someone that she knows."

"Then it has to be someone at the BBC. Maybe a deranged DJ, a crazed cameraman, or a canteen lady that Caroline upset by telling her there were lumps in the mashed potato. Take your pick, Mark, the list is endless."

"No. If it's a Beeb employee, then he or she is contained. We can narrow it down."

"True. Barney can get access to personnel files. Most will be easy to discount. We can flag any likely individuals, then do background checks. See if any have criminal records, or have been under treatment for any form of mental disorder. The field will get smaller."

"That's the long haul. I think we can do it a lot quicker. Barney can have fibres lifted from any Toyota Corolla registered during the relevant years. If we get a match to fibres found at the scenes, then it's a wrap. DNA will tie it up."

"It sounds easy when you put it like that. But we have a deadline; the first Friday in December."

"I'd like to think that one of these two is responsible," Mark said, nodding to the faxes. "But I've got a feeling in my bones that we're on the wrong track."

CHAPTER EIGHTEEN

The passing years and addiction to junk food and cigarettes had not been kind, and had definitely taken their toll. She had always been overweight, but now, at still only twenty-nine, was a gross figure with no curves to advertise her gender.

Laying on her side, awake and facing the window, her stomach was a vast mass nestling on the mattress like a water-filled pink balloon collapsing under its own sagging weight before her, as did her pendulous breasts.

Dawn was heralded not by trumpets or birdsong, but the roar of engines, as a large jet drifted over the rooftops to land at Heathrow. As if in response, the alarm clock buzzed with the sound of an irate wasp in a bottle. She ignored it. It was at Vicky's side. She was content to play possum and let her sleeping partner wake up and rise first.

Vicky snorted, produced a long, rolling fart, then grunted and reached out, swatting the clock and silencing it.

Funny, Ellen thought, (as Vicky sat up, swung her legs out of bed, stretched her arms and yawned), how the demure forty-year-old would die of embarrassment if she were to break wind so freely when awake and in company. She was reserved in all her actions, aside from lovemaking, during which she would vocalise her orgasmic delight by screaming four-letter-words with 'gay' abandon.

Vicky was slim – the antithesis of Ellen – with a creamy complexion and bright cyan eyes; the overall package giving a false impression of youth.

"Good morning, darling," Ellen said, heaving herself over to the middle of the bed in unconscious mimicry of a sea-lion flopping up on to a beach, the rippling fat following along behind the bone structure beneath it, stretching soft muscles to the limit. "You look good enough to eat."

Vicky smiled and walked around the bed, to lean over and kiss Ellen on the mouth.

"Good morning, sweetheart," she said. "I'll go down, let Mr Tibbs out, and make us both a nice cup of tea. How does that sound?"

"Mmmm, good. I won't be long," Ellen said, watching her partner walk across to where her dressing gown hung behind the door. She felt a warm tingle inside at the sight of Vicky's narrow-hipped, boyish figure. Her bottom was tight, still defying gravity, and her small breasts were pert, with large, dark nipples.

Ellen listened as Vicky emptied her bladder and flushed the toilet. She then levered herself up into a sitting position and plumped the pillows against the headboard to rest her back against, before reaching for the pack of cigarettes and lighter that were on the top of the bedside cabinet next to her. She lit up and inhaled deeply, instantly coughing as her lungs rebelled against the hot smoke. It was her habit to wait until Vicky had made the tea before venturing downstairs.

After stubbing the cigarette out, Ellen went into the bathroom to sit on the wooden seat, unmindful of her buttocks overflowing it, or of her stomach resting on the front of her tree-trunk-thick thighs. Looking in the mirror as she brushed her teeth, she acknowledged that she resembled a Sumo wrestler, and promised to contain, then reduce her burgeoning mass. After all, she was far from stupid. Being morbidly obese was putting a strain on her heart, as well as putting her at risk of numerous other assorted ailments that would inevitably shorten her life. 'Be fat, be happy' was a slogan that she had read in some glossy magazine. No doubt whoever had penned it was a fat bitch herself, who thought that shopping in outsize stores and only being able to see her feet by way of a mirror's reflection was in some way chic. Ellen could find no benefits in carrying the equivalent of another human being around in her skin. She so much wanted to be as svelte as Vicky, though would never admit it.

The window reverberated in its frame as yet another several hundred ton of flying steel throttled back and seemed to float over the semi in Stanwell, somehow supported on a raft of cold winter air.

"Only today matters, so be a happy camper," Ellen said aloud, already looking forward to a couple of thousand calories in the mouth-watering form of fried bacon and eggs, accompanied by a stack of toast dripping with butter, and a mug of sweet, hot tea. All thoughts of fighting flab were banished for another day. Tomorrow was always the best time to deal with problems and vexations that dampened the spirit...and tomorrow never comes.

Pulling on a thick, white towelling robe, which would have served as a fancy-dress costume, should she ever want to attend such an event as a giant snowball, Ellen clumped down the stairs, ignoring their creaks of complaint as they bowed grudgingly under her weight.

"It's time we moved away from here," Vicky said as Ellen entered the kitchen and slumped into a chair at the Formica-topped table, panting open-mouthed like an overheated dog.

"Where to?" Ellen said, holding a pudgy hand to her racing heart.

"Anywhere that isn't next to a bloody airport," Vicky said, placing a mug of freshly brewed tea in front of Ellen.

"I'd like to go back up north. Wouldn't it be great to live somewhere in the Yorkshire Dales, or even the Lake District?" Ellen said.

Vicky shrugged. "What about work, which equates to much needed cash?"

"We could open a cafe, or run a small guest house or B & B."

"Absolutely. I'd enjoy that. I'm sick of London," Vicky said, reaching into a pocket for her own cigarettes, and quickly lighting one. "Although I worry about how we would be treated in a small community out in the sticks," she added, opening the fridge and taking out a carton of eggs. "I don't want to be persecuted for being gay."

Ellen smiled. "I may have had counselling and be able to control my anger these days, Vicky. But any moron who gave us a hard time would be given one warning to stay the fuck out of our lives. I wouldn't want any trouble with turnip-eating bumpkins, but if they wanted to go that route, then they'd find me more lethal than foot and mouth."

"ARMED POLICE!" A loud, disembodied voice erupted, causing them both to freeze in bewilderment.

Time bent and slowed in Ellen's mind as both the back and front doors imploded. Vicky dropped the carton, and it seemed to fall with the tardiness of a soap bubble, to disgorge the eggs, which cracked open as they hit the tired linoleum, sending slimy, transparent tentacles of albumen and burst suns of yolks into the air.

"Ellen Garner lives in Stanwell with an ex-air hostess called Vicky Wade," Mike said. "She doesn't drive, but the Wade woman does, and guess what, boss?"

"This isn't a bloody quiz show like The Chase, Mike," Barney said. "Just tell me."

"She owns a Toyota Corolla."

"That makes her our prime suspect, then," Barney said, studying a report from the lab. "Tyler's DNA doesn't match. He's out of the frame."

"You think that these two women are in it together?"

"I don't know. But we have enough to assume that they might be."

"You want to pull them in?"

"Yes, but with appropriate safeguards. I'd rather have an armed unit lift them. If these women are responsible for the park killings, then they're bloody lethal, to be considered as highly dangerous."

"Will the super okay it?"

"Pearce will sign the paperwork if it's put to him properly."

"When will it go down, boss?"

"We'll coordinate it for early Monday morning. We'll keep them under surveillance till then. Organise the team into pairs and arrange for twenty-four-hour cover."

"What about Dr Ross? Are you going to involve him?"

"Yes. He's in it for the duration. I want his input when we interview these two."

Figures in black swarmed into the kitchen, knocking Vicky to the floor as they filled the small room.

Ellen attempted to stand up, but the cold muzzle of an assault rifle met her forehead and forced her back into the chair.

"Just stay on your arse, lady, and put your hands behind your back, now," a young officer with threatening eyes and a tight, nervous expression on his chiselled face said as one of his colleagues moved in with a pair of ratchet cuffs.

Ellen was in shock as she was handcuffed, roughly pulled to her feet and hustled to the door. From the corner of her eye she saw Vicky being held down, with the side of her face pressed into the mess of raw eggs. Frog-marched outside into the grey light, Ellen began to shiver as her robe fell open to disclose her nakedness. At that moment a surge of adrenaline powered into her muscles, and bright red anger misted her vision. She let out a high-pitched shriek of rage, lowered her head and charged, driving the top of her skull into the back of one of her captors.

Officer Chris Buckley thought that the operation had been money for old rope, until an explosion of pain in his spine sent him staggering forward, to fall to the ground in a twisted heap.

Ellen followed up, as hands frantically tore at her robe in an effort to hold her back. She kicked out with her slippered foot and felt a deep sense of satisfaction as her toes smacked into the man's upturned face. She was like a runaway train with a full head of steam powering her. Ignoring the pain that coursed through her toes from contact with the copper's head, she threw herself backwards into the reaching arms behind her. At least two cops went down, falling like ninepins, to be almost flattened as her bulk landed on top of them.

"Eat shit and die, you wankers," she screamed vehemently, before the butt of a rifle was smashed into her temple, cutting off any further thoughts, insults or actions.

Ellen regained consciousness to the sound of her own moaning. The throbbing pain in her head made her feel sick to the stomach, and for a few confused moments she had no recollection of what had happened. As the memory of the incident seeped back, she tried to sit up, but couldn't move. Why not?

With her eyes slitted against the harsh light, she raised her head, looked about her and groaned out loud as a bolt of fire lanced through her brain. She was in a hospital room. A nurse approached the bed, and behind her, standing next to the door was another female, her hands clasped loosely in front of her crotch.

Looking down the bed, Ellen studied the wide, nylon restraining straps, that resembled car safety belts snugly pinioning her across chest, waist, and just above her knees. She croaked, "What the fuck is going on?" Her mouth was bone-dry and her voice reminded her of the cartoon character, Popeye, as she directed the question past the nurse to the other woman, who was now talking in hushed tones into a mobile phone or radio, so was obviously a cop.

"By all accounts, you went berserk," Barney replied to the same question, thirty minutes later, after rushing to the hospital on receiving the call from DC Louise Callard.

Ellen's blood pressure soared, causing her head to pound like a base drum. "Armed men dressed in black like fuckin' ninjas smash down the doors of our house at dawn and attack us, and you have the balls to tell me that *I* went berserk," she said, her words clipped and loaded with venom as she strained against the binds that held her. "I'm going to sue your fuckin' lot for every penny they've got. You assaulted two defenceless women, then compounded it with wrongful arrest. Where's Vicky? What have you done to her; pistol-whipped her senseless, or just put her up against a wall and shot her in the fuckin' head?"

"Ms Wade is fine," Barney said, relieved that the raging woman was strapped down, but still half expecting her to swell up to even bigger proportions, turn green and snap the belts like tissue paper, to rise like the Incredible Hulk and maybe rip his head off and stick it up his arse. "We believe that you and your friend may be able to help us with our inquiries into a serious crime."

"What fuckin' crime?" Ellen said.

"Do you know a woman by the name of Caroline Sellars?" Barney said, ignoring her question.

Ellen frowned and said, "Yes, well, no. I did know a Caroline Sellars a long time ago. Why?"

"That will be all, Officer," a grey-haired doctor said, striding into the room after being summoned by the nurse. "If you want to interview this patient, then I suggest you come back in twenty-four hours. She has suffered a mild concussion and needs rest. I also intend to remove the restraints. This is a hospital, not a prison or asylum."

"Right on, Doc," Ellen said. And addressing Barney. "And tomorrow you'll be talking to my solicitor, you Nazi prick."

Barney turned on his heel and left.

Vicky Wade knew her rights. She refused to say a word without having a solicitor present, because she had not been charged with anything. The experience of the assault on the house, and the way in which she had been restrained and cuffed did not promote an ounce of faith in her captors. Barney could see that she would not cooperate without the counsel of someone she trusted.

An hour later, with a legal beagle at Vicky's side, Barney set the tapes going, and with a WPC and Mark Ross in attendance, started the interview. Mark had been contacted at Cranbrook midmorning by DS Mike Cook, with an invitation to be present.

"Do you know Caroline Sellars, Ms Wade?" Barney said to the woman, who was now clothed in a thick sweater, jeans and trainers, that a WPC had brought from the house in Stanwell.

"I... I've never heard the name before," Vicky said.

"Can you tell me your whereabouts between midnight on Thursday the third and seven a.m. on Friday the fourth of September?"

"Yes," Vicky said. "That's easy. I always go to bed before midnight, apart from Saturdays. And I get up at seven o'clock on Monday through Friday for work."

Barney also quizzed her over October the second and November the sixth, and was given the same answer.

"And what about Ms Garner? Would you know beyond any doubt where she was at those times?"

"Don't answer that, Vicky," Charles Lamont, the solicitor, said. And to Barney. "I am representing both Ms Wade *and* Ms Garner, Detective Chief Inspector Bowen. I would recommend that you ask my other client these questions directly."

"We haven't spent one night apart in over two years," Vicky said, unbidden. "Mr Lamont tells me that you are investigating those park murders, and I am horrified that you would even think that Ellen or I might have anything to do with them."

"We require a DNA swab from you, Ms Wade, and also fibre samples from the carpeting of your car," Barney said. "Do either of those requests present any problems?"

"I don't think—" the solicitor began.

"It's all right," Vicky broke in. "I have absolutely nothing to hide, and neither does Ellen. Take whatever samples you need, Inspector, then please let us go home. Mr Tibbs will be starving and frightened."

"Mr Tibbs?" Barney said.

"Our cat," Vicky said, then started sobbing and covered her face with both hands as her shoulders began to hitch violently.

"I think you can safely cut her loose, once you've got a swab," Mark said after they had left the interview room.

Barney frowned. "You believe her?"

"Yeah, and so do you. Her body language was screaming her innocence. And her answers to your questions were unguarded and obviously truthful."

"She could be a good actress."

"And I could be George Clooney, but I'm not."

"I don't like the coincidence of the Garner woman living in the area. Or the fact that her...girlfriend owns a Toyota."

"If Ellen Garner committed those murders, then I'm convinced that Vicky has no knowledge of it. And how many Toyota Corollas are registered in the Greater London area? If Vicky gets up at seven every morning, then there's no way that Ellen could have killed those women and got home before Vicky was awake and missed her."

"Garner could have drugged her; slipped her a couple of sleeping pills. But if you're right, we're back to square one."

"I don't believe that Ellen is involved, Barney. I think the killer is a man, working alone."

"Let's see what Miss Personality Plus has to say in the morning, when the hospital discharges her."

"I'll stay at Amy's tonight and call you first thing," Mark said, then left the building. He jogged across the windswept car park to JC, climbed in and pondered for a while, letting all the facts of the case separate out. What had Caroline Sellars done? Or what was she hiding from them? She must have done or said something to instigate such dire retribution. No, that was a logical line of thought. He wasn't dealing with logic here, but with psychosis that could not be slotted neatly within normal parameters. He was looking to find a nightmare made of flesh and blood, which could not be treated as a normal, rational man or woman. The killer, who he still thought was a man, did not think or function in any way that could be easily predicted. He was an almost separate species, with thought processes as alien as a scorpion or shark. He was terrorising Caroline from a distance. Her mind was being crushed in a grip of evil, by a person who was without conscience.

CHAPTER NINETEEN

With her head swathed in bandage, and her solicitor sitting next to her, Ellen felt in total control of the situation.

Charles Lamont was more comfortable handling civil gay rights cases, but was confident that his initial representation would be all that was required. He truly believed that his current clients were totally innocent, and was convinced that there would be no charges to answer.

"Is Liberace in there with her?" Barney said to Mike as the DS came out of the interview room.

"Yeah, boss. He makes Graham Norton sound butch. Have you sussed that rug he's wearing?"

"Yeah. It looks like an Astrakhan hat. Where are you floating off to?"

"I was going to organise coffee. Do you want one?" Mike said, looking from Barney to Mark. They both nodded, before bracing themselves to question Jabba the Hutt in human guise.

"Before we get this over with, I want it on record that I think you are all fascist, homophobic pigs," Ellen said as Barney and Mark entered the small, dingy room.

Barney repressed a smile. "Good morning, Ms Garner," he said, unruffled by her comments, having tucked decades of verbal abuse under his belt and developed skin thicker than crocodile hide.

Ellen kept up a tirade of insults throughout the interview, as she chain-smoked and glared at Barney in defiance. "To sum up, copper," she said. "I haven't seen or heard of Caroline since I dropped out of university. I fancied her for a while, maybe because as I recall she was playing hard to get and trying to kid herself that she was straight. As it turned out, I met someone else. Skip forward a few years and I'm into a relationship with Vicky, and love her to bits. I haven't murdered anyone, but if I ever decide to, then you'll be way up near the top of the list. Now, why don't you take a swab, blood sample, bottle of piss, and anything else that floats your boat, and get me the fuck out of this place. I can't wait to start prosecuting you turds for the barbaric treatment that Vicky and I have been subjected to."

"You think the blimp with an attitude is squeaky clean?" Barney said to Mark as they walked out into the car park.

"Yeah. I think it's time to initiate Plan B."

"The BBC?"

Mark nodded. "You should to go ahead and check out all the Beeb's employees who own a Toyota Corolla, and then we can narrow it down to probable suspects. Tyler, Payne and Garner looked good for it, but concentrating on them has just lost us valuable time."

"And what if plan B turns out to be a dead end? The Toyota could've been stolen."

"Then we get more bodies, and have to find another angle."

"I'll get on it. And the team can also check out anyone that works at Caroline's regular watering holes and other haunts. We checked-out and eliminated all the tenants in her apartment block after she received the papers and notes from the killer, but some of them may bear a second look at. I still hope that the hippo in there is bluffing and that her DNA is a match."

"Don't hold your breath."

"I won't, but I can dream."

"I'll be at Cranbrook or home if you get anything you want me to look at."

"When we have a list of all Toyota owners at the Beeb, and their personnel files, I'll give you a bell. I'd like you to help sift through them."

"I'd appreciate that, Barney. I think the killer will fit my original profile. Red flag any single or divorced guys, and do a fibre match on their vehicles first. That might just wrap it for us."

"The coffee is freshly brewed," Amy said as Mark was shown into her office at Sentinel Security. "Your timing is matchless."

Mark poured them both black coffees, carried the wafer-thin bone China cups and saucers across to Amy's desk and set them down on glass coasters.

"Thanks. How did the interviews go? Is the case solved?"

"No such luck," Mark said, moving behind her chair, putting his hands on her shoulders and rolling his thumbs over tense muscles. "The Garner woman is potentially a nasty piece of work, but she's no serial killer."

Amy closed her eyes. If she'd been a cat she would have purred. His hands were working wonders. "It's still the use of the sharpened branches that bugs me," she said. "I can't get my head around the killer using a substitute for his cock. Why doesn't he rape them? Isn't that the ultimate act of control and domination?"

"He has an agenda that's not fuelled by sexual need. His motivation is in creating exhibits that have been executed to primarily scare the shit out of Caroline Sellars."

"He's succeeded."

Mark withdrew his hands and turned to look out of the window behind Amy, to stare at the crooked black fingers of tree branches, whipped by gusts of wind that were far too late to strip the long-gone leaves from them.

"One more," he whispered.

"One more what?" Amy said, getting up and standing next to him.

"He'll take one more before he zeros in on Caroline," Mark said, now fully concentrated, back from what had seemed to be a short mental excursion.

"What makes you think that?"

"Profiler's instincts," he said, raising his eyebrows as if to convey the fact that he had no idea how he sometimes homed-in and received insight. It was as though he was in some metaphysical way able to know how his quarry thought. He had always likened it to the tuner needle of an old radio, scanning the band until a clear signal emerged from the background garble of interference. "I don't try to understand it. If I did, it might leave me. All I know is, he's getting impatient. He knows that he has ruined Caroline's life, and that she's sweating it out in a supposedly safe location. The media coverage is tempting him to do another. Part of him wants the game to go on. His need will be like a fever in the blood. Caroline has been the catalyst and the driving force behind all his actions. Now, he wants her so badly that it will be hurting."

"You really believe that he'll be able to find her?"

"Yeah. I know he will, if we don't stop him first. He knew that she would go to ground when he started this and contacted her. He'll enjoy the thrill of the hunt."

"And that's why you're trying to redirect him."

"In what sense?"

"Today's newspaper. Your interview with Holden is in it."

"I'd forgotten about that. Do you have a copy?"

"Does a bear—"

"Shit in the woods?" Mark finished the saying that he probably overused, and which Amy was now apparently picking up on.

"The photo is flattering. You look like some sixties film star in black and white."

"It's amazing what they can do with an airbrush."

"False modesty doesn't become you."

"Okay, so I'm a hunk. Your mother is a fine judge of looks, if not character."

"Are you staying over tonight?"

"No. I need to be back at Cranbrook early in the morning."

"I'll leave Petra in charge and come back to the flat with you. Is that a problem?"

"You know it isn't. Will you take your car?"

"No. I'll get a cab back tomorrow."

"Last of the big spenders. Business must be good."

"Security is a balm for the paranoid society that we live in. Crime is on the increase, whatever the politicians say. And that makes for nervy punters, all wanting protection from their own shadows. I'm even advertising for two new operatives. There's too much work for Petra, Jon and me to cope with, and I don't like using freelance cowboys."

"It looks as though I'll be able to retire and be a kept man, once we tie the knot."

"You could be my partner in every sense of the word, Mark. You'd find this business a challenge."

"And waste my qualifications?"

"They'd be an asset to the company."

"I'll think about it, once we're hitched."

"Good. Do you want to read that article?" She opened the top draw of her desk and retrieved the newspaper.

"Later," he said. "When we get to the flat."

Dark clouds piled up from the west, pregnant with rain. And rooks tumbled about the sky, screeching discordantly; black and ragged and windblown.

"Looks ominous," Amy said. And as if on cue, lightning snaked out of the angry heavens in front of them, almost instantly followed by a whiplash crack of thunder that split the air.

"Lull before the storm," Mark said, seconds before a violent deluge was unleashed from above, to drum deafeningly on the metal roof over their heads, pound the windows and obscure all vision through the windscreen in a machine-gun peppering of exploding droplets.

"Jesus!" Mark said, snapping the wipers to high speed and turning on the headlights. The wipers fought the tide; demented metronomes slapping to and fro, marking time at a frenzied rate.

Amy's hand – which had been resting on his thigh – gripped him tightly, nipping his flesh.

"Aahh!" he cried out in surprise and pain. "I'm glad you weren't holding anything more delicate."

Amy giggled and moved her hand across his lap. "Shouldn't we stop at the next pub until it passes?" she said.

"No," Mark said, hunching over the steering wheel, straining to peer through the curtain of rain beyond the windscreen. "We should be at the flat in twenty minutes. This storm could hang around for hours."

Nearer to forty minutes later, he parked as close to the entrance door of the flats as possible and cut the lights and engine.

"On three we make a run for it," he said as they released their belts. "One...two..."

Amy didn't wait for three. Just threw open the door and left JC like a bullet from a gun.

"Women," Mark shouted into the wild night as he followed, his card key in hand.

Although only scant seconds out in the open, both of them were drenched. Amy had a laughing fit as they climbed the stairs flat-footed, their shoes squelching as they left a trail of puddles on the all-weather industrial quality carpeting.

"Th... That was fun," she said, when able.

"Getting soaked to the skin by freezing rain is fun?" Mark said, wiping his eyes as droplets ran down into them from his plastered hair.

"Yes. I'd love to stand out in it for a while, if it wasn't for the lightning. Being electrocuted would take the edge off it."

Mark looked at her. She was radiant, with her hair flat to her cheeks, in ringlets on her brow, and with her eyes sparkling with innocent humour. He held that image and stored it in a mental photograph album; a favourite snap that he would cherish and always be able to turn to and study at leisure. When they reached the landing, he stopped, crushed her to him and kissed her wet lips.

"Let's get dry before we catch pneumonia," he said after they had been standing for too long, neither wanting the moment to end, despite the chill seeping into their bones.

Half an hour later they were seated in front of the closed balcony doors, dry and warm, nursing mugs of steaming coffee laced with brandy, and looking out through the mullioned windows, entranced by the fury of the storm which, now unleashed, knew no bounds.

"God, it's beautiful," Amy said, watching mesmerised as nature produced a staggering display of awesome visual and aural effects. An hour passed before the roiling clouds seemed to heal from the lightning wounds that had ruptured their underbellies. The living cinema screen blackened; the spectacle was over, and the travelling circus moved on, to set up its big top farther down the road, to thrill, amaze and entertain new crowds with its awesome and dazzling acts.

"Do you want another coffee?" Amy said.

"A Brandy would hit the spot," Mark said. "You do the honours, while I go out to JC and get that newspaper."

A few minutes later, sitting in front of the coffee-table in the lounge, Mark sipped fine cognac and read Larry Holden's article, while Amy made roast beef and cheese sandwiches. Neither of them had the appetite for a cooked meal.

The photo was flattering. The camera liked him. Strange how some people always seemed to look good on film. He was one of them. The headline made him groan:

AN AMERICAN PROFILER IN LONDON

Mark winced. The connotation to the werewolf movie was painful. Was this piece by Holden going to be a 'bad moon rising'? He read on:

> DR MARK ROSS, PICTURED ABOVE, IS THE CRIMINAL PSYCHOLOGIST WHO MAY BE ABLE TO HELP THE POLICE APPREHEND THE HUMAN MONSTER WHO HAS BEEN TAGGED 'THE PARK KILLER'.
>
> BENEATH A DISCIPLINED AND GUARDED FACADE, I FOUND THIS AFFABLE AMERICAN TO BE A PRINCIPLED AND DRIVEN MAN, WHOSE ALL-CONSUMING PASSION FOR HIS MORBID LINE OF WORK,

DOES, I AM CONVINCED, MAKE FOR A FORMIDABLE ENEMY, SHOULD YOU BE THE TARGET OF HIS REVERED MAN-HUNTING CAPABILITIES.

DR ROSS SEEMED HAPPY TO DISCUSS HIS FORMER CAREER AS A PROFILER WITH THE BEHAVIOURAL SCIENCE SECTION OF THE FBI.

HIS EXPERIENCES ARE THE STUFF OF HOLLYWOOD MOVIES. BUT IT IS TODAY, NOW, AS THE CAPITAL IS GRIPPED BY FEAR OF THE NIGHT STALKER WHO HAS MUTILATED AND KILLED THREE YOUNG WOMEN, THAT ROSS IS CONCENTRATED ON.

THE DOCTOR IS CONVINCED THAT THE PERSON RESPONSIBLE FOR THESE HEINOUS CRIMES IS SUFFERING FROM A CHRONIC PERSONALITY DISORDER. HE ATTRIBUTES THE PERPETRATOR'S CONDITION TO CHILDHOOD IMPRINTING AND AN EMOTIO-PHYSICAL IDENTITY CRISIS THAT IS, TO A DEGREE, INFLUENCED BY A MECHANISM PATTERNED FROM EVENTS LEADING BACK TO HIS EARLY UPBRINGING.

DR ROSS STATED: 'THE MANIAC WE ARE LOOKING FOR IS OF SUB-NORMAL INTELLECT, CANNOT CONTROL HIS SICK URGES, AND WILL NO DOUBT BE OF INSIGNIFICANT APPEARANCE AND INCAPABLE OF RELATING TO OTHERS.

THIS IS AN INSECURE INDIVIDUAL, WHO IS BLAMING SOCIETY FOR HIS OWN INADEQUACIES. HE IS A PATHETIC AND PROBABLY IMPOTENT LITTLE MAN, WHO I IMAGINE MAY WELL BE PHYSICALLY AS WELL AS MENTALLY DEFORMED. HE HAS LEFT SIGNIFICANT CLUES, AND I AM CONFIDENT THAT THE POLICE WILL SOON HAVE THIS MAD DOG CAGED. HIS PREDILECTION TO PICK

ON WEAK AND DEFENCELESS WOMEN GRAPHICALLY SHOW HIM UP FOR THE SKULKING COWARD THAT HE IS....'

"Wow, this should get his attention," Mark said, speed-reading the tail end of the piece, which was just a rehash of the first three slayings.

"You're purposely trying to draw him out," Amy said, appearing at the kitchen door carrying a stacked plate of sandwiches.

"Damn right I am," Mark said. "Most of what I worked out with Larry for this article is bullshit. We're dealing with an intelligent man, not an idiot. But his ego and vanity will bring him down. I doubt that he'll be able to resist contacting me."

"Why would he do that?"

"In an attempt try to convince me that he isn't the sad, moronic piece of shit that I've painted him."

"You've probably put your life on the line, is that professional?"

"No, it's dumb, but we need more time to find him. This might save other women from the fate that the first three suffered. I have to distract him and divide or shift his attention from whatever schedule he's working to. When you leave in the morning, we mustn't see each other till this is a done deal."

"We're in this together, Mark. I—"

"Not anymore. If he knew about us, then you would be his way to get to me. There's no way I want you in the frame."

"You bastard," Amy said, slamming the plate down on the table with such force that the sandwiches flew up a foot into the air and came apart, to disgorge the slivers of beef and cheese over a wide area of tabletop and carpet.

Walking over to the balcony doors to stand facing out into the night, Amy's only view was the reflection of her own angry expression in the glass. "I know that you're doing this with good intentions, and for all the right reasons," she said, her voice controlled as she somehow repressed the urge to run across the room, beat her fists on his chest and scream at him. "But you had no right to risk what we have. This maniac has the advantage. If he decides to take the bait, then he knows who you are. You don't know your enemy."

"It's just a part of the ride on the big, blue, spinning ball, Amy. We all do what we have to. I decided that the only way to break this jerk's focus is to add a new dimension to the game."

"It isn't a fucking game. It's life or death." Amy shouted. "I empathise with his victims but care more about you and me. Survival is like charity; it begins at home. If that sounds selfish, it's because it bloody well is, and I make no excuse for it. You were out of order doing this."

"I'm sorry," Mark said, going to her and hugging her. He could feel the tension. She was shaking, not with cold, but with smouldering rage and deep fear in equal parts. After a while she relaxed a little.

"Too late for sorry. What's done is done," she said. "No point bolting the door when the horse is at least three fields away and running like the wind."

"He'll contact me," Mark said. "Then probably try to take me out. But I'll be ready. Barney will organise a reception committee. I'll be covered."

"You said he'd get to Caroline, and that armed officers and a safe location wouldn't deter him. Why do you suppose that if he decides to go after you it will be any different?"

"Because it's my line of work. Fire-fighters put out fires, bakers bake bread, and I hunt psychos down."

"If you get out of this in one piece, promise me that you'll never get involved with profiling again." Amy said as she pulled back to look him in the eyes.

"I promise that I'll consult you on anything that might come up. That's the best I can do," he said, then covered her lips with his, effectively bringing the conversation to an abrupt end.

CHAPTER TWENTY

Detective Superintendent Clive Pearce was standing behind his desk, tapping out a beat with a pencil on the newspaper that lay open before him as he muttered under his breath. Barney's royal cock-up had brought the wrath of the top floor down on him, and the bollocking was still ringing in his ears, overwhelming the noise of the storm that raged over the city. Tearing a barn-sized strip off Bowen wouldn't change a bloody thing, but might make him feel a little better than he did now. Shit, like everything else, finds its own level, and the DCI was about to find himself up to his neck in it.

"You wanted a word, Clive?" Barney said, rapping once on the office door that had been left ajar, waiting for him like an open and primed gin trap.

"Don't fucking 'Clive' me. Just shut the door and sit down," Clive said, slamming his backside into a swivel chair with all his weight behind the move, almost tipping it over.

"You should get tropical fish in here, Clive. They're good for bringing down stress levels. That's why so many doctors' surgery waiting rooms have them. You—"

"DCI Bowen, shut the fuck up," Clive came back, his face darkening. He broke his pencil in half and gripped the arms of the chair as if he were on a white-knuckle ride at Alton Towers. "The operation you jacked-up to bring in those two dykes was a total disaster. You couldn't organise a piss-up in a brewery. The brass wants to know, on paper, how two innocent women got to be assaulted by a supposedly crack team of armed police."

Barney shrugged. "You sanctioned the action, Clive. I put what we had in front of you and bingo, you said to lift them."

"Both women were injured, for Christ's sake. One of them was hospitalised."

"It's all in my report, Clive. Ellen Garner resisted arrest and went berserk. We have one officer with two or three cracked ribs, and another with a fractured cheekbone."

"Unfuckingbelievable. They were geared up and armed to the teeth," Clive said, shaking his head in disgust. "And the woman was handcuffed. How could she attack them?"

"It's all on video, Clive, as per the book. Our arses are covered. When you see this Sherman tank in human form running amok, then you'll wonder why they didn't just put a bullet up her jacksey."

"Not, funny, Barney," Clive said, though he visibly relaxed a little, happy to know that two officers had been hurt by the suspect, and that it had been captured on video. "Is there any chance whatsoever that the woman could be the killer?"

"Slim to none. Both of them were happy to give samples, and they're in a long-term relationship."

"Where does that leave us?"

"Dr Ross is positive that the perpetrator is male and a BBC employee. We'll be checking out all Toyota Corolla owners for a fibre match of their vehicles' upholstery. Then we can start eliminating and see what we're left with."

"I asked Ross to consult on this case," Clive said, pushing the newspaper across the desk to Barney, as if it was something unwholesome that might infect him. "I'm beginning to regret it. Read this shit."

Barney read the interview Mark had given to Larry Holden. He said nothing.

"Did you authorise this?" Clive said.

Barney shook his head. "Get real, Clive."

"What's his game?"

"I reckon he's trying to buy time, purposely giving the killer something else to think about, to disrupt his plans."

"He should know better. When you chum for sharks you use blood, fish heads or horse meat. You don't throw yourself in the fucking water. The mad bastard could get himself killed."

"I'll talk to him, but it's done now," Barney said.

"OK. Find out just what he's playing at. And let's nail this killer before he rips another woman to bits on our patch."

Barney nodded, quickly got up and left the office. Back in the squad room, Mike, Eddie McKay and three other team members were drinking coffee and reading through reams of BBC employees' details. Initially they were going to concentrate on white males between the ages of nineteen and forty. If push came to shove, they would do a second sweep later. For now, they had more than enough to check with DVLA. The corporation had a list of authorised vehicles owned by employees, which was an aid, but was not necessarily complete, and would not show up any second cars owned by workers.

"I'm calling it a day, Mike," Barney said. "I'll be at home if you need me before morning."

Standing outside, under the portico, Barney rummaged in his coat pocket for his cigarettes, took one out of the crumpled pack and fired up. He sucked in the calming smoke and let the cigarette dangle from his lips as he turned up his collar. The rain was sheeting down, bouncing off the concrete, and retirement in Spain was becoming more attractive by the minute. In his mind's-eye he could see a small, stuccoed villa with tiled floors, a balcony with a fine ocean view, and a swimming pool to cool off in. It was cheap out there. His pension would stretch a lot further, and he and Anna would be able to live comfortably. He felt older than his years. The job was weighing heavily, and his motivation was gradually waning. He felt like a crippled submarine; plates buckling under the building pressure as it slid into the crushing depths. Yes, Spain, good weather, and the shedding of all responsibility was an appealing alternative. But that was something to contemplate in a few months. The brochures and property magazines that Anna was littering every corner of the house with were beginning to wear him down. Before long he might even start to believe that it had been his idea in the first place.

Flicking the end of the cigarette out into the rain, for it to be hammered down, already extinguished before it hit the concrete, Barney ran across the car park to his Mondeo, stabbing the remote door-opener as he neared it, already soaked before he could take shelter.

Driving home, Barney acknowledged to himself that he was approaching, if not already past his sell-by-date. He could understand why Mark Ross had walked away from the escalating inhumanity perpetrated on man, by man. Back in an era not so many years ago, rape and murder were the exception to the rule; headline grabbers that shocked the nation. Time had quickly moved on, and the world had become a much more unsafe, savage place. It was all but impossible to believe that his parents' generation had never felt the need to even lock their doors, back in the late forties and fifties. For some reason, a growing malignancy of far more violent behaviour was escalating out of control. Murder and sex crimes had become daily occurrences. Society was producing more twisted, frustrated and sadistic individuals who were prepared to cast aside all inhibitions and carry out whatever sick, antisocial acts they chose to, apparently without fear of capture or confinement. The culture of crime had changed to become more brutal and perverse. Had there ever really been a time of relative innocence, with less overt evil? Could evil be a spreading disease; an undetectable virus with no cure, which attacked the minds of the susceptible?

Even though it was still raining, Barney spent a few minutes standing at the edge of his pond before going into the house. The pool's underwater lighting enabled him to watch the fat Koi glide uncaringly in a separate liquid universe. The sight of the brightly coloured fish cruising through the clear water calmed him and restored his fundamental belief that there was still a lot better than bad in the world at large. Alarmist and shocking news just got more press. Gloom and doom sold copy.

The glee at having sent Dr Mark a constructed profile, to undermine whatever the Yank's presumptions were, had turned to gut-wrenching, mind-swelling fury. The ex-FBI man stared out from the page of the newspaper with a supercilious smile on his chiselled all-American-boy-next-door face.

He read the article beneath it again, highlighting key words in yellow marker: HUMAN MONSTER, CHRONIC PERSONALITY DISORDER, MANIAC, SUBNORMAL INTELLECT, SICK URGES, INSIGNIFICANT, INSECURE, INADEQUACIES, PATHETIC. IMPOTENT LITTLE MAN, DEFORMED, MAD DOG. SKULKING COWARD.

Blink.

He opened his eyes and felt the pain in the back of his hand. It was throbbing and covered in a mass of smudged yellow squares from stabbing himself with the pen. Thank fuck it had been a chunky felt tip and not a ballpoint. He was dripping with sweat, shaking, and felt nauseous. No one, absolutely *NO ONE* had the right to badmouth him so vehemently. The so-called profiler was well out of line, and would pay dearly for making this personal and painting him as some retarded Neanderthal with a limp dick. He would make the no-good bastard eat his words, literally. He would stuff the newspaper, soaked in petrol, into Yankee Doodle's mouth and light him up like a roman candle, after Dr Mark had apologised satisfactorily for every insult he had uttered.

The article had been written by some scumbag called Larry Holden, who had no doubt taken thirty pieces of silver for aiding and abetting in the false and malicious denouncement. He had called the killer a human monster. Well, Larry the lamb would be duly dealt with, after he had been interrogated at length and divulged everything he knew about the Yank.

Carefully cutting out the picture of his nemesis, he pinned it to the fridge door with his favourite magnet, which depicted the World Trade Center towers. Strange to think that they no longer existed. And funny how priorities shifted. A new plan formed. It was intoxicating. He would take another redhead before the light of another day dawned. All of a sudden, he couldn't wait. Someone had to suffer. There was one bitch who he had stalked for over a month. She would fit the bill admirably. She was physically ideal, though did not do her jogging in parks. But he was capable of adapting. Killing one outside any of the carefully manicured green havens – the lungs of London – that pocked the city, would rattle both the police and Ross. It was time to break the pattern. They may be able to cover the main parks, but not the city at large. His playing field was now without restriction; unbounded. He was expected to strike on the first Friday of the month. So, he would now throw them a curve, as the Yank might say, and confound, confuse and demoralise the enemy.

As though it were a priceless relic or sacred artefact, he removed a single length of sturdy tree branch from the top of the long chest of drawers that stood directly below the gallery of Caroline. He handled the piece of ash with due reverence, then smiled, his eyes sweeping over the photographs, as with a sharp knife he pared, sliced, carved and transformed the innocuous limb into a lethal weapon with a needle-sharp point.

Blink.

He was ready. During the fugue he had cleaned up the wood shavings from the bed and carpet, dressed in black sweats and smooth-soled sneakers, and had slipped the sharpened stake into the extra-long pocket he had made and stitched to the inside of his pants. It was exactly like the stick pockets that screws employed to carry their staves in. The bottom of *his* pocket was thickly padded with cotton wool, though, to stop the point of the stake piercing the material.

The phone book first; a little research. He thumbed to H, then Ho. Ran his finger through the columns of surnames. Holbrook...Holbrough...Hold...HOLDEN. Holden L, address and number listed. The photojournalist was a dead man walking. He would check out the hack's home the following day, break in when he was out and then just wait for the dummy to show up. Caroline could sweat it out for a while longer, as initially planned. Revenge should be taken cold and slowly, to maximise the eventual pleasure it gave. The anticipation of anything he looked forward to doing could be almost as rewarding as the act itself. There was always a certain sense of deflation after the event. He may even take her on Christmas Day. She would make a great stocking filler. Ha! This was one Santa who had his own list of gifts required. And the top item on it was a twenty-eight -year-old redhead by the name of Caroline Sellars.

He became physically aroused. "Impotent, eh, Dr Mark? I think not," he said, picking up his knife, a cellophane packet containing latex gloves, a reel of duct tape and his car keys.

The main force of the storm had shifted farther to the east, and the street and pavement glistened afresh in the glow from the street lamps. He climbed into the Toyota and eased away from the kerb, eager to resume the game and once more assert and demonstrate his power to visit death upon whoever he chose. Behold a pale horse, and the dark rider who stole the living from the midst of life. His acts were uncompromising and pure. He rendered sentient consciousness to profound oblivion. The killings, thus far, had been carried out to curdle Caroline's blood and reduce her to a mental wreck, fearful of even her own shadow. But they had done so much more. The state of terror, and then the stillness that the everlasting obliteration of fellow human beings imbued, caused a previously closed door to open, liberating an inner darkness that had dwelt dormant in the depths of his soul. Killing at close quarters was personal; an exciting activity that like any other stimulant only kept him high for a limited period of time. The stalking and planning maintained the need simmering on a low light. But it was the impaling and the sensation of life being extirpated as his fingers sank into the warm, pulsating flesh of a smooth throat, which gave him what he could only equate to a cerebral orgasm; a numbing gratification that ripped through his neural pathways and caused a million sensual explosions to erupt, taking him to what must be paradise; truly heaven on earth.

He pushed a disc into the deck, searched for track three and cranked up the volume. The CD was The Very Best of Meatloaf, and the track was, *You Took the Words Right Out of My Mouth.* It began with a short conversation, which he spoke the words to as it played:

"On a hot summer night would you offer your throat to the wolf with the red roses?" Bobby said over the singer's voice.

"Will he offer me his mouth?" The seductive, lilting female reply.

"Yes."

"Will he offer me his teeth?"

"Yes."

After the dialogue had run its course, he kept pushing the repeat button, to play the opening to his favourite song a dozen times and talk the words.

Blink.

He had parked on a side street in Chiswick, only a two-minute walk from the riverside path that his prey would jog along in – he looked at the dashboard clock, its glow the same luminous green as a small plastic skeleton which he had kept from his childhood, and that still came to phosphorescent life in the dark – approximately fifteen minutes. At six-thirty a.m. she would be running, alone with her thoughts, perhaps planning her day as she moved sinuously and gracefully, her breathing controlled, her limbs functioning with the fluidity of a mare on the gallop at Ascot. And by six-forty she would be a still and lifeless form.

What *was* death? A reality? A concept? It was beyond his understanding. It was an altered state; a catharsis resulting in a transition. Did thoughts, memories and emotions cease? Or were they independent of the physical shell that they inhabited, and somehow survive intact? That notion was as easy to believe as the possibility of intelligent life on a planet in a galaxy millions of light years from earth, existing in the same bowl of cosmic soup as everything else. It made him realise just how inconsequential his and everyone else's actions and aspirations were. One freak solar flare from the Sun, and spaceship Earth would be flambeau. Nothing lasts forever. And yet the masses were programmed. The human condition allowed them to ignore their insignificance, to be distracted by all things mundane. The main topics of conversation around him at work were fired by greed and vanity. People were *so* small-minded, and he found it both depressing and pathetic.

Just enough time to hear Meatloaf finish off track nine; *Heaven can Wait*. Maybe heaven can, but tide and time wait for no man, and he had a red-hot date to keep. He began to shake at the prospect of what he was about to do.

CHAPTER TWENTY-ONE

"Don't forget to pick up milk and a paper on your way back, darlin'," Charlie Spencer said as Tina left the bedroom, dressed in sweats.

"Have the tea brewed. I'll be back in about forty-five minutes," she said, before walking down the landing to look in on Samantha. It still amazed her how peaceful and serene Sam could look, when asleep. Within an hour the three-year-old would be up, and the house would be filled with her laughter and noisy exuberance for life, that neither herself nor Charlie could now imagine being without. Bending, she kissed her 'little miracle's' forehead. Sam had been born after Tina had miscarried twice. And not a second passed that she and Charlie didn't appreciate the gift of their daughter.

This was Tina's window of opportunity, to fine-tune herself for another hectic day at the local Jobcentre, where she was in the front line, engaged in verbal battle with irate claimants who were not impressed with any explanation that did not result in being awarded some form of allowance or benefit. Running next to the river at dawn was her way of fortifying herself to meet whatever problems and challenges she would no doubt encounter. She had tried yoga and even painting, but both were too passive. She needed to move, to feel unfettered and free.

Descending the narrow flight of stone steps at the side of the road bridge, the light from houseboats with early risers on board painted the Thames in abstract, wavering brushstrokes of white and yellow that danced on the oily black surface. The air was sweet, cool, crisp and invigorating. It was as though the storm had gathered up the polluted air and carried it away, to no doubt dump out over the English Channel.

Flicking her auburn hair back out of her eyes, Tina sped up, increasing her heart rate and pushing herself, not content to jog sedately. There would be plenty of time to be pedestrian in two or three decades. At her age she could afford to extend herself and go for the burn.

Fuck a duck! She was moving like an express train. If she got past him, he would never catch up with her. She was racing like a gazelle with a lion on its tail. No sweat. He would wait and take her on the way back. She would be slower, maybe not spent, but with tiring muscles; easier to overcome.

He moved back behind the broad trunk of the tree he had been leaning against, only ten feet from the path.

A sudden chill flash-froze Tina's spine, to encircle her neck with cold fingers of fear. She looked back, but the path was clear. To her right was the river, to the left, a fifty-yard stretch of mature trees that stood like sentinels in the watery predawn moonlight. She was not given to premonitions, but shivered and was almost overcome by a sense of impending danger. If a figure had appeared from the gloom, she would not have been surprised. But no one rushed out to assail her. All that moved were the bare limbs of the trees, as a breath of wind soughed and whistled through leaf-denuded branches. Unsettled, she ran on, regaining some control and pushing back the irrational panic that had pervaded her. Maybe the subconscious thoughts of the recent murders in Regent's and Hyde Park were playing on her mind. She knew that her qualms were unfounded, but the presentiment had spoilt her run and made her wary and anxious.

She ran on for another half mile and then stopped to hold the rusted railings that separated her from the now ominous looking river. She breathed deeply, evenly, and gradually calmed herself. Never before had she experienced such a potent sensation of unease. All she wanted now was to be back home and in the light with Charlie and Sam. Every second alone in the darkness was a second too long. She set off, back along the path, not as fast on the return trip, watching for movement and feeling foolish, not able to comprehend why she was teetering on the edge of a panic attack.

The shadow sprang out at her, detaching itself from the tree, independent from the background that spawned it. In a heartbeat she realised that it was a man. He was dressed all in black, – Johnny Cash – dashing towards her, brandishing something in his hand, and it wasn't a guitar.

Oh, Jesus, no, please, her mind shrieked as she swerved sideways and slammed her hip into the palisade of rigid iron.

Yes...Yes...Yes...Yes. Now, now, he thought as the bitch faltered and reeled sideways, banging into the railings and falling to one knee.

Tina felt stupefied, unable to move. Numbness permeated throughout her whole being. Her mind was frozen like a bloom being withdrawn from a canister of liquid nitrogen; the petals brittle, changed to a state of petrifaction. She was beyond having the ability to assess or consider any options, but knew on some fundamental level that she must act, do something...anything. *Do not just kneel here to accept defeat and die.*

The face was large, inlaid with wide eyes that appeared to be black pools; inhuman and without expression. The mouth was wide open in a demonic grin, and the tongue that curled out from its depths, flicked back and forth over the bottom lip, as a snake might taste the air to locate its prey. In the figure's hand was a stick; a sharpened piece of wood.

DO SOMETHING, NOW! A voice commanded Tina from the very core of her brain, to limbs that languished in slack, perfidious mutiny.

He lashed out at her head with the branch to club her, needing to daze her so that he could pull her pants down, spread her legs and impale her while she was incapable of struggling. Once staked, she would be too preoccupied with the subsequent agony to resist as he slowly strangled her. He would look into her eyes and enjoy a spontaneous ejaculation in his pants as all embodiment drained away to leave the deadpan, vacuous expression of a stuffed animal on her face. It was all going to plan. His life was a series of plans that he viewed as screenplays for movies, to then act out while a part of his mind stood back, meticulously directing the proceedings. He had worked at the BBC, involved with both radio and television productions for long enough to pick up on how the overpaid shirt lifters operated. This was a two-hander; just him and his victim. He had scrolled through his mental screenplay while standing against the rough, damp trunk of the tree:

ACT 1

FADE IN ON:

EXT (exterior). THE RUNNER. CU (close

up).

She is running along the riverbank on the dark

side of dawn, her red tresses streaming behind

her, breasts jiggling up and down, bra-less under her sweat top.

SOUND, BG (background).

The slap of the runner's soles on the wet path. Her breathing becoming louder as she approaches. The wind whipping through the bare tree branches.

THE CAMERA DRAWS BACK.

Through the trees we can now see the antagonist, waiting, watching. CU of his right hand shows that he is gripping a sharpened tree branch.

THE CAMERA TRACKS WITH KILLER as he darts out, rushing at the runner, knocking her backwards against a barrier of iron railings.

THE CAMERA SWINGS TO THE RUNNER. She puts her hands up in defence.

CU of her face, as an expression of startled horror forms. Her mouth opens wide – ECU (extreme close up) – but no sound escapes it.

THE CAMERA DRAWS BACK as the killer clubs her to the ground and then pulls her sweat bottoms and panties down to her ankles. He kneels between her legs, forces them apart and plunges the sharp length of hand-hewn wood into her.

ECU of penetration. SOUND. Agonised scream of pain from victim.

THE CAMERA DRAWS BACK as killer strangles runner. SOUND. Choking.

Killer pulls knife from sheath on waistband and hacks heart from the now limp corpse. SOUND. Ripping, sucking, as heart is excised. This scene is filmed from killer's POV (point of view).

THE CAMERA TRACKS ACROSS TO THE

TREES as killer walks into them.

FADE TO BLACK.

Tina's muscles surged with adrenaline, releasing her from the torpor that had threatened to assist her attacker in his venture. She shifted her weight onto her left leg and straight-kicked with her right.

"Yesss," she hissed through clenched teeth as her foot connected with the oncoming figure's kneecap.

It had been almost four years since Tina had taken her course in self defence. She had noted the rising assaults against women in general and one in particular, which had prompted her to make the decision to be prepared and able to defend herself of paramount importance. Should some man ever decide to mistake her for an easy target, then he would hopefully learn a valid and painful lesson. A friend at the office, Katy, had been date-raped. Allowed a man who picked her up at a nightclub to drive her home. She had found him well spoken, with a good sense of humour and of above average intelligence. He was just the type of guy she was looking for, or so she thought, until he stopped on waste ground, broke her nose with his fist and took her by force. Tina remembered Katy saying that he had not seemed the type who would become violent. That concentrated Tina. A lot of assaults on women were reportedly carried out by men known to them. With that in mind, she had attended evening classes at a local sport centre every Wednesday for eighteen months, to be instructed by a hard-arsed physical education instructor, who by day worked in the PE department at Wandsworth prison. The rigorous training had instilled in her an ability to react against physical attack.

The man grunted and fell back as his leg gave way. He dropped the stake and clutched at his knee with both hands as he rolled on to his side.

Tina knew better than to risk any further contact. She had disabled her assailant and given herself the time needed to escape. Without any hesitation she sprinted away, glancing back every few seconds, expecting to see the man bearing down on her. A last view of him – as the pathway curved and a hedge obscured her sight line – was just a dark shape rising clumsily to its feet in the gloom.

With her heart pounding so fast that her sight dimmed, robbing her of peripheral vision, and her head throbbing as if on the point of bursting, she headed for home. She felt sick to her stomach as vivid pictures of what might have transpired flashed through her mind. And yet simultaneously she was elated, on a high; a thin thread of conceit at having foiled the man mingled with curling waves of fear.

"Jesus...Jesus...Jesus," she said with every footfall, until she finally turned into the gateway of her semi on Garfield Road.

Tina's lungs burned as she staggered, panting like an overheated dog, into the kitchen, where Charlie was drinking tea, still in the T-shirt and boxer shorts that he had slept in.

"What..." he began, looking away from the early morning news on the portable television.

"P... Police...Charlie," Tina gasped, sinking into the chair opposite him. "Phone the police...now. I think I was just attacked by the Park Killer."

CHAPTER TWENTY-TWO

He hobbled-limped-dragged himself back through the strip of trees that bordered what had once been a towpath, and struggled along a dark side street to the car.

"Christ Almighty!" Tears of pain and frustration spiked his eyes as he jerked the door open and it slammed against his injured leg. The bitch had fractured, or at least displaced his fucking kneecap. It felt as though a white-hot nail had been hammered into it.

Have to get away from here. The cow will ring the police as soon as she gets home. She may even have a mobile. Oh, God. Every second counted. Move, move, move. Ignore the pain and get the fuck out of the area. He cranked the engine into life, released the brake, then screamed out as he depressed the clutch and his leg seemed to fragment like a hand grenade going off.

"I KNOW WHERE YOU FUCKING LIVE," he shouted hoarsely at the windscreen as he pulled away from the kerb. "I'll deal with you later, you...you whore."

His mental screenplay had not just been adapted or slightly modified. It had been totally rewritten and bastardised by one lucky kick. He could imagine the camera tracking him as he drove along the wet, city streets. His carefully choreographed one act teleplay had been fucked-up beyond all recognition.

Blink.

Home. Thank Christ, or George the auto pilot who was his alter ego and somehow took care of things while he was...away. He was parked outside the house with no memory of the past half an hour. It amazed him that he could function with no awareness of his actions.

Unmoving for a minute, he waited until an old guy walking his dog had reached the end of the street and vanished around the corner. Then, sure that the coast was clear, he opened the car door and put his right foot out on to the pavement. His left leg wouldn't bend. It felt like an overfilled sausage skin, with the added ingredient of live nerves that were bombarding his brain with messages of pain...in stereo...with the volume wound up to the limit. It seemed to take forever to negotiate the few yards between the car and his front door. Every step was excruciating, and his stomach was churning. It reneged and forced its contents up, out of his mouth; a geyser of steaming, half-digested food. He kept moving as he retched and gagged, unmindful of the mess down the front of his clothing.

Inside at last with sweat popping from his body, he limped into the kitchen and swallowed six Nurofen down with Scotch, which he chugged straight from the bottle. He undressed, which was a painful exercise. After stuffing the soiled clothing into the washing machine, he took a tray of ice cubes from the fridge, to crack them out onto a tea towel and hold the makeshift ice pack to the damaged joint as he smoked cigarettes and sipped more Scotch.

By midmorning he had emptied the bottle of Bells and taken a total of twelve painkillers. Armed with another make-do ice pack, and feeling drunk and tired, he somehow made it to the bedroom and lay out on the bed, facing his gallery.

"Change of plan, Caroline, you arrogant, supercilious cow," he slurred. "No more rehearsals to get your attention. I'm going to deal with that journalist and Ross, and then I'm coming for you, ready or not."

Wanting more Scotch, needing to urinate, and feeling dizzy and sick, he passed out, and as usual began to dream of his dear, dead mother...

...Linda Cain had cherished her son. He had his dead father's high cheekbones and inky black eyes that held the faraway look of a dreamer who could travel anywhere without moving from his chair.

Without Bobby, Linda would have had no sense of purpose or focus. Life had been hard enough, and worsened considerably when her husband, Donald, had died. It was the love for Bobby that had given Linda the fortitude to work long hours at the tannery, and somehow make ends meet. The hardest part had been not knowing why Donald had committed suicide. Sometimes there are no answers, just questions.

In his dream, his mother spoke: "You'll never find another woman to look after you the way I do, Bobby, and that's a fact," Linda said, standing in the kitchen – as it had been back then, so clean and homely – ironing clothes that were shiny and thin and worse for wear.

"I know, Mum," the teenage Bobby Cain of yesteryear answered.

A part of his psyche knew that it was a sleeping vagary, and watched the mother and son re-enact a sliver of life, with him as a spectator at the other side of an illusory room.

He studied the mature, matronly woman wearing a floral-patterned housecoat, who had rollers in her netted hair, and who paused to stand the brown-bottomed iron upright on the – God forbid – asbestos end of the board for it to spit and hiss steam as she sipped black, syrup-sweet tea from a cup that was part of a service which had belonged to her mother.

"I found a magazine in your room, Bobby," Linda said. "You worry me, son. You're at that age when the sight of a woman's naked flesh will play havoc with your hormones. If you get yourself too excited, your acne will get worse and never go away. You'll have craters on your face like the surface of the moon for the rest of your life. Do you know what I'm sayin'?"

"Yes, Mum," Bobby said, not having the slightest idea of why thumbing through an old dog-eared girlie magazine – that he had traded for a wonky-bladed penknife – or wanking would cause his zits to escalate or become a permanent feature. Ralph Pibus, his pal, had a stack of much more explicit magazines, was always jacking off, and had skin as smooth as a baby's arse. What did mothers know?

"Most girls are sluts, Bobby. Remember that, son. If you let your urges rule your life, some loose little bitch will make sure you get her in the family way. Before you know it you'll be tied down, raisin' kids and payin' bills. All your hopes and dreams will come to nothin'. You'll be a Mr Middle-age, trapped in a way of life that you would hate. Is that what you want, Bobby? Is it?"

"But, Mum—"

"But, nothin'. Don't be a meal ticket for some grabbin' whore. Keep your emotions under control. Best when you get older if you just...just have your way with them. I know a man has desires that he can't ignore, but there's no need to commit yourself to the first tart that lets you get inside her knickers."

"Dad was married to you."

"Your dad found one in a million, Bobby. I encouraged him in everythin' he did, and was always there for him, whatever his need. When he died, a big part of me died with him. You're all that keeps me goin', son. You know that, don't you?"

Died? The watching thirty-five-year-old dreamer thought, oh, yes, his dad had died all right. He'd topped himself in the old wooden garage at the bottom of the back garden.

The dream shifted, to become much darker as more years melted away. "Go and tell your father his tea is ready," Linda said. And at just nine-years-old he had gone out and opened the side door of the garage, to stand in profound shock and with pee running down his leg as he stared up at the still-swinging figure of his dad.

He was now that boy again inside the garage. He couldn't move; mesmerised by the human pendulum and the attendant squeaking of the blue nylon rope which was chafing against the wooden crossbeam above, that it was tied to. His father's eyes were bulging. Bobby had seen a snake coiled around a mouse on a nature programme just a few weeks earlier, and the rodent's eyes were the same, almost popping out of its head under the pressure. His dad's mouth was wide open, tongue out, unnaturally long and as blue as a grape. Bobby may as well have been set in concrete. He was not only rooted to the spot, but could not avert his eyes from the horrific sight. Small tendrils of macabre fascination blended with a sense of fear and revulsion as he studied the single, long string of viscous spittle that hung from his now late father's bottom lip and chin. He took in the whole picture. The little finger of the corpse's right hand was still twitching. It was much later that Bobby realised that the last sight Donald Cain had, must have been of his son entering the garage and looking up at him.

Bobby might have remained there forever, or at least until his mother had come out to see what was keeping them both, had the hot, malodorous stench of human waste not made him recoil and stumble out into the fresh air.

The dream advanced, instantly devouring the years. Bobby was now over twenty years old, and it was Christmas, though his mother was oblivious to the festive hullabaloo.

At first, Bobby had cared for her at home, bathing, feeding and dressing her. But even a doting son can only do so much; what with work, and the fact that it was becoming unsafe to leave her unattended as her diseased brain robbed her of all intellectual power. He had no choice but to off-load the problem to an NHS nursing home.

"Do you know who I am, Mum?" Bobby said, sitting next to the bed and holding her liver-spotted and claw-like hand on the last occasion he had bothered to visit the depressing Victorian institution, which he believed had not been afforded an iota of modernisation or redecorating since it had been built.

"Of course, Donald, my darlin'," Linda said, now trapped back in the seventies in a time that spared her the harsh reality of her current condition.

He had only seen her once more, lying pale, waxen and coffin-bound at the local Co-operative's chapel of rest. It was at that moment, standing and looking down at her empty husk that he had decided to 'do his own thing'. From that day on, now alone, he had allowed the dark side of his personality to blossom, without the restrictive influence of his mother to cramp his style. He was inflamed, casting aside all inhibitions that had dictated how he should behave, if not think. Now enlightened, he determined that only his own instincts could be trusted. In the confused world about him, he would be true to his own doctrine, not constrained by any concepts that had hitherto suppressed his free spirit.

Awake now, and the nightmare of past events evaporated. The pain in his knee was no more than a dull throb; manageable, bearable. More ice required. Only a couple of hours had passed. It had felt so much longer than that. The bad dream had seemed to be in real time. He'd read somewhere that the average dream was of only a few seconds' duration. But that was probably drivel. You couldn't believe anything you read. Slowly, carefully, he made his way through to the kitchen and took another two pain killers, washing them down not with alcohol, but with a glassful of cold water. Feeling better, he lit a cigarette and eased himself into a chair with his left leg stuck out, ramrod straight. It was time to consider his options and prioritise them.

Time and the element of surprise were on his side. He would rest up for a couple of days and let his leg heal. He gingerly manipulated the kneecap with his fingers and decided that it was not fractured. Perhaps the cartilage had been compressed. He would keep it chilled, and supported with a crepe bandage. Just his luck to pick on some bimbo who obviously practised karate or something. Martial arts would not save her the next time they met, though. He was an idiot to underestimate women. He would have to appreciate that survival was a powerful instinct, and that prey – given half a chance – were unpredictable and could turn like cornered rats.

He reached across the tabletop for a notepad and pencil, then paused and looked at himself in the small, free-standing circular mirror that he had been using to inspect the back of his knee. His eyes were tar-black, almost hypnotic, even to himself, and his nose was broad and straight. Mouth...maybe a little thin-lipped and purporting a hint of cruelty, which was fitting. Chin...strong and dimpled. His face was wide, and the top of his head was bald, as smooth as a snooker ball; the hair at its sides kept ultra short. It was fair, with a hint of ginger and even some grey; not the fiery red that his mum's had been.

Overall, he was a more muscular, heftier and much younger version of Patrick Stewart, the charismatic captain, Jean Luc Picard of *Star Trek: The Next Generation* and *X-Men* fame. He was certainly not deformed or of subnormal intellect. His brain functioned just fine, and although he was physically a tad shorter than he would have liked at five-seven, he maintained that good things came in small packages. Women had always lusted after him. Even when they pretended not to be interested, he knew different, and could see the desire in their eyes. Some needed to be taken aggressively, and would even struggle and accuse him of rape. Strange creatures, women, to resist that which in their hearts they desired, but he was neither fooled nor distracted by their posturing and sham rejection of his advances. He could smell the subtle scent of secretions that gave away their stimulated state of arousal.

Caroline had been different. He liked all women, and would accommodate them whatever their age, colour or shape. His taste was catholic. But Caroline had captivated his heart and stirred emotions that he had never experienced. He came to adore her from afar, and foresaw a special relationship blossoming between them, that would be unique and of a lifetime's duration.

She had smiled at him in the lifts, when they crossed paths in the corridors, and even on occasion when queuing for meals in the canteen. He was positive that she was smitten by him, but when he engaged her in conversation, six months ago now, his dreams had been shattered. He recalled what had been said word for word, incorporating all the nuances and inflections of syntax that had conveyed her lack of sensibility and tainted his love for her, transforming it into an equally powerful emotion: hate.

"The play was terrific Ms Sellars," he had said on that Monday, back in May, confronting her after she had finished talking to some assistant head of drama.

She had continued walking along the corridor, towards her office. "Thank you, er..."

A charade. Pretending that she did not know his name.

"Bob Cain, sound effects," he said, flashing his most sincere smile.

"Well, Bob, it's the writer, actors and director, and even your department that deserve any praise. I just produced it."

"You have a lot of control over the whole production, though."

"I won't argue. I thought the sound effects of the house burning down at the end of the play were stunning. I closed my eyes in the booth and could almost smell the smoke."

"All on tape nowadays, I'm afraid," he said. "At one time the sound of faux fires was usually achieved by crumpling cellophane and splintering pieces of wood. Now it's a lot more sophisticated."

"That's interesting, er...Bob."

"Perhaps you'd enjoy discussing it at length, over a drink in the bar?"

Her eyes almost talked. They hardened. They said; 'You must be fucking joking coming on to me, mister. I'm a top producer, and you're just a sweaty little sound effects nerd, one step up from rattling coconut shells, breaking glass, and playing with a wind machine'.

Probably because he cared so much for her, he saw the truth. This woman, who he had chosen above all others, deemed him unworthy. He would never be welcome into her heart, bed or body.

"Goodnight," Caroline had said, summarily dismissing him as she reached her door, opened it, and turned her back on him.

"Yeah, goodnight, Ms Sellars," he said, his heart thudding against the cage of his ribs. In that instant, what had been a bright, delicious fruit, turned dark and began to rot in his mind. He had never...ever experienced the pain of rejection before. It embittered him, and a deep fissure of molten hurt overflowed and cooled to form a solid wall of profound animosity.

It had been in the space of a second, as her office door closed, that he had decided to fuck up her life, then her, before ripping her traitorous heart from her living body.

He had not approached her again, though had smiled on the odd occasion that their paths had crossed. He was invisible to her, not a part of her insignificant little life. With time she would have even forgotten their one brief conversation, let alone his name. The months passed, and he monitored her life closely, recording her movements by way of a camera with a telephoto lens. He was obsessed, and harboured an unwavering aim to destroy the cause of his chagrin.

Back in real time. Concentrate. The notepad was still blank. He rose slowly, wincing as he walked across to the corner unit above the microwave and withdrew a fresh bottle of cheap Safeway own-label Scotch, which he opened and poured himself a large measure of. It would help to dampen the pain in his leg, and also ease the shit-awful frustration of the situation he was in. He needed closure re the matter of Larry Holden, Dr Mark and Caroline. He was being screwed around with, badmouthed, and had even been physically attacked and injured by the psychotic bitch in Chiswick. How could he be expected to ignore so much hostile provocation? And what if the murderous runner had had the presence of mind to study his face? Slim chance. It had been pretty dark. Surely, she would have just seen a shape rushing at her. And then she had kicked out, got lucky and ran away. But there was a half chance that she had given the police at least a rough description. And even if she hadn't, what if someone had seen him struggling to get into his car? They could have clocked the make and even made a note of his number plate.

"Bastards!" he shouted as he lifted the mirror and threw it across the kitchen, for it to shatter against the refrigerator. The best sound effect for breaking glass was breaking fucking glass.

CHAPTER TWENTY-THREE

Mark had snail mail on his desk, and e-mail waiting on his computer. First things first. He switched on the coffeemaker and set the strength selector to maximum. Life, he decided, would be so much worse without java in it.

While the coffee bubbled and filled the room with what was probably his most favourite aroma, he sifted through the envelopes. Most were work related; journals full of psychobabble and other dross, which he tossed aside to look at later, maybe. One, a smaller blue envelope, looked interesting. Opening and reaching into the top drawer of his desk, he pulled out an old FBI letter opener and slit along the top of the envelope. Inside was an invitation to the Oxford Union, where an address was to be given by Dr Stefan Friedman, a much-revered clinical psychologist, who he had played golf with on several occasions when they had met up at seminars. All being well, he would attend. Stefan had a wicked sense of humour, and enjoyed a drink or two. And his lectures, given without the aid of notes, were always fresh, innovative, and laced with dark, witty analogies. Stefan looked a lot like the movie director Mel Brooks, with a shock of dyed hair and a strong New York City twang.

Mark stiffened, in the way that he would have if a rattlesnake appeared on his lap, poised and ready to strike. The last item of post was a buff manila envelope, which in itself was innocuous. It was the sight of his name and the hospital's address written in red capital letters that rang alarm bells. There were no prizes for guessing who it was from. He knew that there would be no latents, but left the office and purloined a pair of latex gloves from a storeroom, to which he held a key.

Back at his desk, he inspected the writing more closely. He had no formal training in forensic document examination, but had picked up a lot of pointers from the professionals at Quantico. An expert could put together a psycholinguistic profile from a ransom note or sample of an unknown subject's handwriting. All Mark had to work with was his own name and Cranbrook's address. Not enough to study the way in which sentences were constructed, and the grammar used in their composition.

Opening the envelope, he withdrew the copy paper with the tips of a glove-clad finger and thumb and carefully unfolded the sheets.

The sender was not stupid. He had used a printer, so was computer literate. The top sheet was a note:

Dr Mark,

You really shouldn't be poking your EX-FBI nose into THIS rabbit hole. It might just get bitten off.

Enclosed is a profile ON ME, which I worked up just for the pure hell of it. Obviously, YOU will have access to police and autopsy reports that I haven't. BUT overall, I think I'M on the money. What YOU have is WORTHLESS. I WON'T keep going till I'm caught. It's NEARLY over.

I enjoyed your book, Dr Mark. It says as much about YOU as the killers you used to hunt. YOU also inhabit the DARKNESS.

This has been an amusing aside. DO NOT continue to search for me, or I will be forced to take DIRECT action against YOU.

Mark studied the letter and the accompanying psych profile, looking for an insight into the mind and soul of the killer. Only an unbounded arrogance was evident. The unsub was brash, which was a bonus. If he thought that he was too clever to be caught, then in all likelihood he would be apprehended. The most successful killers did not underestimate the authorities that were trying to close them down. They made no contact, and in some instances were only caught through their inability to stop. Insatiable bloodlust brought about their downfall. There was no reason to suppose that this creep would prove to be the exception to the rule. He might truly believe that after killing Caroline, should he succeed in doing so, that he would stop. But he was either lying to or deluding himself. Once started, serial killers invariably kept going, compelled by their sick minds to keep on, until, like lemmings, they eventually fell over the cliff's edge. There was no off switch in the mindset of an established pattern or ritual murderer.

Pouring himself a fresh cup of coffee, Mark realised that the unsub had not read the interview he had laid as bait. This communication had been written and posted as a result of the original press photo taken by Larry in Hyde Park, together with the attendant article. His quarry had been drawn out by egotism to enjoin in a psychological battle with a stranger who he perceived to be an adversary with special skills. Mark was hit by a sudden welling tide of relief. His decision not to see Amy for a while had been timely. This unsolicited response from the killer justified his belief that he was up against a game player. God knew how he would respond to the insulting character assassination that Mark had put together with Larry. But Mark *did* know. This psycho would strike back, and it would most likely not hit his spot to retaliate by mail. He didn't want to be a pen pal. It was now a very personal secondary diversion. It had not taken a lot to distract the killer.

Closing his eyes, Mark withdrew into himself and felt his way into his quarry's mind. On some unfathomable level, that he had never understood or questioned, lest he lose the ability, he became the man he hunted. He mentally reviewed the content of the article from the other man's perspective. A sense of rage and emotional turmoil inhabited him. He needed to attack the source of his vilification; to release the internal pressure that only killing would mollify.

"Larry," Mark said, his eyes snapping open as with logical insight he knew that Larry Holden was, initially, in more danger than himself. At this juncture the reporter would be a soft target whom the killer could make an example of to cause Mark to sit up and take notice of what happens if someone pissed him off enough.

Larry was fully dressed, curled up on top of the bed in a deep stupor, courtesy of a full bottle of Johnny Walker. He was dreaming, bringing his hands together with joyous enthusiasm; applauding.

The school hall was packed, and before him on the raised stage was the choir. His daughter, Annette, walked out to centre stage, resplendent in her maroon and grey uniform; face peaches and cream, her hair a golden shining mane under the spotlight. This, to Larry and Hannah, was the high point of the service. And as Annette sang like a songbird in perfect pitch, Hannah found his hand and squeezed it gently.

Everything was as it should be. But dreams lacked the reality of conscious life. The hall faded, to become the murky interior of a pub, where he had endeavoured unsuccessfully to drown his heartbreaking sorrow on the day that his divorce became absolute. Behind the bar, a phone rang and rang and rang, but the landlord ignored it and continued to mechanically and maniacally wipe the same patch of marble counter with a grey, beer-sodden dishcloth.

Coming to, slowly, Larry felt wetness on the pillow, where he had drooled and spilled tears while asleep. Bile burned at the back of his throat, and his head pounded as he sat up too quickly. The empty Scotch bottle rolled across the floor as his feet, still encased in shoes, inadvertently caught it.

The dream shone brightly for a second, then receded to fade beyond recall, leaving him feeling empty, wretched and without hope.

Making his way through to the living room, he picked up the receiver to still the strident ringing that had woken him and was aggravating his 'bought and paid for' headache. "Yeah," he said.

"Larry, it's Mark Ross."

"What do you want?" he said, his words clipped and terse. Almost as sour as his breath.

"I think that you're in real danger. I just got post from the Park Killer, which was obviously written before he got to read the piece you and I cooked up."

"So?"

"So, I believe he'll come after you, Larry. He'll want to show me that he doesn't take kindly to ridicule."

"No sense of humour, eh?"

"Not that you or I would laugh at. You need to pack up and haul ass out of there, now."

"You don't really think—"

"What I think is that he will kill you, Larry, just to make a point. He won't contact you, warn you, or stalk you. He'll just fucking kill you, as soon as he can."

"Christ, Mark, do you expect me to move out into a hotel that I can ill afford, on the off chance that some mad bastard might take time out to waste a second-rate stringer?"

"I don't consider it an off-chance risk. You just spelt it out. He's a mad bastard, and that sums him up, in layman's terms. Check his curriculum vitae, Larry. He kills people. That's what pops his cork."

"Okay, I get the picture. I've got some stuff to print up, and then I'll decamp."

"Don't get whacked over some crummy photographs, Larry."

"Worry not, Doc. I'll watch my back and find somewhere to hole-up."

"Just don't get smashed and decide that it's not important. I honestly believe that you will be his number one priority."

"I hear you loud and clear. Thanks for calling." Larry said, then disconnected and returned to the bedroom, where he undressed and dumped his shirt, underpants and socks into a raffia basket that was already overflowing with dirty clothes, before going into the bathroom to shower and shave.

Twenty minutes after receiving the call from Mark, Larry was feeling more human as he sipped black coffee and reflected on what the American had said. The more he considered the likelihood of some homicidal maniac targeting him, just because of an article he'd written that the guy probably hadn't even read, the more ridiculous the premise seemed. The killer's penchant was for redheads. He was fixated on the female of the species, not any Tom, Dick or Larry. Mark Ross meant well, but seemed a little paranoid and irrational. Commonsense told Larry that he was far more likely to die as a result of drinking and smoking to excess, than at the hands of the so-called Park Killer.

Having dismissed the warning, Larry went into the small, cramped second bedroom, which he had converted into a darkroom, and closed the door. He should have gone wholly digital by now, but the familiar smell of developer and fix mildly seared his nostrils, and at once sheathed him in a cocoon of familiarity. In a world of uncertainty and fluctuating fortune, this environment of: chemicals, trays, enlarger, and boxes of photographic paper was a constant. Since being a teenager, he had found a sense of escape and almost seductive wonder in the red glow of a darkroom. He had never tired of watching an image magically appear as he gently agitated a seemingly blank sheet of paper in a fresh batch of colourless fluid. The new digital technology was soulless, and did not offer the same level of satisfaction.

Lost in a warm, womb-like retreat that dispelled his problems and the acute self reproach at having fucked up his life and alienated the only two people who had given it substance and meaning, Larry developed, fixed and rinsed a film, then cut it into manageable strips and clipped them on to a length of cord that hung over the bench. He then printed up a few 8x10's of an ex-boy band singer who had just launched his solo career with a hit single, and was flavour of the month. Larry had snapped the young man as he staggered out of Stringfellows in Covent Garden and fell over, pissed, with fresh vomit on his shirt front. The prat had an idiotic expression on his face, and was offering up his middle finger to the camera lens. Pure gold.

Larry shrugged. He may not be the new Litchfield, or ever be invited to 'do' the Pirelli calendar, but the spontaneous and candid reality of what he shot was, in his view, far more credible.

At noon, Larry left his refuge to relieve his bladder, have a cigarette, and dispel hunger pains with a quickly made and even more quickly devoured sandwich, made up of stale bread and a single slice of sweaty, out-of-date ham that he liberally smothered with mustard. He then returned to his sanctum, where space and time seemed suspended, and the pain and inability to cope without the crutch of alcohol dissolved.

Larry was still working under the safety light an hour later, too absorbed to hear the creak of floorboards at the other side of the darkroom's door.

CHAPTER TWENTY-FOUR

Amy taxied to a stop. The flight had given her the space to think, but the altitude had not lifted her spirits a centimetre above ground level. The emotional weight of the danger that Mark had intentionally placed himself in had deflated the blossoming joy that had initially bloomed at the thought of being with him, committed wholeheartedly to another person for the rest of her life.

Taking the morning off to 'reach for the sky' had been a ploy to clear her mind and rise out of the dark hole of self-pity she had allowed herself to sink into. It hadn't worked. She had soared above the earth, but had felt shackled to it by morose and fearful thoughts.

Back home, Amy phoned Petra at Sentinel and told her she was taking the rest of the day off; one of the perks of being the boss, but she felt guilty as hell. She was being too self indulgent. Her absence would substantially increase Jon and Petra's already heavy workload. She determined to make it up to them and work extra hours, when events permitted.

After finishing her call to Petra, she phoned Cranbrook and asked to speak to Mark.

"Hi, Amy. Is everything okay?"

"In a word, no," she said. "I feel as though I've been dismissed, and I don't like it one bit. Our relationship has always been based on mutual respect and consideration, up until now."

"What're you trying to say?"

"That you have no right to hang me out to dry. I realise that you're doing it with the best of intentions, but I'm an ex-cop for Christ's sake. I can take care of myself."

"No, you can't, Amy. That is exactly why you are an ex-cop," Mark said, pulling no punches. "He sent me a letter. Even compiled a goddamn profile on himself. The asshole has fixated on me, and that's just in response to knowing that I'm involved. If he has seen Larry Holden's latest article, he'll have gone ballistic."

"So, we'll deal with it as a team. I'm not going to sit back and be a spectator."

Mark sighed with exasperation. "I've just told Larry that he'll be a target by association. And that goes for you too, kiddo. If he finds out that you're close to me, then you'll go straight to the top of his hit list."

169

"You don't know that for a fact."

"Yes, I do, Amy. It's what I would do if I was him. I'd dismember his life around him. That's what he's done to Caroline, but in a different way. He's isolated her, and killed look-alikes to terrorise her. Common sense dictates that—"

"Fuck common sense. I'm driving down. I'll see you at the flat, later."

He had the sinking feeling that he was fighting a losing battle, and had already lost a lot of ground, and before he could put up further argument, she ended the call. The dead line purred in defiance. He loved her for her many qualities, one of which was her fiercely independent nature. He just wished that for once she could have got the smarts and backed off, or at least compromised. Protecting his own ass might be hard enough, without the liability of having her far shapelier one to cover.

As he hung up, the phone immediately rang again.

"Amy?"

"No, Mark, Barney."

"Are you psychic? I was just going to call you."

"About what?"

"The Park Killer just sent me some fan mail, including a do-it-yourself profile. The dickhead has checked me out and read my book."

"I'll have whatever he's sent to you picked up. I phoned you because the bugger's crawled out from under his rock. He attacked another woman this morning on a towpath in Chiswick."

"Same M.O.?"

"I said attacked. The girl managed to disable him and run off. She left him rolling around on the ground with a damaged leg."

"What makes you think it was our boy? The date and location don't fit."

"Because he was carrying a sharpened tree branch. He dropped it at the scene."

"Could be a copycat."

"Don't rain on my parade, Mark. I've got forensics doing a comparison with the other stakes. It's ash, the same length, and if the same knife or tool was used to sharpen it, then the striations will match. Bingo."

"Did she get a look at him?"

"Yeah. She's positive that she'd recognise him again. Said that she would never forget his face. There's a police artist with her now, working up a likeness. She said the guy was average height, stocky, dressed in black sweats, and that he looked a lot like the bald guy in one of those Star Trek series."

"Patrick Stewart?"

"That's what she said. We're looking for a fuller-faced Starfleet captain lookalike. She wasn't sure about his age, though. With his being bald or shaven-headed, she guesstimated that he was anywhere between thirty and forty-five."

"That's great, Barney. If it is him, and he works for the Beeb, then it could be game, set and match."

"It looks that way. I talked to Caroline Sellars. She says the description fits a sound engineer. She doesn't have a name for us, but I've got detectives checking it out."

"It's a race against time, now. He may run."

"Explain."

"He knows that he's been seen. He might just go to earth like a fox. Identifying him is one thing. Finding and lifting him is another."

"You're a real party-pooper, Ross. I'm hoping that we can ID and locate him before he has chance to think it through. He may believe that she didn't get a good look at him. It was dark, and the incident was over within a few seconds."

"I just love optimism in a cop," Mark said. "But I like to always consider the worst-case scenario."

"Which is?"

"That he dumps his car, finds a new base, and changes his appearance."

"We'll still find him."

"Maybe. But will that be before or after he kills again?"

"What do you think his next move will be?"

"He'll feel at risk. That might make him go straight for Caroline, to complete what he thinks of as a mission, and finish the job."

"That would be irrational. Even if he could find out where she is, which I don't buy, then he must know that she's being protected by armed officers."

"He isn't rational. Think of him as being like a lame-brained suicide bomber. As long as he takes his intended victim out, he won't give much thought to walking away from it. Survival isn't a be all and end all priority. Killing Caroline is."

"I'll keep that in mind."

"Do. And let me know if you get lucky. I'll feel safer when he's cooling off in some mortuary drawer."

"I'm hoping it doesn't come to that."

"And I'm hoping that it does, Barney. I like a done deal."

"You also like throwing shit at fans."

"Uh?"

"I got carpeted by Pearce over that interview you did. You went out of your way to goad our boy, without letting us know. In Pearce's book that makes you a loose cannon. If you want to top yourself, why not just find a high building to jump off."

"It seemed like a good idea at the time. I wanted to—"

"You wanted to piss him off and bring him out. He may have tried to murder the girl this morning as a result. Have you thought about that? You could have been the catalyst for an impromptu attempt to kill again; wound him up and sent him off at a tangent."

As Mark opened his mouth to answer, Barney hung up. It seemed that no one was going to let him have the last word. His mind was reeling with input. Amy was his main concern. He wanted to see her, but the emotion was mixed with a fear for her safety. He hoped that current events would negate any threat. He had no doubt that Barney would know the killer's identity within the hour. A lot of cases needed a lucky break, and the failed murder attempt was as lucky as you could get. He wondered if the girl who had faced the unsub and survived had any idea just what a horrific fate she had so narrowly escaped. His thoughts were unsettled. It was now impossible for him to feel what the killer would do next. Logic told him that the guy must know that the net was closing, and would put all other considerations aside, to concentrate on his prime target. Larry and himself would have been little more than side dishes, that may have been tempting, but were not the main course. Surely the impetus would be to seek out the safe house. Hopefully, they were coming down the back straight with the tape in sight.

He left the office and let himself through the security gate, then took the stairs down into the main residential area. In the common room, six patients were assembled, seated on plastic chairs in a semicircle, waiting for him to preside over the group session.

"Good morning, gentlemen," he said, looking from face to face to assess their moods as he took his seat front and centre.

"G... good m... morning, Dr Ross," Billy Hicks said.

Frank Marshall and Tony Skerrit nodded. Gordon Shaw gave him a toothless grin. Barry Fuller continued to pick his nose with gusto, while staring at the dark screen of the television that was bolted high up on to the wall behind Mark. Old Walter Stubbs just kept rocking, as he had done for the past six years, since drowning his wife in the bath before setting fire to the house that they had lived in for over forty years.

The sessions followed a pattern. Billy would be attentive, but not contribute, while the others, apart from Walter, would bicker like school kids. It rarely came to blows, but with due respect of the fact that each of them had committed violent, murderous acts, an orderly was always present, ready to press an alarm bell or intervene, should things get out of hand.

"Who's going to start the ball rolling and share a few thoughts with the group?" Mark said, attempting to put his own problems to one side as he studied the way his patients interacted.

"Come, mourn with me for that I do lament," Gordon said, standing up and closing his eyes. His words sounded slushy without the benefit of his dentures, which reposed in a Perspex beaker on the bedside table in his room. He only wore them on Sundays, when he made a special effort to be presentable for the service in the institution's chapel. "And put on sullen black incontinent. I'll make a voyage to the Holy Land, to wash this blood off from my guilty hand." Finished, he blinked rapidly as tears spilled out and ran down his creased cheeks.

"Is that Shakespeare, Gordon?" Mark said, knowing that all the small, gaunt man's quotes were from the Bard's works.

"Yes, Richard the Second."

"And what's the meaning behind it?"

"It means that I'm sorry for what I did, Doc. But being sorry doesn't count for shit. You bastards are going to keep me locked up in this funny farm with all these loonies until I fucking die."

Absolutely, Mark thought. Gordon believed that he was the reincarnation of Jack the Ripper, and had set out on a quest to reconstruct the nineteenth-century mystery killer's murders. When apprehended after just one savage killing, the police found a mass of literature on the original Ripper, that Gordon had collected since being a teenager. He would – in Mark's estimation – never be mentally well enough to be released back into society.

"Are you calling me a loony, you mad bastard?" Frank Marshall snarled; a plump vein throbbing at the centre of his forehead like a caterpillar, and his face flushed bright red with anger.

"Hey guys, this is an open forum," Mark said in a firm voice. "You know the rules. Anyone can off-load their thoughts and feelings without any comeback. Let's not get personal."

"Okay," Frank said. "But if Jumping Jack Flash calls me a loony again, I'm going to stick a pencil in his ear and push it into whatever substitutes for brains in there."

"Will you tossers keep the noise down?" Barry Fuller said, removing a bloodied finger from the depths of his right nostril. "I'm trying to watch some golf."

Apart from old Walter, they all looked up to the blank TV screen, half expecting to see Tiger Woods teeing up.

"It was my hands," Walter said, staring down at his gnarled hands, which were swollen-jointed and deformed by severe arthritis. "They do what they want. I have no control over the fuckers," and as if in confirmation, one moved with lightning speed from where it had reposed on his lap, to scratch at his unshaven cheek, leaving red welts but not breaking the skin, due to his fingernails being kept ultra short. Walter had pleaded not guilty at his trial. He blamed his hands for murdering his wife, and for then torching the family home. He had asked that the offending appendages be removed, amputated, to prevent them from committing further mischief, and had even tried to damage them himself on numerous occasions, but they wouldn't let him.

"You don't fool any of us with that shit about your hands havin' a life of their own," Tony Skerrit said, smiling sardonically at Walter. "It's time you faced up to the fact that you're a fuckin' psycho. You drowned your wife because she was a pain in the arse, not because your hands took a personal dislike to the bitch."

"Thanks guys. Same time, same place, next week," Mark said, standing, relieved once the hour session was over. It had followed its normal course. A lot of repressed angst had been got rid of, and the patients seemed more relaxed for expressing themselves in a controlled situation. They needed to let off steam.

"You're st... still in danger, Dr Ross," Billy said, following Mark out into the corridor.

"I don't think so, Billy," he said. "Things have changed, and I believe the danger's past."

"N... No. It's getting n... nearer, stronger."

"Do you still see an aura around me, Billy? Is that it?"

"Yes. It's vivid. Blood r... red."

"Thanks for the warning. I'll be careful."

Billy just hung his head and shuffled off in the direction of his room.

Mark felt extremely unsettled. There was something in Billy's manner that said, 'Being careful doesn't always cut it, Doc. What's ordained will happen, ready or not'. Believing anything that Billy said might be a dumb call, but Mark *did* believe. A part of his mind knew that the young man's supernatural ability was the genuine article; the real deal. It wasn't something that he could rationalise, but in his bones, he accepted that the killer out there had plans for him that would not be abandoned.

It was after lunch. He was updating the files of the patients who had attended that morning's session when he received another outside call.

"Hello."

"Good afternoon, Dr Mark. I'm calling to give you fair warning that due to your insulting comments in that article, I'm going to make you wish that you were just suffering from terminal bowel cancer."

Jesus! It was him. He sounded calm, buoyant. His voice was raspy, dry, and full of menace.

"How's the knee, dickhead?" Mark said, hoping that he sounded unfazed. "You don't expect me to be intimidated by some retard piece of shit who gets taken out by a defenceless woman, do you?"

"Trying to wind me up won't work, you sad FBI dropout. Have a quick word with a friend of yours."

Unbridled fear tore and gouged at his mind. He was truly terror-stricken. It had to be Amy. Images of the obscenities committed on the other victims sprang to the fore.

"Mark...Mark. Oh, Christ, no, stop. Pleeease..."

Larry. It was Larry Holden's voice, full of fear and pain. God help the man, but thank the same god that it wasn't Amy.

"Still feeling like the cock of the north, huh?" Bobby said.

"What do you want?" Mark said, knowing that bar a miracle, Larry was a lost cause. Nothing he might say would save the man now. The poor schmuck should have stuck to chasing celebs with his camera, or listened to Mark's warning.

"What I want, I take. I just thought you should know that I don't forgive or forget...ever. I'm going to kill you, Ross. Larry is just, what would you call it? An exemplar. You're on borrowed time, courtesy of me. First, I'll take everything that you value away. And finally, when you have nothing left to lose, I'll cut your fucking heart out."

"You're just a pathetic, psychotic little no-hoper," Mark goaded. "Don't threaten me with what you intend doing. Just come on in when you're ready. I'll be happy to put you out of your misery."

"You...You—"

Mark slammed the phone down, then lifted it again and punched in Barney's number. He felt sick to the stomach, and helpless. He was going through the motions, but knew that it was way too late to save Larry from whatever the killer was doing to him, which Mark didn't want to even attempt to contemplate. Why for Christ's sake hadn't Larry listened to him and left his flat? Although the psycho had probably had him under surveillance and would have followed him. This was no dummy who had now declared war on Mark. He was cunning; a calculating son of a bitch who appeared to be one step ahead of them at every turn.

"Yeah, Mark, what's the problem?" Barney said.

CHAPTER TWENTY-FIVE

Ignoring the ball of fire that raged in his knee, he dressed, filled a training bag with necessary items, and left the house. He was almost certain that the woman had not seen his features clearly, but the fact that she had escaped him was a worry. He had to consider her a threat to his continued anonymity and freedom.

Reversing into a tight space fifty yards along the street from where Holden lived, he parked and then eased himself out of the car and limped along the pavement. Beads of sweat pricked his scalp, saturating the band of the baseball cap that he wore to cover his baldness. He grunted with every laboured step, and sighed with relief as he reached the door of the large Victorian terrace house which, as so many others in the area, was now converted into flats.

Built into the wall was a large mailbox with four hinged flaps and attendant label holders that advertised the occupants' names on slivers of paper beneath clear plastic. L. HOLDEN was the tenant of flat 3. The entrance door was closed, but not locked. He entered and checked the ground floor. 1 and 2. The inconsiderate bastard lived on the first floor, and the stairs seemed to stretch upwards, endlessly before him, making his knee complain in reluctance at the prospect of having to mount them.

At the top, on the landing outside number 3, now bathed in sweat from head to foot, he put his ear to the door and listened. There was no sound from within. After donning a pair of cellophane gloves, he took a lock knife from a pocket of his quilted parka, released the serrated blade and slid it into the narrow gap between the jamb and door edge. It was a Mickey Mouse lock, and within seconds he was closing the door behind him. He moved silently through the flat and found only one internal door closed. A sliver of red light escaped from the narrow gap at the bottom of it, and from behind it, as if on cue, someone sneezed, making Bobby smile, despite the discomfort he was in.

Larry was feeling more optimistic than he had done in years. The exclusive shots and interview with Mark had been very lucrative and had been syndicated around the world. The Park Killer was now international news, and he had the goose – in the shape of Mark Ross – that was laying the golden eggs. This was an upturn in fortune that he had not envisaged in his wildest dreams. Maybe he could get back on track. He suddenly had a name that editors of city desks were sitting up and taking notice of. Funny how from being a pariah one day, he could be in such demand the next. Knowledge is power that can open doors, and in this case was generating funds to dramatically bolster his overdrawn bank account. If he could just get off the sauce, then he may be able to put things right, as they should be. If he could convince Hannah and Annette that he was a changed man, then he might just get a second chance. It would take time, but he wanted his life back, which equated to being with his wife...ex-wife, and daughter.

With a smile on his face and hope in his heart, Larry pegged up a wet print of Bruce Willis, who had been in town to promote his latest movie. The star was doing nothing outlandish, and knew how to handle the press and paparazzi. His eyes were hidden by the long bill of a baseball cap, and the lopsided smile beneath it showed that the temperamental actor was in a mellow frame of mind.

Larry had no time to formulate any constructive thought as the door swung open. He turned towards it, mouthing 'shit' as natural light threatened to ruin an open box of highly sensitive and expensive photographic paper. In the instant after he saw the figure and a blur of movement, a bright detonation robbed him of all sensibility.

Bobby dropped the empty whisky bottle, which he had found on the bedroom floor and employed to swing one-handed against Larry's forehead. He then grasped the fallen man by the ankles and dragged him through to the kitchen, to ready him for a pleasant chat.

When Larry regained consciousness, he was sitting with his head slumped forward on his chest and pounding with a splitting pain that made him cry out. He opened his eyes slowly, couldn't focus, but recognised the top of his kitchen table, which was only a few inches from his face.

The combined flash and familiar whir of a camera made him lift his head, to where a figure was sitting at the other side of the table, his face obscured by an old 35mm Nikon. Larry tried to stand, but could not move. His arms had been secured behind the chair's back, and his ankles were bound to its thick wooden legs.

"Say cheese," Bobby said, grinning broadly as Larry squinted across at him, trying to clear his vision. Whir. "That's another one for the album."

Larry coughed, and a paroxysm of nausea made him gag and swallow hard. When able, he said, "Who are you?"

"You know who I am, Larry. The one you chose to call a human monster. The one who you wrote all those lies about, that were fed to you by Ross," Bobby said, placing the camera down next to an ugly knife, its blade glittering blue and silver under the fluorescent tube that hummed above them.

"Oh, God!"

"I guarantee that God can't hear you, Larry. He doesn't do fuck all for the righteous or anyone else, so what chance have you got of divine intervention? Only I can hear your confession and decide what might be a suitable act of contrition."

"W... What are you going to do?"

"Whatever I choose to. My choices are limitless, whereas yours are extremely limited, in fact nonexistent. What do you think I might do?"

"I think you're going to kill me," Larry murmured, before losing the fight with his stomach, to throw-up on the edge of the table, which acted as a splash back, resulting in the front of his shirt and trousers being soaked.

"You've been out cold for over half an hour," Bobby said in a conversational tone. "I thought for a while that I'd hit you too hard with that empty bottle. Do you have a full one?"

Larry finished retching, spat strings of bile from his mouth, and then nodded towards a wall unit. "In there," he croaked.

Bobby poured a large measure of the Scotch into a glass that he first rinsed out and dried with a sheet of kitchen towel, before sitting back down and sipping it.

"Don't I get one?" Larry said, needing a drink more now than he had ever needed one in his life. "I thought a condemned man got to pick his last meal."

"Maybe later," Bobby said. "After you've told me all about Ross, and what he and the police have got on me."

"I don't know anything," Larry protested, but the lie sounded unconvincing, even to him.

Bobby set down the glass, lifted a thick roll of duct tape out of the bag at his feet, and getting up, moved behind Larry. He wound the tape around his captive's head, covering his mouth and nostrils, to then hold Larry's shoulders and wait until the frantic thrashing became weaker, and the head stopped jerking from side to side, before ripping the tape free as Larry lost consciousness again.

Pouring another drink and lighting a cigarette, Bobby waited until Larry once more surfaced from the safety and respite of dark unawareness, to face his inescapable plight.

"This is a learning curve, Larry," Bobby said. "I'm feeling a little tetchy, so the quicker you grasp the ground rules of the game, the better. When I ask you a question, you answer it, honestly, fully and immediately. If I even think that you're lying or holding out on me, I'll start cutting pieces off you."

To make his point, he picked the knife up and stroked the keen blade across Larry's cheek.

Initially, Larry felt less pain than a paper cut might cause, but a lot of blood ran out from the laceration, to merge with the puke already on his shirt.

Bobby swapped the knife for the camera, taking another shot of Larry, hoping that the lens would capture the stark fear in the man's eyes; to record it faithfully on the emulsion coated film behind the shutter. He then went back to his chair, in no hurry, content to let the nonentity fully appreciate the gravity of the situation he was in.

Blink.

Larry waited, confused as the maniac stared unblinking, as though he were in a trance. After a few seconds he said to his captor, "What do you want to know?" No reply or reaction. Please, Christ, let him have just suffered a massive heart attack or stroke and died.

Leaning forward until his head was no more than an inch from the surface of the table, Larry strained, pulling his arms up behind him, to try to slip them over the back of the chair. So near, yet so far. With his legs taped to the chair, he could not raise his arms the extra fraction required. His shoulder joints cracked in protest. He tried to stand, heaving forward, but lost his balance and fell sideways, crashing to the floor and crying out as his right arm was crushed between the edges of the chair's back and the unyielding surface.

"What happened?" Bobby said; a synaesthesia taking place as the scream stimulated his mental processes and brought him instantly back to full awareness.

"I fell over," Larry said.

Bobby went to him, lifted him back up into a sitting position, then poured two fingers of Scotch into a second glass and held it to Larry's lips.

The spirit burned its way down into his stomach, scouring away the sour residue that being sick had left.

"Let's start again," Bobby said. "And remember that the truth will out, and that telling it is good for your soul. Do you want to live through this?"

"Y... Yes."

"Good man. Now, in your own time, tell me all about the Yank."

"He's an ex-FBI profiler. The police asked him to consult on the Park Killer case."

"I know that. Who's in charge of the case?"

"A DCI by the name of Barney Bowen."

"Tell me about Ross. Who he is, not what he does. I know his profession. Start with his home address and telephone number."

"In my address book. It's on the top shelf of the bookcase in the living room."

Bobby had already searched the flat while Larry was out cold, and had been surprised not to find an address book in the vicinity of the phone.

"A little paranoid, eh?" Bobby said, going through to the small living room and retrieving the book from where it had been squeezed between Bill Bryson's: *A Walk in the Woods*, and Kurt Vonnegut's *Hocus Pocus*.

"What does he drive?" Bobby said, returning and pushing the book into his bag.

"A black Jeep Cherokee."

"Is he a queer?"

"What?"

"Is he a fag, homo, fruit, pufter, shirt lifter, faggot, gay, shit stabber? You know what a queer is, don't you, Larry?"

"No... I mean, yes. Ross is straight."

"And does he have a lady friend?"

"I don't know."

The glass hit him in the mouth, thrown full force, whip lashing his head back. He felt his lips burst and his front teeth shatter.

"Your eyes can't lie, Larry. Forget about trying to protect anyone. Just be sensible and concentrate on saving your own stinking, worthless skin. Now answer the question."

"Yes. She's an ex-cop," Larry slurred through lips that he could feel swelling. "Her name is Amy Egan. I think she lives in Richmond, but I don't have her address."

Bobby believed him. "What does our gallant American friend think he has on me?"

"He believes that you work for the BBC, and that you drive a Toyota."

"Why a Toyota?"

"The police found carpet fibres at two of the scenes."

"Clever. Why did Yankee Doodle do the interview with you?"

"To bait you. Bring you out."

"Well, it certainly worked, my friend. I think I'll call Dr Mark, now. Let him know that we're getting acquainted, and maybe let you have a few words with him. Does that sound good?"

"Then you kill me, right?"

"Not necessarily. While you were taking a nap, I had a look around this shithole. I found a framed photo of you with a good-looking woman and young girl. Who are they?"

"My ex-wife and daughter."

"If I let you live, would you believe that they would be in mortal danger if you ever described me to the police?"

Larry nodded. *Please...Please, not Hannah and Annette.* He had already hurt them enough, without being responsible for introducing this raving lunatic into their lives.

Bobby made the call, talked to Mark, and then held the receiver to Larry's ear.

Larry wailed, "Mark...Mark. Oh, Christ, no. Stop. Pleeease," as the blade of the knife was being slowly thrust into his side; the point of it puncturing his right kidney.

After Ross slagged him off and hung up on him, Bobby had to vent his rage, to leave a graphic reminder of just what he was capable of doing to another lesser being. "Time for some serious atonement for your sins, Larry," he said, once again reaching for the duct tape. "Any last words before I start the wet work?"

"Rot in hell, you sick bastard," Larry said before Bobby wound the tape several times around his bleeding head, to cover his mouth and suppress the unbridled screams that he would be unable to stifle, given the pain that he was about to endure.

Bobby went through to the living room, to undress and leave his clothes folded on a cushion of a grubby two-seater settee; not wanting them to be covered in what he knew would be a very large amount of blood.

Naked and standing in front of Larry with the knife held loosely in his hand, he smiled. "You're a lucky son of a gun, Larry," he said. "I'm pressed for time. I'd have preferred to make a real meal of this, but you'll appreciate that your good friend Dr Mark will be calling the police as I speak. Just take this last thought to the grave with you. I'm going to make a point of looking up your ex and your daughter, and introducing them both to Mr Knife."

Showtime. He was euphoric at the look of pure primal dread in his intended victim's eyes, as he set to work with a vengeance.

CHAPTER TWENTY-SIX

After phoning Barney, Mark punched in Amy's landline number on his mobile phone as he ran across the staff car park to JC. Her recorded voice invited him to leave a message.

"If you're in, pick up, Amy, it's urgent."

No response.

"Call me soonest. I have to talk to you," he said, then climbed into the Cherokee and tried her mobile number. It was turned off.

"Jesus H Christ!" he shouted at his phone, throwing it aside as panic spiked his heart. He viciously plunged the ignition key into the slot and wrenched it clockwise. The engine fired. He grated the gears in haste and accelerated away so fast that he left two lines of black rubber on the grey asphalt road surface.

The unsub had killed Larry, of that there was absolutely no doubt in his mind. But first he would have made the poor bastard talk, and would now know everything that Larry knew. Mark's mind raced, and his fingers hammered on the steering wheel with impatience as he waited what seemed an age for the facility's gates to slowly slide apart. Miscalculating, he shot forward too soon, clipping a wing mirror, inciting the security guard in the gate-house to shake his head in disdain, as he sped away, leaving a cloud of oily exhaust fumes and shattered glass in his wake.

What could Larry have given up? Too much. Mark's home address and phone number. He did not know Amy's address, but knew of her, and her name. Since leaving the force she was not ex-directory. He had to presume that both of their lives were now on the line. They could be in imminent danger, at the whim of a creature whose next move could not be determined, and who might not even know himself what course of action he would take. Playing cat and mouse on the killer's terms was a weak position to be in, and now Amy was involved. In effect she was his Achilles heel. Protecting her was far more important than going head-to-head with an unpredictable psycho. All Mark could hope for was that the killer was lifted soon, or that he would make a play for Caroline next, where armed protection squad officers were ready and waiting. Mark also knew that hopes were like wishes, and in the real-world wishes had a bad habit of not coming true.

Barney and Mike climbed the stairs to find half a dozen uniformed officers on the landing outside an open door that had a plastic 3 hung upside down, fastened to the wood surface by a single loose screw.

DC Eddie McKay appeared out of the pack to meet them, his face pale, and an unlit cigarette gripped tightly between bloodless lips. "Jesus, boss, it's like a fucking slaughterhouse in there," he said, stepping over to the banister, removing the cigarette from his mouth and taking deep breaths to try to settle his nerves and stomach.

"Give me a clue, Eddie," Barney said.

"We have one victim, tied to a chair. I assume it's the stringer, Larry Holden."

"Meaning?" Barney said.

"Meaning, it's a mess, boss."

Followed by Mike, Barney entered the kitchen. From where he was standing, he could see the rear view of a man slumped in a wooden chair, restrained to it by tape that bound his wrists behind the ladder-back. Blood pooled beneath the still figure, and also striped the walls, units and ceiling in abstract spatters.

Barney breathed through his mouth to lessen the heavy, still warm and cloying smell. Approaching from both sides, and staying far enough back to not step into the sanguineous slick, he and Mike almost crept up alongside the corpse, to be met by a scene from a horror movie or hell.

Mike emitted a strangulated choking sound, then stepped back, turned and gripped the edge of the dish-filled sink tightly with both hands.

Barney fought to pull his gaze away from the two staring eyeballs and the bared teeth, that were the only facial features left to distinguish the pulpy red mass as having been of human origin. It was with difficulty that he finally looked away from the ghastly yet hypnotic sight, to see a sheet of paper on the table, held in place by a small canister which he recognised as being the container for a 35 mm roll of film. Fumbling in the inside pocket of his jacket, he found his glasses, put them on and leaned forward to read the hand-written note. It said, in block capitals:

HI THERE, BARNEY,

THE HACK DIED BADLY. YOU MIGHT

WANT TO HAVE

THIS OLD FILM DEVELOPED TO SEE A STEP-
BY-STEP GUIDE

TO FACIAL FLENSING IN FABULOUS
FUJICOLOUR.

GIVE DR MARK AND AMY MY REGARDS. I
INTEND TO MAKE

THEIR ACQUAINTANCE WHEN TIME
ALLOWS.

"Eddie," Barney shouted.

"Yeah, boss," the DC said, appearing at the door, but making no move to cross the threshold.

"I want Jane Beatty here. She dealt with this nutter's first three victims."

"Okay, boss, I'll see to it," Eddie said, vanishing from view as he reached for his smart phone.

"Come on, Mike, let's get out of here, I've seen enough," Barney said, removing his glasses and stepping back, away from the body that he found more abhorrent than any dissected cadaver he had ever seen in an autopsy suite. A fully dressed man bound to a chair with no face was an incongruous spectacle; the stuff of nightmares.

"What's your name, son?" Barney said to a young PC as he and Mike walked along the landing to the top of the stairs.

"PC King, sir."

"First name?"

"Steven, sir."

"No kidding?"

"No kidding, sir, but spelt with a V, not a P."

"Well, with a name like that, this sort of horror shouldn't faze you."

The young cop said nothing, but looked as sick to the gut as Barney and Mike felt.

"Is this floor secure, Steven?"

"Yes, sir. Only two flats. And I'm advised that the other one is unoccupied at the moment."

"Good. Stay outside the door. Only the forensic team and the pathologist are to be allowed in for the time being."

"Right, sir," Steven said, wishing that he was on nights, patrol, or preferably off duty and at home with his wife, watching something banal on TV.

Out on the pavement, Barney and Mike waited for Jane, not going back into the house when the CSI team arrived. Barney made two calls; one to Clive Pearce, to ruin his day, and the other to Mark Ross, to let him know that the Park Killer had indeed murdered Larry Holden.

"Did he suffer?" Mark said, now at home, still unable to contact Amy on either of her numbers, punching them up every couple of minutes, cursing her for purposely staying incommunicado. He had phoned Sentinel Security, but Amy was not at work.

"It was as bad as it gets," Barney said. "Holden died hard. I want you to go into siege mode. I'll have armed officers at your place within the hour. The bastard left a note, asking me, by name, to give you and Amy his regards, and to let you know that he intends to look you both up when he has time."

"Thanks for calling, Barney. I can't reach Amy by phone. Could you arrange for officers to swing by her place, and get back to me? I'm going crazy here with worry."

"I'll have the Richmond police check her out, then give you a bell. Just sit tight, Mark."

As Barney pocketed his phone, the pathologist arrived, stepped out of her car and walked over to where he and Mike were waiting.

"Tell me about it, Barnaby," Jane said, nodding to Mike as she stopped in front of them. She was already in her jumpsuit, and carrying her familiar green case.

"We've got a middle-aged white male tied to a chair in the kitchen of a first-floor flat. The only obvious injury is that his face has been removed. The offender is without any doubt the Park Killer."

"No stakes this time?" Jane said.

Barney shook his head. "Looks as if he made do with just a knife."

"Let's go up and see what we've got," Jane said, reaching into a pocket and withdrawing two packets; one containing surgical gloves, the other, elasticised overshoes. "Are you any closer to catching this creep?" she said as they entered the house.

"It's looking touch-wood-good, Jane," Barney said, tilting his hand back and forth in a so-so gesture. "We've got an eye witness who he attacked. She got away unscathed. Caroline Sellars is sure that the description fits a guy who works at the Beeb. It should only be a matter of time now."

Half an hour later they were back outside on the street.

"He had only been dead for a very short period of time," Jane said. "Probably just a few minutes before your officers arrived at the scene. There is a deep penetration wound to his right kidney that would have resulted in significant internal haemorrhaging, and of course his face was cut and ripped off. That's all I can tell you until after I do the autopsy."

"Thanks, Jane."

"I'll phone you with my preliminary findings when I finish up. I know the written reports baffle you."

"True. There's always too much medical jargon in them for an old dinosaur like me to digest," Barney said, taking out a slim, leather-bound notebook, jotting down his mobile number and handing it to the pathologist.

The sky was darkening prematurely, heavy with the promise of more rain as Mike jinked the car through the official vehicles that littered the street.

"Find a pub, Mike, I need a drink," Barney said, once they had pulled out on to the main road. "I've got a taste at the back of my throat that I can't get rid of."

"Right, boss," Mike said, scanning the road ahead. He still felt nauseous. The sight of the faceless man had etched itself into his psyche, to become yet another hideous, unwanted, but permanent image that he knew would haunt him for the rest of his days. He had seen numerous atrocities during his years on the force; lives extinguished by accident, suicide and murder. But out of the many, only a very few of the most appalling equalled this outrage. He knew that in the dark, alone, he would have to deal with it a thousand times. In that twilight zone between sleeping and waking, he would see those eyes turn to him; watch the exposed, red jaw muscles flex, and the broken and blood-stained teeth come apart. The seated corpse, in the manner of a demonic, grotesque ventriloquist's dummy, would begin to talk. If there was a God, Mike hoped that his prayers would be answered, and that he would never have to hear the words that the apparition might say.

"There, Mike, that'll do," Barney said, pointing to a rundown looking public house.

Mike pulled away from his disturbing thoughts and parked in the side street next to the Ship Inn, which would have been better named the Shit Inn, judging by the interior, which warranted a government health warning.

They settled in a corner booth, the faux leather upholstery of the bench seats ripped and grimy. The tape that covered the tears was lifting, and it escaped neither of them that it was almost identical to the duct tape that had bound the corpse of Larry Holden. As they both reflected on the day's events, an antiquated jukebox churned out an equally dated and eclectic mix of crackling and less than golden oldies.

The shrill tone of Barney's phone was a welcome interruption that they were both glad of.

"Bowen," he said.

"It's Gary, boss," DC Gary Shields said, his voice full of urgency.

"If it isn't good news, hang up," Barney said.

"We've identified the Park Killer. His name is Robert Cain. He works for the BBC, and he drives a Toyota."

"How sure are you?" Barney said.

"Caroline Sellars confirms that she has run across him at work. And Tina Spencer positively identified him from a photo out of his personnel file. It's him."

"Good work, Gary. Do we have an address?"

"Yeah, boss. It's a terrace property south of the river, in Lambeth. Louise and Geoff are en route now, to stake the place out till you jack up an operation."

Barney made a note of the address and told Gary to instruct the two DCs to stay well back and observe only.

As Mike drove away from the pub, hoping that the vinegary pint would not give him dysentery, Barney made calls. He arranged for a response unit to roll, then put Pearce in the hot seat, giving him a chance to call the shots.

"You're a hundred and ten percent sure this time?" the Chief Superintendent said.

"It's him, Clive. And he's just topped the reporter who did the interview with Mark Ross. We need to move, now, to stop him killing again."

"How do you want to play it?" Clive said, with no intention of allowing the buck to stop on his desk. As a kid at parties he had never been the one left standing without a chair to sit on when the music stopped, or been caught holding the parcel. If there was credit to be had, then he would grab it with both hands, but if things went pear-shaped, then he made sure that he always had a fall guy to feed to the wolves.

"There are two DCs on the way to keep a watch on his house. And an armed response unit will soon be there. I want a tech team in the house next door with listening devices. We need to establish whether he's in or not. He isn't at work. He phoned in sick over a week ago. I don't want to force entry and scare him off."

"Good thinking, Barney. Play it how you see it. You have my backing."

Barney managed a wry smile. Yeah, verbally. Backing that would be denied if the shit started to grow wings and take flight. "Only problem I foresee is if he thinks the girl that he attacked in Chiswick eyeballed him," he said. "He may have already quit the house and ditched his car."

"Let's hope not. Keep me posted, Barney," Clive said before ending the call.

"Worm wriggled off the hook, eh, boss?" Mike said with a smirk on his face.

"Yeah, he's got more moves than a pole dancer."

After the sight of the faceless corpse, Mike had thought he may never smile or laugh again. But as an image of the balding Chief Super wearing only a posing pouch and gyrating to *Simply the Best* in a Soho dive took shape in his mind, he found that his sense of humour was still intact.

"Jesus, boss, what a thought," he said.

They both cracked up at Pearce's expense.

"He'd have to keep the day job," Barney said, wiping tears of laughter from his eyes. "I don't think he'd make a living at it."

"I don't know," Mike said. "He thinks he's a mover and a shaker. He might go down well at rest homes for the elderly, and blue rinse hen nights."

Barney sniggered. "Don't underestimate the more mature women, Mike. Although they would prefer a young guy like you, with a bit of muscle and a firm arse."

"Don't, boss," Mike howled. "I'll have to stop the car if you keep this up."

When composed, Barney made one more quick call, to update Mark with what he knew about Robert Cain, and the method he had employed to kill Holden. Just the telling of what had gone down drained all the humour from him.

CHAPTER TWENTY-SEVEN

After finishing up with Larry, Bobby took a quick, tepid shower, then dressed. He rewound the film, removed it from the camera and placed it back in the plastic canister, to stand it on the table in front of the corpse, on top of a quickly scribbled note, then left the flat. Apart from a lone teenager on a skateboard, the street outside was empty, and with his knee screaming out for relief, he limped across it to a large double-fronted house directly opposite. It had also been converted into flats. Taking his time to ascend the stairs, he knocked on the first door he came to. No answer.

"They're not in," a reedy voice erupted from the partly open door of the next street-facing flat, making his heart skip a beat as he whipped his head sideways to face the speaker.

Dorothy Dwyer missed nothing. She monitored all comings and goings, spending much of each day in a recliner chair next to the bay window, feet up and fervently knitting, yet vigilant. She had watched the stocky man in the baseball cap climb out of his car and, favouring one leg, limp along the pavement to enter the house opposite. And when he reappeared some time later, she was intrigued to know what his business might have been. He didn't go back to his car, instead he made a beeline for the property that she was watching him from, to vanish from sight and presumably enter the house.

Dorothy was far too feisty and inquisitive for her own good. She had scorned the air-raid shelters as a youngster during the Blitz, to sleep in her own bed, as undaunted as her parents were by the sound of exploding bombs or antiaircraft fire. And still, now in her nineties and just a few months younger than the Queen, whom she had always referred to as Liz, she was afraid of nothing, having determined that the good Lord would take her into His fold when He was good and ready, and not a moment before.

"That's nice to know," Bobby said, moving as quickly as his crocked leg would allow, pushing the old woman back into her flat, shutting the door behind him and locking it.

"There's no need to hurt me, young man," Dorothy said. "You're welcome to wait here till Brian and Marjory get home. Would you like a nice cup of tea? You look pale."

Bobby paused, his hand on the knife in his pocket. The old girl reminded him of photographs of his maternal grandmother, who had died when he was three, and who he had no actual memory of. Only stories about her, told to him by his mum, had given her a semblance of reality in his mind.

"Tea would be nice," he said. "I'll need to stay here for an hour or two. Then I'll leave."

"Are you in trouble?" Dorothy said.

"No. Others are. But you'll be safe. I'm not going to rob or harm you."

"That's a relief, son. My name is Dorothy, what's yours?" she said, thinking that his dark eyes were sincere, and that his voice held conviction.

"Bobby," he said.

"Well, Bobby, I'll put the kettle on. Would you like something to eat?"

"No, er, Dorothy. A cup of tea will be just fine."

See, I'm not some out of control killer, Dr Mark; he thought as he relaxed in Dorothy's chair by the window and looked out, unseen, well back from the thick net curtains. You would expect me to kill this old woman. Wrong. I have no reason to. I choose to let her live as testament to my humanity. I have the capacity to be merciful. Death is mine to mete out as I see fit, to those who further my undertaking, and to those, such as yourself, who would malign me and bear me malice.

Within two minutes, police cars streamed into the street from both ends, the flashing blue of their roof lights reflecting off other vehicles and house windows as they gathered below him like so many ants.

Dorothy put the tea on a small occasional table next to him, then pulled up another chair, to sit by his side and watch the frantic activity. "Are they looking for you, Bobby?" she said.

"Not yet, Grandma," he said, unaware of how he had addressed her. "But they soon will be."

Driving her Nissan through the failing afternoon light, Amy switched on the headlights, as the transition from day to early evening took place.

She had switched her mobile phone off, and was listening to a Neil Diamond CD: *The Movie Album - As time goes by*. The singer's roast almond voice helped her to put aside the sense of guilt that she felt. Mark would be angry, and worried at not being able to contact her. She was compromising an already perilous situation, but would not stay on the outside looking in. There was no way that she could bring herself to employ common sense; to sit back and hope that Mark would not be the killer's next victim. There was strength in numbers. Together they could watch each other's backs. And anyhow, the psycho had other fish to fry. It was too ludicrous to even contemplate his actually turning on his pursuers.

As she pulled into the car park and stopped next to JC, Mark ran out to meet her. She turned the CD off and cut the lights and engine as he opened the car's door.

"Amy—"

"My case is on the back seat, Mark," she said. "If you're going to lecture me, wait till we get inside."

He leaned forward and kissed her on the lips, to then stand back and smile before opening the rear door to pick up her soft, leather suitcase.

"So, let's get in out of the cold," he said as she frowned at the unexpected warm reception.

"No reading me the riot act for being a stroppy bitch, then?" she said as they climbed the stairs to the flat.

"Would it do any good, or change anything?"

"No."

"No point in kicking a dead horse, then. You know that you've raised the stakes. I don't have to lay it out for you."

"That's right. I feel much better now that I'm here with you. Let's have a brandy and get warm."

"You'll need a brandy for more than warmth," he said, entering the flat, depositing the case behind the sofa and following her through to the kitchen.

"Why?"

As he poured two large measures of Remy Martin, Mark told her of the day's events, which had culminated with the death of Larry Holden.

"He killed Larry just because of the article?" Amy said.

"Yeah. I think he cut his face off while he was still alive. He left a note for Barney, asking him to give us his regards and tell us that he planned to visit with us."

Amy drained her glass in three gulps, but the warmth of the alcohol failed to stop a chill run up and down the length of her spine.

"There are two armed cops outside in the car park," Mark said, going for the bottle and refilling their glasses. "They'll stop him if he decides to make a house call. And they have a description of him. He's no longer anonymous."

"Who is he?"

"A nobody, Amy. A sound engineer who must have fixated on Caroline Sellars at the BBC. His name is Robert Cain. The guy is just a nonentity who has flipped his lid and will more than likely burn out like a fire starved of oxygen."

"It's as good as over, then?"

"No. He won't go back to his place. He's on the loose, making decisions on the hoof. He could be lying low anywhere, or be on his way here, now. Whatever Larry knew, he'll know."

"He may believe that the girl he attacked didn't get a good look at him. He could be at home and feeling safe; maybe watching the telly, or microwaving himself a limp lasagne."

"I wish. He's too smart to take the risk."

"What do you think he'll do?" Amy said as she reached out for and gripped Mark's hand.

"Try for you or Caroline. It won't take him long to look up your address. We know that he has your name. Larry won't have been able to hold anything back."

"You think he'll also know where Caroline is?"

"Maybe. If he doesn't already, then he'll find out."

"How? Her boyfriend, Simon Payne?"

"No. He would credit the police with more sense than to let Payne know where she is. He now knows that Barney is in charge of the investigation, so the weak link is Barney, or one of his team."

"Does Barney realise that?"

"I don't know. He may have thought of it, but I'll give him a call and check."

Bobby chuckled as the Mondeo arrived and the middle-aged cop and his sidekick stepped out. He recognised the DCI from the newspapers; Barney Bowen, Barney the Bear, an old and tired looking grizzly, out of his league with this case. He watched the two plainclothes pigs enter the house and felt a twinge of disappointment at not being able to see their reaction to his handiwork.

Sipping his tea, he enjoyed the show. The forensic team arrived and filed into the house, looking like snowmen dressed in their white overalls. Barney the Bear and his deputy dawg were now back outside, both looking suitably ashen. Another car pulled up and a blonde climbed out of it, also wearing overalls and carrying a bulky, green case. She talked to the cops for a minute or two and then went into the house with them. At a guess, he pegged her as being a pathologist. He had always enjoyed the early series of *Silent Witness* on the box. The sight of Amanda Burton almost caressing stiffs and pronouncing them as being 'well nourished' corpses, was a turn-on. He just wished that the sexy actress had smiled more often. She came across as a miserable cow. He knew what *would* put a smile on her face, but had enough on his plate at the moment, without turning another fantasy into reality. Knowing that he could, if he wished, was enough.

Finishing his tea, he reluctantly got up and moved away from the window. The uniforms were spreading out like a dark rash, going door-to-door to interview neighbours, obviously to ask them if they had seen any strangers in the vicinity. That several of the boys in blue had gathered around his car, was significant. It confirmed that they knew it belonged to him, and were therefore aware of his identity.

"Come on, Grandma," he said to Dorothy, helping her up with a firm grip under her right forearm, to lead the old dear through to the bedroom.

Dorothy said nothing as he taped her arms behind her back. And she stretched out on the bed as directed while he bound her ankles together and finally fixed more tape over her mouth. He then gently arranged her on top of the patchwork quilt with her head on the pillow.

"When the police have left, then so will I," he said. "Just try to relax. When I'm out of the area I'll give them a call and you'll be set free. Okay?"

Dorothy nodded. She sensed that the man had the capacity to be as cruel or kind as he chose to be. And that he might well be unstable. The large police presence was telling. They were not responding to a burglary or minor crime. Intuition told her that someone across the street had died at this man's hands. She was also positive that if she remained quiet and still, then he would just leave. He had no reason to hurt her. And she would not give him one.

The police came, knocked at the door, waited, knocked again and then moved on. An hour later only three police cars and the forensic team's van remained in the street. It was time to go. He left by the rear entrance, opened a gate that led out on to a narrow alley, and when satisfied that the coast was clear, limped away. Fifteen minutes later he had broken into an Astra, hot-wired it and was heading towards his own house. He had used the time at Dorothy's place to plan his next move. He needed to outthink the enemy. They would circulate a flyer of him to all airports, ferry terminals and railway stations. He had to act as if every copper on the planet was looking for him. Now was the time to find a safe refuge. He stopped once, swapped plates with an old Ford – that appeared to be falling apart from a terminal case of rust – and phoned 999 to alert the filth to Dorothy's situation.

CHAPTER TWENTY-EIGHT

DC Louise Callard knocked at the door and stepped back, clipboard in hand, making sure that she was to a side and not obstructing the hidden marksman's line of sight.

The tech team in the house next door to Cain's had established that if anyone was in the house, then they were either dead or asleep and breathing very shallowly. The sensitive equipment was picking up nothing but the electric hum of household appliances and the ticking of a clock.

Louise knocked again, rapping her knuckles on the grime-covered glass panel of the door.

"Okay, Lou, walk away, now," Barney said into the lip mike he was wearing.

Louise put her hand up to the ear piece as her boss's voice almost deafened her, then with a small sigh of relief, she gladly obeyed the order.

Barney was disappointed. He had hoped that Cain would have returned home and been caught cold. The OIC of the ARU was looking to him for a decision. Barney's choices were to either go in, or stake the place out. If the suspect returned, then the street would be sealed in seconds. Going in could not jeopardise his capture. And they needed to see inside the house.

"Do it," Barney said to the officer in charge of the Armed Response Unit.

The house was entered and pronounced clear within less than sixty seconds, and Barney, Mike, Eddie, Louise, and Gary moved in to search the premises for clues.

Barney entered the bedroom and surveyed it. His eyes were drawn to the shadowy back wall of an alcove that was plastered with what seemed to be hundreds of photographs, all of Caroline Sellars. He also found a copy of Mark Ross's book on top of the bedside cabinet. Any lingering doubts as to whether Robert Cain was the Park Killer were dispelled there and then.

Downstairs in the kitchen, Eddie discovered wood shavings in a swing top waste bin. There was also a newspaper picture of the psychologist pinned to the fridge door by a magnet. They had everything but the killer; almost.

Lifting the lid of a chest freezer, Eddie glanced at the sparse contents, noticing handwriting on adhesive labels that were affixed to three freezer bags that held roughly oval-shaped contents.

"Boss! Boss!" Eddie shouted, recoiling as he realised what the unsavoury items he had found were.

Barney and the others converged on the kitchen from other areas of the house.

"What is it?" Barney said to his shocked looking DC.

Eddie pointed to the open freezer, and Barney stepped up to it, looked in, reached down and let the heat of his fingers dissolve the fine coating of frost that almost obscured the writing beneath the layer of white crystals.

The information on each of the labelled bags was as chilling as the frigid air that rose to numb his face: Elaine Stanton 4/9/20, Karen Perry 2/10/20, and Judy Prescott 6/11/20. It didn't take Sherlock Holmes to work out that the contents were the solid frozen hearts of the killer's victims.

"Get the forensic boys out here, Mike," Barney said. "This whole house needs processing. And arrange for someone from the coroner's office to deal with these," he added, closing the lid down to preserve the physical evidence.

On the way out, Barney's mobile rang.

He checked the caller ID. "Yes, Mark," he said.

"Amy's here with me, now. She's safe. But that's not why I called you. I think Cain will lock-on to you or one of your squad. He's a stalker by nature, and so it seems highly likely that he'll find out where Caroline is from someone who knows her location."

"And just how do you suppose he'll do that?"

"I believe he phoned me from Larry's to set the ball rolling; to ensure that Larry was found quickly. He'll have been near the scene, waiting and watching to eyeball who turned up."

"We're at Cain's place now. You might want to see it, Mark. He has a shrine to Caroline. There's a wall covered in photographs of her, as well as a copy of your book, and even a picture of you stuck on his fridge door. And we found the hearts of the three female victims in his freezer."

"I don't need to see it. We already know who he is and what he's capable of doing. Just advise your officers that they are in as much danger as Caroline, Amy or me. Be aware that his priority is to find out where Caroline is stashed, and that anyone who knows her whereabouts is a potential victim."

"For Christ's sake, Mark. All told there are dozens of detectives working on this case."

"He could single out any one of them, or you, Barney. Remember, he's focused on one main objective. His obsession will drive him to take whatever measures he has to, to find her."

"Thanks for the warning, Mark. I'll get my team together and run it past them."

Parked on the busy road within sight of the entrance to his street, Bobby waited until the Mondeo nosed out, to speed away, closely followed by a dark blue Xantia. He tailed them, keeping his distance as they sped through the early evening traffic. He had no real need to keep them in sight. He knew that Barney the Bear and his minions were heading back to base, to plot further against him.

DC Gary Shields listened as his boss brought the roomful of detectives up to speed on the case, before telling them of the Yank psychologist's warning, that they may be in personal danger from Robert Cain. Gary didn't buy it. He thought it was a knee-jerk reaction, bordering on scare-mongering. He found it completely outlandish to even consider that a wanted killer would turn his attention to the police who sought him. He felt under no threat whatsoever. In any event, only the boss had been mentioned and pictured in the newspapers. He and the others in the squad were anonymous.

Later, on leaving the station, Gary found himself checking the rear-view mirror as he headed north towards home. Now, away from the pack, he was a little nervous, more accepting of the boss's warning that a psycho needing information that he among others had, might feasibly be crazy enough to follow and try to intimidate a copper who was on his own, like a lone steer away from the herd.

Almost home, Gary pulled into the car park of his local. A few beers and the therapy of being in the company of people talking about sport and telling dirty jokes would be welcome respite from the narrow and depressing world of serious crime that filled his working hours.

After a couple of pints and a double Scotch, he was chilled. He wanted to really hang one on, but was on standby. Being off duty was a misnomer. Murder cops took time out when they could, but were always just a phone call away, and were obligated to be fit to work twenty-four/seven.

Fuck it. One more pint wouldn't hurt. It was his only pleasure, now that Jill had walked. Funny how it had been her that did all the crying, as she'd packed a couple of suitcases and waited for her brother to pick her up. She had kept apologising; told him that she still loved him, but couldn't stand coming a poor second to his job. And she was right. He was a cop first. She'd known what he did when they'd got together, so he wasn't about go on a guilt trip. Most of the lads he worked with were single, divorced, or their relationships were heading for the rocks. It wasn't like a regular nine-to-five job. It owned you. Working a case was like a hot wire in the blood. And there was always a shitload of cases. Murder was all part of a day – or night – in the city.

Reluctantly, having rushed another pint, Gary said goodnight to Cyril, the landlord, and after calling in the gents, walked out of the rear door into the small and ill-lit gravelled car park. He felt mellow and tired, ready to hit the sack as he thumbed the car key fob and heard the clunk of the locks disengaging. He hoped that the phone wouldn't ring. He could use a solid six or seven hours kip.

He opened the door and was about to climb in the car when a voice stopped him dead.

"Have you got a light, pal?"

Gary turned to see the shadowy form of a small guy wearing a bulky parka and a baseball cap. He was holding up an unlit cigarette in his hand.

"Sure," Gary said, relaxing, though his heart had gone into overdrive. He reached for his lighter, and...

...it was pitch black. His head throbbed with pain. He was horizontal, on his side, knees up to his chest, and could not move his arms or legs, or open his mouth. Engine noise and the bouncing – caused by a springy suspension – told him that he was in a moving vehicle. Suddenly stone-cold sober and back in cop mode, he suppressed the rising panic, bit it back and took deep breaths through his nose. His last memory was of putting his empty glass on the counter and saying goodnight to Cyril, before going for a slash and then walking out of the rear door into the cold night air. Then what? He stopped trying to think and gave his befuddled mind time to settle and search for the answer. He knew that his brain would still be scrolling through recent data, and that it would recall events a lot quicker without his consciously trying to force the issue. *Have you got a light, pal?* It flooded back. A short, stocky guy had appeared from nowhere with a cigarette held up in front of his face. The stranger must have slugged him, tied him up, and bundled him into the boot of a car. There was no other explanation.

Oh, Jesus fucking wept. Nooo, he thought in screaming off the dial surround sound that ricocheted around his skull as he faced the only logical solution to the position that he was in. This was the ghoul who had hacked out hearts, and who had just removed the face of the newshound.

Bobby drove out on the A104 to Epping Forest and found a suitably narrow track that led off from the main road into the depths of the tree-packed tract. He cut the lights and continued driving over the rutted surface at no more than walking pace. When the ground inclined down to the side of a small stream, he stopped the car and switched off the engine. Got out and drew his knife.

Opening the boot, he let his eyes acclimatise to the ambient moonlight that filtered through a veil of high, insubstantial cloud. He hesitated. There was something about the moon that fascinated him. Maybe it was because he knew that every human being who had ever lived, if not blind, had gazed upon that cold, bright lunar face. From the hunter-gatherers of bygone millennia, through to Jesus Christ, Hitler, Frank Sinatra; everyone. It was awesome to acknowledge that looking at a piece of rock floating in space was a common denominator; a universal image that in some way linked everybody that had ever been, or ever would be.

The young copper looked up at him, fear carved in deep shadows across his upturned face, with good reason.

"My name is Cain," Bobby said, holding the knife out for his prisoner to see. "Like the biblical character that killed his brother. I'm going to uncover your mouth and ask you some questions. If you tell me one lie, then I will know, and you will suffer the same fate as befell Abel; more than Larry Holden did. Nod if you understand the seriousness of your predicament."

Gary nodded theatrically, his eyes fixed on the shape of the knife's blade, which was silhouetted; black against the backdrop of moon glow.

"Good man," Bobby said, reaching into the boot to grasp an edge of the duct tape and rip it away from Gary's mouth. "What's your name and rank?"

"Gary. DC Gary Shields," Gary mumbled, the fear within him now a solid, living entity that was sliding and writhing in his guts like a muscular, headless eel in its death throes.

"And you're one of Barney the Bear's squad, assigned to track down the Park Killer. Am I right?"

"Y... Yes."

"Well, you've found me, Gary. Does that make you happy?"

"No."

"I thought not. And the truth of it is, *I* found *you*. Maybe I should have been a copper. What did you imagine? Maybe capturing me mob-handed, like a murder of crows hiding behind a few heroes with automatic rifles? Was that a more appealing scenario?"

"Yes."

"Tell me, are Dr Mark and his slut being guarded?"

"You mean, Ross?"

"Who else?"

"Yes. They're under protection."

"Now for the 64,000-dollar question, Gary. Where is Caroline Sellars stashed? I need to know everything. Give me a detailed report, including how many of your lot are with her? Don't leave anything out, no matter how trivial you may think it might be."

Gary gave him the address in west London, and told him that four armed cops were protecting Caroline around-the-clock; two inside the bungalow, one in a van out front, and the other in a shed in the back garden.

"Anything else I should know?" Bobby said.

Gary shook his head.

Leaning over the cop, Bobby wound fresh tape around his head, covering his mouth and nose in several layers. Standing back, he lit a cigarette and looked off into the trees, from where he could hear the haunting hoots of a tawny owl. He loved owls. Like so many other predators they were stone killers, devoid of any emotion.

After a surprisingly long time, the cop's feet stopped drumming against metal, and the grunting ceased. He had put up a laudable though futile fight for life. Bobby lifted the body from the boot, draped it over his shoulder and carried it into the trees, where he shrugged it off into a natural hollow in the ground. He covered it with dead branches and a thick layer of the matted pine needles that carpeted the forest floor, after first removing money from the cop's wallet, and a mobile phone from an inside pocket, that he would destroy and dump away from the scene. The corpse would rot down, and the skeleton would no doubt remain unfound until the following spring, or even later. Winter was upon them, and the body was secreted away from the beaten track, to decompose as the temperature eventually rose. Nature would devour it in a thousand efficient age-old ways, as insects, carrion crows and small mammals were drawn to the scene by the smell of slowly putrefying flesh.

Driving back along the A104, Bobby saw a sign for the Forest Glade Caravan Park and turned into the lane that led to it. He parked the car under cover of thick evergreen hedging that bordered the site, found a gap in the fencing that fronted it, and pushed through the natural barrier. Making his way to the nearest static holiday home, he forced open the door and smiled at his good fortune. Being out of season, the park and its units were deserted. This was not an all-year-round operation. Within minutes Bobby was in bed, snuggled under blankets that he had found stacked in a closet. He drifted off to sleep, tired and contented after such a long, eventful and satisfying day.

Caroline's face filled his mind's eye. She would soon be were she belonged, with him. It was destiny. Nothing or no one could or would keep them apart.

CHAPTER TWENTY-NINE

Mark lay beside Amy in the darkness and listened to her steady, even breathing. They'd both had too much brandy and then gone to bed and made love. Amy had fallen asleep with her head on his chest, and her left arm draped across his waist. That had been two hours ago he confirmed, glancing sideways to see the clock's glowing display, which read 2:20 AM.

He was wide awake, his mind a swirling vortex of disjointed thoughts, to be transported back to his youth on the family ranch in Colorado, almost able to smell his mother's freshly baked pecan pies, that stood cooling on the counter in front of the open kitchen window. Only as an adult could he look back and truly appreciate the childhood he had enjoyed; the small things that had made his youth such a rich and wonderful time. He recalled a melange of many fond memories, and imagined trotting down the wide porch steps with Red, his mongrel dog, at his heels. The mountain air was sweet and clear, devoid of pollution, and with a fishing pole and a sandwich box, he and Red had had fine old times, fishing for brown trout down on the banks of the South Platte River.

Back in the present, in self-imposed confinement, and with a chair wedged under the already double-locked and chained door of the flat, he had never felt so out of control of a situation. This killer was not running scared, but had turned like a wild and wounded animal, and was now at his most dangerous, still intent on carrying out his mindless mission. He was out there, scheming, with his next move known only to himself. Mark would have felt better with the comforting weight of a Smith & Wesson pistol in his hand to protect Amy with, should, against all odds, Cain managed to get to them.

Lifting Amy's arm from his stomach, he slid slowly out of the bed, so that her head was gently transferred on to the pillow, and watched as she turned onto her back without waking. God, she was so beautiful. Outside, clouds parted as if on cue, and soft, yellow moonlight pierced the gaps in the Venetian blinds to paint her naked upper body in slats of light and dark, creating a sensuous and abstract living work of art. He studied the contours of her firm breasts, tipped with nipples which cast their own thumb tip shadows. Her tummy was a smooth valley, and the old bullet wound scar on it was highlighted; a small, many-pointed star that enhanced the perfection around it. Shivering a little, he leaned over and pulled the duvet up to her shoulders, and then kissed her smooth brow, before putting on his robe and heading for the kitchen.

Switching on the coffeemaker, Mark ran through what he determined would be Cain's immediate priorities, and the order in which he might attempt to execute them. After a while he poured the fresh brew, and went to sit at the table, armed with a pencil and notepad to make a short list of what Cain might do:

1. Abort plans and fully concern himself with

avoiding capture.

2. Follow up his murder of Larry by attempting

to kill Amy/me.

3. Find and deal with original and primary

target: Caroline Sellars.

Taking the offender's twisted aims into

consideration, I will be left till last.

What would I do? I AM HIM...

Mark stopped writing, closed his eyes and withdrew into a room in his mind that had always offered a measure of enlightenment. In it, he let the imagined voice of the killer talk for him: *I will kill Caroline under their noses. Demonstrate that they are powerless to stop me. Gloat over their ineptitude to protect her from me. And then I will take Amy Egan, which will destroy Ross, to punish him for his unforgivable insults. Do a 'Larry' on the woman he loves and save the manhunter till last, and...*

"What are you doing, Mark?" Amy said, appearing at the kitchen door, now wearing one of his towelling robes, that was oversize and simultaneously made her look both comical and childlike.

Her unexpected voice made him jump as his eyes snapped open. And the point of his pencil snapped off as it dug into the notepad.

"I couldn't sleep. You want coffee?" he said, his heart racing.

"I'll get it, but caffeine won't help you to sleep. What were you writing?"

"Just putting thoughts on paper. I need to figure out some course of action. Cain has taken full control of the situation, and that's getting to me."

"He's up shit creek," Amy said, pouring herself a coffee, and freshening Mark's before sitting down across from him, to cradle the steaming ceramic mug in both hands.

"Maybe, but the bastard still has a paddle."

"He's out in the cold, Mark. We know who he is, and what he intended to do. He'll be digging a deep hole somewhere and trying to bury himself in it."

"No, Amy. That's what he knows we'll expect him to do. This is a man who has allowed his festering inner feelings free rein. He won't be able to stop. He's snapped like a broken twig. The person that he was, who worked, paid his bills and functioned in society within acceptable parameters, has stepped out. What is in control now is a man at odds with the world, bursting with accumulated anger, hatred, and an iron will to mete out his own warped conception of justice on anyone who he deems guilty of acting against him in word or deed."

"What do you think his next move is likely to be, then? You're the expert."

"He'll want to show that he can't be stopped or swayed from carrying out what to him has become an obsessive undertaking. He'll find Caroline, and kill her."

"You really think that he's mad enough to try and get past armed police?"

"Yeah. It'll be a challenge to him that he won't be able to resist. And he'll know that they won't expect him. He will have the element of surprise on his side."

"There's nothing that we can do, Mark. All we can hope for is that he gets caught before anyone else is murdered."

"That's what kept me awake, knowing that I *can't* do anything. I'll call Barney again in a few hours' and talk it through."

"Let's finish our coffee and go back to bed," Amy said. "Start in on it fresh, later, huh?"

He nodded and closed the notepad. He didn't want her to know just how scared he was for her safety.

Officers in a patrol car only a couple of minutes from Dorothy's address were instructed to check out the anonymous report of her being bound and gagged in her flat.

"Most likely some kid making a hoax call," PC Dennis McAvoy said, climbing out of the car and putting his cap on.

"Should bring back the bloody birch," PC Norman Bates – who was likely to take a swing at anyone who made any reference to the Psycho movies, after a lifetime of being subjected to moronic, tasteless jokes – said. "Soon sort out all the muggin' stabbin' and car theft. A lot of kids today have no respect and no discipline, just a fuckin' habit to feed. When I was at school there were no bloody drugs. And no one beat up pensioners for a few quid. Smokin' behind the bike sheds, and maybe coppin' the odd feel of a girl's tits on the back row at the flicks was about as bad as it got. Nowadays, rape doesn't even rate headlines like it used to. And murder is rife."

"Those days are gone forever, Norm," Dennis said, leading the way up the stairs to the old woman's flat, to walk along the landing and knock at the door.

"Yeah, thanks to liberal elite snowflakes who decide on what's best for a population who in the main are so sick of politicians' lies and double-dealin' that they don't even turn out to bleedin' vote anymore. It's not apathy, it's a statement of resentment and mistrust. The bastards take billions off us in fuckin' taxes and then make a pig's ear of everythin', and have the bloody front to come back for even more soddin' money."

"Do we break in, or try to find out who the landlord is and get him here with a key?" Dennis said, giving up trying to raise anyone, and determined not to get embroiled in a political argument with Norm.

Norman took a step back and kicked out. The door flew open with a loud splintering crack as the wood disintegrated around the lock.

"I guess that answers my question," Dennis said, entering the darkness and running his hand up the wall to locate the light switch and illuminate their surroundings.

Norman entered the bedroom to find Dorothy on the bed. He reached into a side pocket of his uniform jacket for the penknife he always carried, and carefully cut through the tape, before helping the old woman up into a sitting position.

Dennis went into the kitchen, switched on the light and was faced with something that his mind could not immediately comprehend.

Stretched and clinging to a large, round cabbage – that had been placed at the centre of the Formica-topped table – was what at first appeared to be a joke shop rubber mask. Only the drying blood prompted Dennis to step nearer, to lean forward and examine it more closely. He saw stubble on the cheeks, chin and upper lip; eyelashes sprouting from drooping lids, and nasal hair protruding from the narrow, pinched nostrils. It wasn't a mask. It was a *real* face.

"Norm. Nooorm!" he shouted, drawing his baton as he backed away from the obscene human remnant. "You won't believe what I've just fucking found."

Later, sitting by the window and drinking hot tea, having refused to go to the hospital for a check up, Dorothy answered Barney's questions as best she could.

"I knew he'd done something terrible," she said, nodding to confirm that her visitor had indeed been the man who now stared back at her from the flyer that Barney held out for her to see. "I made him a cup of tea, and he sat by the window, in this very chair, and watched all the goings-on in the street. He chuckled a lot, as though he found it all very amusing. Then he took me through to the bedroom and left me trussed up, just how your nice constable found me. He was very gentle, though, and told me that he would make a call and tell the police to come and release me."

"Is there anything else that you can remember about him?" Barney said.

"He was in some pain. He was limping. I think he must have hurt his leg. And he had a large bag with him, but I don't know what was in it. Oh, and he called me grandma. I think he was a little confused."

"Did he say where he was going, or anything else that might help us to find him?"

Dorothy gave it some thought before shaking her head. "I'm sorry, no, he didn't tell me anything."

"Okay, Dorothy, thank you," Barney said, leaving her with a WPC. They had a description of what Cain had been wearing, and confirmation that his leg was damaged. Nothing else.

"The bugger's got some neck," Barney said to Mike. "He stayed here, right under our bloody noses and watched us from a front row seat. He sat tight, even when they did a door-to-door. Then, after we'd left, he scarpered."

"He must have lifted a car. I can't see him walking far if his leg is banged-up," Mike said. "I'll get Louise to check on all vehicles reported stolen in the area."

Barney sighed. "If he nicked one, then it might not be reported missed until morning. But it's worth a shot."

"Where do we go from here, boss?" Mike said.

"I wish I knew. He could be anywhere. He knows that we're on to him, so he'll have gone somewhere he thinks is safe to lie low. We've lost the advantage. All we can do is wait for him to surface, and hope that we get lucky."

"You don't think that he'll still make a play for the Sellars woman, do you?"

Barney started rubbing-twisting-pulling at his wedding band. "If Mark Ross is right, then we can't outguess him. Nothing about this bastard is predictable."

CHAPTER THIRTY

At four a.m. Bobby was awake, staring up into the gloom. He loved the darkness. He remembered being a little boy and then a teenager in his small box bedroom. It had been his private place. He even resented his mother cleaning it. She would mop the paisley patterned linoleum, dust every surface and change his sheets and pillowcase once a week on a Monday, which was washing day, when the lines in the neighbourhood back yards and small gardens would be festooned with breeze-blown curtains, bedding and clothing.

That small room had afforded him a window out on to a view that had imprinted itself indelibly on his mind. Through that thin pane of glass, he had been a watcher from behind the net curtain; an unseen voyeur on the people that lived within his sight. He would study the bras and panties that swung to and fro on the lines, and sometimes he would open the window an inch to shoot pigeons from the ridge tiles of the terrace roofs that were within range of his old Diana air rifle. But it was the nights that enthralled him. The young woman opposite would take a bath on a Friday evening, unaware that he could see her fuzzy naked shape through the frosted glass as she stepped into the tub, and again when she climbed out and dried herself. And couples would sometimes stop in the alley and have it off against the wall of old Mrs Carson's yard. He missed being a boy. Youth was so much more of an adventure than adulthood; more carefree, and without the tribulations that age and responsibility brought. He felt so alone at times. Everyone that had been close to him had died. His grandparents, parents, and his favourite aunt, Cordelia, were all gone. His life was like a book with missing pages. He wanted everything to be as it was; wanted time to have stood still at a point when everything was just perfect. He had kept his toys, comics, annuals, and all the bric-a-brac of those wonder-filled days. He even had his parents' spectacles, most of their clothes, his fathers old Ronson lighter, and his mother's dentures. If he could not return to the house, then even the material residue of his past would be lost to him. He felt so alone and downtrodden, but would regroup, achieve his objectives, and turn his life around. Next year would be a new beginning. Everything would be just wonderful again.

He let the darkness soothe him for a while longer, then left the unit and made his way back to the car, through an early morning fog that clung; a white undulating blanket swirling around his feet. He thought of it as Cloudwalking. He was refreshed, hyper, and eager to meet the new day, and Caroline. The swelling around his knee had reduced, and although still painful, he could bear more weight on it.

It was easy to imagine the scale of the manhunt. But neither the police nor the Yank would have the foggiest idea where to begin looking for him, or be able to outguess his next move. It was odds on that they would assume he would run and hide. The last thing that they would expect would be a daring assault on the safe house. And knowing who he was would be of no help to them. All they had was a name, and the picture of a face that could be altered. He could blend in and be anonymous. No one could get inside his head. He was a law unto himself, and they were powerless to stop him from doing whatever he wanted to. He felt in total control again, without any doubts or fears. Maybe he should feel nervous or paranoid; after all, everybody *was* after him. But in fact, he felt incredibly buoyant. He would be calm, careful, and would triumph. He was invincible against an enemy that could not fathom out what drove him. It was emancipating to act on impulse and turn fantasy into reality.

Stopping at a garage, he left the car parked in shadow, away from the brightly lit forecourt that would be covered by CCTV. Pulling the bill of his cap well down, he entered the shop, picked up a large bar of fruit and nut chocolate, paid the dopey looking bird behind the counter and then went over to the drinks machine and selected coffee, black and sweet. Back in the car, he ate all the chocolate and drank the hot, gritty coffee, before heading for his destination.

He parked in the avenue running parallel and behind the road that the bungalow was situated on, after first doing a drive-by to fix the geography of the immediate area in his mind. He was almost convinced that the now dead copper had not lied to him. But it was more prudent to keep an open mind. 'Trust no one' was a very sensible saying.

A footpath between houses brought him to within sixty feet of the safe house, which was becoming – unbeknown to its occupants – less safe by the second. He kept low against fencing and privet hedging as he approached.

The wrought-iron rear gate was standing partially open. He turned sideways and slipped through the gap, stepped off the flagged path and ducked behind the garden shed, that he knew was far from being as innocuous as its exterior suggested. This structure was a temporary home to more than rusting tools and perhaps a mower hibernating until spring incited the dormant grass to grow and once more give the machine purpose for its existence.

A sudden rush of adrenaline almost overcame his caution. He put his ear to the thin tongue and groove cladding and could hear the light snoring of its lone occupant inside. He breathed in deeply through his nose to calm and steady himself, and relished the piquant fumes of creosote, that he found almost as stimulating as the smell of petrol, burning rubber, and a woman's sex and blood.

With total confidence and purpose, he walked around to the side door, opened it, took two steps forward and plunged the blade of his knife up under the ribcage and into the heart of the seated copper, who came awake fast, but far too slow to save his complacent skin.

"Bad career choice, pal," Bobby said, standing back to watch as the young guy took one last wheezing, pain-filled intake of breath and clawed at his chest before slumping forward and falling to the floor.

On an upturned wooden crate, next to the now vacated plastic contour chair lay: a paperback book, a large pump-action thermos flask, two-way radio, and a real prize; a matt-black pistol with an extension to the muzzle, which was a silencer.

"Thoughtful," Bobby said to the body at his feet. "You didn't want to wake the neighbours up when you took pot-shots at me, right?"

As if in answer, a red bubble popped on the dead man's lips, to be followed by a thin stream of blood that ran down from the slack mouth, to be hungrily absorbed by the parched wooden boards beneath his head.

Bobby paused, pumped some of the coffee out into the cop's plastic cup, and drank it. Less haste, more speed. This was his game, his rules. He was in absolute control.

Keeping to the solid darkness of night shadow provided by a mature row of thirty-feet-high conifers screening the back garden from the view of neighbours, he reached the bungalow and stepped over to the kitchen window. Streaks of light shone out on to the small patio through narrow gaps between the slats of the blind. Looking in, he could see both of Caroline's woefully inadequate bodyguards. They were facing each other across a small table in a dining nook, playing cards and armed with handguns that hung from shoulder holsters. He supposed that they no doubt believed that there was far more chance of winning the lotto than being paid a pre-dawn visit by death in human form.

Inspired, Bobby tucked the pistol under his belt and withdrew a reel of duct tape from his pocket. He bit off two six-inch lengths and pressed them to the glass, overlapped in a cross. A radio was on inside, and the music playing drowned out any slight sound that he may have made.

Not familiar with handguns, and unaware that the heavy pistol was a SIG-Sauer P226, he held the weapon two-handed, hoping that no safety mechanism was on to lock the action. He took a deep intake of breath, held it, aimed, slowly exhaled, and smoothly squeezed the trigger, to fire through the tape at the two seated men.

The shots made no more noise than polite coughs as the silencer's unused baffles absorbed eighty percent of the reports. The tape stopped the whole window from shattering.

Bright crimson rosettes formed on the back of the nearest cop's white T-shirt, and he jerked forward to involuntarily head butt the tabletop. His partner came up off the bench like a Jack-in-the-box, reaching for his gun, only to be driven backwards and stopped by the wall behind him. He collapsed sideways, slowly, like a felled tree. The bullet had drilled through his forehead, instantly robbing him of life. It penetrated his skull, cut through his frontal lobe and cerebellum, and exited to imbed in the wall amid a spatter of bloody brain tissue. The cop was clinically dead before he hit the floor.

Without pause, Bobby tried the door. It was locked. He removed his parka, bunched it up and held it to one of the small windows, then hit it with the gun's butt, hoping that the fourth cop – out in the street at the front of the house in a van – would not hear the muffled tinkle of breaking glass.

Reaching inside, he turned the key in the lock and entered, closing the door behind him. A quick but unnecessary check confirmed that neither of the cops presented any further threat. Out in the hall there were three doors; two on the right and one to the left. He opened the nearest and smiled broadly at the sight of Caroline, who was awake, cowering on the bed, unmoving and facing him. The semi-darkness had stolen the flaming red from her hair, which hung in thick tresses about her shoulders. She was a vision of loveliness in black and white; no less beautiful for being denied the light that would illuminate her skin tones, sparkle in her emerald eyes, and embrace and enhance her crowning glory. He looked on her as being *almost* perfection, because he knew that nothing and no one was wholly perfect. His pent-up anger and resentment dissolved as he feasted his eyes on the only woman he had ever truly loved.

At last, she is mine, utterly and completely, to cherish or destroy; to possess in every way; to venerate or despoil as I see fit, he thought, walking across the room to sit next to her.

CHAPTER THIRTY-ONE

"Do I have your full and undivided attention, Caroline?" Bobby said as he settled by her side.

Caroline somehow found the strength of will to nod in affirmation. Her voice had deserted her, and her limbs had seized up, in the manner of a car engine bereft of oil and rusted-up in a breaker's yard. She had not known what brought her awake so suddenly. Sitting up, she had listened to the faint music emanating from the radio in the kitchen, and on some instinctive level became aware that she was in imminent danger. She had almost called out to her protectors, whom she knew to be out there, but bit back the shout of alarm as an overpowering state of panic held her still and silent.

As the door opened, she had prayed that it would be one of the policemen who appeared, but was not surprised when the stocky, familiar shape of Cain filled the doorway, to then approach and sit down next to her. She felt like a mouse in the shadow of a cat that was waiting for movement to galvanise it into action and initiate a sudden and deadly attack.

He reached out and stroked her cheek, letting his fingertips meander down the side of her face to her jaw line, and lower, to caress her slender, milk-white neck. A surge of power manifested within him, filling him. Not just power, but an emotion that he had never known before. He had been driven to find her, to make her repent for the torment that she had caused him to suffer, before raping, mutilating and killing her. But that would be of fleeting pleasure, to leave him an empty vessel, soured by regret. Keeping her alive offered the far greater challenge, and the promise of lasting reward. With time and training she would learn to love and need him above all else. All of this he came to realise in the space of a second.

"Listen to me, Caroline," he said, his voice catching with excitement. "I'm prepared to give you a chance to redeem yourself. Do you want to live?"

"Y... Yes," she managed to whisper.

"Good. We need somewhere to go. Where will we be safe? Think quickly, your life really does depend on it."

She frowned. Her mind was a mass of milling pixels. Fear forced out rational thought. And then the whirling particles slowly coalesced into a three-dimensional form. "The houseboat," she said.

215

"A friend of mine owns a houseboat. It's moored on the Thames at Laleham."

"Friend?" Bobby said, his fingers and thumb now biting into her neck, to feel the beat of blood throbbing through pinched arteries. "Be more fucking specific, you whore."

"S... Simon. Simon Payne."

"Ah, yes. The Romeo of Russell Square. Doesn't he use it?"

"No, not in winter," she rasped, feeling the pressure building in her face as her senses began to reel.

"Is it private?"

"Yes. Very."

"Then that's where we'll go," he said, relaxing his grip and running his thumb tip lightly across her bottom lip. "Get dressed, quickly. And remember, Caroline, if you try to escape or shout for help, I *will* kill you."

She pulled off her nightie and tossed it aside, to then dress and await his instructions. He reached out, gripped her wrist tightly and led her through the bungalow, past the two dead cops in the kitchen, where he paused to frisk them, taking their handcuffs and a spare magazine of bullets for the handgun.

Outside, walking beside him, Caroline tried to summon up enough courage to do something. It would be easy enough to bob her head down and bite the hand that held her wrist, to then run away screaming for help. The only problem being, that her legs felt weak and leaden, and she believed that her teeth sinking into his flesh would not cause him to release his grip, and that he may even enjoy the pain. A debilitating fear crushed her spirit and prevented her from taking any action against him. She felt a lost soul, beyond salvation, being led through the darkness, not to Simon's houseboat, but to a sleek and glossy-black gondola which would be manned by the skeletal, cloaked and hooded figure of Charon, waiting to ferry her to a place worse than hell.

At the car, Bobby opened the rear door, pushed her down into the foot well, then cuffed first her wrists and then her ankles together, and covered her with a throw from the back seat.

"I want you to be as quiet as a church mouse," he said. "Don't move or talk unless you are asked to."

He drove at just above the posted limit, at a speed that was neither too fast nor slow to draw suspicion, and he sniggered at his good fortune and accomplishment as he headed west. He stopped at a small newsagent-come-grocery store in Ashford. Told Caroline that he was parked outside a shop, and that if she should sit up, scream, or try to leave the car, then he would shoot the store's owner, and then her.

He purchased milk, bread, eggs, bacon, coffee, an assortment of canned goods, and cigarettes, then drove to nearby Laleham, describing the surroundings and asking Caroline for directions. On reaching the road that fronted the river, he stopped again and transferred her to the front passenger seat, for her to guide him in to the houseboat, which was situated off a private lane away from the road, moored in a short inlet at least fifty yards from its nearest neighbour.

After parking and freeing her ankles, he slipped out of the car, went around to her side, helped her out and pushed her ahead of him.

Boarding the floating home, Bobby used the blade of his knife to quickly disengage the simple lock on the sliding door that led into the main saloon. Once inside, he shackled Caroline to a pillar that was bolted to the floor and was the central support of a large, round teak table. He then taped her mouth and went back to the car for the groceries and his holdall.

Perfect, he thought, studying the immediate surroundings. The houseboat's port side was screened from the lane by tall evergreens, and its starboard side faced the river. Back on board, he shut the door and closed the ceiling to floor blinds. The interior of the vessel comprised a large kitchen/living area, two bedrooms, and spacious bathroom with a shower, toilet and washbasin. Simon Payne must be worth a few quid, judging by the expensive furniture and fittings throughout the glorified riverside sex den. Even the side windows were solid brass portholes, curtained for privacy.

"Together at last, sweet Caroline," he said, kneeling on the thick, lush carpeting and removing the tape from her mouth with a sudden jerk that made her cry out in pain.

"Sorry. But it's like Elastoplasts. My mother, God rest her soul, always said it hurt more if you peeled them off slowly." He then repositioned the strip across her eyes, smoothing it to her temples.

"I want you to know that this is the most satisfying moment of my life," he said, sitting back cross-legged to feast his eyes on his newly acquired possession. "I don't want you to spoil how I'm feeling, so please keep in mind what I did to those other women. They died for you, Caroline. I vented the anger I felt for you on them. I know that you're very scared, and that underneath that fear is a rage fuelled by hatred waiting to surface. You must suppress, then rid yourself of all counterproductive thoughts. You will come to accept that through sparing your life, I now own it. You have to understand that we will live or die together. Do you realise that any future you might have will be with me?"

"Y... Yes," she said.

The blow to her stomach folded her in half. She cried out in agony as a breathtaking pain brought tears to her covered eyes, bathing and stinging them, but trapped, with no exit to escape on to her cheeks and run away.

"That was a lie, Caroline. It may seem inconceivable to you at this moment in time, but you will learn to love me. Take deep breaths and listen to my voice. Absorb and remember what I say."

Caroline gasped, mouth open like a fish out of water, and after a while the fiery pain in her stomach died down to a dull ache.

"Sit up," he said, and she obeyed. "There are two very important points that you have to get your pretty head around. The first is, that you must not attempt to escape or signal for help in any way. Secondly, do not at any time be foolish enough to interpret my feelings for you as a weakness that can be used against me. If you abuse my trust and belief in what we may become together, then you will only have yourself to blame for my actions. Have you a problem with any of that? Do you need any clarification?"

"No, I understand," Caroline murmured. "I'll do anything you want me to. Just please don't hurt me any more."

"I don't want to hurt you, my love," he said, unlocking the cuffs and releasing her from the table. "Stand up."

He led her to the bedroom, undressed her, and gently pushed her down on to the bed. She heard the rustle of clothes, the clink of a metal belt buckle, and a zip being pulled down, before the mattress gave as he climbed on to the bed and lay alongside her, his skin against hers, sending ripples of revulsion through her.

A hand squeezed her right breast, kneading it like bread dough. She wanted to scream, to kick, to fight him, but was too afraid to retaliate. She was in survival mode, enduring what she had no way of preventing.

"No, please, no." she said as a hand found the inside of her thigh and eased her legs apart. Hate, shame and humiliation enveloped her. It was as though she were a laboratory animal being inspected and manipulated without consent or concern for her feelings. She now fully came to realise how it felt to be deprived of all rights. And as he touched her and slipped a finger into her vagina, she was overwhelmed by the imagined sight of his previous victims being penetrated by sharpened spears of wood. Tensing and gripping the bedclothes with her hands, she waited blindly for the pain.

"Tell me you love me," he said.

"I... I love you," she whimpered, unable to convey any feeling or emotion to the words.

"Bobby. Say, I love you, Bobby. And say it as if you mean it. Humour me."

"I love you, Bobby," she whispered, trying to believe herself an actress in one of the countless radio plays that she had produced. Christ, it seemed a lifetime ago that she had led a relatively normal life. It was as though she was now another person. She felt changed, no longer the successful woman that she had been. All that had gone before was now fading memories, dislocated from this new and harsh reality.

"No, you don't, yet," he said. "But you will, princess, believe me, you will."

He was gentle, taking her as though she were a fragile and priceless work of art made of fine, rare crystal that would shatter if handled roughly. The coupling was, to him, a physical consummation of countless dreams that he had never thought would be realised in the flesh.

Impotent am I, Dr Mark? I dare say that Caroline would vouch for my virility, he mused, scant seconds before arching his muscular back, stretching his vein-corded neck up to face the ceiling and howling like a wolf as he came.

Finished, he stroked her body, face and hair, and then kissed her tenderly on the lips. "Don't move," he said, climbing off the bed.

Caroline kept still and could hear nothing. He may have been standing next to her, watching her, waiting for her to disobey his order, to give him an excuse to punish her. Although unfettered, she may as well have been chained to the bed. She did not dare to even close her legs to retain any shred of dignity.

He found nylon rope coiled in a locker near the saloon door, returned to the bedroom and spread-eagled her, tying her to the solid brass bed posts by her wrists and ankles. He then removed the tape from her eyes and smiled down at her as she squinted up at him, blinking rapidly as she attempted to focus.

"I'd rather not have to do this, my love," he said. "But it's for your own good. You'll hate me for a while, and then you'll come to rely on me and need me. And finally, you will love me, as I love you."

She said nothing, and fought to keep the disgust for him locked in her mind; to not express it on her face.

He discarded the strip of damp tape and leaned forward with the reel, then paused and said, "How is the good ship Lollipop powered, Carrie?"

"It... It's connected up to mains water and electric. There are also bottles of propane gas in a locker on deck, and batteries under a cover outside the main door," she said.

"All mod cons, eh?" he said, lifting her head and winding the tape around it twice, to cover her mouth, before quickly severing it with his teeth. "Even if you can work this free, don't," he warned. "Just stay as sweet as you are."

As he left the bedroom and slid the door to, Caroline's bone-deep loathing for her captor gave her a small, diamond-hard feeling of inner strength. He could rule her body, for now, but he could not control her mind or know her thoughts. She had a certain integrity that he could not touch. Her spirit was strong, and she knew that she would never, ever be brainwashed into feeling anything but absolute revulsion, utter contempt and pure unbounded hatred for the deranged killer.

After what seemed a small eternity, Caroline forced away the hideous sensation of his hands on her skin, and the feeling that his engorged penis was still inside her. Her rage was amplified by the sense of violation. She had been terrorised, almost lost her identity, and had now been abducted, raped and left tied up, as though she were no more than a meal to be enjoyed when his hunger returned. He was intent on breaking her morale, draining her resistance and conditioning her. His plan was to alter her way of thinking; to programme her to be his ideal woman.

As she dozed, a cold and dispassionate plan for survival took shape in her mind. She would use his arrogance and self-belief as a weapon against him. She would lull him into believing exactly what he wanted to believe; that she was putty in his hands, to be moulded as he saw fit. At some juncture she would gain his trust and wait for him to make a mistake. She would have to be ready. Only one single, split second chance might present itself. And when it did, she would escape, or die in the attempt.

CHAPTER THIRTY-TWO

Something terrible has happened, Mark thought.

The clock showed 7:00 A.M., and the phone was ringing. It would be bad news. He knew it. Thank God that Amy was with him. Whatever had gone down, she was asleep, warm and safe by his side. He did not hurry to answer. Bad news didn't go away, ever.

"Yeah," he said, steeling himself.

"The no-good bastard has killed three officers and taken Caroline," Barney said, his voice full of pure vehemence.

"He took out an armed protection unit?" Mark said, incredulity apparent in his voice.

"That's right. I need help. I have no idea where he might have gone to ground."

"Any sign of a struggle?"

"No. He knifed one external officer, who had been hidden in a garden shed, then took the officer's gun and shot the two in the bungalow through a kitchen window, that he took the time to tape first, to stop it shattering. He's got two pairs of handcuffs, a silenced handgun, and a spare mag. It looks as if he even took the time to let Caroline get dressed. There was no sign of a struggle."

"He won't kill her immediately, then," Mark said. "He'll take her somewhere that he considers to be safe. Somewhere very private."

Barney sighed audibly down the phone. "He has no friends or relations, Mark. He's a loner, who is apparently close to no one."

"What about Caroline's flat? Is it still under surveillance?"

"Yeah. No one has been near it."

"It's a paper chase, Barney. You need to look for addresses at Cain's. When you find the right one, you'll know it. He isn't going to abduct her and then drive around aimlessly. He'll want to spend some quality time with her. I would imagine that he'll keep her alive for several days, maybe even longer. If he had just wanted to kill her, then you would have found her at the bungalow, mutilated and dead."

"What does he want from her, sex?"

"Everything. He wants everything from her. It's all about power, control and domination, remember? He doesn't just want to rape and kill her. He needs to possess her completely, body, mind and soul; to make her return the love that he believes he feels for her. If she cottons on to the game and has the balls to play it, then she'll be able to buy some extra time."

"If he loves her, then he might not kill her."

"Oh, he'll find a reason to kill her. Even if she is able to live up to his expectations, which is doubtful. In the end, when he truly believes that he owns her totally, then he will freeze that moment forever by destroying her."

"What makes these sick bastards the way they are, Mark? Did you ever work that one out?"

"It was another Mark, Twain, that said that like the moon all men have a dark side. I choose to believe that many sociopaths are born evil with no control over their actions. It might be a chemical imbalance in their brains, but the bottom line is that the safety valves that most of us use to repress our baser instincts are nonexistent in these freaks. I don't buy the pitch that they all get that way purely because of abuse or deprivation in their formative years. It may account for some of them, but not the majority. I once had dealings with a guy who raped and then chopped up over twenty teenage girls. It turned out he was a twin. His brother was an Assistant District Attorney, married with three kids; a regular guy. Both men had enjoyed a stable, middle-class upbringing. But even as a kid, this creep had tortured animals and got his rocks off hurting his peers. I sometimes believe that evil is an entity that cohabits with some people from birth, or before. It's like a virus. They're gripped by it, and it runs its course.

"Then again, I could be totally wrong. Psychiatrists talk about how parts of the brain can be wired-up wrong, or suffer physical or emotional damage that alters personality. There are areas of nerve cells that govern social behaviour and emotional response."

"Which reminds me, Mark, we found Holden's face. Cain left it for us in a flat opposite the crime scene. He'd watched us while he sipped tea and waited for us to leave. He tied up and gagged the elderly tenant. Even phoned the police when he'd quit the area. The old girl said that he was gentle, but seemed a little intense."

"Intense! She was one lucky lady."

"She said he called her, 'grandma'."

"Old age does have its compensations, then. If she'd been younger and a redhead, I think she would have seen a different side of him."

"Yeah, he's full of surprises. I'll keep you up to speed."

"Good...One other point. How did Cain know not only where the safe house was, but details of where the men were positioned?"

"I don't know. He may have been watching the bungalow for a while and clocking all the procedures."

"I hope you're right."

"What now?" Amy said as Mark put the phone down.

"The heat's off us for a while."

"How come?"

"Cain just capped three protection officers at the bungalow."

"Caroline?"

"He took her. But there was no blood or sign of a struggle. It looks as though he made her get dressed and abducted her."

"How do we find him?" Amy said as she tried to imagine the terrible plight that Caroline was in.

"It might be impossible. Barney's checking for any addresses left at Cain's house. But the truth is, he could be holed up anywhere; a hut in a forest; a lockup garage, or any abandoned, empty building. Remember Donald Neilson?"

"The Panther?"

"Yeah. He hid in tunnels under the ground, like a fucking rat. He abducted a girl; Lesley Whittle, and she was found hanging naked in a drainage shaft. Cain will without doubt be au fait with all M.O.s of past serial killers."

"But the Panther wasn't a serial killer."

"I know. That was just an illustration of what unlikely places can be used as lairs by these animals. And Neilson had killed in cold blood while robbing post offices. He was a sociopath who murdered without compunction. Had he not been caught, he would have kept killing."

"Are you saying that there is nothing we can do?"

Mark shrugged. "Just hold tight and wait for the wave to break."

"That's not good enough. That won't stop him from—"

"He'll turn up, Amy," Mark said, taking her in his arms. "Whether it will be in time to save Caroline is anyone's guess. Sometimes all you can do is pray for some luck. Barney and his team are doing all that they can."

"Let's go to my place. I need more space."

"There's still an element of risk, honey. He'll know your address."

"He found a safe house, dealt with armed officers, and walked away with a woman. In my book, that says that we're not safe unless we pack up and catch the next plane out of Heathrow."

"Do you want to do that?"

"No. I don't intend to run away from some lowlife who may be satisfied now that he has his prime target stashed somewhere. I want to go home, feed the squirrels and pretend that everything is better than it really is."

"You make the coffee, then. I'll go and tell our minders the new game plan."

"Thanks," Amy said. "And dress first. You might give the old dear downstairs a funny turn if you go outside in that robe."

"I don't think the sight of my legs would cause her any permanent emotional damage."

"It wasn't your legs I was worried about. It looks windy out there. Those two cops might end up nicking you for indecent exposure."

"You've got a dirty mind. And you're obviously insanely jealous of Mrs Cicero."

"I am not jealous of the widow downstairs, even if she is a sucker for a Yank accent. And as for having a dirty mind...guilty as charged," she said, reaching out to slip her hand inside his robe.

"Aghh! Your hand's cold."

"Be brave. It'll soon warm up."

"I can't raise Gary, boss," Mike said, cocking his wrist and frowning as he looked at his watch for the umpteenth time.

"It's only eight-fifteen," Barney said.

"He was due in at eight, and he's always early," Mike said, hitting the redial button and trying to will Gary to pick up. "He would have phoned if something had come up."

Alarm bells started to ring in Barney's head. Ross had said that each and every member of his team was at risk. Until the safe house got hit, he had thought it an extreme and highly unlikely supposition. But how had Cain known so much?

"Get local uniforms to check out Gary's place, Mike," he said with an edge of urgency in his voice. "If he isn't home, tell them to do a door-to-door."

Mike's brow furrowed. "You think—"

"I don't think anything, yet. But we need to be sure that he's okay, right?"

Within thirty minutes, Mike got a call-back with news that made him believe the worst. Gary could not be located. A neighbour was certain that Gary's car had not been outside the house overnight. It was subsequently located in the car park of his local pub, and the landlord affirmed that Gary had called in the previous evening, but that he had not actually seen him leave the premises. It had to be assumed that something had happened to him between the rear door of the pub and his car.

"Do you really think that he was snatched, boss?" Mike said, finding it hard to believe.

"Yeah," Barney said. "I think Cain got to Caroline through Gary."

"That means—"

"That in all probability, Gary is dead."

"Oh, Christ."

"I know. It just gets worse at every turn. All we can hope is that he's in the sack with some bird. Contact the rest of the team, Mike. I don't want them to hear this second-hand. Tell them what might have happened."

While Mike made calls, Barney paced the office, feeling more frustrated than he had for more than four years, since the Fisher case. He recalled that it had been at noon on a red-hot day in mid July when Andrea Fisher had gone missing. He had headed up the hunt for her, and after twenty-four hours had got that lead-in-the-gut feeling that they were looking for a body, not searching for a lost but still living nine-year-old.

Andrea had set off from where she lived in a terrace house in Putney, to walk less than a hundred yards to a shop at the corner of the street. She had not returned, and her divorced mother was hysterical with fear for her daughter's safety.

At first, they had hoped that the ex-husband had abducted Andrea. He was the prime suspect, after it became known that he had fought unsuccessfully for custody. But he was eliminated within hours. At the time Andrea had vanished he had been in a snooker hall across town, and at least a dozen other players and drinkers confirmed his alibi.

Within six hours they had picked up a registered sex offender who had only been released from prison two months prior to the crime, and had previously lived in the next street to the Fishers'. Although in a halfway house, the suspect had a certain amount of free time, and

Barney was convinced that some of it had been spent with the missing minor.

Graham Balfour was thirty-six, and had been molesting young girls since being a fourteen-year-old. Barney believed that perverts like Balfour, who could not control their urges, should all be physically or chemically castrated, and locked up ad infinitum. But even monsters had rights and kept being given the chance to fuck up law-abiding people's lives, until they pushed the envelope so far out of shape that some judge eventually saw the light and was given no choice but to hand down a meaningful, lengthy sentence. They had tried to sweat Balfour, but he would not be drawn, and with no physical evidence he was back on the street within forty-eight hours.

It had been a week later that Andrea's body was found. Two lads had seen bubbles rising to the surface of the local canal, and then watched as a large black bin-liner breached like a whale. They had thrown stones at the partially air-filled bag, only stopping when a pale, bloated arm slipped out through a tear in the plastic.

Hairs, fibres and DNA samples found on and in the corpse linked Balfour to the murder. Faced with the overwhelming amount of forensic evidence recovered, he broke down and admitted that he had abducted, raped and strangled the little girl. He had weighted Andrea's body with a breeze block, before pushing it out into the canal, where it had sunk into the oily, polluted and stagnant water. The weight had been insufficient, and the trapped air and resulting body gases had finally brought Andrea up, to bear witness against her killer.

"The super wants a word," Mike said for a second time.

Barney left his bitter reverie, took the proffered phone, and thought how best to placate his irate boss.

"My office," Clive ordered, and slammed the receiver down.

Barney went up in the lift, reflexively twisting his wedding band. He closed his eyes and tried to get a handle on the rage that was cramping his stomach. He needed at least an hour by the side of his fishpond to put him in the right frame of mind to deal with Pearce without blowing up big-time. He visualised the Koi rising to the surface to take the food pellets from his hand. It helped a little, but not enough.

"Yes, Clive?" he said, entering the superintendent's office without knocking.

"Sit," Clive ordered, without looking up from the open folder in front of him.

"I'm not a fucking dog, Clive. I don't sit, roll over, or lick my own balls on command."

Clive brought his pudgy fist down too hard on the top of his desk and could not help but wince at the instant, bruising pain. "I'm going to ignore that kind of remark, Barney. I know you're having a bad day, but—"

"A bad day! Is that how you see having an officer abducted and probably tortured and murdered? It's a fucking horrendous day."

"Enough," Clive said, his face turning puce, and his eyes bulging. He appeared to be in imminent danger of having a stroke or heart attack as his anger reached critical point. "We don't know that DC Shields has come to any harm, yet. What we do know is, that three armed officers have been murdered, and that the Sellars woman has been snatched."

"And you're getting it in the neck, so you've stopped me doing my job and summoned me up here to hand the shit parcel to. Right?"

"Let's just look at what we've got, Barney," Clive said, his voice softening. "Do you want a cup of coffee?"

Barney nodded, and Clive used his intercom to ask his secretary to rustle up coffee for two.

Barney slumped into the chair that he had been standing next to. "We know who the killer is. We just don't know his whereabouts, yet," he said. "We're doing everything we can to locate him."

"Such as?" Clive said.

"Searching his house for any leads. And computer section is looking at his machine. There may be something on it or the hard drive. It's just a matter of time, Clive. Believe me, we'll lift him."

CHAPTER THIRTY-THREE

The house was cold. Amy switched on the central heating and the coffeemaker before going out into the back garden to fill the depleted bird feed holders with peanuts and seed. She also pressed hazelnuts into the drilled holes of a log, which was screwed to the rustic post that held the bird table aloft. She smiled, thinking back to when Mark had blamed a totally fictitious weevil infestation for his failure to buy any nuts. Being home, in the comfort of familiar surroundings – and her habits within it – filled Amy with an erroneous sense of normality. She could immerse herself in routines that forced back and lessened the unwanted thoughts of Cain, and the vile acts that the man had committed.

Mark poured the coffee. Walked over to the kitchen door and looked out to watch Amy juggle with brown paper bags and feeders.

A hoar-frost still clung tenaciously to every surface. The temperature was so low that it would no doubt persist for much of the morning, until slightly milder air dispatched it.

Finding a large Perspex jug in a wall unit, Mark filled it with water and went out to join her. He removed a thin layer of ice from the ornamental, pre-cast concrete birdbath and filled it to overflowing.

"That should hold them for a while," Amy said, breaking up some stale bread and scattering it on the stiff, white-coated grass.

Mark grinned. "Yeah, it'll be cat heaven in a few minutes."

"Uh?"

"You attract the birds, and Sylvester will come running for his takeaway Tweety Pie."

"What are you saying, that I shouldn't feed them?"

"No, Amy. I just accept that the birds are a magnet to predators. It's called nature. There's nothing you can do about it. For the odd bird lost, the many will survive."

"It's all life and death, isn't it?" Amy mused, dropping the last two slices of bread to the ground intact, her prior enthusiasm instantly depleted.

"Yeah," Mark said. "Everything has its day. It's all short term, so you have to make the most of now, and not dwell too much on what's gone, or what's up ahead."

"The philosophy doesn't make it any less depressing," Amy said, heading back to the house. "Wrap it up anyway you like, but it still sucks."

"I don't know. Being alive wouldn't be so precious if we were immortal. It's the knowledge that you're on a journey that has a beginning, middle and ending that makes it so meaningful."

"Say that to me again in forty years time. See if it's as meaningful when you're wrinkled, balding, and full of aches and pains, wishing that you could do a tenth of what used to be a walk in the park."

"You're saying we'll still be together in forty years?"

"Unless you get the hots for some young piece of skirt half your age and go walkabout, yes."

"I don't think I could find another mug like you to put up with me."

Amy punched him on the biceps. Mark grimaced and pretended that it had hurt him.

Once back inside, they paused to kiss, as out in the garden the birds appeared and started to feed, and a lone squirrel ran along the top of the panel fencing, eager to prise a nut from the log, to no doubt attempt to relocate in the rock-hard ground.

Savouring the hot coffee, they skirted around the issue that was foremost on their minds.

"Why did you join the FBI, Mark? What made you want to be involved with violence and death?" Amy said.

"TV," he replied with a rueful expression. "As a kid I watched all the cops and robber shows on the tube. It was the mystique about the men in grey suits who usually wore shades that hooked me. Fidelity, bravery and integrity seemed ideals that went hand in hand with an adventurous life. I just got channelled. The only other line of work that appealed to me was being an oceanographer, like Hooper, the character that Richard Dreyfuss played in *Jaws*."

"Why did you decide on the bureau, and not a life on the ocean wave?"

"I get seasick."

They both laughed, and the mood that had threatened to darken the day, lightened.

"Sounds like you wanted a gung-ho, macho career?"

"At first, yeah, to a degree. But that soon wore thin. The weight of responsibility to try and make a difference brought me down to earth."

"You found it a noble cause, then?"

"I came to believe that there is a dark side that has to be opposed. And before you say it, I'm no Luke Skywalker. If utilizing whatever skills I had to fight the good fight was being noble, then I suppose I'm guilty as charged, ma'am. You were a cop. Why did you do it?"

"I guess I was always a tomboy. Dolls, prams and pretty dresses were wasted on me. I was forever climbing trees, playing football, and fighting. I was going to join the armed forces, but thought it a bit mindless to be told who this week's enemy was. I wasn't prepared to kill strangers, who like me would be tools of the government of the day. I'm an individual, not expendable fodder. I had an uncle who was a copper in CID, and I thought he had an exciting and rewarding career. And I came to believe that it was. But after I got shot, I had a lot of questions and not many answers. I don't know if in the end it was fear or just a reaction to the whole sordid business, or both, but I couldn't go back to it."

"Do you ever miss it?"

"For a while it was as though I'd lost an arm, and there was a lot of guilt. I felt a coward, who'd run home crying after having my eye blackened."

"You're no coward, Amy. You just knew when it was time to move on."

"We both chose a new path to follow, and look at us now, up to our necks in what we walked away from. It must be kismet."

"It's not destiny. I didn't make a clean break. I still work with convicted killers. And for some reason I can't say no if I'm asked to consult on pattern or ritual murders. There's a side of me that still wants to be in the game; a part that I can't deny. You're only involved in this case through association...because of me."

"I could have kept my nose out of it. I wanted to be included."

Mark got up and poured more coffee for both of them. His face and mood were equally grave. "I should have given more thought to your safety," he said. "I was stupid. I drew Cain out and put you in danger."

"The next time you agree to work up a profile, don't cross the magic line, then. Distance yourself from it."

"I'd like to think that I could say no, period, if I'm ever approached again. But I might not be able to."

"I know. We are what we are. How do we go forward with this case? There has to be something we can do."

"I don't think there is. It's up to Barney and his team to flush Cain out."

"But they don't have what you've got. They can't get into his mind."

"I can't either. I couldn't foresee him executing three cops. He even took the time after he'd killed them to let Caroline get dressed," Mark said, and then fell silent, suddenly consumed by intense rumination.

Amy watched as Mark figuratively detached himself from his surroundings and drew inward, to another place; a corner of his mind that allowed him to see more clearly what eyes could not.

"Billy!" Mark said after less than ten seconds had elapsed, almost causing Amy to spill her coffee. "It's insane, but I've got a real off-the-wall idea."

"What? Tell me."

"Billy Hicks at the hospital. You know, the young guy who sees auras around people. I'm wondering if he can do the same with personal effects."

"Such as?"

"I'm not sure. Cain made Caroline get dressed. She was in bed when he broke in, with cops in the house. She would have most likely been wearing a nightdress, T-shirt or something."

"True. I doubt that she would have been starkers with armed police in the next room."

"Even if she was, the pillow or sheet that she was lying on would do."

"Would do what, Mark? Explain where you're coming from."

"I want Billy to see and hold something that Caroline had contact with when Cain went into that bedroom and was with her."

"You think he'll have some psychic vision?"

"I don't know. It may be the most stupid and way-out idea that I've ever had. But when there's nothing to lose, then what the hell. Police forces world-wide have used psychic investigators and clairvoyants. And some have proved uncannily helpful."

"It's better to have tried and failed—"

"Than to live life wondering what would've happened if I *hadn't* tried," Mark said, finishing off the Alfred Lord Tennyson quote.

Not allowing himself time to change his mind, Mark phoned Barney.

"You want the nightie she was wearing?" Barney said, taken aback by Mark's request.

"Yeah," Mark said, glad that he could not see the expression on the veteran cop's face. "I need to play a hunch."

"Give me some more, Mark. I don't understand how it will help with the investigation."

"I know someone who gets insights. Just run with this, Barney. It can't do any harm, and there's a chance we might get a break."

"You're talking about a bloody psychic. We don't recognise or rate them."

"You use me and other psychological profilers. This is just one step beyond that. And you wouldn't be compromised. The person I plan to approach would not be given any details of the case."

"The garment is with forensics."

"Get it back off them, for Christ's sake. Fibres and hairs won't help you. We already know who he is. We need to know *where* he is."

Barney evaluated the situation. It was true what Mark had said. Currently they had nothing that would help them home in on Cain.

"Where are you?"

"I'm at Amy's."

"Stay put. I'll get it to you ASAP."

"Thanks, Barney," Mark said before the line purred.

Forty-five minutes later, a patrol car pulled up at the front of the house. Mark went out to take possession of the paprika coloured cotton nightie, which was stuffed into a transparent, zip-locked plastic evidence bag, which he had to sign for.

Minutes later, Mark was ready to go. "Make sure that the doors and windows are locked," he said.

"I'll be fine," Amy said as they walked over to where he had parked JC. "I want to soak in a hot bath. And I may even go into the office later. They'll be starting to think that I'm taking the urine."

"Okay. I should be back before dark," he said, climbing into the Cherokee and keying the engine.

She kissed him, then closed the door and stepped back, watching until the four-by-four reached the end of the street and vanished from view. Back inside the house, she noticed that Mark had left his mobile phone on the kitchen table. In his haste, he had forgotten it.

It was over an hour later when it rang.

"Hello," she said.

"Hello. You must be Amy," a pleasant male voice.

"Who's speaking, please?" she said, knowing that it wasn't Barney's voice, but believing it to be the police trying to contact Mark.

"Is Dr Mark there?" the caller said, ignoring her question.

CHAPTER THIRTY-FOUR

The guard in the gatehouse raised his hand to Mark, recognising the doctor and his vehicle, but still checking the plate number against his list before pushing the button to activate the opening of the large gates, and hoping that the doctor would allow them to open fully this time.

Mark gave a lazy salute and drove through, to skirt the lakeside, having to almost brake to a stop as a couple of geese waddled unconcernedly in front of him, oblivious to what the effect of impact with a Jeep Cherokee would result in.

Entering the building, Mark collected his security keys, went to his office and draped his navy fleece over the back of a chair, before heading for the residential wing on which Billy was located.

Dr Jeremy Pank, a rotund little man in a too-tight white coat – and wearing what were deemed nowadays to be John Lennon glasses, with a pink cast to their lenses – approached him. "The director is infuriated, Mark," he said with a smug smile. "He doesn't like the attendant publicity that your article has brought to his door. I wouldn't be surprised if he suspends you."

"Jeremy, fuck off, why don't you?" Mark said as he shouldered past him without breaking stride.

"You can't just come and go as you like, and treat people with such disrespect," Jeremy called out, his face flushed with anger.

"Sit on it," Mark said, raising his right hand and extending the middle finger, but not turning.

Making his presence known to the orderly in the wing office, and telling him that he was there to visit Billy, Mark went to the young man's room.

"Hi, Dr R... Ross," Billy said, a smile lighting his face at Mark's surprise visit.

"Hi yourself, Billy. What kind of day are you having?" Mark said.

"A g... good one. I've been reading some Shakespeare," he said, holding up a thick copy of the bard's complete works. "I don't really understand th...that much of it, but I like the old-fashioned w... words. I have the feeling that he was a very special and g... gifted person."

"He was, Billy. And so are you, in a different way. I've come to ask you for some help."

234

"I'll help you in any way I c... can, Dr Ross," Billy said, and with a fleeting, guileful look added. "Would it merit another walk b...by the lake?"

Mark smiled. "Yes, Billy, it probably would." He was not offended by the request. If you don't ask, chances are you won't get.

"What d...do you want me to do?" Billy said.

Mark took the nightie out of the bag and held it out. "I want you to take this, and tell me any thoughts or impressions you have about it."

Billy reached out and gently took the garment, to close his eyes and crush the material between his hands, then to his face, to smell the fabric.

Billy had sometimes experienced 'vibes' from inanimate objects. It wasn't a sense like the auras he saw around people; that was a constant facility he possessed. The images that touching articles could induce were haphazard and periodic; another talent he had never mentioned to anyone. Now, holding the flimsy nightie, his mind was filled with a rush of powerful emotions, and images that made him moan aloud.

Mark neither spoke nor moved. He did not want to break the concentration that was etched on the young man's face, as Billy lowered the nightie, but kept his eyes tightly closed.

Billy was transported. He was sitting on another bed in another room, which was dark and full of oppressing shadows. A figure moved towards him from an open door, and he felt numb, rooted to the spot, entangled in an invisible net of fear. Someone, a woman, was in mortal danger. Then a few scattered, random images from the woman's memory banks half-formed in his mind; of people's faces, a collie dog, the BBC and a houseboat. That was all. He had gleaned all residue of events that had somehow been conveyed by the fabric, which had become like chewed-out gum; bland and bereft of all flavour, and now no more than the sum of its fibres. He was wholly back in the safety of his room with Mark, relieved to be away from the distressing situation that he knew was real and ongoing.

Mark waited.

"I was in another place, Dr Ross," Billy said, his voice now fluent and without the trace of a stammer, as he reported his experience. "I was wearing this nightie. Someone came for me in the darkness, and I was terrified. But it wasn't me. I was looking out through the eyes of a young woman in grave danger. I think her captor is going to kill her."

"Anything else, Billy? Anything at all?" Mark said, though he was more than impressed by what he had already been told.

Billy seemed to shrink visibly, his shoulders sagging as his head dropped forward.

"Only that I f... felt the presence of great evil, Dr Ross. The person who t... took her has no conscience. He believes that life is a c... commodity, which he has the right to take as h... he sees fit. And I don't know how b... but I got a glimpse into the he woman's memory and saw images of people, a dog, and a boat among other things."

"Can you describe the boat, Billy?"

"No. It was j... just a quick flash of white on water. I think it could have been a houseboat."

"Okay, Billy. Thanks for what you just did. I'll arrange for us to take that walk in the next day or two. You've earned it."

"I'll look f...forward to that, Dr Ross. Be careful, though. You're still in g... great danger."

"I'll watch my back, Billy. I'll see you soon," Mark said, taking the nightie back and stuffing it into the bag. He then let the orderly know that he was leaving the residential wing, and headed back to his office.

Writing down all that Billy had said, he was unable to begin to understand what power enabled the young man to somehow see what he had from holding the nightie that Caroline had worn. Could it all be just a figment of Billy's strange mind? As he pondered what seemed to be an impossible feat with no rational explanation, Mark noticed the blinking red light on the phone. There was one message. He hit the play button and listened to Amy's voice. She was trying to keep it even and controlled, but the pitch and tone gave away the underlying agitation: *'Mark, phone me, it's urgent. I've just spoken to Cain'.*

Snatching up the receiver, he punched in Amy's number. The presentiment of imminent disaster enveloped him, with what would prove to be good reason.

CHAPTER THIRTY-FIVE

"Who is this?" Amy repeated the question, although deep down she had no need to ask. She knew that it was Cain.

"You know exactly who it is, sweet lips. Now be a good girl and put Dr Mark on."

"I can't do that."

A pause. "I understand. You aren't with him, but you have his phone. Where are you, Amy? Tell me."

"If you really expect me to do that, then you're more insane than I thought, if that's possible."

"Be very careful, Amy Egan. Don't say things that you will regret if we happen to meet. Tell the Yank that I will dedicate Caroline to him. She will be punished for his past insults. Larry lost face because of him, literally. And now he can add what Caroline will shortly suffer to his guilt-ridden conscience. His inefficiency is mildly disappointing. I expected much more from him and thought he may at least live up to his third-rate book."

"You can tell him all this yourself, when he finds the hole you've crawled into, you sad, out of control, pathetic little shit," Amy said, finding some small pleasure in badmouthing him.

"I am in *total* control, you stupid slut. Think of the pleasure and sense of well-being that fulfilling your own pathetic needs gives you, and try to comprehend that what I do gives me tenfold the gratification that you have ever experienced. I am unrestricted in my actions, and allow myself to indulge in the ultimate game, without fear of retribution. It all comes down to different strokes for different folks."

"Normal people don't get their rocks off by mutilating and killing, Cain," Amy countered, her anger rising, overcoming the initial shock and fear of his disembodied voice. "You are one seriously fucked-up disease. Why don't you just put your sick head on the nearest railway line and wait for the next train to hell?"

"You interest me, Amy," he said, not rising to her artless bait. "You have grit, over the phone that is. I wonder if you would be so forthright in the flesh, face to face. I think not. Perhaps we'll find out. When I have a spare hour or two, I might just make your acquaintance. I'd enjoy that, but you most certainly would not. For now, just give the good doctor my regards, and let Barney Bear know that young Gary is rotting in a shallow grave, somewhere in Epping Forest. If he starts looking now, he may come across the bones in twenty years or so."

The phone went dead, and Amy began to shake. The killer, albeit only his voice, had entered her home unbidden. And like a rat that had died behind a skirting board, it had fouled the atmosphere, contaminating every inch of it with its stink.

Blink.

He was driving through Laleham, on his way back to the houseboat. He had left Caroline tethered to the bed and driven away from the area to phone Ross, but had ended up speaking to Amy Egan. And then another fugue had robbed him of awareness.

Back on board, he sat in the murky saloon, blinds closed, staring unseeing into the shadows. A thin, glistening slug-trail of saliva ran from the right corner of his open mouth, and his expression was one of untenanted lunacy.

After a while, the storm in his neural pathways subsided, and normal service resumed. He looked about, as though he were seeing the interior of the houseboat for the first time. The episodes were becoming far more frequent. Maybe he just needed sleep, he thought, absently wiping the drool from his chin. Standing up, he massaged his temples and then went across to the fridge, took out a four-pint container of milk and drank over a pint of it.

Ross would no doubt think that his having abducted and being preoccupied with Caroline would buy him some breathing space. Wrong. Now was the perfect time to up the anti and really hurt him. Mr Ex-FBI had not answered his home number, and was not with his woman. Amy Egan was alone. He would drive to Richmond, check the local phone book, and if she wasn't listed, then find her through the electoral role. The psychologist would soon need extensive counselling himself, if he were ever to come to terms with what he would find. The love of the shrink's life would be the living palette; the walls of her house the canvas on which he would produce a masterpiece in blood, and entitle it: The Art of Death.

"Amy?" Mark said, weak with relief when she picked up.

"Thank God you got my message, Mark," she said. "Cain called me. He rang your mobile number."

"What did he say?"

Amy had written down as much of the conversation as she could remember, and read it to Mark from the notepad in front of her.

"Did you call Barney?" Mark said.

"Yes. I told him what I've told you. He's trying to trace the caller number from your phone."

"Okay. Don't go to the office, or anywhere. Just stay put. I'm leaving Cranbrook now."

"He wouldn't come here, Mark," Amy said. "He's got Caroline. You said that the heat was off us for the time being."

"That was before he called you. The son of a bitch might do anything. We have to believe that you are in his firing line. The guy is totally unpredictable."

"Hurry, Mark. I need you here."

"I'm on my way. I love you, Amy."

She went through the house and made sure that every window was both closed and locked. She then double-checked the front and back doors. Still feeling like a goldfish in a bowl, she withdrew a teak-handled carving knife from the block next to the bread bin, immediately feeling better for having the heavy, razor-sharp knife gripped tightly in her hand.

Mounting the stairs, with the feeling that she was overreacting to a nonexistent situation that was not about to happen, Amy tried to calm down and evaluate the facts. It was broad daylight. Cain was not going to appear like the unstoppable guy in the Halloween movies. And he wasn't the fucking Terminator...*Tell Larry Holden that*, she thought, not able to stop hearing the killer's voice, or the things he had said, which kept repeating over and over in her mind.

Standing on the landing, Amy felt irrationally vulnerable and defenceless. If Cain came, then a knife would in all likelihood be useless against him. Barney had said he had a gun. She needed to hide...but where? He would systematically search the house; every room, cupboard, wardrobe, and any other place that was big enough to conceal her.

Retracing her steps downstairs to the kitchen, she rummaged through the cupboard under the sink unit and pulled out a canister of Raid. 'Kills bugs dead', the label proclaimed. Cain might not be the type of insect that they had in mind, but a shot of the spray in the eyes would temporarily blind him, giving her enough time to follow up with the knife. Her instincts told her to run, get the hell out of the house and drive away. But what if he was already out there, watching and waiting? Better to face any danger on home territory. At that moment, soaring through the skies in the Cessna would have been the only place where she would have felt truly safe.

A quick stop at an internet café was all it took to find Amy Egan's name and address in the UK online phonebook. He drove to the location and could see no sign of police in the area. He would have seen or sensed them as he cruised the streets in the proximity of Amy's house near Richmond Park.

There was a Nissan standing at the kerb outside the well-kept Georgian gaff, which he presumed was Amy's. She would be at home alone, of that he was positive. The police would not be watching her; would believe that having abducted Caroline, he would be fully, if temporarily engaged.

He parked almost a hundred yards away, behind a Volvo estate, then walked – his leg now only sore, not causing him to grimace with pain as he put weight on it, or to limp – past her house, turning left at the bottom of the street to find a passageway that separated one row of back gardens from those opposite.

The loud noise was sudden; a crash that only lasted for half a second, but Amy knew that it was the back door exploding open. There was no doubt in her mind that it was Cain. She felt panic rising, threatening to paralyse her and prevent her from taking any evasive action. She bit down on her tongue, hard enough to make her grunt with a level of pain that freed her locked limbs.

Moving fast across the first-floor landing, she entered her bedroom and quietly eased the door shut behind her. He would come, that was as sure-fire as night following day. Shit! She had forgotten to pick up Mark's mobile; had isolated herself. Stupid bitch. No matter. When he opened the door, she would be behind it, ready to spray the mace substitute into his eyes, and to bury ten inches of Sheffield steel into his chest.

After what seemed an interminable length of time, a board on the landing creaked under weight. He had obviously searched the ground floor and satisfied himself that she was not there. Now, he was only a few feet from her. Almost crippled with terror and knowing exactly what he was capable of doing, she raised both the knife and canister, to see them shake in her trembling hands. This was not a burglar, or someone that she could talk down and deal with rationally. Cain was a monster, infinitely more dangerous than any run-of-the-mill thief or rapist. His motive was known, and his past crimes only too graphically illustrated what he would do to her, given the chance.

With nowhere to run, she would have to face death head on, and hope that she could thwart it.

The round, crazed porcelain knob began to turn, and Amy watched; breath held and heart thudding, spellbound as the faded rose that decorated it slowly revolved through 180 degrees. She readied herself, biting back a cry that was aching to be released.

The door burst open and was thrown against her, knocking her hands back, sending the can of Raid flying through the air, and pushing the edge of the knife's blade into her face to produce a short, deep cut down the centre of her chin.

He was fast. He rounded the now wide-open door, and his left hand snaked out, gripped her by the wrist and jerked her brutally away from the wall, to throw her across the room. She pirouetted off balance and slammed into the edge of the solid oak wardrobe, crying out as the bone-jarring collision between her back and the unforgiving wood winded her, causing her to sink to the floor in a splay-legged sitting position. Instinctively, she attempted to push herself up, simultaneously thrusting her hand out, only to discover that it was empty; the knife gone, now lying four feet away on the carpet, out of reach.

With her lungs cramping, Amy looked up into the black, emotionless eyes of the Park Killer. He was of average height, broad, and wore a black parka, blue jeans, and a long-billed baseball cap with a patch of the Warner logo 'What's up, Doc?' embroidered on to the front of it. The expression on his wide, high-cheeked face was one of undisguised delight, as he pointed the silencer-equipped pistol at her chest.

"Where's Ross?" he said, taking a step towards her.

"Where's Caroline?" she countered.

"Under all your noses on her now ex-boyfriend's houseboat," Bobby said, grinning, happy to give up information that would never find its way out of the bedroom. "Your turn. Where is Ross?"

"On his way, and so are the police," Amy said, annoyed to hear the tremor of fear in her voice.

"In that case, I'd better hurry," he said. "Stand up, Amy, and take off your sweater. Be aware that if you try to fuck me about, I'll gut shoot you."

"Please, don't hurt me," she whimpered, climbing slowly to her feet and cringing back into the niche formed by the wall and the side of the wardrobe. If he thought that she was too scared and intimidated to offer any resistance, then a chance might present itself.

"The sweater," he said. "Let's see what you've got under it that the Yank finds so attractive."

Amy pulled the sweater off over her head and dropped it at her feet.

He moved closer, grasped the front of her blouse and ripped it open, popping buttons. As the garment came apart, her breasts, unfettered by a bra, spilled out. She wanted to knee him in the crotch, or make a bid to jam her fingers into his eyes, but the cold, steel end of the silencer on the gun was pressed against her now bare midriff, almost on the scar left by the bullet wound. She remembered the agony she had suffered, and the blood in her veins seemed to thicken into syrup and render her incapable of any action.

His free left hand reached out and latched on to her right breast, causing her to draw even further back, to shudder with revulsion as he massaged the flesh, then squeezed hard enough to make her yelp.

"Nice tits," he said, his breathing quickening as he moved his hand down over her flat stomach, to release the stud on her Levis and lower the zip. "Take them off, Amy."

His voice was catching, full of urgency as he became aroused. She slid her jeans and panties down over her hips, and he backed up as she bent forward, which gave her room to manoeuvre. She stepped out of the garments, kicked them aside and then straightened up.

He moved in close again and began to thrust against her. She responded. Jabbed her hips forward to meet the bulge at his crotch with simulated ardour, and reached behind him to hold his quivering buttocks in her hands.

"Yes, baby. Yesss!" he groaned, and his gun hand went behind her lower back, to crush her to him as his mouth found her lips.

Loathing welled up as she smelled his sour breath.

I don't want to die. He wants to fuck me, and then kill me. Stop it from happening. Do not become another of his victims.

Amy reacted on automatic, spontaneously, channelling her whole being into a single all out bid to survive. As his left hand slipped down between their bodies, she clamped her teeth on to his bottom lip and bit down hard, positioning her right leg between his legs and bringing her knee up simultaneously with all the force that she could muster.

He bellowed with the sudden pain that knifed through his mouth and testicles, and before he could recover his wits, Amy wrenched her head sideways, slicing her teeth through his lip. She gripped his gun hand and brought it up, transferring her bloody mouth to his wrist, to bite deeply, to the bone.

He made a whining sound, hardly recognisable as human, then dropped the gun and stumbled backwards. And as he did, Amy bent her arm and brought the edge of her hand scything across his throat.

Yes! Yes! She had beaten him. Breathless, she watched as he sank to his knees, clutching his throat with both hands and making wheezing, gagging noises as he fought to breathe.

He, or in this case, she who hesitates, is lost. For just a split-second too long Amy admired her work, and even contemplated retrieving his gun and shooting him dead. The urge to flee won out, though, and she moved around him to the door.

The pain was excruciating, and he thought he might pass out. His vision was darkening as he sucked small amounts of air into his windpipe, which felt as though it was going into spasm. Only the fear of being caught gave him the willpower to react. The bitch had seemed too scared and demoralised to present any problem. He had wanted to screw her, as a precursor to dismembering her for the Yank to find. And his lust had cost him dearly.

As she darted past him, he regrouped, ignoring the pain, to throw himself sideways, tripping her with his body, reaching out blindly and managing to grasp her ankle with his uninjured hand.

Face down on the carpet, Amy felt his weight on top of her, as he crawled, dragged himself up her body. Her unexpected cunning and ferocity had saved her once, but now his hands had reached her neck and were digging into the flesh. She knew that he would not let go until she was unconscious or dead.

CHAPTER THIRTY-SIX

The seat belt saved Mark from going through the windscreen. He slammed into the kerb in front of Amy's house, brakes squealing as the discs reneged against the amount of friction they were subjected to. The whiplash hurt his neck, but he ignored the discomfort and left JC on the run.

Unlocking the door, he entered the hall and paused to take in the surroundings. He almost called out, but stopped himself. In the thick silence that pervaded the house, he looked about, saw spots of blood on the floor. His heart sank. He moved quickly through to the kitchen. The back door stood ajar, and the damage to it was proof that it had been forced open. More teardrops of blood laced the vinyl floor covering, the tails of their elongated pear shape evidence that whoever had been bleeding had been heading out of the house.

Knelt on one knee, Mark touched a crimson spot with his fingertip. It was fresh. He ran back, through the hall and out on to the street, but there was no sign of anyone, and no vehicle suddenly pulled away at speed.

In almost blind panic he checked every room on the ground floor, then mounted the stairs and immediately saw a red smear on the jamb of Amy's open bedroom door. He walked in stiffly, heart thumping, fully expecting to be confronted by his worst fears. There was no body. But this had been the scene of whatever had transpired. He could see patches, streaks and spatters of blood on the carpet, a wall, and lacing the side of the bedspread.

Staring at Amy's discarded clothing, Mark fought back hot tears, trying to hold on to the thought that she had been taken, not killed. Logic told him that if Cain had murdered her, then he would have left a macabre calling card in his wake; an exhibition of his work. But if he had abducted her, why no note to taunt him? Or a message scrawled on the wall in her blood. It didn't add up.

The only logical conclusion he could come to, was that Amy was injured, bleeding, incapacitated and probably unconscious. Cain must have risked taking her away in broad daylight, and decided that the bloody scene and the fact that she was missing was message enough. He would no doubt make contact when he was good and ready. Mark smashed his fist into the wardrobe door in frustration, tormented and almost overcome by misery at the thought of Amy being tortured and probably made – when Cain called him – to scream into the mouthpiece of a phone, in much the same way as the bastard had forced Larry to, before butchering him. He had never felt so alone or so desperately helpless. If he couldn't find Cain, and quickly, then the only person who mattered in his life and gave it meaning, would be lost to him forever.

Think, damnit. Cain has found somewhere safe to keep prisoners. And if by handling Caroline's nightie, Billy had really experienced some weird form of second sight, then the killer's new lair may well be near or on water. But where? Who did Caroline know who owned a boat?

The rich boyfriend, Payne. Could it be that simple? Doubtful. But when you're drowning at sea, anything that floats by is a possible lifesaver. Just shake the dice, pray for a gambler's lucky streak, and throw a seven.

Back downstairs in the kitchen, Mark phoned the Yard and asked to be put through to Barney's extension, for it to be answered by Mike Cook, who gave up Payne's landline and mobile numbers without subjecting him to an inquisition.

"Simon Payne speaking." An Oxbridge accent.

"Mr Payne," Mark said. "This is Detective Sergeant Mike Cook."

"Have you heard anything? Have you found Caroline?" Simon said, his voice full of concern and anxiety.

"Not yet, sir. But you might be able to help. Do you own a boat, or any property near water?"

"Yes, why?"

Mark's grip on the phone tightened, and his stomach rolled as he picked up a ballpoint and made ready to write an address on a Post-it notepad.

"It may help with our investigation, sir."

"You think he may have taken her to my houseboat...the Pandora?"

"Tell me its location, sir. And then wait for us to get back to you. Under no circumstances must you take any independent action. It could very easily cost Caroline her life," Mark said, hoping that Payne had enough commonsense to keep out of it.

Armed with the location, the name of the houseboat, a tyre iron and his mobile phone, which he had found on the coffee table in the lounge, Mark drove to Laleham. He knew that he should call Barney with what he now knew, and twice picked up the phone from the passenger seat next to him, but tossed it back. If he involved the police, then he would lose control of the situation, and Amy's life would be further compromised. Cain would not respond to negotiators. Should he find himself surrounded and with no possible avenue of escape, then he would kill Caroline and Amy, and in all probability eat a bullet, rather than spend the rest of his life in prison without a cat in hell's chance of parole. Mark was certain that independent action was the only game in town, and that what he did would be the deciding factor as to whether the women, if still alive, would remain so.

Parking at least a quarter of a mile from the houseboat, he approached it on foot, glad of the fading afternoon light. He stayed close to the trees on the river side of the lane, using other craft and foliage as cover.

Hunkered down amid a sprawling thicket of gorse, Mark surveyed the unlit houseboat. He had the gut feeling that the Pandora – as the box of Greek mythology – would, in addition to hope, still be holding the blessing of life. The only ill on board was Cain, who he counted on not surviving their meeting to be let loose again on mankind. He had come prepared to use extreme prejudice if necessary, deeming Cain's life totally irrelevant, when measured against saving the lives of the man's two prisoners.

"It's Jane, Barnaby," the pathologist said. "I was expecting you to give me a call over the PM report on Larry Holden."

"Events have overtaken Larry, Jane," Barney said. "Our killer has murdered four officers and abducted Caroline Sellars since then. We know who he is, but not where he is."

"I'm sorry to hear that, Barnaby. I'll let you get back to it."

"Was there anything about Holden's death that I should know?"

"Only that you're dealing with a devil. Larry's face was excoriated...peeled off while he was still alive. It wasn't the stab wound to his kidney, or the removal of his face that killed him. He died as a result of a ventricular fibrillation of the heart."

"He had a heart attack?"

"Yes. You could say that he died of fright."

"Thanks, Jane. I'll let you know if we get the bastard."

"Do, please."

Barney hung up as Mike entered the office. "Anything?" he asked his DS.

"Not yet, boss. There was no paperwork with any addresses at Cain's that could be relevant to his whereabouts. And nothing from Caroline Sellars' flat is paying off. We can account for all her friends and work colleagues from her address book. I think Cain must have found an empty house, or maybe a closed down factory or warehouse to hole up in."

"If that's true, we're fucked," Barney said, stooping and crushing out the cigarette he'd been smoking on the inside of the metal waste bin next to his desk, before immediately lighting another.

"You're chain-smoking, boss," Mike said.

Barney just glared.

"I'll keep on it," Mike said as he retreated back through the door, to return to the squad room.

Mike had been close to Gary Shields. They had been firm friends from way back, when they had roomed together at the training school in Hendon. Should the opportunity arise, Mike had made the decision that he would forsake his career for just five minutes alone in a cell with Cain, when the psycho was apprehended. The killer needed some of his own medicine. Sod right and wrong. Mike wanted a large portion of good old-fashioned revenge. Prison was too good for the likes of Cain. The best he could do for Gary and all the other victims was to paralyse Cain from the neck down. Spending the rest of his life as a quadriplegic might concentrate his mind to the fact that there were worse things than being incarcerated and coddled behind bars. The pressure within Mike had to be released. He picked up his coffee mug and hurled it at the wall. It shattered, and shards of pot showered the top of a filing cabinet and bounced off on to the floor, as the coffee fanned out and ran down the wall; brown rivulets on once white emulsion. He didn't feel any better for the physical expression of his overwrought emotions, and none of the other team members in the room said a word. Mike's action reflected how they all felt; angry, exasperated, and almost choked with a need to get their hands on the psycho that had murdered Gary.

CHAPTER THIRTY-SEVEN

"You're going to die now, you bitch," Bobby lisped through his torn and swelling bottom lip; his voice harsh and gruff, due to the blow that had struck his throat.

His hands locked on to Amy's neck, and his thick fingers sank into the flesh, cutting off her air supply.

Her heartbeat raged in her ears; the pulsing of ventrium and atrium pounding so loud within her skull that all thought was nullified by the booming, echoing resonance. Red motes appeared, dancing in front of her eyes, and a growing enervation robbed her muscles of all strength.

I will not die like this, Amy's mind screamed in defiance, and she summoned up the last ounce of her depleted vigour, to snap her head up and back, to hear a loud crack as Cain's nose fractured under the impact.

His hands disengaged from her throat to cradle the new source of pain, and she scuttled crab-like, sideways, out from under him, then flipped over, coughing, fighting to push back the greyness that threatened to overcome her.

He was knelt, an eerie keening issuing from his bloody mouth as he tried to contain the fresh agony.

With no hesitation whatsoever, Amy snatched the tall and heavy bedside lamp from the top of the cabinet next to the bed, and with a sweeping round-house swing brought the oak base full force against the side of his head. He keeled over and was still. But his eyes were wide open; black, staring, blood-chilling.

Lifting the gun from where it lay on the carpet, Amy crawled back out of range, climbed shakily to her feet and levelled the weapon at his head. Her hands shook as the silenced barrel wavered on and off target. It was not easy to kill someone in cold blood. She took up the small amount of slack on the trigger, ground her teeth together and determined to finish it and be done with him; to end it there and then. If he had been conscious, still attacking her, then she would not have faltered in emptying the pistol into him. But to premeditatedly execute a defenceless, unconscious man, however evil she knew him to be, was an act beyond her capability. Tears of frustration ran down her cheeks as she lowered the pistol.

He groaned, and she fled from the bedroom, paused for a second outside the door, and then went up the stairs to the top of the house, not down to the ground floor. She knew that he was coming around, and that he would no doubt rush after her when he was able, expecting her to run out into the street and call for help.

On the top landing, Amy looked up at the trapdoor to the loft. She needed stepladders to climb up to it, and they were out in the garage. But where there's a will there's a way. Climbing up on to the bannister rail, she was able to stretch out, reach the hatch and push it up and backwards one-handed without losing balance and falling. Tossing the handgun up into the gloom, she then somehow found the strength to grip the edge of the frame with both hands and lever herself up after it. Within ninety seconds of having left the bedroom, she was huddled in the darkness of the loft, next to the hissing water tank, her bare back against the cobwebbed bricks, with the gun pointing at the now closed trapdoor.

Blink.

Where was he? He moaned aloud and the pain from his groin, throat, nose, head, wrist and mouth brought back images of the dire struggle that he had evidently lost.

There was no time to nurse his wounds. He looked around for the gun, but there was no sign of it. No surprise there. He had no idea how long he had been unconscious, or in the grip of a fugue. The bitch would have called the police. They may already be outside, approaching the house, or inside, on the stairs, armed and trigger-happy. All he could do was attempt to escape, and hope that only seconds had elapsed, not minutes.

In a fit of near hysteria and fuelled by savage ferocity, he ignored the combined pains that caused a greasy nausea to swirl in his stomach and chest and made his way down the stairs, reeling from side-to-side like a drunken sailor on a rolling ship, to go out through the kitchen and head back to the car, expecting to hear the sirens of police vehicles with every step he took.

He reached the car and drove away from the scene. Opened the glove compartment and removed a handful of tissues from the box inside, to clamp against his nose and mouth, which were still bleeding profusely.

What the fuck was happening? One minute he had been in total control, with the bitch almost naked and at gunpoint in front of him.

She had been shaking with fear, begging him not to hurt her. They had been kissing, thrusting against each other. Everything had been going just fine, and he had been only seconds away from screwing her stupid against the wardrobe. And then she had almost fucking killed him. His injuries were to say the least painful, but not life-threatening. He ascertained that his nose was definitely broken, his bottom lip felt like chopped liver, and his balls ached, on fire, sending tines of agony up into his stomach. His wrist was pounding and his head splitting. He was in a deep, dark place and needed to return to the houseboat, tend to his wounds and get some rest.

In the aftermath of the violent struggle – which had resulted in him being knocked unconscious and simultaneously suffering one of his episodes – he had no memory whatsoever of telling Amy, in passing, that Caroline was on Payne's houseboat. Unbeknown to him, Amy knew his hideout, as did Mark, following his phone call to Payne.

She grunted and came awake shivering and sore. Her throat was swollen and tender, and the muscles in her back were contracted and aching from the collision with the wardrobe.

Myriad beams of light shone through small gaps in the tiles and pinprick holes in the roofing felt above, reminding her of stars on a trip she had once made to the Planetarium. Making her way across to the trapdoor, she eased it open a fraction, saw that the landing was clear, and lowered herself down, to drop to the carpet in a crouch. If Cain was still unconscious on the bedroom floor, she would tie him up and then call Barney. If he had gone, she would still call Barney and tell him what she now knew. She had let panic take the reins and had fled when she could have ended it. Hard to imagine that she had been a copper. She had acted more like a frightened schoolgirl; should have bound Cain up when the chance presented itself. It had been an opportunity thrown away.

Slowly, edging down to the first floor with the gun held out two-handed in front of her, its barrel moving in coordination with her eyes, she approached the bedroom door, summoned up the courage and kicked it open.

He was gone. She followed a trail of blood that showed his passage, down the stairs, into the kitchen and out through the back door.

Still holding the gun, Amy lifted the phone, then paused as she saw the Post-it pad and recognised Mark's handwriting: Pandora, Bridge Lane, Laleham.

Jesus! Mark must have returned while she was in the loft, and after Cain had left. He had obviously called someone, and written down the address of Payne's houseboat. What had Mark thought? That Cain had taken her? Of course. The blood, and the lamp with its cord ripped from the wall the shade crumpled and bulb broken. He had seen the evidence and come to the wrong conclusion.

Dropping the phone, Amy ran back upstairs, planning as she dressed, ignoring the drying blood that had run down her body from the cut to her chin. She knew that Mark would be heading for Laleham, and not in a cool, dispassionate and professional state of mind, but with a sense of urgency that might make him reckless. She was tuned-in to how he thought. He would not have phoned Barney; wouldn't risk her life by putting Cain's back against a wall with nowhere to go and nothing to lose.

She drove fast but carefully, concentrating on holding her emotions together, fighting the panic and instinctively slipping back into police mode. She reached within herself and found a measure of the cool composure that had made her a good, hard-arsed vice cop. The gun, ugly but reassuring, was on the rubber mat between her feet with a bullet chambered, ready to go.

The cold water made him cry out as he rinsed the blood from his nose, mouth and wrist. He gently patted the wounds dry with a towel and then searched the units and drawers until he found a well-stocked first-aid box. After gingerly applying iodine with a wad of cotton wool – which made his eyes water as the yellow antiseptic burned into raw flesh – he used butterfly stitches to hold his torn lip in place, and finally bandaged his bitten wrist, before going aft to check on Caroline.

She raised her head, and her eyes widened at the sight of his puffy, discoloured face. A blow that had obviously broken his nose had given rise to swollen purple bruising that had also blackened and slitted his eyes. She thought he looked like a boxer; how Stallone had appeared at the end of most of his Rocky movies, after receiving a brutal pummelling before ultimately being victorious.

As he studied Caroline's naked body, Bobby suddenly wanted things to be as he had once envisaged. A part of him craved a normal life. He could imagine his Caroline framed by sweet-smelling climbing roses, standing in the doorway of a picturesque country cottage, welcoming him home from work, and maybe cradling their child in her arms. That was what he *really* wanted and believed he deserved. Could he make that dream come true?

He went to her and used his knife to cut the tape away from her mouth.

"W... What happened to you?" she said, having decided that in a bid to live, she would offer him the illusion of unswerving affection and obedience.

"It doesn't matter," he mumbled, talking without moving his lips a fraction more than absolutely necessary, like a ventriloquist. "Do you need anything?"

"I need to go to the bathroom," she said. And to her surprise he untied the ropes that bound her wrists and ankles.

"Go on, then," he said. "But leave the door open. And don't do anything that would make me hurt you, Caroline."

"I won't, I promise," she said, rubbing her wrists, which throbbed with pins and needles as the circulation returned to her hands. She climbed off the bed and hobbled past him; her feet almost unfeeling. He seemed different. His mood had changed, and an unexpected melancholy and gentleness in his manner gave her renewed hope. His bruised eyes said it all. The bottom line was that in his own warped way he really *did* love her. If that all-powerful emotion wasn't enough to use as a weapon against him, then nothing else would be.

In the bathroom she relieved herself, washed with scented soap, cleaned her teeth and brushed her hair. Finished, she stood at the open door and waited for him to tell her what to do.

"Put a robe or something on," he said, speaking from where he was now seated in the gloom. "Then make some coffee for us both. And if you're hungry, get something. But no lights."

She went back into the bedroom, took a silk kimono from the wardrobe – a gift from Simon – and slipped it on, then returned to the spacious saloon.

"You remind me of my mother," he said, a wistful quality to his voice. "As she looked when I was a young boy. She's dead now."

"I'm sorry," Caroline said.

"No, I don't think you are," he said, the trace of a pained smile on his face. "You're understandably too preoccupied with your own predicament to give a shit about my mother, my life, or anything else. But please don't patronise me, or I'll have to tie you up and gag you again."

"Why do you hate me so much, Robert?" she said. "What did I do to make you so angry?"

He stared at her for an age before answering. "I tried to reach out, to be close to you. But you made it quite clear that I wasn't good enough for you. I cared for you, and...and wanted your friendship; to be a part of your life, and you treated me with disdain. You made me feel unworthy, and I realised that you were just the same as all women; a taker."

"That's not true," she said. "I was in a relationship. I had no idea how you felt. And I certainly didn't think that you weren't good enough. If I upset you unknowingly, then I'm truly sorry."

"That's easy to say, now. But it's too late, Caroline."

"Why is it?"

"Because there's nowhere for us to go, to be together. And I could never trust you."

"I can start afresh, if you can," she said.

"Make the coffee," he said. "I need to think."

She made them both a mug of instant coffee and then went to sit next to him, as though they were a couple and not two individuals; one a gaoler, the other a prisoner.

"This is nice," Bobby said, sipping his milky drink through the left side of his mouth, which was not as damaged as the right. "Hold my hand."

Caroline reached out, took his hand in hers and imagined that she was role-playing; acting out a part in a play. Whatever she might do to try to save herself, she would deem as not being reality, but the enactment of a script. She would have to become a character that was separate and apart from the real Caroline Sellars. And the performance would have to be of BAFTA winning quality, or he would see through it and no doubt punish her severely.

After a while, Bobby put the mug down and leant his head on her shoulder. She could feel his whole body shaking slightly; Robert Cain, the Park Killer was crying.

Putting her arm around him, Caroline held him close, rested her cheek against his bald head, and prayed long and hard for a miracle to happen.

After a while, he raised his face and looked into her eyes, searching them, plumbing their depths. In them, he saw fear, but also compassion. She did *not* hate him. Could it be that she understood that it had been his love for her that had caused him to strike out at others, rather than harm her? God she was so beautiful, and now she would belong to him, forever, however long that might last. He needed a plan, but was tired, hurting and could not concentrate. Maybe it would be better if he just cut her throat now, then his own wrists, to end it all in the peace and quietude. That might be the only way for them to stay together.

CHAPTER THIRTY-EIGHT

It was bitterly cold and almost dark. The waiting had been a necessary ordeal, but Mark was now on the move, keeping low as he covered the last few yards towards the houseboat. He had begun to lose hope. There were no lights or sounds or sign of life to suggest that the craft was inhabited. And then he saw a car parked in the shadows and doubt was replaced with the conviction that his initial suspicion was well-founded.

The moment was nearing when he would meet Cain face to face. Mark's whole being was now charged with deadly intent. He looked at the ground around him, found a heavy length of windblown tree branch and hurled it through the air with the action of a circus knife thrower. The gnarled limb pin-wheeled end over end and crashed into the bonnet of the car as Mark stepped aboard the houseboat as lightly as possible and made his way forward, to where he expected the cabin door would be located. When Cain came out to investigate the noise, he would strike swift and hard with the raised tyre iron that he held.

Bobby's head snapped sideways at the loud sound, and without a word he pushed Caroline down, beneath the table, withdrew a set of handcuffs from a pocket and once more cuffed her to the single central leg.

"Not one sound," he whispered, and then moved away from her towards the door.

No response. Mark took shallow sips of breath through his mouth. Had Cain stolen another car and moved on, with the two women bound and gagged in the boot? Or were Amy and Caroline inside, and dead?

He waited and then edged forward to the corner of the cabin, bending low to look around it, so as not to present himself at an expected height.

Nothing.

Using his left hand, he pushed the edge of the sliding door, and it began to move. Why wasn't it locked? But then, Cain would have no reason to lock it when he left.

Still no sound or movement from the darkness within. His adrenaline rush began to recede. He now thought he had made a mistake. Cain was not here. He wouldn't have been stupid enough to use a refuge that could be linked to Caroline through Payne. It had been too much to hope for, and the sickening sense of disappointment crushed him. But no, he caught the aroma of coffee escaping from the cabin, a fraction of a second too late.

The door squealed back on its runners, and something dropped over his head, to be drawn tightly around his neck and immediately begin to choke him. He struggled, lashed out with the tyre iron, but was hauled forward, face down into the saloon.

Dropping the weighty tool, Mark put both hands to his neck and felt the rope that was biting into it, but could not find space to insert his fingers to relieve the crushing force.

I'm about to die! The words screamed through his mind as the pressure on his carotid arteries cut off the blood supply to his brain, causing the world to spin, to carry him down, rushing at dizzying speed into a bottomless pit.

Amy's heart skipped as her headlights swept across the rear of Mark's Cherokee. It was parked on a wide grass verge, nose in, up against a mass of thorny bushes. She pulled in next to it, got out and tucked the handgun under the waistband of her jeans, then zipped up her blouson.

Taking her time, she moved furtively along the lane, approaching each houseboat in turn, to check the names on their hulls.

Pandora. She sucked in her breath. She had found it. Now what? Fear pricked her, and the scar tissue on her stomach actually hurt and began to itch and burn as though a stinging nettle had been pressed up against it. Closing her eyes, she took deep breaths and remembered an old quote: 'Courage is resistance to fear, mastery of fear– not absence of fear'. She would harness the negative qualms that threatened to immobilise her, and convert them into positive action. She had the advantage. Cain did not expect her.

Shedding the bulky blouson, she stepped into the river and waded out around the side of the houseboat with one hand resting on the edge of the deck for balance, with the other now holding the gun above the water's surface; water so cold that it penetrated her bones and sapped all feeling from her legs. Clinging mud sucked both of her trainers off after just three steps. She pushed on, then lost her footing and slipped back, down under the surface. The frigid water took her breath away. She regained her feet and fought against the urge to cough and splutter aloud.

Low, muffled male voices carried through the cabin's wall, but the words were unintelligible. Mark would not be talking to Cain in the dark. The only explanation was that Mark was in trouble, and that Cain had got the better of him.

Another few laboured steps and Amy came to an opening in the railing that edged the deck. The houseboat sat low in the water, and although awkward, she managed to ease herself up on to it, turn, swing her legs inboard, and then stand without causing any noticeable movement to the substantial floating home. Creeping forward, she was consumed by self doubt. Could she gain entry, identify Cain in the murk and shoot him without risk to Mark? Should she back off now, call Barney and wait for the cavalry to arrive? And what if Cain killed Mark in the meantime? The bottom line was that she had no alternative but to go it alone. She would have to draw on the ruthless side of her personality and rely on her basic instincts. She could not afford to let emotion get in the way. Cain was injured. She had faced him once and outsmarted him. And now she had the gun, and would not hesitate to use it this time. Pumping herself up, she visualised what was about to take place. She would enter fast and low, search out the shape of Cain, who was smaller and broader than Mark, and empty the magazine into him.

On three, she thought, hand now on the handle of the tempered glass door, which was open a couple of inches. One...two...

CHAPTER THIRTY-NINE

"We've got two possibilities, boss," Mike said as he strode into the office brandishing a single sheet of paper.

"What?" Barney said, tossing a file that they had compiled on Cain to one side.

"A fellow producer at the Beeb, Marsha Reynolds, is an old friend of Caroline's. She owns a holiday cottage outside the village of Bank in the New Forest. She says that Caroline has visited it several times in the past and spent weekends there."

"What else?"

"The boyfriend, Simon Payne."

"Christ, I'd almost forgotten he existed."

"He has a houseboat on the river at Laleham. Eddie gave him a call, and Payne asked if the left hand knew what the right was doing. He said that DS Mike Cook had phoned him earlier, asking him if he owned property near water, or had a boat. And I didn't phone him."

"Who would...? Ross would," Barney said, answering his own question as it took shape in his mind. "It has to have been Mark Ross. Why in God's name would he elect to go after Cain by himself?"

Mike shrugged.

"Get on the blower to Hampshire CID, Mike. Give them the address of that cottage, and tell them who might be there, and all relevant details. Then give Amy Egan a bell. If you can't get hold of her, have the nearest unit check out her address. I'll try to locate Ross."

"You think—"

"I think Cain's on the houseboat. I'll jack up some firepower, and we'll go find out. I also have a bad feeling about Amy. Ross wouldn't have gone it alone without a damn good reason."

Barney and Mike worked the phones. They couldn't contact Mark or Amy. When he was almost set to head for Laleham, Barney gave Pearce a call, to bring him up to speed and tell him what he intended to do.

"You're implying that you may be faced with a multiple hostage scenario, am I right?" Clive said.

"Yes. I think that it's as bad as it gets. Cain may be holding Caroline Sellars, Amy Egan, and possibly Mark Ross. He could have already killed them all. I can't contact Mark or Amy."

"What's our best chance of salvaging something out of this, Barney?"

"Initially, I'm putting the houseboat under surveillance. We can use a laser mike to ascertain who, if anybody, is on board."

"Then?"

"Make contact and try to negotiate, if Cain is on board and holding hostages. I also intend to give the ARU team leader the green light to take Cain out the second an opportunity presents itself. We're dealing with a maniac who is now in possession of a handgun. And we know exactly what he's capable of doing."

"You don't think he might have gone to ground at the Hampshire address, then?"

"No. All my money is on the Laleham location."

"And you expect casualties?"

"With any luck, just one."

"Okay. I want to know what you know, five seconds after it happens."

"I'll keep you briefed," Barney said before hanging up.

"We've got a probable crime scene at Richmond, boss," Mike said after taking a call from the Surrey constabulary. "Someone broke into Ms Egan's house. There was plenty of blood, but no body. And they found the name of Payne's houseboat scribbled on a notepad."

"Let's hope we can get there in time. And that when we do, we can make a difference," Barney said as he frantically twisted his wedding band.

They left the office on the run, coats flapping in their slipstream; shades of Batman and Robin in civvies.

Mark's consciousness returned slowly. He was face down against the carpeting, and he was gasping for breath, with pressure still around his neck.

"Try not to move too much, Dr Mark," a voice said from somewhere behind him. "There's a rope from your neck to your ankles. I'm sure you get the picture. If you try to straighten your legs, you'll top yourself. Understand?"

"Yeah. Not very original, but effective," Mark croaked, gauging the tension of the rope as a hand withdrew from his ankles and he felt the noose tighten. He transferred his weight and fell over on to his side, letting the floor assist in keeping his legs drawn up in a position that afforded a certain amount of slack in the rope.

In the semi-darkness he could see Caroline. She was crouched under a table, attached to it by handcuffs. Looking up, to her left, he saw Cain for the first time. The man was sitting on an upholstered bench seat, leaning forward with his forearms on his knees. A wicked looking knife dangled loosely from one hand. He stared back at Mark; the large, black irises of his eyes as reflective as mirrored sunglasses, showing nothing of the spirit or state of mind that lurked behind them.

"Where's Amy?" Mark said, ignoring the painful sensation of broken glass in his throat that talking generated.

"Good question," Bobby said. "But you're the smart-aleck profiler. You tell me."

"I found her blood, you—"

"You found *my* fucking blood, Yank. Your bitch went berserk and almost fucking killed me," Bobby raved. He leapt to his feet, took a step forward and kicked Mark viciously in the stomach.

Mark's cry died in his throat as his legs jerked involuntarily, causing the noose to bite deep, robbing him of his lifeline to air.

The knife blade flashed, cut through the strands and opened a shallow two-inch long gash in Mark's neck as the rope parted.

Gasping, Mark straightened out on the floor. His ankles were still bound, as were his wrists, behind him, but he was no longer totally helpless. A ray of hope shone through the dark clouds of despair.

"Don't move a muscle, you insignificant, small-minded wanker," Bobby said. "You'll die soon enough, without rushing it. Tell me how you found out that I was here."

"It was easy. I just followed the raw smell of sewage, and here I am," Mark said, hoping that Cain would attack him again; ready to kick out and take his chances against the knife. Doing nothing wouldn't save himself or Caroline. He had to somehow disconcert and throw his enemy off balance.

Bobby smiled, before ducking down and running the blade of his knife along Caroline's arm, shallowly slitting it from just below the shoulder to the wrist. Blood seeped through the flimsy material of her Kimono and dripped on to the carpet. She gasped in pain, and tears glittered in her eyes.

"Wrong answer, dickhead," Bobby said. "Try again, and bear in mind that Caroline gets to lose an ear next, if you get comical or call me names."

Mark had just lost another psychological round on points, and knew it.

"I worked out that you hadn't planned on having to run. And that being a fucking sociopath; a loner with no friends, you wouldn't have anywhere to go," he said. "It seemed logical that you might ask Caroline if she knew somewhere that would be safe. I gave her boyfriend a call, and he told me that he owned this houseboat."

"Who else knows about it?" Bobby said.

Mark could have lied and said that the police knew, and that they were on their way. But that might just panic Cain and bring things to a head too quickly. He needed to buy as much time as possible in an attempt to try to turn things around. All that was in his favour was Cain's contempt for everyone, and his need to flaunt what he thought to be a superior intellect. The guy needed an audience to play to, whether he realised it or not.

"No one," Mark said. "I thought you had Amy as well as Caroline. I didn't want to risk their lives by having half the Met joining the party."

Bobby chuckled. "You thought you would just be able to sneak up and blind side me, huh? You didn't give me any credit or respect, Ross. You overestimated your piss-poor capabilities, and now you get to suffer and die for your amour propre."

"Your time will come, Cain, and soon."

"Death doesn't hold any fear for me. I find a certain degree of solace at the thought of nonexistence, with no awareness. It's life that is the vexation. Take it away and you remove all misery, pain, regrets, unfulfilled dreams, and the sadness of shattered expectations. Death is a release from suffering; a door to oblivion. Being born is the punishment; the beginning of a long, hard struggle along a road strewn with rocks."

"Very eloquent, Cain. I take it you don't believe in a final judgement? You have some smart-ass way of knowing that you won't be condemned to eternal purgatory for the unforgivable, barbaric acts that you've committed?"

"Shut the fuck up."

"No, Cain. Why should I? You can't threaten a dead man. You're going to torture and kill Caroline and me whatever I say. I bet you pulled wings off flies, and then graduated to mutilating neighbourhood pets when you were a kid. You're a sad, brain-damaged little fucker, who has never known love. You can't..."

"SHUT UP! SHUT UP!"

"...stand to be in a world where other people can find a happiness that you haven't the power to tap in to. You should have been stillborn for your own and everyone else's sake. You're a disease, Cain; one that has the ability to kill, but is itself condemned by its own malignance."

Bobby felt the blood throbbing at his temples as the psychologist reviled him. He allowed hate in its purest form to bubble up and fill his brain. He would gag Ross, then make his last minutes of life an experience of heretofore unrivalled agony. The man would suffer unimaginable fear and pain before he finally died.

Mark saw that Cain was readying himself to attack. The knife shook in his white-knuckled grip, and a tic in his swollen left eyelid was reminiscent of the exaggerated wink of a kerbside whore.

Blink.

Something was wrong.

All expression instantly drained from Cain's face. He became totally calm and impassive. His eyes were still fixed on Mark's, wide open now, and flat, glazed looking. It was as if he had entered a state of serenity and composure that a Tibetan monk might spend a lifetime attempting to achieve. He appeared to be unfazed, in total control of his emotions. But it was no more than an illusion. To dispel it, his mouth gaped open, his head fell forward, and it became apparent that something was very off beam.

"He...he's having some sort of seizure," Caroline whispered. "He's like a television set on standby."

"Can you hear me?" Mark said to Cain.

No reply. The man was inert, reminding him of a lizard basking on a rock in the morning sun; needing to warm its sluggish blood before it could function properly.

Mark eased himself up on to his knees and then shuffled across the floor to the table and ducked under it, turning so that his bound wrists faced Caroline. She reached forward, as far as the cuffs would allow, and began to pick at the knot without needing to be asked.

Her tongue curled out over her bottom lip as she squinted at the intertwining tangle of rope and concentrated fully on which part of it should be worked on to loosen it. And as she frantically worked at the assemblage, breaking fingernails on the tough sisal, Mark looked up from underneath the table, his attention wholly on their captor. There was movement. Cain was flicking the blade of his knife back and forth across the back of his left hand, striping it with superficial cuts that flowed with blood as he unconsciously mutilated himself.

"Yesss!" Caroline said in a triumphant whisper. The rope loosened, and Mark pulled his hands free. He could not risk taking more time to untie his ankles. Rolling away from Caroline and standing up, he looked around for a weapon. A small fire extinguisher was clipped to a wall bracket that was screwed to the side of a unit. With his feet still pinioned together, he hopped over to it, amazed that even in such a dangerous situation a part of him could feel foolish at his lame-assed 'Skippy the bush kangaroo' impression. Pulling the extinguisher free, he turned...to find Cain lurching to his feet, in the same instant that Caroline cried, "Look out!"

He had planned to hit Cain over the head full force with the heavy metal cylinder, to brain the bastard and not worry unduly as to how much physical damage he might inflict. But now, as his adversary lumbered towards him, he pulled the locking pin free and depressed the lever as he aimed the extinguisher's nozzle directly at Cain's face.

The white, chemical stream found its mark, but not in time to stop the blade of the knife from sinking into Mark's side. He felt the steel grate against his ribs, and the piercing barb of pain made him double up, to lose balance and crash forward over the table, before rolling off it to impact with the floor.

Bobby was temporarily blinded and began to retch, fighting for breath as the poisonous mix of chemicals filled his open mouth and was inhaled into his lungs. He lashed out with the knife, sweeping the blade back and forth in every direction, unable to see Mark or anything else, but still hoping to connect with flesh and bone as he blinked frantically and rubbed at his sore eyes with his free hand.

Caroline saw a small window of opportunity open as Cain fell back against the sink unit, gagging and wiping at the mass of foam that swathed his head. As Mark hit the tabletop, the handcuff keys were dislodged. They fell to the carpet in front of her. Using her right foot, she dragged them to within reach of her hands, and with shaking, fumbling fingers, managed to find the small keyhole and release her wrists from the ratcheted cuffs.

Glancing at Mark, Caroline saw a trickle of blood running down his face from a gash on his temple. He was moaning and badly dazed, having caught his head on the corner of the walnut frame that the seat and back cushions of the bench were affixed to.

"Wake up, please wake up...Help me," she pleaded, shaking Mark, then pulling her hand back from his jacket as warm blood coated her hand. She was on her own. Mark had been stabbed and was wounded; maybe even dying.

"You bitch," Bobby wheezed, now able to see the blurry, distorted image of Caroline crawling out from beneath the table. "It's over. I'm going to cut your rotten heart out and hold it in front of your eyes. It will be the last thing you see before you die."

Gripping her by the hair, he pulled backwards, so that she fell, to lay face up, legs trapped under her. For a few seconds, as the kimono fell open, Bobby blinked rapidly, and though his sight was still impaired, he studied the indistinct, exquisite body beneath him, and looked into her fear-filled eyes to feel an overpowering sadness at the sense of loss he knew would overwhelm him when she was gone. The dream of what might have been was over before it had begun.

Tears of sorrow further misted his vision as he drew back the knife.

CHAPTER FORTY

"**Stop**," Barney said as he spotted the rear ends of the vehicles protruding out of the foliage.

Mike braked, pulled up on to the wide grass verge and skidded to a halt just inches from the Cherokee. The innocuous looking Transit van, that had been following, parked behind him, and several black-clad figures emerged from its side; stubby automatic rifles held close to their Kevlar-protected bodies.

"Those cars belong to Ross and Egan," Barney informed the team leader, who then nodded to two of his men, prompting them to move in and check the Jeep Cherokee and Nissan. Using a lock gun, they entered both vehicles, satisfied themselves that they were unoccupied, then signalled 'all clear' and withdrew.

A few minutes later the Pandora was covered on all but the river side by the Armed Response Unit.

"It always sends a shiver up my spine to see these guys at work," Mike said to Barney, following him to a position under the cover of trees at the far side of the lane. "It's like a Darth Vader convention, all tooled-up with Heckler & Koch's instead of light sabres."

The team – wearing infrared night sight goggles – operated in total silence, using hand signals to communicate as they closed in on the houseboat. The officers had been given a description of Cain and Mark Ross. The plan was simple. Once in position, they would throw a flash grenade into the dark cabin to blind anyone on board, and then storm the craft and shoot Cain on sight.

Barney had decided that to attempt negotiating with the killer was a luxury he could not afford to do. He believed that given warning of a police presence, Cain would execute his hostages without hesitation. The operation was now fully under the command of the ARU leader, who was trained to contain a situation by eliminating its root cause.

...Three, Amy thought, throwing the door back one-handed, before adopting a shooter's stance; her right hand holding the pistol cupped in her left, and the left side of her body slightly forward of the right. She entered the cabin and moved to her left, so as not to be silhouetted against the ambient light of the evening sky.

Bobby reacted fast, somehow staying the descent of the knife, he pulled Caroline up on to her knees in front of him as a shield, hunkering down behind her and holding the edge of the blade firmly pressed against her neck, just below her left ear.

Amy found her target a split second too late. She could not risk taking the shot. Cain was too obscured by Caroline, and there was no guarantee of being able to hit him in the gloomy surroundings.

"Welcome aboard, Amy," Bobby said, his voice like gravel, due to the tissue of his throat doubly inflamed by the blow to it, and the chemicals he had breathed in. "As you can see, we started without you. But better late than never. Toss the gun over to me by the butt, or I'll cut sweet Caroline's throat from ear to ear."

Behind Cain, Amy could see Mark slumped on the floor, facing her. She saw everything in slow motion, almost like individual photos being shown as a slideshow on a computer screen. Mark's fleece had ridden up almost to his chest, and the light-coloured sweatshirt beneath it was covered in a dark bloodstain. She couldn't tell if he was alive or dead. She wanted to run to him, check for a pulse, and summon an ambulance.

"Get fucking real, Cain," she said, her voice loaded with venom that only the strongest cocktail of fear, anger and hatred could produce. "I don't have the time to listen to your threats. Use the knife and I'll have no reason not to empty this gun into you."

"You're bluffing, bitch," he said. But he could see the truth of her words in both the stony expression on her face and the intensity in her eyes.

"Unless you're totally brain dead, you must know that blowing your head off would make my fucking day," she said.

"Shoot him!" Caroline cried out, twisting sideways, away from the knife.

As Amy's finger tightened on the trigger, and an instant before the SIG spat a bullet at Cain, the interior of the houseboat exploded in brilliant, all-encompassing light, which seared her retinas with brightness she imagined to be ten times more powerful than that of a camera's flash gun.

Bobby leapt forward as Caroline moved. The slug punched a channel through the air next to his head, and as he slammed into Amy, blinded by the explosion of light that robbed him of sight, he gripped her in a bear hug and his momentum carried them both out through the open door, across the narrow deck and over the low guard-rail, into the dark, icy waters.

"Go...go...go!" the team leader whispered into a lip-mike, and the shadowy figures boarded the craft, their helmet visors down as the leading officer lobbed the flash-bang through the partly open door. A second following the effusion of light that floodlit the cabin, and also the low bark of a silenced gunshot, two figures teetered out on to the deck as though in a lovers' embrace, to topple over the rounded prow of the houseboat's hull.

Amy kicked out and clawed at Cain's face as they hit the water. They struggled beneath the surface, weighted down by their now sodden clothing.

She was drowning, and knew it. Her lungs cramped with the amount of water that she had sucked in, and her will to survive was diminished. She ceased to fight, and through a fog, over Cain's right shoulder, the small figure of a child appeared. It was Darren, her dead son, smiling and beckoning to her from the radiant glow that he was suspended in.

The pressure in her chest increased, and she was tantalisingly close to opening her mouth and inhaling for what would be the last time. On the brink of having to gulp for air that was not there, Cain released her, and with a supreme last-ditch effort she propelled herself towards the golden apparition of her late son, upwards, with limbs that felt too heavy to obey her muddled brain's instructions. Like a runner stretching forward to cross the finish line, she thrust her face up into air, but was jerked back down; an unseen hand around her ankle. She kicked out instinctively, felt something solid give beneath her foot, and was at once free again.

Amy came to her senses laying face down, head turned to the side. She was coughing water out on to the grass. A helmeted officer knelt at her side, pumping her back with his hands.

"Mark?" she spluttered.

"Dr Ross is being stabilised," the officer said.

Barney was squatting down in her line of sight, lighting a cigarette, his face ashen and etched with concern.

"What happened, Barney?" Amy gasped, twisting over and pushing herself up into a sitting position, to wrap her arms around her aching chest.

"Mark got himself stabbed, but he'll be okay. It looks worse than it is," Barney said, hoping that he was right. "Caroline is in a state of shock and has a nasty cut on her arm, but will be fine. Cain is missing."

"Missing?"

"You both went overboard, and only you came up. We're searching for him now."

"I took a shot at him," Amy said. "But I don't know whether I hit him or not. Somebody turned floodlights on and blinded me."

"It was a flash grenade," the officer by her side said.

"Dead or alive, we'll find him," Barney said, taking a long drag from his cigarette, before dropping it on the grass and crushing it underfoot. "We've got divers and a helicopter on the way. I'm hoping the bastard did us all a favour and drowned."

CHAPTER FORTY-ONE

Bobby lost his grip on Amy. He made a grab for her as she rose to the surface, grasped her by the ankle, but was kicked off. His desperate need to breathe forced him to let her get away from him. He swam powerfully under the water, ignoring the compulsion to surface and relieve his pounding lungs, which were starved of oxygen. He eventually surfaced, drew in a single deep draught of sweet, cool air, got his bearings and then ducked back underwater and headed out into the swift flowing river.

Each time he surfaced, torch beams were searching for him, sweeping the black waters. But he was not seen. His luck held, and going with the strong current and keeping close to the far bank, he was soon a long way from the houseboat and the police that were hunting for him.

Finding his feet on the muddy bottom, Bobby waded ashore, gripping the pilings of a small jetty to keep his balance as the soft mud clung to his legs. In front of him was a beer garden at the rear of a country pub. Shivering and suffering from the numerous injuries and the effects of the blast from the fire extinguisher, he fell to his knees, crawled up on to the bank and lay on the damp grass for a few minutes to recover his breath and muster the strength to go on. All he wanted to do was curl up and escape into sleep.

Blink.

He came out of the trance, seizure or whatever the fuck it was with new resolve. In some way the mental break had worked like a battery charger. He felt infused with new strength and determination.

Rising in a crouch, he made his way over to a high brick wall that bordered a long lawn. Keeping close to the wall, he scurried like a half-drowned rat scampering through a sewer. The Thames was reputedly cleaner than it had been in decades, with a burgeoning fish population; even wayward dolphins and whales had been sighted on several occasions in recent years. But the stink of his sodden clothes from the muddy water contradicted that finding.

The sound of laughter and music drifted from the open rear door of the pub, so he veered away from the building to a gate that led from the garden into an ill-lit car park at its side. He staggered from vehicle to vehicle, eventually found an unlocked Audi, and paused to give his predicament some thought. He felt vulnerable. He now had to improvise and dig himself out of a mess, without having the luxury of being able to plan in advance. If he was to have any chance of evading capture, then he would have to think clearly and foresee the actions of his enemies. His first impulse was to hot-wire the car and drive away. But no, he could not risk the chance of being stopped at a police roadblock. They may believe that he had drowned, but would seal off the area on the off chance that he had survived. He would only make good his getaway if he outthought them and kept calm. If the game was to continue, which it must, then he had to outmanoeuvre the slow-moving, witless plods who were hell-bent on ending it.

Exiting the car, he closed the driver's door and went to the rear. He was freezing, and hurting from head to foot, but ignored the discomfort and put it out of his mind. There would be time enough to worry about his physical condition when he had found a suitable place to lie low and recuperate. His sight was the main cause of concern. The compound from the fire-extinguisher had fucked up his vision. Everything appeared to be on the other side of a thin sheet of dirty ice, distorted and blurred. Hopefully, the river water – polluted or not– may have diluted the chemicals in time to save his eyes from any permanent damage.

He opened the boot, climbed in, pulled the lid down until he heard the lock mechanism click into place, and then curled into a foetal position and waited in the pitch-black metal womb of the car.

The slamming doors woke him from a dream in which he was chasing a naked female runner around Nelson's Column in Trafalgar Square. He was also naked, wielding a sharpened branch, and was gaining on his prey. Her mouth was open and she was screaming, but could not be heard above the noise of traffic and the chatter of tourists. He and his quarry were in a world a fraction out of sync with their surroundings. He could pass through people, and they were unaware of his presence. Only the concrete under his feet was solid. Increasing his pace, he reached out, grasped the prey by its flowing red hair, and pulled. The woman lost her footing. Her feet shot forward, and she left the ground in the same way that someone slipping on a banana skin would go down. Her back hit the unyielding grey paving stones with a loud smack. He knelt in front of her, and made ready to impale her, only to find that his short ash wood spear had become a bouquet of red roses. The young redhead began to laugh at him, as her features rearranged into those of his late mother.

The absurdity of dreams was their attraction. It did not occur to him that in reality it would be ludicrous to be in this position. He could smell the roses, hear the masses of pigeons cooing, despite all efforts to banish them from the square, and could see the corpses of his prior victims shuffling towards him, to encircle him and reach out to claw at him with green-skinned fingers.

"Now you'll be sorry, Bobby, you're a naughty, naughty boy" the apparition of his mother said.

He awoke, back to suffer and shiver in the darkness. But not for long. The engine started and the Audi began to move.

A magical mystery tour, he thought. Someone was unwittingly aiding his escape, taking him to their home, where he would be able to find warmth, dry clothes, food, and most importantly, sanctuary. With any luck the police would be convinced that he had drowned. The dumb bastards might spend days searching the Thames for his body. The relief of having escaped diminished the anger that he felt towards Caroline, Amy, and Dr Mark. He would hopefully have another chance to kill all three of them. The thought of the expressions on their faces when he 'returned from the grave' to take care of business made him snigger, like when he had been a schoolboy, up on the flat roof of the gymnasium block, looking down through a skylight into the girls' shower room. He and Charlie Dodson had got away with it at least a dozen times. They would never have been caught, he believed, if Charlie hadn't taken some Polaroids of the naked thirteen-year-olds and started showing them to classmates. Old 'Dinger' Bell, the music teacher, had caught him with them, and Charlie had not only admitted to having taken them, but grassed him up as being his accomplice. That was a valuable lesson, and was an incident that, with others, resulted in him trusting no one. He had been quite pleased when Charlie crashed a stolen car two years later, to be burned to death, trapped in the resulting wreckage. The bitch who had fried in the car with him was Pamela Briggs; one of the girls that he had photographed in the showers.

Geoffrey and Felicity Collins were both retired school teachers, financially secure and living out their 'golden years' in a secluded cottage that backed on to the golf course at Esher. It had been the occasion of the sixty-fifth birthday of their dear friend, John Goodwin, another retired teacher, which had resulted in them driving over to the pub near Chertsey for a celebratory meal with John and his wife, Eileen.

Geoffrey limited himself to a couple of small glasses of red wine with the meal, not prepared to risk losing his driving licence by being over the limit. The evening went well, and the four of them discussed the possibility of taking a cruise together the following year.

"You didn't lock it, again," Felicity said, opening the passenger door of the Audi, climbing in and slamming it shut behind her.

"It must be an inherent trust in my fellow man," Geoffrey said, buckling up, starting the engine and turning the lights on before driving across the car park to the road.

"I think it's more likely to be one of those senior moments; an early sign of dementia," Felicity said, slapping him on the leg, and then leaving her hand on his thigh. She felt horny. Funny how the older she got, the more she enjoyed sex. Maybe without the pressure of work, or their son living at home, her libido was responding to the lack of other stimuli. She wanted to sit on Geoffrey and work off the need that was demanding release, and hoped that he would be in the mood, and could get it up. He wasn't impotent, but neither was he the ever-ready stud he had once been. She let her hand move up and over, and was rewarded by the feel of a healthy erection straining against cavalry twill.

Blink.

He was alone in a cocoon of darkness, and knew that he had suffered yet another of his fugues. They were becoming far too frequent, and his fear of one kicking in at an inopportune moment made him ill at ease. Had one taken place while he had been in the river, then he would almost certainly have drowned, unless his trusty auto pilot had stepped in to save the day. There was no way of knowing how long he had been 'away'. The tink of hot metal cooling, and the stillness, told him that his unwary chauffeur had completed the journey. He counted to a thousand, twice, then kicked out the back of the rear seat, hoping – but not unduly worried – that the noise would not be heard and cause alarm.

The car was garaged. He exited it and then took the time to strip off his still dripping clothing and dry himself with a tartan throw that had been on the rear seat of the Audi.

Opening the garage's side door, he investigated his surroundings. The detached cottage was in large, secluded gardens. A light shone from an upstairs window. He returned to the garage, wrapped the damp blanket around himself and climbed back in the front passenger seat of the car. He decided to wait for a while, to give them time to go to sleep, before breaking in.

He dozed. It had been a hectic day, and he had much to contemplate. Not least the fact that Amy Egan had nearly been the end of him, not once, but twice in the space of a few hours. He fell asleep with the image of her pointing the gun at him. The dazzling flash had undoubtedly been his salvation, by spoiling her aim.

When he woke again, he left the garage, having no idea what time it was. At the rear of the cottage he held the blanket over a small window of the kitchen door and punched it out. The sound was negligible, and the falling glass fell on to a thick coir doormat, which dampened the noise. He reached in, turned the key, which had been left in the lock, twisted the door handle and pushed. There was hardly any give. He stretched his arm up to the elbow inside the door, found the bolt, slid the bar back from the staple to release it, and entered the house.

There was no knife rack to be seen on any of the tiled counters, but a cutlery draw offered a wide selection of weapons. The house was quiet, save for the tick tock of a grandfather clock that stood sentry-like in the hall, as if guarding the stairs. He was suddenly hungry and thirsty, but that would have to wait. First things first. He would secure the area, as Mr FBI would probably say in cop speak. He climbed the stairs, and the act of stalking human prey dulled his pain and aroused him. All the negativity was dispelled. He was yet again fired-up and totally focused. What really turned him on, was that he had no idea where this was going, or what he might do next. He could outguess most people, but not himself. He felt charged, and the air seemed to spark around him. A manic excitement swelled in his mind. All his senses were heightened.

Felicity had gone to sleep thoroughly sated. Geoffrey had risen admirably to the occasion, and with hardly any foreplay she had positioned herself over his turgid member, lowered herself on to it, and began to move, slowly at first, then faster and faster, crying out with unrestrained pleasure as the burning need within her was satisfied.

She came awake to the nightmare, moonlit vision of a naked man standing at the side of the bed, holding a gleaming knife in his hand.

As she watched, frozen and incapable of movement, he lowered himself next to her and put a finger to his lips, implying that she should not make a noise. She tried to scream; to break free from the bonds of fear that pinned her to the mattress, but might have been struck dumb; a state that no doubt saved her life.

"What's your hubby's name, sweetheart?" Bobby said, touching the cold blade to her throat.

The harsh voice released Felicity from her fright induced torpidity. "Geoffrey," she whispered.

"And yours?"

"Felicity."

"Okay, Felicity, wake Geoffrey up."

Unable to turn away from the stranger, Felicity reached out a trembling hand behind her, to grasp a sleeve of Geoffrey's pyjama jacket and shake him into wakefulness.

Bobby smiled. Older people were easier to deal with, as a rule. Most of them had lost the boldness of youth, were less impetuous, and did not have the physical strength to resist. He could not foresee any problems with the couple. He pegged them both as being in their late sixties or early seventies.

"What?" Geoffrey murmured, turning to face Felicity. "Was I snoring?"

"No, Geoff, you were sleeping like a baby," Bobby said. "I need somewhere to stay for a couple of days, and whether you survive my visit or not is dependent on just how sensible you both are. Are you sensible, Geoff?"

Geoffrey had angina, and the shock of the naked man up close to Felicity on the bed and holding a knife to her throat, brought on chest pains stronger than he had suffered in over two years. And the fact that he had enjoyed a rather strenuous bout of sex less than an hour before did not help.

"We'll do whatever you say," he said, pressing the heel of his hand to his sternum, trying to keep calm and slow his racing, diseased heart.

"I had every intention of just killing you both," Bobby said matter-of-factly. "But there's no need to have you stinking up the house, if you do exactly what you're told."

"We will," Felicity said. "Geoffrey has a heart condition. We are no threat to you."

Bobby studied the woman. She was matronly, with greying hair and loose skin at her eyes, jowls and throat. But she had pleasant features, and still appeared shapely beneath the voluminous cotton nightie she wore. He leaned back against the headboard and considered taking her in front of her husband. Would Geoff's ticker be able to withstand the sight of his wife being raped? He imagined that Felicity let her eyes rove over him to linger for a second on his crotch. Maybe...No, not maybe, he just knew that she wasn't getting it, or enough of it. There had been the shadow of lust in that look. She may love her husband, but like Tina sang; *What's love got to do with it?* Sex and love were two different animals, and she wanted the former. There was no way that she could eyeball his firm body and poker-stiff penis without being turned on. But first things first. She would have to wait. Later, he would see to her needs, and his own.

He asked the couple several questions, and by the time he escorted them downstairs, he knew all about their lives and habits. They were basically homebodies, happy to be in each other's company, with few close friends. Reading, doing jigsaws, going on Saga cruises and gardening were their main distractions. Sad bastards. They offered no resistance, and obeyed his every instruction immediately and without question.

The cottage had a cellar, reached by way of a trapdoor located under a faded Persian rug in the living room. There were no exits to the dank underground chamber, and so he ushered them down the wooden steps, allowing them to take blankets, pillows, Geoffrey's medication, and a jug of water. He then left the trembling couple to their own devices, after first warning them not to make a sound. After bolting the trapdoor, he hustled a weighty sideboard over it for extra peace of mind. He had no inclination to harm them, yet. They were not a part of his immediate problem.

Back upstairs in the bathroom, he showered under piping hot water with lavender-scented soap, to cleanse himself of the river, which he imagined harboured countless diseases. After towelling dry he returned to the master bedroom to take his pick of clothes from Geoff's wardrobe. He dressed quickly in a loose sweater over a casual shirt, baggy chinos, belted tightly, sports socks and loafers. The guy was almost his size.

Downstairs, he made himself a ham sandwich lathered with mustard, and a mug of instant coffee, and began to relax.

Once finished eating, he checked that the answer phone was switched on, then lay down on the settee and drifted off into a deep, dreamless and much needed sleep.

It was a little before seven a.m. when he woke, turned on the TV and watched the early morning news. There was footage of yet more conflict in the Middle East, and then news of a lame-brained suicide bomber who had walked into a school playground in Hounslow and detonated a large nail bomb, killing himself, six children, a teacher, and wounding twenty others. That was followed by the report of a multiple pileup on the M25. After that, the talking head reported that the man known as the Park Killer was believed to have drowned in the Thames, after being located and cornered by armed police. The picture flashed to a previously recorded outside broadcast, and none other than Barney Bear appeared, standing with the houseboat ill-defined at the outer range of the camera's lighting.

"Detective Inspector Bowen," an unseen interviewer said. "Can you verify that the Park Killer was drowned while trying to evade capture?"

"No," Barney said. "I can tell you that during an operation to apprehend the suspect, he dived into the river. We have had police boats and divers searching for him throughout the night, and believe that in all probability he has not survived."

"What makes you think that?"

"His clothing will have made it difficult to swim, and bearing in mind the freezing water temperature at this time of year, and the currents, it is highly unlikely that he could still be alive."

"Wrong, Barney," Bobby said, about to laugh, but frowning instead. A photo of him – stolen from his house by the pigs – suddenly filled the screen. The police were looking for Robert Cain, a thirty-five-year-old white male, balding and clean shaven, with black, menacing eyes.

More chance of finding a pot of gold at the end of a fucking rainbow, Bobby thought. As a kid he had tried to do just that on several occasions, but had never even found the spot where a rainbow met the ground, much less a pot of gold.

"And what can you tell us with regard to the other man and two women that were on board the houseboat?" the disembodied voice continued.

"Apart from the fact that we had a hostage situation, I'm afraid at this time I can give no details that might compromise our ongoing inquiries," Barney said.

"Just what *can* you tell our viewers, Detective Inspector?"

"That if anyone knows or has any information regarding Robert Cain, then please contact the police immediately. And though highly unlikely, if Cain has not drowned and has somehow managed to flee the area, I stress that he is extremely dangerous and should under no circumstances be approached by members of the public."

Bobby switched off the television. He was buzzing. This had to be how all the great 'most wanted' gangsters must have felt, living within a society that loathed yet were intrigued and, in some way, stimulated by characters who were at large, still enjoying their reign of terror. He was famous, or to be more precise, infamous, which had more substance than the former. It was poxy pop idols, movie, soap and sports stars, and even the new breed of royals that were famous. He had more je ne sais quoi than all of them put together. What he did was meaningful and real. He was up there with The Yorkshire Ripper, Fred and Rose West, The Black Panther, Harold Shipman, Hindley and Brady, and many other big-name killers that had gripped the nation's attention in a vicelike grip. But surely it was quality and not quantity that counted. He had found his way into the mainstream conscience. He was the embodiment of the bogeyman, who from childhood was a part of everyone's deepest inner fears. He was a dark figure of the night that preyed upon and ripped the beating hearts from his prey. Who would not be in awe and terrified of someone like him?

He searched the cottage and, from photographs and the contents of a metal home file, he put together a reasonably accurate picture of Geoff and Felicity Collins. He had picked the best possible car to hide in. This had been a retired couple, living in the sticks. They had one son, Cameron, now residing in Melbourne, Australia. Should anyone call at the house over the next few days, he could always let Felicity out of the cellar to allay suspicion. It might just pay to keep the couple fed, watered and in good health for the time being. Yes, this was perfect. He had a roof over his head, a well-stocked fridge and freezer, and had found a large steel gun safe bolted to the utility room wall. A subsequent search for the keys was fruitful. The thoughtful Mr Collins had hung them with other assorted keys on one of several brass hooks that were screwed into a wooden baton on the kitchen wall. The gun safe held a 12 gauge over & under Browning shotgun, two boxes of cartridges, and a cleaning kit. A framed certificate on the wall proclaimed that Geoffrey Collins had been a regional winner of some clay shooting competition.

After cooking and eating a fried breakfast, Bobby took the shotgun out to the garage, and with the aid of a hacksaw, carefully remodelled the weapon, sawing down the barrels and stock to convert it into what looked like a large, bulky pistol that could be concealed easily about his person.

Over the following days, he made plans. The police and media were now convinced that he was dead, and commonsense decreed that he should move away from the area, perhaps up north, to assume a new identity. But first he needed to deal with Dr Mark and Amy. They had ruined his game, and were now, no doubt, feeling smug in the false belief that he was fish food. They had to pay for the pain and problems that they had caused him. Once he had killed them, Caroline could spend the rest of her life waiting, knowing that he was out there, never able to enjoy a moment's peace of mind. She would always expect him to turn up, and who knows, one day he might just roll up at her door like a bad penny, to finish what he had started. In fact, he knew that he would.

It was almost ten o' clock on the evening of the fourth day after his escape that the banging on the trapdoor disturbed him as he packed to leave.

"What?" he said, lifting the door to be faced by Felicity, who was wild-eyed and crying, with snot running from her nostrils.

"It's Geoffrey. You've got to get him help...Please. It's his heart. I can't wake him up."

There would be no help.

"Let's have a look and see how he is," Bobby said, motioning for her to go back down the steps.

"But—"

"Just move, bitch. Get your fat arse back down there."

He followed her, and needed only to glance at the man's slate grey face to know that he had expired. "He doesn't need help, you stupid cow, can't you see that he's dead?"

Felicity moaned, knelt down distraught and cradled her late husband's head.

Bobby enjoyed the moment. It was poignant, charged with significance and solemnity. The death experience was profound, and he stood, relishing the incomparable intensity of the woman's grief, and her outpouring of pitiful sentiments, that were falling on deaf ears.

He was aroused, in the same inexplicable way that being confronted by his father's body swinging in the garage so many years ago had infused him with an electric fascination. He pushed Felicity down over the still warm body, pulled up the now grubby nightie, unzipped his fly, and forced his cock between her plump thighs.

It was a mercy killing. His strong hands choked her to death as he found relief. She had fought, but with no real conviction. Geoff's sudden passing had obviously taken all the wind out of her sails; broken her spirit. Now, the couple were together again, and she had been saved the misery that the loss of a loved one evoked. He had been her benefactor, whether she appreciated it or not.

Before leaving the cellar, and after having spent himself once more in the slack body so recently vacated by Felicity, he laid the couple side by side and adjusted the woman's nightdress to preserve some dignity. After all, this couple had done him no harm. He bore them no malice, but did not have the capacity to mourn their passing. They were just dead strangers. Sitting with them for a while was invigorating. The state of death was so peaceful. For the first time since their birth, these two people were totally still. All of their combined experiences had led to this moment in time; to a point when they ceased to be anything. They had gone, to where he did not know, and didn't care. To ponder what came next was a fool's errand. It was the lack of animation of the dead that fascinated him. They were like broken watches beyond repair, totally useless; so much junk to be disposed of.

He was elated as he drove away from the cottage in Esher. He felt totally liberated and, in some way, reborn. He had crawled out of the Thames to a new beginning. All that had gone before was in preparation for what was to come. His every outlandish act would dominate the media, and he would be immortalised in print in perpetuity. He was about to leave his bloody footsteps in history, and determined that he would never be forgotten, and that his deeds would leave a lasting stain on humanity.

There was a sense of urgency within him which, like hunger, demanded to be fed. It was almost impossible to remain calm. His sweating hands were slipping on the steering wheel, and he had to wipe them in turn on the late Geoffrey's chinos. He needed to be in control, and so took deep breaths, then lit one of the long, slim panatelas' that had belonged to Geoffrey, who had surely been foolhardy to indulge, knowing that his pump was shot.

Christ, he was up for this. Most of his victims had only been stalked from afar, and were virtual strangers to him. With Dr Mark Ross and the ex-cop Amy Egan it was splendidly different. He had connected with them, and had cause to despise them both on more than one level. Firstly, they had gone up against him, and had nearly brought about his downfall. And secondly, they had a meaningful relationship; a bond of love that he had never enjoyed. Their fullness highlighted his emptiness and alienation. He wanted to belong, to be loved, to experience what they had, and to cease being a man apart. And he might, one day. But in the meantime, he would erase any hopes and dreams that they envisaged fulfilling.

His cheeks were now heavily stubbled with beard, and he wore suitably warm winter clothing and a woollen watch cap. He was prepared, like every good Boy Scout should be. Everything he needed was in the Audi, which now had false plates.

Once finished with the couple in Richmond, he would feel free to venture to pastures new, forge a new life and find another perfect woman to live out his dream of domestic bliss with, while at the same time perfecting his art.

CHAPTER FORTY-TWO

"**What** do you think?" Barney said, looking from Mark to Amy and back to Mark again.

It was the day after the couple, along with Caroline, had miraculously escaped with their lives. Mark was sore from the stab wound that had grazed a rib, but he was otherwise fit enough to attend Barney's office to give a statement.

"I think that until I see Cain tagged and bagged, then I'll go on believing that he survived, is out there, and is still a very real threat," Mark said.

"Caroline has decided to move away from the city and stay with friends in Bristol for the time being," Barney said. "She feels the same as you. She said that she doesn't believe he drowned, and is going with her instincts."

"Thanks," Amy said, accepting a Styrofoam cup full of milky coffee from Mike Cook. "I have to agree with Mark and Caroline, Barney. I'm not convinced that it's over. I'll need to see the creep on a slab before I can get past this and accept that it's a done deal."

Barney nodded. "I can understand how you both feel, but I don't think he slipped the net."

"Think, doesn't cut it by a country mile. You're not on his people-to-kill list," Mark said. "You can sleep easy at night."

Barney shrugged and said, "What do you intend to do?"

"Take all due precautions, and watch our backs until he turns up."

There was no closure. Mark and Amy were uptight, needing resolution. They made Amy's house their base, and without being conscious of it, kept in sight or sound of each other at all times, as though they were teenage lovers who could not bear being apart for more than a second.

After four days, the pressure of the wait became untenable to Amy. "I can't stand this, Mark," she said, pushing away yet another meal, which she had just picked at and moved around the plate with her fork. "Let's go away. I need to feel safe, even if only for a couple of weeks."

"Where do you suggest?" Mark said.

"Anywhere. Let's just go to Heathrow in the morning and catch a flight out to somewhere warm and sunny. Maybe the Caribbean. A resort in Barbados. We could go scuba diving, sailing, make out on the beach, and drink too much rum."

Mark grinned. "The making out on the beach sounds good. But what if they *don't* find Cain?"

"They will. He's on borrowed time. Life is like tossing a pebble into a pond, it leaves ripples. And if he doesn't show up, then I'll move house, dye my hair blonde and change my name."

"To Ross?"

"Of course. We'd already decided to tie the knot." Amy said, looking at Mark with a quizzical expression.

"Being together and being married are two different things."

"Lots of folk seem to think that marriage is an old-fashioned institution that's dying out."

"Not me, Amy. It's a commitment, in that you are morally dedicating yourself to something permanent."

"So how come the divorce rate is so high, and more and more couples just shack up together without the need to make it official with a piece of paper?"

"Because they approach it with the same undertaking as if they're buying a bloody car; something they can trade in down the line. I don't believe they really get their head around the 'till death do us part' vow. They look at the state of the modern nuclear family, and deep down they treat a relationship as a disposable item. I don't think that enough people realise that anything worth having and keeping needs working at. You've got to take the good with the bad and tough it out together when things get a little rocky. What do you reckon?"

"That you're right. Let's talk about it when we get on that beach, okay?"

"Okay," Mark said, more than a little disappointed that Amy now appeared to be reticent. Initially, on one level, he felt rebuffed and wondered if she loved him with the same all-consuming adoration that he felt for her. But the psychologist in him read her body language, and saw a certain underlying fear. Both of them had been lucky to escape with their lives, and the threat may still be out there, ready to pounce and rob them of a future together, in the shape of a homicidal psychopath who they were both convinced was still alive. He knew then that until this episode was resolved, their waking thoughts would be filled mainly with the spectre of Cain.

"We'll have to go to my place first," Mark said. "I need to get my passport, and pack."

"Fine. Let's go to bed, and get an early start in the morning."

"Why? Are you tired?"

"No, I'm feeling randy. I want your body, Ross, if your side is up to it."

"Your wish is my command," Mark said, putting his hand to where spots of blood were seeping through the dressing under his shirt. "Just be gentle with me."

They were still laughing at that remark as they snuggled up together, naked in the darkness, though the mood quickly changed to one of concentrated passion. They kissed and touched; the tactile feast arousing them both to a state of urgent need.

The lovemaking relaxed Amy in both body and mind. She nestled her cheek on Mark's chest and allowed herself the luxury of contemplating waking up next to him every morning for the rest of their lives. Maybe they could adopt, she thought, fingering the scar, immediately dispirited. She had lost Darren, and then the ability to function as a normal woman and bear another child. A lowlife's bullet had effectively ended her bloodline for the rest of time. *Don't go there. Make the best of what is. Bemoaning your lot is a lost cause. You've got to work with what you've got.* Minutes later, within the safety of Mark's arms, Amy fell asleep.

Many miles away, in Bristol, Caroline lay in the strange bed of a friend's house. She had not even told Simon where she was going, and her life still felt on hold. She was running scared. The monster had intimidated her to such a degree that she could not function properly. He had raped her mind as well as her body. The memory of her abduction and the time kept in captivity on the boat obsessed her. Each terror-filled second replayed endlessly, looping around continuously in her brain. Even with her eyes closed, it was as if the inside of her eyelids were screens that showed continual repeat performances of the atrocities. The anger, fear and sense of total subjugation had melded and fused a part of her mind. Her suffering remained vivid, and even when exhausted and able to sleep, her nightmares were of Cain, his hideous eyes, and the abhorrent sensation of him holding, touching, kissing, and invading her on every level.

Tucking her legs up tight to her chest, Caroline cried quietly into the pillow. She wanted to be strong, clear her mind of the incident and get her life back on track. But she knew that he was out there, fixated on her, determined to possess and kill her. She had escaped him once, thanks to the doctor, Mark Ross, and Amy Egan, who had arrived in the nick of time to save her life. Unfortunately, while Cain was still on the loose and unaccounted for, every minute was potentially her last. There was no alleviation from the unseen threat. He had effectively stolen her life. It was impossible for her to believe that he had drowned. Something about him was inhuman, and therefore indestructible.

He parked almost half a mile away, leaving the Audi between two other nondescript cars on a quiet avenue. He then walked in, wishing that he had a dog on a leash to give him an even lower profile. At the house, once satisfied that there were no police sitting in unmarked vehicles close by, he made his way around to the rear, climbed the fence and took stock of his surroundings. There was only the harsh whisper and scrape of a cold vociferous breeze whipping up dead leaves; chasing and herding them into swirling, restless drifts in damp corners. The windows were blank and black, and he had no sensation of being watched from behind them. Nothing but sounds that belonged to the night could be heard. He approached the newly hung kitchen door, smiling in anticipation, removing a reel of tape from his bag, to bite strips of it off and stick them to one of the six small windows in the top half, before quickly etching a circle around it with a cutter he had found in the garage at Esher and taken, along with a steel jemmy; a short crowbar that could be innocuously employed to open the tops of nailed wooden crates or pry up floorboards, or be carried by a burglar to force open a window or door. Holding a loose edge of the tape, he tapped the glass once, firmly, and pulled the circle free. The window was double-glazed, and so he had to repeat the operation on the inner pane, before reaching inside, only to find that there was no key in the lock. The smile died on his face. But no matter, he would have to risk making a little noise. After inserting the curved chisel end of the jemmy in the small gap next to the lock, he pulled it back with a quick and powerful jerk, and the door burst open.

He remained still for a long time, listening to the house as his eyes adjusted to the darkness. The only sounds were a low humming and occasional liquid gurgle from the fridge and freezer. When satisfied that his entry had not been overheard, he moved silently out into the hall, entered the lounge to take a cushion from the settee, and then went to the stairs and ascended into the gloomier reaches of the first-floor landing.

Holding the sawn-off shotgun one-handed, heavy and comforting in his grip, he felt himself harden like a steel rod. The imbeciles obviously thought that he was rotting in mud at the bottom of the Thames, with fish and fresh water shrimps picking the flesh off his bones, and his eyes from their sockets. They were in for the biggest surprise of their pathetic lives. Death had come-a-calling.

Dr Mark's Cherokee had been parked outside the front of the house. The couple had been foolhardy enough to deem it safe to return to whatever they considered as being normality. It was a mistake that only one of them would live to regret. He was now totally relaxed, focused, and ready to deal with them. There would be no more cock-ups on his part. He'd fucked up by using Payne's houseboat, and had then compounded the mistake by being far too arrogant, underestimating the enemy. Perhaps he was his own worst enemy. Overconfidence was a weakness that he would have to somehow come to terms with.

At the partly open door of the first bedroom he came to, he folded the cushion over the muzzles of the Browning's shortened barrels, which would hopefully dampen the sound to an acceptable level.

The new plan was simple. There was no way that he was going to take any more chances with these two. He would initially disable both of them, and then shoot Amy in the face while the Yank looked on. Leaving Ross wounded but alive, and with the image of his slut's head exploding like a melon, would be mind-blowing for them all, especially the split-arse ex-cop.

Entering the bedroom, he could see the shapes of the couple lying as close to each other as two peas in a pod. Moonlight penetrating through thin curtains at the large window was all the illumination he needed.

He took aim near the foot of the bed, deciding to shoot them both in the lower legs or feet. That would be an attention-getter.

The first blast brought Mark and Amy wide awake. Sitting bolt upright, and without pause, Mark rolled out of bed and grasped the World War Two bayonet – which he had purchased on impulse in a militaria shop three days earlier – from where he had leant it up in the corner behind the bedside cabinet. He rushed out of the small spare room that they had moved into just in case precisely what was happening now should transpire. Paranoia has its place, especially when someone really *is* out to get you.

Bobby giggled as he aimed at where the other feet should be and triggered the second barrel. He then frowned when his only reward was an unnatural stillness. No one reared up screaming in agony. The realisation that the bed had been padded to appear occupied, and that he had been expected, hit hard as a voice came from the open doorway behind him.

"Glad to see you could make it, Cain," Mark said.

Bobby spun around, lashed out blindly with the spent shotgun, but teetered off balance as he connected with no more than thin air.

Mark lunged at the spinning figure, felt the rusted, pitted blade of the old bayonet sink into the killer's body, and thrust deeper.

Bobby howled in surprise and pain as he released the shotgun, pulled back to disengage himself from the blade, and without hesitation attacked, throwing a punch that caught Mark on the cheek, knocking him backwards. Bobby followed up, got in close and gripped Mark around the waist in a bear hug, simultaneously biting into his chest like a crazed, rabid dog.

The air was forced from Mark's lungs as the man's powerful arms crushed his ribcage. Christ, he's strong, Mark thought. He had to react instantly, or his initial advantage would have been for nothing. At some point he had dropped the bayonet. Both of his hands were free. He scrabbled at Cain's bald head, which was attached to him like a leech, by his teeth, and Mark's fingers found the nose with one hand and an eye with the other. He dug his thumb into the man's left eye, hooked the first two fingers of his other hand into the wide nostrils, and jerked back with all his might.

The result was instantaneous. Bobby released his grip with arms and teeth, screamed out and put his hands up to the two fresh seats of pain.

Mark drew his fist back and struck Cain a tremendous blow to the chin.

Blink.

Bobby's senses deserted him. He tottered backwards on his heels, eyes rolled up to show the whites, his momentum taking him across to the window, which he crashed through, to tumble out into the night amid a shower of glass.

The ornamental fleur-de-lis-shaped points that tipped the palisade posts of the steel fencing below, broke his fall. One sank into his right buttock, another into his back.

Mark looked out and down through the shattered window to see Cain fixed like a marshmallow on a toasting fork. His shoulders slumped as relief swept through him.

"Is it over?" Amy said, standing naked at the open bedroom door, her arms folded across her breasts, fists clenched.

"Yeah," Mark said, going to her and holding her close. "He's finished. Call Barney."

Amy went across to the window to look down and see for herself, while Mark unhurriedly went back to the bedroom at the rear of the house for his robe and slippers, not knowing that Cain was *not* dead.

Mark went downstairs and out of the house to approach Cain, the soles of his moccasin-style slippers crunching on shards of broken glass. He was unashamedly pleased to see the dying man's lips drawn back in a rictus grimace, and his black eyes still animated, aware, and full of pain, fear and hatred.

Bobby had been snapped out of his fugue as the pointed tips of the railing posts punched into his body. Red, frothy blood bubbled from his lips, and he began to make small, wet, whimpering sounds as he arched his back in an agonising and futile attempt to free himself.

Mark could feel no measure of compassion. This man was a creature who personified death, and who, without conscience, fed off the terror and agony that he had visited upon others. Standing just a yard away, Mark was a witness, waiting patiently and expectantly for nature to take its course.

"Fuck you, Ross," Bobby managed to say; his voice a liquid slur, as blood leaked up into his throat and mouth from a skewered lung.

"No, Cain, fuck *you*," Mark said, as with a final shudder that ran the length of his broken body, the homicidal psychopath's hands clawed at the air, and with a whistling last breath he drowned in his own escaping lifeblood and ceased to be a danger to anyone.

After phoning Barney, Amy pulled on a sweater and jeans as Mark lingered outside and watched as blood seeped out of the body before him and ran down the iron railings to pool on the concrete and fan out in small streams to follow the camber of the pavement and flow into the gutter. He felt weak, on the verge of being overwhelmed by a melange of emotions; the most powerful being that of incredible relief. This was the closure that they had needed.

Putting two fingers to Cain's neck – half expecting the half-closed eyes to snap wide open and stare at him – he confirmed that the man was dead. Whatever evil was, it had left this now limp, untenanted vessel. A line from Shakespeare's Julius Caesar came to mind: 'The evil that men do lives after them; the good is oft interred with their bones'. The iniquitous and vicious force that had driven the man was now loose, without a physical body to work like a marionette. Did evil exist as a separate entity? Could it survive the death of the host it dwelt within, to move on, perhaps to invade and inhabit a newly born infant? These were considerations that Mark had pondered for most of his adult life, and was still no nearer to having the answers to.

He went back inside the house to the kitchen, where Amy was just racking the phone.

"You want a cup of coffee?" Mark said.

"Hug first," she said.

He held her until the distant sound of sirens drew nearer, louder, and then he left her and once more walked down the hallway to the still open front door. Amy switched on the coffeemaker and let the sense of anxiety dissipate, as if it had been a physical, oppressive weight. The death of Cain was her salvation. It was as if she had been set free to walk out into bright sunlight after being confined in a dark, stinking dungeon. It was both an uplifting and meaningful moment.

EPILOGUE

Two weeks later.

The sky appeared as a conflagration; the sun a massive golden globe rushing down to the western horizon, signalling an end to another day with a breathtaking display of orange, crimson and purple that gladdened, warmed and inspired the spirit.

Mark and Amy wandered hand in hand along the sugar-white sand. They had decided on having a break in the Sunshine State, so had flown to Tampa from Heathrow, rented a car and driven south on I-75 to a small key north of Sarasota on the Gulf of Mexico.

Mark had made a call to an old 'Agency' friend in D.C., and had accepted the offer to use his beach house in Florida for three weeks.

"Look," Amy said, pointing out beyond the surf to where dorsal fins knifed the surface just fifteen or twenty yards away from them, as several dolphins indolently slipped by, in no hurry to reach their destination, should they have one.

"You like it here?" Mark said.

"I love it here," Amy said, stopping to face him and search out his lips with hers. "I can't think of a better place to be."

The almost unbearable tension had melted away with Cain's last breath, and life had suddenly returned to some semblance of normality, whatever the hell that was. In the immediate aftermath, Caroline Sellars had resumed her career with the BBC, and was back in her London flat. Barney Bowen had accumulated his leave, and would not return to duty before his official retirement date in March. He and Anna had gone out to Spain for a couple of months, but only for an extended holiday. They had decided that their home and Barney's beloved pond and Koi carp outweighed a permanent move abroad.

The body of DC Gary Shields was found by a Forestry Commission work crew in Epping Forest, which at least afforded his family the solace of being able to give him a proper burial. The police turned out in force for the funeral; he was one of their own.

Mark had cleared his desk at Cranbrook, and had resigned a week after the incident at Amy's house, pre-empting the hospital's governors' intention to let him go, due to his high-profile involvement in the Park Killer case. The media had made him out to be some kind of super hero; the definitive manhunter. He saw the writing on the wall and beat the board to the mark. He didn't condemn or resent their attitude. He had brought unwelcome publicity to their door. An upside, he supposed, was that his book had been given a new lease of life. The publishers were quick to cash in on his unsolicited fame.

The tormented and strangely gifted Billy Hicks found peace. A few hours after enjoying a lakeside walk with Mark, he had packed up his meagre belongings in a cardboard carton, lay down on his bed, and died. The cause of death was officially recorded as being due to heart failure. Mark doubted it was that simple. The discovery of a dead, jet-black barn owl on the ground outside, below the window of Billy's room, was as inexplicable as the young man's demise. To Mark's knowledge, there were no black owls, apart from the Visitor whom Billy had talked about. For the sake of his own sanity, Mark consigned the episode into his mental filing cabinet labelled 'crazy shit', and closed the drawer.

To put things into perspective, or to gather in the corn, as his father had always said, Mark decided that he would write a second book. It would be entitled: The Park Killer, and would document the case from his personal viewpoint. He also made the decision to be involved with Amy's security company, and to take on a limited amount of consult work for the police. All in all, he should be kept fully and gainfully employed.

The shimmering sun turned the now placid, plate-glass smooth surface of the Gulf of Mexico to burnished copper, before it appeared to slip into the ocean and be extinguished, leaving the rising, glowing moon on night watch.

Amy thought of her present situation as a happy ending, and then her dark side reminded her that the only happy endings were in books and movies. This was just the start of another chapter in her life, which held a fragile promise of being better than the last one.

The abomination that had been Cain affected her deeply. She could not factor-in and embrace the view of psychologists like Mark. In her mind, Cain had been a malformed item that had somehow gained a stamp of acceptable quality and found its way into the marketplace. Either that, or Mark was right and pure evil was an ever-present force that raised its ugly head whenever it found a suitable host. They had been pitted against something truly maleficent that masqueraded as Bobby Cain. It struck her that without morality, a person like Cain did not have the capacity to weigh a conflict of principles and make balanced, ethical decisions. The absence of an ability to empathise with others' feelings made it impossible to contemplate such qualities as kindness, love, or mercy. Maybe evil was just a total absence of compassion.

Clearing her mind of negative and depressing speculation, Amy turned to Mark. And said, "You want to go skinny-dipping?"

"Bearing in mind that sharks feed mainly at dawn and dusk, do you really want to risk one taking a bite out of your cute ass?" Mark said, grinning broadly.

"No way, Jose," she said, wincing as she recalled Spielberg's famous movie, that had made swimming in the sea a no-no for countless millions of people. "Let's drive over to the Dockside Grill on the mainland and have a steak meal and a cold beer, instead."

About The Author

I write the type of original, action-packed, violent crime thrillers
that I know I would enjoy reading if they were written by such
authors as: Lee Child, David Baldacci, Simon Kernick, Harlan
Coben, Michael Billingham and their ilk.
Over twenty years in the Prison Service proved great research into
the minds of criminals, and especially into the dark world that serial
killers - of who I have met quite a few - frequent.

I live in a cottage a mile from the nearest main road in the Yorkshire
Wolds, enjoy photography, the wildlife, and of course creating new
characters to place in dilemmas that my mind dreams up.

What makes a good read? Believable protagonists that you care
about, set in a story that stirs all of your emotions.

If you like your crime fiction fast-paced, then I believe that the
books I have already uploaded on Amazon/Kindle will keep you
turning the pages.

Connect With Michael Kerr and discover other great titles.

Facebook
https://www.faccbook.com/MichaelKerrAuthor

Kindle Store
http://www.michaelkerr.org/amazon

Also By Michael Kerr

DI Matt Barnes Series
A REASON TO KILL
LETHAL INTENT
A NEED TO KILL
CHOSEN TO KILL
A PASSION TO KILL
RAISED TO KILL
DRIVEN TO KILL

The Joe Logan Series
AFTERMATH
ATONEMENT
ABSOLUTION
ALLEGIANCE
ABDUCTION
ACCUSED

The Laura Scott Series
A DEADLY COMPULSION
THE SIGN OF FEAR
THE TROPHY ROOM

Other Crime Thrillers
DEADLY REPRISAL
DEADLY REQUITAL
BLACK ROCK BAY
A HUNGER WITHIN
THE SNAKE PIT
A DEADLY STATE OF MIND
TAKEN BY FORCE
DARK NEEDS AND EVIL DEEDS
DEADLY OBSESSION
COFFEE CRIME CAFE
A DARKNESS WITHIN
PLAIN EVIL
DEADLY PURPOSE

Science Fiction / Horror
WAITING
CLOSE ENCOUNTERS OF THE STRANGE KIND
RE-EMERGENCE

Children's Fiction
Adventures in Otherworld
PART ONE – THE CHALICE OF HOPE
PART TWO – THE FAIRY CROWN

Printed in Great Britain
by Amazon

54590953R00180